THE CURSE

A Novel of the Breedline Series

by SHANA CONGROVE

Cover Design by: Covers by Christian Artworks

Published by: Shana Congrove

Signed copies @ shanacongrove.com

Novels of the Breedline Series by Shana Congrove

Sweet Chaos

Total Chaos

Unleashed Chaos

Sins of Chaos

The Immortal

The Curse

Living Nightmares & Vampirism in Manhattan... *up next!*

Available on Amazon, B&N, shanacongrove.com

or wherever books are sold online

Author's Acknowledgments

Dedicated to all my talented friends on FanStory.com, especially Roy Owens, Neal Owens, and AJ McCall. Without your helpful advice and continuing support, none of this would exist. Supportive friends are hard to find. Thank you for being mine. YOU make a difference!

As always, immense gratitude to God's loving grace. Thank you for giving me guidance and courage with everything I do.

To all the readers, family, and friends: Thank you for stepping into my fantasy world of the Breedline. I appreciate your support!

Mom, you are my guiding light and my rock! I love you!

To my "Drakon," *you know who you are*, thanks for everything you do. I love you!

Chocco boy, although you're just a ten-pound Chihuahua, you fill my heart with so much joy. Love you, little buddy!

Most importantly, to my son, Nathan Gage: Always remember, having a weird mom builds character. *Love you to the moon & back!*

The Legend of the Breedline

Imagine all the myths, legends, and folktales that both captivated and terrified you as a child—*the monsters under your bed, the boogieman in the closet, werewolves, vampires, witches, demons, ghosts, and so on*—really existed.

The story I'm about to tell you goes beyond unbelievable.

This is the legend of the Breedline.

Story goes that a secret species of humans born with an identical twin had the power to shift into wolves.

Some say it to be an old tall tale... an ancient lore derived from Native American legends, known mainly as stories of shape-shifting creatures.

For the Navajo and other tribes of the southwest, each has their own version of supernatural creatures called Skin-walkers—but each boils down to the same thing—a majestic being capable of transforming itself into a wolf, coyote, bear, bird, or any other animal. When the transformation is complete, the human inherits the speed, strength, or cunning of the animal whose shape it has taken.

So the question remains...

Do supernatural beings really exist among our mundane, humdrum existence?

The thing about myths, legends, and folktales are...

Sometimes they're true.

How do I know, you ask? Because... I'm their queen, and this is our story.

Chapter One

While he sipped his brandy, he looked around the bar, taking in all the half-naked bodies gyrating on the dance floor to the voice of Marilyn Manson, singing something about beautiful people. The Cat Club was packed tonight, full of freaks and wannabes dressed in a ghastly fashion between gothic black leather, tight miniskirts, and ripped jeans. To him, they all appeared as rejects or outcasts who did not fit in with normal society.

But then, he wondered, what was considered *normal*? If indeed there were a checklist, he would not fit into those categories. No, he was something else. Something dark, sinister... *cruel*. Going by the diagnosis of his childhood psychologist, he suffered from a chronic mental disorder with violent tendencies, an inability to love, and a lack of remorse. At age thirteen, he showed all the traits of a psychopath. And that was just the beginning.

Although it wasn't like he had the best upbringing. His father was an abusive drunk, and his mother felt trapped, fearing if she left, he would track her down and kill her. He'd witnessed firsthand all the threats and abuse his mother endured. If she answered his father in a tone he regarded as disrespectful or even looked at him the wrong way, he'd beat her. At times, his father used him as leverage, threatening punishment, even death. Many times, his mother would take the beating meant for him, while he looked on, feeling completely helpless. His mother did her best, gave him all the love she could, until she took her last breath.

Growing up in an abusive household was just something he learned to cope with. No matter how hard he wished it, he couldn't change the hand that had been dealt. He couldn't stop himself from wishing things were different though. That maybe he could have been born into a *normal* family.

As he dredged up those painful memories, his body responded to the remembered horror of his mother's battered and bruised body. His heart ached just thinking about it. He brought his hand up and touched the center of his chest. He would never forget that one horrific day. The worst day of his life.

It was a cold and rainy Saturday afternoon. He was only five years old at the time, but he remembered that tragic incident like it was yesterday. His mother was late coming home after a run to the liquor store to appease his father's addiction. By the time she arrived, he was already in a drunken stupor. In a fit of rage, he repeatedly kicked and beat her. No matter how much he pleaded and begged his father to stop, the bastard continued his brutality. Before his father beat his mother unconscious, she dragged herself over to him and reached out. She could barely open her swollen eyes. She said one last thing before he watched the light in her eyes dim and then go out.

"Don't ever forget... Mommy will always love you."

He could still hear himself calling out to her over and over.

That was the day his life changed forever, and when he shot his father. Although he was surprised he was even capable of firing his father's 9mm semi-automatic at such a young age. It didn't kill his father, but he had meant for it to.

When the neighbors heard the blast from the gun, they called the police. As they arrived, he still had it in his hand and aimed at his father. He would never forget the female officer that arrived at the scene. She had a dark complexion, braided hair, and big brown, caring eyes. He kept her face and the sound of her voice embedded in his memory.

"Put the gun down, honey." Her voice had been soft and comforting like his mother's. *"I know you didn't mean to hurt anyone. We're here to help you."*

"He hurt my mommy," I remember hearing myself tell the officer. *"I won't let him hurt her anymore."*

"I know," the officer soothed, her expression softening with understanding. *"What's your name, honey?"*

"Joseph," I answered, looking at the officer with troubled blue eyes that seemed to carry a lifetime of violence and pain behind them.

"Okay, listen to me, Joseph. My name is Officer Katie Mendoza, and I'm here to help you. Do you understand?"

When I nodded an understanding, she continued to say, *"I promise I won't let anyone hurt your mother, but I need you to do something for me."* She got down on one knee and held out her hand. *"Please, Joseph. Please give me the gun."*

"I can't," I told her. *"He'll kill her."*

Back then, he wasn't the cold and calculating person he was today. He was just a scared little boy trying to protect his mother. It took almost thirty minutes, but finally Officer Katie coaxed him into giving her the gun. Then he remembered watching as the paramedics loaded his mother into the back of an ambulance and drove away.

The next day, she suffered from an aneurysm, caused by all the blunt force, and died in the hospital. Immediately following her death, police arrested his father. Charged with aggravated assault in the first degree, the judge sentenced him to twenty years. During his father's trial, and with no other living relatives, he'd been placed in foster care. Spending most of his childhood in the system wasn't exactly any better than what he had at home. He'd gone through ten foster families before he was carted off in a straitjacket—due to his psychopathic behavior—and put into a mental institution where he spent most of his adolescent years.

Twenty-one years later, here he was, rehabilitated and back in the real world. During the years he'd spent in the mental hospital, he quickly mastered the skills of manipulation. He said all the right words and all the things his therapists wanted to hear. For good behavior and therapeutic reasons, they allowed him to take online college courses. The day the institute finally discharged him, believing he'd been cured, it wasn't long before he landed a job as a freelance journalist at the San Francisco Chronicle. For the first year, it was mandatory to check in with his therapist on a regular basis.

Soon after, he discovered his father's whereabouts. A year prior, after doing his time, dear ol' dad was now living as a civilian. His father should have killed him when he had the chance, or better yet, made his mother abort him before he was ever born. No amount of therapy, drugs, or shock treatment could cure what he was.

His mind took him back to that day, to the memories of when his father took his last gurgling breath. He'd sliced his throat so deep that it nearly severed his head. There was so much blood. He was gratified to watch his father's life drain in a pool of red. He had been planning to kill him the day a social worker delivered the dreadful news of his mother's death. At that moment, it was as if something evil—a dark, soulless entity—clawed its way inside of him and inhabited his body. It was the day he heard the voice whisper in his head. It introduced itself as the *Shadow* and spoke to him in a way that was both soothing and malicious. Although he was just a child at the time, the Shadow gave him courage, taught him things, helped him survive, and kept his mind focused for all those years. Focused on one thing: to *kill*.

While he reminisced on the past, and before his imagination got the best of him, someone caught his eye. Across the crowded dance floor, a young girl with long, blonde hair, dressed in a pink strapless top and a pair of tight jeans, stood by the bar, observing all the social misfits.

He leaned back in his chair and simply watched her. The short distance that separated them, he studied every detail, every curve. Regardless of the high-heeled boots she wore, she couldn't have been any taller than five-foot-two, and no older than twenty-five. The smoothness and flawless lines on her sun-kissed skin gave her a youthful glow. She had that girl-next-door look to her. Pretty, but not overly attractive. She looked out of place, like she didn't belong here. He noticed the way she chewed at her bottom lip and the swell of her breasts as she took each breath. And she appeared to be alone.

"She's perrrrfect," the Shadow whispered to him in a soft purr. *"Pick her, Joseph."*

Joseph briefly closed his eyes and drew in a wavering breath. The Shadow was his driving force to take lives, always in his head, always picking out their next victim. It was like having an evil twin inside your head twenty-four seven. Sometimes it was exhausting. *God,* he thought, *how have I made it all these years without going mad.*

"Well, you are clinically insane," the Shadow said. *"Admit it, Joseph. You need me. You're weak without me."*

In a flash, he recalled the day the Shadow gave him the courage to go back to his parents' home one last time, to avenge his mother. God, he could still remember how his father begged for his pathetic life. But mostly, he looked back on the memory of watching the house go up in flames with his father's body burning inside. As he savored that moment, he felt reborn.

Yes, Joseph silently agreed. *I need you, Shadow.* Then he smiled, his eyes growing hooded as his gaze lingered on the girl's lips. But to his surprise, she wandered off, probably heading for the ladies' room. His smile disappeared.

"Don't let her get away. Follow her, Joseph."

Joseph tossed back the rest of his drink, swallowing it whole. The minute he rose from his chair, a waitress wearing skintight leopard pants, and four-inch heels came up to his table, working her hips as if they were double-jointed. She swirled her tongue over her black-coated lips and muttered, "How 'bout another round, sweetheart?"

For a brief, lapsing moment, the Shadow's voice came back to him. *"Hurry, Joseph. The girl is leaving the bar."*

Joseph quickly reached into the front pocket of his jeans and dug out a twenty-dollar bill. "No thanks." He placed the money on the table. "I was just leaving."

* * *

The blonde-haired girl swiped her phone on her way out of the bar. After a few rings, it went straight to voicemail. "Dammit, Kevin," she cursed under her breath, and ended the call. This had been the fourth time her boyfriend was a no-show, and this time she'd make damn sure it was his last. He was a total loser, and she had a sneaking suspicion that he was a cheater. And to make matters worse, he'd made promises for a *supposedly* romantic Valentine's dinner.

It was already after midnight, and she should probably call for an Uber, but her apartment building was only five blocks away. Besides, she was angry, and the walk might do some good.

As she walked along, she noticed some of the businesses were hopping. Other than the Cat Club, there was Dino's Bar and Grill, JJ's Smoke Shop, and a hole-in-the-wall pool hall further down the main strip. Across the street was a tattoo parlor, a Mexican restaurant, a pizza place where you could make your own pies, and a little burger joint around the corner. Above the Cat Club, there were loft rentals that suited the local bartenders and servers. Most of the places seemed safe enough. Although there were a couple she didn't care for like Ziggy's pool hall. It mostly brought in a rougher crowd that usually involved the police before closing time. The Cat Club had been the other place she disliked. If it weren't for Kevin, she wouldn't have set foot in the place. The clientele that hung out easily stereotyped as members of the Vampire-Goth subculture, and not exactly her type. She stuck out like a sore thumb.

When she rounded the corner and walked past Biggy's Burgers, she got an uneasy feeling in the pit of her gut. It was as if someone was following her. As she turned to look, expecting to see someone stalking her, she was relieved no one was there. Then, as a noisy crowd of people came out of the burger joint, she relaxed even more. With her nerves still intact, she hurried across the street toward Sunset. By the time she got on Richmond, she noticed it was unusually quiet. The street looked deserted, but her apartment complex was only a few blocks away.

A thick fog hung in the air, but the streetlights overhead and the headlights from an occasional passing car made the visibility tolerable. She slowed when leering whistles caught her attention.

Don't look back, her inner voice warned her. *Keep your eyes forward and stay focused on getting home.*

She paid no attention to the obnoxious catcalls and kept moving.

Suddenly, two men hurriedly crossed the street and jogged up to her. Quickly, she reached into her purse and dug around for her Taser. It had been a gift, along with a container of pepper spray, from her Uncle Frank, who was a homicide detective for the San Francisco Police Department.

"What's a pretty girl like you doing out at this hour all alone?" the guy who stood taller than his buddy said. As he walked alongside her, she noticed his eyes trailing up and down her body.

She ignored him, preparing to defend herself by any means necessary.

"Damn, girl," the other guy said, his beady eyes focused on her hips. "You're fine as hell."

Not far down the street, Joseph stopped in his tracks when he caught sight of two men ogling the blonde-haired girl he'd spotted in the bar. It looked as though they were taunting her, and maybe contemplating assaulting her. In irritation, his hands fisted at his sides, noticing how the taller guy moved in closer.

"Need a lift, sweetheart?" the guy said, winking at his bug-eyed buddy. "It's no trouble. Our car is just across the street."

She picked up her pace, her hand continuing to fumble aimlessly inside her purse. *Where in the hell is that Taser?* Then a knot formed at the back of her throat. She remembered she'd left it in her gym bag and the pepper spray at home. *Shit!*

"We are not going to just stand back, and do nothing," the Shadow said, bringing Joseph back to focus. *"She belongs to us."*

"It's too risky," Joseph said, keeping his voice low. "Besides, there's two of them."

"But there's two of us."

"I don't know." Joseph furrowed his brows, contemplating the idea. "One of them could have a weapon."

"Don't be a pussy, Joseph."

He closed his eyes, desperate to drown out the Shadow's voice, and let out a deep breath.

Joseph's lids flew open at the sound of a high-pitched scream. One of the men had his arms wrapped around the girl's waist, proceeding to drag her off while the other man watched for onlookers. The girl continued to scream, putting up one hell of a fight, kicking and punching, but was unable to break free.

The guy quickly put her into a choke hold. "Shut up," he said through gritted teeth.

The girl stopped struggling and lowered her voice to a whimper.

Joseph felt the Shadow inside of him, itching to be released. *"Follow them. Don't let them kill the girl. She's ours."*

He obeyed the Shadow's demands and followed the two men as they forced the girl further into the shadows, toward an abandoned building.

Joseph watched in disgust as the taller man pushed the girl up against the bricks of the vacant building. While he pinned her wrists above her head, his beady-eyed buddy slipped his hand underneath her blouse. The girl screamed and, for a moment, the man looked as if he was about to strike her. Instead, he reached up and grabbed her by the throat. "You scream one more time, and I'll cut you," he said as he produced a knife with his other hand, flashing it in her face.

Joseph's temper flared as the guy placed the edge of the blade close to her cheek. "Are you going to keep that trap of yours shut?"

The girl, her eyes stricken with fear, quickly bobbed her head.

"Good girl," he murmured, finally relaxing his grip. Then he lowered the blade and replaced it with his tongue, swiping it over her cheek. "Mmm..." he purred deep in his throat. "You taste sweet."

By the way the girl recoiled, Joseph could tell she was on the verge of becoming sick.

"I bet the rest of her tastes even sweeter," muttered the other guy, pressing his groin up against the girl.

She instantly tried to lash out, but the other man caught her by the wrist and backhanded her.

"Kill them," the Shadow called within Joseph. *"And take the girl."*

Adrenaline surged through Joseph, and an overwhelming sense of power washed over him. Inside his mind, the Shadow stirred. As it clawed its way to freedom, Joseph felt a familiar rage emerging, starting off from a grain of irritation, until it fed itself and became a living thing that made his breathing irregular and pulse race. He welcomed the evil entity and the strength it brought him. He let go of everything, freeing his mind, so that only a single thought remained. And that was to kill.

Then he felt something shift inside of him. The sensation was almost too overwhelming. It was like being reborn, seeing the world through someone's else eyes. Eyes that wielded knowledge and power. He felt like a god. Within seconds, the change began. His handsome features twisted and reshaped, transforming into a mask of demonic horror. His skin paled like a corpse's, webbed with dark veins, and his perfect teeth were now shaped like ivory fangs. Black soulless orbs, blazing with hunger and utter malevolence, replaced his piercing blue eyes.

As Joseph started forward, preparing to kill, two glowing eyes shone out from the darkness, and a deep, guttural growl echoed around the thick veil of fog. The sounds were nothing like he'd ever heard. More like a beast than that of any dog. With a roar, an immense creature burst from the shadows and hurled itself at the men, knocking them off the girl, and onto the ground.

Joseph backed away. "What the—" His mind reeled as if trying to process what had just happened. He focused his line of vision on the hulking creature standing no more than a few away. He had never seen an animal of its size before. It had to be at least seven feet tall. Its massive frame was covered in sleek black fur, with triangular lupine ears poking out of its hideous head. It looked like a wolf. Not really a wolf though. An elongated snout like a wolf with sharp canines, the kind to eat you. Huge claws to rip through flesh. Its hindquarters were like a wolf's, but the thing stood upright like a man.

"It's a werewolf," the Shadow muttered.

Falling to her knees, the girl screamed into the palm of her hand.

Under the light of the full moon, Joseph could see it perfectly. The sight would have been magnificent if it hadn't been so terrifying. It was just standing there, ignoring the terrified girl, and kept its yellow orbs trained on the men. From his vantage point, he saw as it pulled back its wolfish lips into a vicious snarl like it was waiting for them to make a move. Yet worst of all was the hunger in its glowing gaze.

The taller man finally scrambled to get to his feet, wavering on the edge of consciousness, until he heard the growl. His eyes fluttered open, but before he managed to scream, sharp claws tore through flesh and jaws crunched through bones. The man's mouth bobbed like a fish out of water, releasing wet gurgles while the ground beneath him pooled in red.

With his heart hammering against his heaving chest, the dead guy's buddy tried to crawl away. His efforts were halted when something grabbed him by the ankle. He screamed as sharp claws dug into his flesh. The second he craned his head to look, he cringed at the pair of murderous eyes gazing back at him. Then a pungent smell of urine was thick in the air.

"Oh no... oh no... oh no..." he sputtered over and over.

The wolfish creature cocked its head, as if studying its prey. In a matter of seconds, it lowered its jaws and clamped down on the man's face. Blood spurted from the werewolf's mouth and mingled with the puddle of urine at its feet. The guy's body twitched and convulsed, until finally he went limp.

The girl was afraid to run, but more terrified to stay. With a bolt of adrenaline, she got to her feet and ran, her screams filling the alleyway.

To Joseph's surprise, the creature did not chase after her. Although it seemed inconceivable, he could have sworn that it was somehow here to protect her. *But why?*

"What are you waiting for, Joseph?" the Shadow said. *"Go after the girl."*

Chapter Two

The girl didn't stop running until she was at the door to her apartment. Her hands shook and her lungs screamed inside her chest. She felt as though she was going to hyperventilate before she ever made it inside. It wasn't until she reached for the door that she realized it was locked.

Keys, she feverishly thought as she dug into the pockets of her jeans. *Dammit, where are my keys?*

At that moment, she remembered where they were. Her apartment keys and her phone were in her purse. *Shit!* It was in that alley where she'd been attacked, and there was no way in hell she was going back there.

"Jessica!" She shouted and pounded on the door, praying her roommate was home. "Please, Jess... Open the door!"

When she finally accepted the fact that her roommate wasn't home, she leaned against her apartment door as panic and terror quickly took hold. She blinked her eyes, trying to get the nightmarish images out of her head. God, she could still see all the blood and hear those awful screams. And that *thing*... What was *it*? It looked like a *werewolf.* Whatever attacked those two creeps wasn't human. No matter how hard she tried, nothing made sense. Although whatever it was, it kept her from getting raped and most likely saved her life. That's when the tears started. They streaked down her cheeks in what seemed like an endless river. She wiped at her eyes, feeling as though she had stepped into an alternate universe where nothing seemed real. Then she placed both hands over her face and fell apart.

"Carrie?"

At the sound of her roommate's voice, she lowered her hands and cleared her throat. "Oh, thank God."

Jessica came forward, realizing her friend was in a state of distress and reached out to her. "What's wrong, Carrie?"

Carrie pushed her long blonde hair out of her face and wiped her tear-stained eyes. "I-I'm locked out."

"Where's your keys?"

"I-In my purse. And I lost it."

"Where?"

"I-In an alley."

Jessica's brows spiked in confusion. "What in the world were you doing in an alley?"

"I was attacked."

"Oh my God, Carrie." Jessica took hold of her hand. "Are you okay?"

Carrie slowly nodded. "I just need to sit down."

"Come on." Jessica went to unlock the door. "Let's get you inside. And we need to file a report. I'll be damned if whoever did this gets away."

While Jessica guided her inside, Carrie thought of what her friend had said as she stretched out on the sofa. And it wasn't far from the truth. The fact of the matter was those two creeps were certainly not going to get away. There was no doubt about it. They were no longer able—or living for that matter—to prey on the weak and helpless ever again.

Jessica looked down at Carrie, concerned. "Do you want me to get something for your lip?"

"Thanks." Carrie shook her head. "It's fine."

"Want to talk about it?"

Carrie sighed and scooted higher on the couch. She tucked her legs in close, making room for Jessica to sit down. "Jess, you'll think I've gone mad." She exhaled a sigh. "And I'm not entirely sure I haven't."

Jessica plopped down next to Carrie and placed her hand on her shoulder. "Remember, it's me you're talking to. How long have we known each other?"

"Since kindergarten."

"That's right." Jessica smiled. "And we've always told each other everything. Besides, nothing you say will make me think you're crazy. You trust me, don't you?"

Carrie nodded. "Of course, I trust you. It's just so..." She paused and shook her head. "...hard to talk about. It makes me sick just thinking about it."

"Oh God, Carrie." Jessica lightly squeezed her shoulder. "You weren't raped, were you?"

"No. I got away before it went that far."

"Thank goodness." Jessica let out a sigh of relief. "Do you know the person who attacked you?"

"There were two of them, and no, I've never seen them before."

"Jeez, girl. How did you get away? Did you use that Taser your Uncle Frank got you?"

"Hell no, but I was going to. I forgot it in my gym bag."

Jessica shrugged. "So, how did you manage to get away?"

"This is the part that doesn't make any sense."

"I'm listening," Jessica said.

Carrie leaned in close and looked her friend square in the eyes. "You promise you won't think I'm crazy?"

"I swear." Jessica made the sign of a cross. "Cross my heart."

"Something attacked those guys and *killed* them."

Jessica straightened. "Are you serious?"

When Carrie nodded, Jessica said, "Did you see who it was?"

"I know this is going to sound insane, but I swear, I saw it with my own two eyes."

"Come on, Carrie." Her voice sounded impatient. "What did you see?"

"It was some kind of animal."

"An animal? What kind?"

"Jess, it looked like a damn werewolf."

"Really, Carrie?" Jessica rolled her eyes. "A *werewolf*?"

"I knew it." Carrie huffed. "I knew you wouldn't believe me."

"Now wait a minute." Jessica held up a halting hand. "Maybe it was just a big dog or a coyote."

"I know what I saw," Carrie said firmly. "And it wasn't any dog or a coyote for that matter. It stood at least seven feet and ran upright."

"Okay, okay. I believe you."

Carrie narrowed her eyes. "Are you sure?"

"Yes, Carrie. I know you. If you say that's what you saw, I don't doubt you. So, what are you going to do? Are you going to report this?"

"I've got to. Although those creeps got what was coming, I still need to tell someone. I mean, hell, my purse is somewhere in that alley. Whoever discovers those bodies, they'll eventually find out I was there."

"Maybe you should call your Uncle Frank."

"My phone is in my purse. Would you mind calling him?"

"Of course I will," Jessica said. "You just sit back and try to relax. And don't worry. We'll figure this out."

"Thanks, Jess."

"It's no biggie, girl. That's what friends are for. Besides, you'd do the same for me."

"Hey, I forgot to ask," Carrie said. "Did you and Ryan have that talk?"

With her phone in her hand, Jessica turned toward Carrie with a gloomy look on her face.

"Uh-oh." Carrie frowned. "I know that look. What happened?"

"I broke it off."

"Great timing, Jess. Why the day before Valentine's?"

"I know, I know." Jessica groaned. "I'm horrible, right?"

"Well." Carrie shrugged. "You could have waited a few days. He probably had something romantic planned."

"Yeah, but it was for the best. I mean, we've only been dating a few months. Besides, he's been acting strange lately."

Carrie raised a brow. "Strange how?"

"It's hard to explain. It just seems like he's hiding something. Every time I bring it up, he acts like nothing's wrong and changes the subject."

"You think he's seeing someone else?"

Jessica shook her head. "No, it's not like that. He spends a lot of time with me, but when we're together, I can tell something is off, like he's keeping a big secret."

"That's too bad. I thought you two made a cute couple. And I have to say, Ryan is easy on the eyes. All that gorgeous blond hair and those baby blues."

"Jeez, girl." Jessica frowned. "You're killing me here. I've been trying to erase those perfect images of him from my head, and now—"

"Sorry." Carrie shot her a look of sympathy. "Anyway, I'm sorry it didn't work out. If it makes you feel any better, my love life isn't all that great either. Kevin stood me up *again*."

"I told you that guy was no good. Sure, Kevin's loaded, but still, he's a total loser."

"Yeah." Carrie rolled her eyes. "You were right. I should have taken your advice."

"Oh well." Jessica placed her hand over Carrie's. "Maybe someday we'll find the right guys."

Carrie laughed a little. "When hell freezes over."

"You're probably right," Jessica said with a smirk. "Well, it looks like it's going be a rotten Valentine's for the two of us."

"Ain't that the truth," Carrie grudgingly said. "I've got a bottle of wine I was saving. Now that we're both technically single, and I hate to see a good red go to waste, let's drown our sorrows in it."

"That sounds like a great idea. But right now, we've got more important things to worry about, like making that call to your uncle."

* * *

Detective Frank Perkins turned off his computer and reached for his jacket. The cubicles and desks in the precinct were quiet, the staff normally at a bare minimum at this hour. Before he left for the night, he went over to his partner's desk with his brow furrowed. "You're not pulling another all-nighter, are you?"

Manuel looked up at Frank. In his hand, he had a box of chocolates in the shape of a heart.

"What's the occasion?" Manuel asked. "Is it your and Missy's anniversary or something?"

"Did you forget, buddy? According to my watch, it's technically Valentine's Day."

Manuel cursed under his breath. "It completely slipped my mind. You think I still got time to get something for Kathryn?"

Frank arched a brow. "Nothing like waiting until the last minute."

"Give me a break." Manuel rolled his eyes. "This dating *thing* is all new to me."

Frank set the box of chocolates on Manuel's desk. "Missy bought these for you to give to Kathryn. She figured you'd forget."

"I told you." Manuel sighed. "I'm not good at this stuff. Tell Missy thanks and I owe her."

"You can tell her yourself. Or did you forget about the dinner reservation we made at DeVito's?"

"For Pete's sake." Manuel threw his hands up in defeat. "Where the hell is my head? I totally forgot we had a double date."

"It's time to slow your roll, partner. You're working too many late nights."

Manuel groaned. "I think I'm just getting too damn old for all this."

"Are you referring to dating or this job?"

Manuel shrugged. "Maybe both."

"Come on, buddy." Frank chuckled. "You're an excellent detective. Besides, you and I both know you can still give a young man a run for his money. And not to mention all your charisma and charming personality."

Manuel cocked a brow. "Are you taking a jab at me?"

Frank laughed again. "The part about you being a great detective is true. And I've seen you kick some ass in the ring. You nearly knocked out Detective O'Brien last week. I admit you're no longer a spring chicken, and neither am I, but you got one hell of a left hook, partner. But the charming personality part was definitely a jab."

"Yeah." Manuel smirked. "I guess you're right. I'm not exactly Mr. Charming."

"All I'm saying is you could use a little work in that department. Don't take everything so serious all the time. Learn to relax a little."

"Okay, okay," Manuel grumbled. "I'll work on it."

Frank nodded. "And try smiling more. I'm sure Kathryn wouldn't complain."

Manuel shot him a fake smile. "So, I guess I'll see you later. Oh, yeah. What time is our reservation again?"

Frank shook his head, and just as he was about to reply, Manuel's phone rang.

"Hang on, partner," Manuel said, reaching across his desk. "I better take this call."

"Detective Sanchez," he answered, realizing it was almost two o'clock in the morning, which ruled out telemarketers and suggested either dispatch calling or a wrong number.

"Hello," a nervous voice said on the other end. "This is Jessica Phillips. I'm Carrie Randall's roommate. I'm trying to get in touch with her Uncle Frank. I tried earlier, but he didn't answer his phone, so Carrie had me call you."

"He's right here," Manuel said. "Is everything okay?"

There was a moment of silence, and then Jessica finally said, "I need to report an incident. Carrie was attacked tonight."

"What?" Manuel shot to his feet. "Is Carrie all right?"

"She's shook up, but physically okay, I think," Jessica said. "She doesn't feel comfortable talking to anyone else but her uncle."

Manuel nodded against the receiver. "I completely understand. Hold on, Ms. Phillips. I'll give the phone to Frank so she can speak with him."

Before Manuel handed Frank the phone, he put the call on hold. "It's your niece's roommate, Jessica Phillips. Carrie wants to talk to you. She's been attacked. That's all I know so far."

"Oh, my God." Frank gasped and took the phone from Manuel. He went pale and his insides shuddered at the mere thought of some bastard attacking his niece.

He nodded at Manuel as he put the phone up to his ear.

When Manuel took it off hold, Frank said, "Are you okay, sweetheart?"

"I-I'm okay, Uncle Frank," Carrie said in a small voice. "Can you please come to my apartment?"

"Of course, honey. Do you need any medical attention?"

"No, no. I'm not hurt. I managed to get away before..." Her voice trailed off for a second. "Please, just get here quick. It's better if I explain in person."

"Just sit tight, honey, and keep the doors locked. Manuel and I are heading your way."

"Okay," Carrie muttered.

When Frank handed the phone back to Manuel, he said, "Whoever hurt my niece is going to regret the day they were born."

* * *

One minute the wolfish creature was feasting on its fallen prey, devouring the two men almost entirely, and next, it disappeared as though it had shifted somehow, mixing with the thick fog, and drifted away.

Now, more than ever, Joseph wanted to find the girl. The *Shadow* demanded it of him. But unfortunately, she got away. How was he supposed to find her now? His shoulders sagged in defeat. The moment he'd seen her he'd wanted her just as much as the Shadow. He wondered what her name was. The shameful truth of it was he wanted to know more than her name. He felt drawn to her in a strange way. For a split second, he recalled the terrified look on her face when those two men attacked her. An awful chill sank into his bones. It brought back the memory of his mother and the terrified look she got during his father's drunken benders. *Would the girl have looked at me the same way?*

"Yesss," the Shadow said.

Joseph thought of the number of times his father had gotten drunk and had beaten his mother. His first memory was at age three. Afterward, his father always promised he'd never do it again. Although there had always been a next time. And a next time. Always with the same outcome in the end.

"Do you remember how that made you feel?"

"I hated him."

"Your father got what was coming to him in the end, did he not?"

Joseph nodded. "Yes."

"Tell me, Joseph... Why did you let the girl get away?"

"I'm sorry. That *thing* distracted me. I don't understand. What was it?"

"An extraordinary creature. The last of its kind."

"Why did it not kill the girl?"

"It only hunts evil."

"What keeps it from attacking us?"

"It does not bestow the power to destroy us."

"Then what can?"

"Do not worry, Joseph. Together, we are invincible."

Joseph smiled and nodded a silent understanding. As he turned to leave, something on the ground caught his eye. It wasn't until he moved closer that he realized what it was. The girl's purse. The white, small handbag glistened under the light of the full moon. He bent over and plucked it from the grass that was wet with morning dew. While he searched the contents inside, he found a cell phone and a photo ID. *Bingo!* He had her name and address.

"Her name is Carrie Randall," Joseph said. "She lives at 1477 Fillmore Street."

"Exxxceeellent... She's ours for the taking."

Chapter Three

The mind-numbing phone conversation with his niece just moments ago sliced through Frank's heart like he'd been cut with a knife. He'd never be able to get Carrie's terrified voice out of his head.

"Buckle up, partner," Frank said as he hit the lights on his unmarked car and floored it.

It was raining and the roads were wet, so when he hit the gas, his Ford Taurus fishtailed a little. The car then sprang forward as he exited the precinct's parking lot and bolted onto the interstate.

Manuel shot his partner a look. "I'd like to get there," he sputtered, bracing his arm against the car's dashboard, "in one piece, if that's okay with you."

"Come on, buddy." Frank chortled. "Where's your sense of adventure? You used to love this stuff."

"That was twenty years ago. Before we got old."

"Aw, now." Frank shrugged with his hands tight on the wheel. "Age has nothing to do with it. You're only as old as you feel."

Manuel glared at Frank. "How old is dirt? 'Cuz right about now, that's how old I feel."

Frank glanced toward the passenger's seat and cocked a brow. "That's not what I hear."

"What in the hell is that supposed to mean?"

"Our women are friends," Frank said. "They talk."

"Whaddaya mean *they talk*? About what?"

"Well, you didn't hear this from me, but Missy said Kathryn told her you remind her of that Spanish actor, Antonio Banderas."

"Really?" The corner of Manuel's lips curled up a little. "How so?"

"She meant you *look* like the guy."

"I take it that's a good thing?"

Frank raised a brow. "According to Kathryn it is."

Manuel's smile broadened. "Well, that's not the first time I've heard that. The last time your wife set me up on a blind date, which seems like a decade ago, the subject may have come up in conversation."

"Yeah, I also recall Jena saying something like that the first time we met her in the hospital." Frank took his eyes off the road for a second to look at Manuel. "Come to think of it, I think they're right. You do resemble the guy."

Manuel rolled his eyes, his thoughts going back to the day he and his partner met Jena. Back then, she was just a frightened, innocent girl—who had been bitten by a creature and cursed—and now she was the most courageous person he knew. After Jena destroyed the creature, she was doomed to take its place, except she would never harm an innocent person. She would only kill evil. Which in turn rid the city of the worst criminals. As he came back to focus, he said, "I wonder how Jena is adjusting to her new life? I mean, with the curse and all. Have you heard from Nicolas?"

"As a matter of fact," Frank said, "I talked to him the other day. They just got back from their trip. Nicolas said it's taking her some getting used to. You know..." He took one hand off the wheel and made finger quotations. "...with the *werewolf thing* and *killing people*."

"Yeah, but she's killing bad people."

"Still..." Frank grimaced. "...the whole thing is kind of morbid when you think about it. I can't imagine having to live with a curse that drives me to eat people."

"Eat *bad* people," Manuel corrected as though he was making light of the situation. "Besides, remember what the battle angels said? Jena will be helping them by eliminating Satan's future soldiers, and it saves the city tax money. That's less evil the battle angels will have to fight and a lot less offenders we'll have to deal with. Think about the number of criminals, and I'm talking about the worst kind, who are sent to prison. Our tax dollars support those SOBs. If it was up to me, I'd give Jena the key to all their cells." He laughed a little. "Think of it like this: It'd be an all-you-can-eat buffet to her."

Frank frowned. "That's just messed up, buddy."

"That's a matter of opinion, partner."

Fifteen minutes later, as they pulled into the parking lot where Carrie lived, they noticed someone dart around the building wearing a black hoodie.

Manuel's eyes rounded. "What the hell?"

"My words exactly," Frank said, switching off the lights. "It's after two o'clock, and too damn early for a morning stroll."

Manuel reached for the passenger's door when the vehicle skidded to a stop next to Carrie's Volkswagen Beetle. "Let's check it out."

The second they got out of the car, Manuel signaled toward Frank, pointing to the rear of the apartment building. "You head toward the back while I go around the front. Maybe we can block him in from both sides."

Frank gave him a thumb's up and took off toward the back of his niece's apartment complex. As he made it to the rear of the building, he pulled his gun from his holster and peered around the corner. He could hear the ping of footsteps against the metal stairway that led to the second floor. When Frank spotted his partner, he waved him over and pointed to the stairs.

Manuel nodded and motioned for him to go up while he covered him from the rear.

Frank came up behind the hooded stranger, who was moving toward the sliding glass doors at the back of his niece's apartment. "Hold it right there." He held his gun steady. "Don't make another move."

When the hooded guy spun around and saw Frank and his partner with their weapons drawn, he instantly held up his hands. "What the—"

"Keep your hands where we can see them," Manuel directed. "And don't make a move."

"What's going on?" the hooded man sputtered, keeping his hands high.

"Keep your pie-hole shut," Frank gritted out. "I'll be the one asking all the questions. Do I make myself clear?"

With a shocked look on his face, the guy quickly nodded a silent understanding.

"What are you doing at this apartment building?"

"M-my girlfriend lives here. And I live on the top floor."

"What's your girlfriend's name?"

"Jessica Phillips. Well actually," he swallowed hard, "she's my ex-girlfriend. She broke up with me earlier and I just wanted to talk to her."

"What's your name?" Frank asked, continuing to grill the guy.

"R-Ryan Grayson."

"Mr. Grayson, do you have an ID on you?"

Ryan nodded at Frank. "Yes, sir. My wallet is in my back pocket."

"Have you been drinking tonight?"

"I've had a few drinks," Ryan said. "But I haven't been driving. I took an Uber."

"Can you tell us your whereabouts tonight?"

"I was at the Alibi. You know?" He shrugged. "That popular bar off Main Street. I met Jessica there for drinks earlier."

"Yeah, I know the place," Frank said. "What time did you last see Miss Phillips?"

"About an hour ago." Ryan clenched his brows in confusion. "Why? Is something wrong?"

"Listen to what I tell you, Ryan," Frank urged. "Using one hand, I want you to *slowly* reach into your back pocket and pull out your wallet. Then I want you to toss it over to my partner. Do you understand?"

"Yes, sir."

After Ryan carefully took out his wallet and tossed it to Manuel, Frank said, "Do you know Miss Phillips's roommate?"

Ryan nodded again. "Yeah. I mean, yes, sir. I know Carrie. Please, Detective. Is Jessica all right?"

"Looks like he checks out," Manuel said.

"Mr. Grayson, your ex-girlfriend is fine," Frank said. "We got a call from her about twenty minutes ago. Carrie was attacked tonight, and we're here to get a report of the incident."

Ryan's eyes rounded. "Oh my God. Is she okay?"

Before Manuel replied, he looked at the sliding glass door as it made a whooshing sound when it came open.

Jessica's mouth dropped when her eyes caught sight of her ex-boyfriend with his hands above his head. "Ryan—" Her head swiveled back and forth between Ryan and the two detectives. "What's going on here?"

The detectives lowered their weapons and Frank said, "You can drop your hands now, Mr. Grayson."

Ryan slowly lowered his hands and gave Jessica a despairing little shrug.

"We caught your boyfriend going around the back when we arrived," Manuel said. "At this hour, he looked suspicious, so we followed him. He says you two were together earlier. We're just checking his story to make sure he's not giving us a line of BS."

Jessica crossed her arms and sighed. "For starters, he's my ex-boyfriend. And he's telling the truth. I was with him about an hour ago. We had drinks at the Alibi tonight."

"Well, that's what he told us," Frank pointed out. "It seems he came back to talk to you, but considering the situation, I think it best that lover-boy comes back to chitchat another time. Of course, he'll stop by at a *respectful* hour of the day." He shot Ryan a look. "Isn't that right, Mr. Grayson?"

Ryan quickly bobbed his head. "Yes, sir."

As he turned to leave, Jessica said, "If you still want to talk, I'm free for coffee later this morning."

Ryan's face instantly brightened. "That would be great, Jess." He smiled and waved at her. "I'll see you then." After he turned to leave, he briefly looked back. "I hope Carrie is okay. Call me if you need anything."

Jessica nodded. "Thanks, Ryan."

Manuel rolled his eyes and Frank said, "How's my niece?"

"Much better than I would be," Jessica said, shaking her head. "Especially after what she's been through." She motioned them inside. "Carrie will be glad to see you. And man, she's got one crazy story to tell you. But please, keep an open mind. What she's about to tell you goes beyond reason."

* * *

With his mind still focused on the girl, Joseph was about to cross the street when the sound of humming caught his attention. As he turned to look, he spotted a woman not far down the sidewalk, moving in his direction. She had long, blonde hair like Carrie's, but this girl was a lot taller.

"Well, heeello," the Shadow purred. *"I like her, Joseph."*

"What about Carrie?"

"Save her for later." The Shadow smacked his lips. *"I'm starving. This one will do."*

Before he approached the girl, his eyes searched the surroundings, making sure the streets were clear of any onlookers or eyewitnesses. When Joseph saw the coast was clear, his upper lip curled up into a snarl and his face twisted into a mask of horror. His breaths came out deeper and more guttural, as though another person was inside of him breathing. He was changing quickly. Already the shape of his face was less human and more demonic. His eyes were like black, soulless pits.

"Take her, Joseph. Do it for me."

He started forward, moving with long strides and a determination to please the Shadow. But his efforts availed him nothing. It was like some sort of magic trick. The girl simply vanished before his eyes, leaving nothing behind but a thick veil of fog.

Joseph's eyes bulged. "How—?"

"Look out, Joseph. She's behind you."

When Joseph spun around on the balls of his feet, he came face-to-face with the girl. Her eyes were flat reflective disks under the light of the moon and the lines of her face looked distorted. It was stretching and bulging as though her features were reshaping themselves. Her body continued to crack and shift. He could hear the distinctive sounds of bones snapping and reforming. Panic threatened to overwhelm him, and for a second, he froze, watching in disgust as black hairs began to bristle from her skin.

The Shadow cursed in irritation. *"The girl is the creature."*

Her blouse ripped apart as her chest quickly expanded and her arms and legs began to lengthen, growing at an alarming rate. She now stood at least a foot taller than him, and her features were entirely unrecognizable. What was once a feminine mouth was now a muzzle, full of razor-sharp teeth. Atop her hideous wolf-like head were two lupine ears.

Rendered speechless, Joseph took a few steps back. For a moment, he stared at her in disbelief, caught between his fight-or-flight response.

"Hold steady, Joseph."

The wolfish creature took an inquisitive step forward. "Who are you?"

Joseph peered up at the hideous thing and replied, *"We are the Shadow."*

"We?" The wolfish creature spoke in a guttural voice. "I only see one of you."

Before Joseph could respond, the sound of voices caught him off guard. As he turned to look, he saw a man and a woman engaging in a conversation not far down the street. It had only been seconds, but when looked back, the creature was nowhere in sight. It was as if it had magically disappeared in thin air.

"What now?" Joseph asked the Shadow.

"We find another."

"What about Carrie?"

"Oh, we'll have her. Sooner or later."

Chapter Four

When Carrie told Frank and Manuel what had happened to her earlier, including the part about the *werewolf*, it completely rendered them speechless. Although, if she had told this to anyone else, she'd have been hauled off to the looney bin and put in a straitjacket. Considering what the two detectives had experienced in the last year—discovering a secret species of humans with the ability to shapeshift into wolves, as well as real live battle angels and much more bizarre creatures—they believed her every word. Nevertheless, they told her to keep the incident, especially the werewolf part, under wraps until further notice.

After they took Carrie's statement, promising they would check things out and search for her purse, they drove to the crime scene. Even though they didn't know her attacker's identity, they had a pretty good idea who saved Carrie. By her description of the wolfish creature, it had to be Jena. However, they still weren't a hundred percent sure. There was a possibility it could have been someone or *something* else.

By the time they arrived, the area was completely deserted. As Frank parked alongside the street, Manuel said, "You think we should contact the Breedline Covenant?"

"Let's check the crime scene first. Besides, it's three o'clock in the morning. There's no reason to wake the Covenant until we get the facts. If we call Tim Ross, he'll have to notify Tessa. I hate to wake her at this hour since she's got her hands full with twins."

Manuel checked his watch and sighed. "Yeah, you're right. Let's go see what kind of mess we're dealing with."

"This is the part I hate about my job," Frank said as he took the keys from the ignition. "Although by now, you'd think I'd be used to bloody body parts."

Manuel reached to open the passenger's door. "And it's not going to get any better."

Frank sighed and stepped out of the vehicle.

Manuel directed a flashlight toward a dark alley. "Carrie said those bastards dragged her over there."

When they got closer, the glare from the light displayed spray-painted profanity and obscene gestures all over the front of an abandoned building. As they searched the area, Frank shook his head. "I just wish one of those bastards were still alive so I could…"

"Me too, partner," Manuel said as Frank's voice trailed off. "But I've got a feeling if this was Jena, she didn't leave much behind."

"Good lord," Frank muttered, pointing toward the ground. "Is that what I think it is?"

When Manuel shined the flashlight in the direction Frank was pointing, they both cringed and took a step back. Lying in the grass were two severed heads. One of them stared blankly at nothing with dead, glassy eyes, and the other one was barely recognizable. His skull was crushed like an elephant had stomped on it.

Manuel nodded. "I believe it's as good time as any to make that call."

"We better do it soon," Frank said. "It'll be daylight in a few hours and we sure as hell don't want this reported in. Captain Hodge will have a coronary if this gets out to the press."

"You got that right," Manuel said. "While I call Tim, go on ahead and look for your niece's purse." He handed Frank the flashlight. "We don't need her connected to any of this. If word gets out, we'll have another panicked outbreak on our hands."

After Manuel ended the call, he told Frank, "Tim's on his way. And he's bringing backup."

Frank sighed in relief. "Did he say who?"

"Drakon and Roman."

"Speaking of Roman," Frank began, "how's it going with him and your sister?"

"By what Lailah tells me, they've been talking about tying the knot."

Frank's eyes widened. "Already?"

"Yeah. I guess some things are just meant to be."

"Are you okay with your sister marrying Roman?"

"Of course," Manuel said. "Roman's a good guy. In addition, he treats Lailah like a queen. If it stays that way, he's got my blessing. Lailah deserves happiness after everything she's been through. Although I can't believe my sister is back from the dead. I always felt like it was my fault for not doing more to stop her from leaving with a total stranger."

"You can't blame yourself," Frank said. "You were just a kid. Put all that in the past now that she's back. And just think, your sister was an actual battle angel for crying out loud. It's hard to imagine something like that. Plus, Lailah had some kick-ass powers. Never in a million years would I envision angels having wings that could be used as weapons."

"You and me both," Manuel said.

Frank focused back on the current situation and said, "What did Tim say?"

"As soon as they get here, they'll take care of this. So, did you find your niece's purse?"

"I've looked everywhere," Frank said, "but unfortunately, I came up empty. I wonder if Jena picked it up after she—"

"Ate those guys?"

Frank gave Manuel an unsettling nod.

"She could have," Manuel said. "But we still don't know for sure if it was her."

"You think we should call Nicolas?" Frank asked. "He is the closest person to Jena."

"It wouldn't hurt to try."

"I'll wait to see what Tim says when he arrives with the others," Frank said. "I just hope this isn't going to be a habit with Jena."

"She's not going to stop killing bad people. Jena is cursed for eternity."

"I know," Frank said. "But what are we supposed to do? We can't just follow her around and clean up all the mess she leaves behind."

"You've got a point there, partner. I guess that's something we need to discuss with the Covenant. We can't have pieces of dead bodies left all over the city."

* * *

Carrie flinched when a loud knock sounded at the front door. She looked at Jessica wide-eyed. "Are you expecting company?"

Jessica shot Carrie a look. "It's freaking three o'clock in the morning."

"Carrie…" came a loud voice, followed by another round of loud knocks that sounded more like pounding fists. "Open the door. It's me, Kevin."

Carrie groaned, rolling her eyes.

"Seriously?" Jessica put her hands on her hips. "Who does he think he is?"

"I'm not talking to him," Carrie said. "He can just stand out there all night."

"Carrrieee…" Kevin pounded on the door, slurring his words. "Come on. I know you're in there."

"He sounds drunk," Jessica grumbled. "We ought to call the cops."

"He won't last long," Carrie said. "He has a problem with that sort of thing." She looked at Jessica with a raised brow. "If you know what I mean."

Jessica snickered. "What a loser. I guess his mommy and daddy's money can't buy him stamina."

They both burst into laughter. Shortly after, Kevin finally gave up.

Carrie grinned. "See, I told you."

Jessica chuckled. "I'm glad you're finally getting rid of that jerk. You deserve so much better."

"I totally agree. So, what did Ryan want earlier?"

Jessica's face lit up. "He said he wanted to talk."

"Really?" Carrie looked at Jessica curiously. "Maybe he wants to tell you about the so-called *secret* he's been keeping."

"Maybe." Jessica shrugged. "We'll see."

"Well, whatever it is, don't be holding out on me. I want details later."

Jessica batted her brows. "You know it, girl."

Carrie yawned. "So, are you ready to turn in?"

"Yeah." Jessica's shoulders sagged. "It's been a long night."

Meanwhile, as Carrie and Jessica got ready for bed, Kevin—who had had way too much alcohol—staggered back to the parking lot where he half-ass parked his Porsche, taking up two parking spaces in the process.

When he finally made his way over to his shiny red sports car, he reached inside the front pocket of his designer jeans and fumbled around for his keys. He was oblivious to his surroundings and the dark figure that came up behind him. As he looked up to unlock the door, his eyes rounded in sheer terror. The image staring back at him through the car's tinted window nearly brought him to his knees.

Then he felt something with an immense force punch through his chest. He opened his mouth, but instead of a scream, out came a gurgling sound. Blood spurted like a crimson geyser, coating his expensive car. He gasped at the bloody hand protruding from his chest, gripping his still-beating heart. As Kevin went limp, he collapsed forward, triggering the car alarm.

"*Mmmm...*" purred the Shadow as Joseph devoured Kevin's heart, relishing the taste of the blood as the organ burst between his teeth.

The blaring car alarm echoed, the sound drifting through the parking lot and into Carrie and Jessica's apartment.

"Un-freaking-believable." Jessica let out a frustrated groan. "That better not be your stupid-ass boyfriend."

Carrie frowned. "You mean, stupid-ass ex-boyfriend."

"Sorry," Jessica said. "I swear, though, I'm fixing to go out there and kick his spoiled, rich ass."

"I second that," Carrie said as she went into the coat closet and grabbed the Taser from her gym bag. "I'm bringing backup."

Jessica snatched up her phone. "Oh, I'm getting a photo of that."

Carrie laughed. "Come on." She threw open the door. "I'll bet you fifty bucks he's passed out in his car."

"You're on," Jessica said. "I doubt the jerk didn't even make it that far."

It didn't take long for them to locate Kevin's car. The sound coming from the car alarm led them straight to it. When

Carrie and Jessica came up to the Porsche, they saw Kevin lying on his back next to his car. He wasn't moving and there was blood everywhere.

"Oh my God." Carrie gasped into the palm of her hand. "Kevin—"

"Shit," Jessica spouted, noticing the giant hole in Kevin's chest. Her insides churned at the gruesome image. "How in the hell did that happen?"

"I-I can't believe it." Carrie's voice trembled. "Who would do this?"

"Well," Jessica said, shrugging, "I guess you owe me fifty bucks."

Carrie faced Jessica with a shocked expression. "What?"

"Sorry. I didn't mean—"

"For crying out loud, Jess... Please, just call my Uncle Frank."

Chapter Five

It wasn't long before the bright headlights of a black SUV pulled in behind Frank's unmarked car. Then came the sounds of doors opening and closing, followed by several heavy footsteps. When Manuel caught sight of a black Mohawk, he sighed in relief, realizing it was Drakon Hexus, which meant the members of the Breedline Covenant had arrived. Manuel remembered the story on Drakon. He'd been born a Breedline, but when he disobeyed one of their True Laws, he'd been banished to live as a rogue wolf. For years, he did not possess the ability to shift back to his human form. But when Drakon helped the Breedline destroy the Chiang-shih demon, he'd been granted a full pardon by the Covenant. And there was one peculiar thing about Drakon's rogue wolf. It was not exactly what you'd call an ordinary Breedline. Although it was as big as a horse, it also resembles something out of the Mesozoic era.

Roman Kincaid, who belonged to a Special Ops group, trained in military tactics and allies to the Breedline, followed close behind Drakon. Roman, on the other hand, was not born a Breedline. Instead, he shapeshifted into an Adalwolf, inheriting both features of man and wolf.

So far, Manuel was still getting used to the Breedline. Finding out that there were people who could turn into wolves blew his mind. Aside from that, not long ago he'd found out he was also born with the Breedline genetics. Since he didn't have an identical twin, he didn't possess the *wolf thing*.

A tense muscle worked in Tim Ross's jaw—who was born a Breedline and was the council head of the California Covenant—as he and his comrades took in the gruesome scene.

"Explain to me again what all happened here," Tim said.

"Well, to make a long story short," Manuel began, gesturing toward the two severed heads, "we *think* they're the remains of Jena's last meal."

"How did you find them?"

"They attacked my niece tonight," Frank said, his eyes shifting between the three intimidating men.

Drakon's and Roman's expressions became visibly alarmed, and Tim shook his head, muttering something under his breath.

Tim looked at Frank, concerned. "Is she all right?"

"One of them hit her," Frank said. "But she managed to get away with just a split lip. She's pretty shook up. She called me right after the attack."

"How did she get away?" Roman asked, chiming into the conversation.

"Manuel and I believe it was Jena who saved her," Frank explained. "By my niece's description, we instantly thought of Jena's creature."

"Shit," Tim gritted out. "Your niece saw Jena's creature?"

"If it weren't for Jena," Frank said, "those creeps would have raped her, or worse."

Tim wore a look of understanding and placed a hand on Frank's shoulder. "I'm sorry, Frank. The important thing is your niece is safe. And if this indeed was Jena, she did a good thing tonight."

Drakon came forward. "You didn't mention anything about Jena's identity to your niece, did you?"

"No, no," Frank said. "We just told her we would check it out and for her to keep what she saw between the four of us."

"The four of you?" Tim frowned. "Besides you two, and your niece, who else are you referring to?"

"Carrie's roommate, Jessica Phillips," Frank said. "She was at the apartment when Carrie rushed home after the attack. Jessica is her best friend and someone she trusts."

"This could create a problem if this gets out," Tim said.

Frank shook his head. "I don't think they'll tell a soul. I mean, who'd believe a story like that?"

"You'd be surprised," Drakon said. "Reporters would eat this up."

"Yeah, I guess you're right," Frank said. "Last time something like this got out, it was all over the media."

"Sorry to change the subject," Manuel said. "Although I don't think we have to worry about Carrie and Jessica saying anything to anyone. Before you arrived, we found the assailant's vehicle across the street. I ran their tags and got an

ID on those two guys. It looks like one of them did some time for assaulting a minor. It's only been a month since he's been released from the penitentiary. The other guy, the one who looks like his head has been through a meat grinder, is a felon with a long criminal history. In my opinion, whoever killed these SOBs did everyone a favor. It's less garbage we'll have to deal with."

"Well, it looks like Jena's MO all right," Drakon said. "Roman and I will get this cleaned up. Besides, I don't think anyone will be missing these two jokers, or what's left of them anyway."

"That's another thing we want to talk to you about," Manuel said. "Are we going to have to continue to clean up what Jena leaves behind?"

"I don't know, Detective," Tim reluctantly said. "That's something we'll all have to discuss."

"There's something else," Frank mentioned. "Carrie said she dropped her purse around here somewhere, and I can't seem to find it. Would you ask Jena if she picked it up?"

"Of course," Tim said. "I'll let you know as soon as I get some answers."

As the two detectives started for their car, Frank's cell phone went off. When he looked at the caller ID, he recognized the number. He looked up at Manuel wide-eyed and said, "It's Jessica."

"Well, see what she wants."

Frank swiped to answer. "Jessica, is everything all right?"

After a few moments of silence, everyone noticed that Frank's face grew pale.

"Stay inside the apartment," Frank finally said. "And keep the doors locked. We're on our way."

When he ended the call, Manuel said, "What's going on?"

Frank's stomach churned as he traded glances with Manuel and the others. It sickened him to think what his niece had been through. "The girls just found Carrie's boyfriend lying in the parking lot of their apartment building. And he's covered in blood."

"What...?" Manuel's jaw dropped. "Is he dead?"

"Going by Jessica's description, I believe so. She said it looked like the guy's chest has been ripped open."

"We better head that way," Manuel said.

"You two go on ahead," Tim said. "We'll meet you there as soon as we can."

Frank nodded and followed Manuel as he headed for the car.

Tim's phone went off right after Manuel and Frank drove away. The moment he retrieved it from his back pocket he saw it was Tessa calling. Realizing no decisions were made without her approval, this would save him the trouble of having to contact her.

He quickly answered, "This is Tim."

"I know you guys are busy," Tessa said, "but we've got a bit of another situation on our hands."

"What's going on?"

"I just spoke with Jena. The Detectives were right. She's the one that killed those two men. Jena said she had no choice. Her instincts drove her to save a young girl from being attacked. But that's not the only reason I'm calling." Tessa exhaled a deep breath. "Not long after Jena saved the girl, she came in contact with something strange."

"Strange how?"

"It's hard to explain," Tessa said, "but Jena described it as something supernatural. She said it looked inhuman, like a man with demonic features."

"Did Jena kill him?"

"No," Tessa replied. "But she spoke to him."

"What did he say?"

"When she asked who he was, his answer was odd. It was like he was addressing himself as more than one person, saying *we* are the Shadow."

"That is odd," Tim said.

"Jena and I thought so too. Unfortunately, she didn't get the chance to stick around. There were people not far away and she didn't want to be seen, since she was forced to shift into her creature."

"That is interesting," Tim said. "I wonder why he didn't try to attack Jena."

"That's a good question."

Tim nodded against his phone. "Did Jena happen to mention anything else about the girl she saved?"

"No, why?"

"Her name is Carrie Randall. She's Frank's niece. And there's more. Her roommate just contacted Frank right before you called. The two girls found Carrie's boyfriend in the parking lot of their apartment building, and by the description, I don't think he's alive."

"Oh, no," Tessa said. "Do you need me to send more help?"

"Between me, Drakon, and Roman, I believe we got this covered. I'll let you know what we find out."

"I'm just a phone call away if you need anything."

"There's one more thing," Tim said. "Could you ask Jena if she picked up a purse where Frank's niece was attacked?"

"Sure. Does it belong to her?"

"Yeah, and it's missing. Frank said his niece told him she dropped it when those guys attacked her, but now it's not here."

"I'll ask her."

"Thanks, Tessa."

There was a moment of silence and then Tessa finally said, "How are we going to deal with Frank's niece? She obviously saw Jena's creature. I'm worried she'll stir up the press if word gets out. We sure don't want talk about another werewolf sighting."

"Frank seems positive his niece will keep this quiet," Tim said. "But there's also another person who knows."

"Who?"

"Carrie's roommate. Her name is Jessica Phillips, and she was the first person Carrie confided in after the attack."

"There's nothing we can do about it now," Tessa said. "We'll discuss all this later."

When Tim ended the call, muddled pieces of the conversation with Tessa kept surfacing in his brain as he drove to Carrie's apartment complex, which now was a crime scene. His nerves, along with Drakon's and Roman's, were on edge. His fingers gripped the steering wheel with enough force that his knuckles bulged white. What in the hell were they dealing with now? Was this *demonic thing* a new creature they'd never heard of? And what did it want? Could it be destroyed? If so, how? To make matters worse, they had to deal with Frank's niece and her roommate. It was crucial that their species remained secret from the outside world. Although there had been a few exceptions in the past. The two detectives knew about their secret, along with some other human Breedline family members. While Tim tried to come up with a solution to their current dilemma, the Covenant's True Laws suddenly came to mind. And that's when he realized what was most important. Their rules were designed for a good reason. But unfortunately, sometimes rules had to be broken.

"So, this demon-possessed person," Drakon spoke out, breaking the silence, "did Jena find out what it wants?"

Tim shook his head. "Right now, we haven't a clue."

Roman focused on Tim from the back seat. "Do you think this demonic thing had something to do with the situation with Carrie's boyfriend?"

"Who knows?" Tim shrugged. "I'm not throwing the possibility out the window."

As always, Tim's faith in God remained strong, but now, as he pulled into the parking lot and parked by Frank's unmarked car, he decided that today was a great time to call upon *His* help.

When Tim stepped out of the vehicle, his heart filled with dread. He spotted an area roped off with yellow tape where officers were working the crime scene. Obviously, Manuel and Frank had already reported the incident.

Their surroundings grew more gruesome as they got closer. A wide stain of red covered the window of a Porsche and over the ground where a body lay behind the roped-off crime scene. Then Tim noticed two young women standing away from the dreadful scene. One of them appeared to be crying. She was leaning for support against the other girl.

Frank approached Tim, Drakon, and Roman with a grim look on his face. "We made a positive ID on the victim. His name is Kevin Russo. He's the son of Russo's Exotic Car Dealerships."

"What happened?" Tim asked.

"It's the damnedest thing," Frank said, shaking his head. "There's an entry wound beginning at the upper portion of Mr. Russo's back that exits clean through his chest cavity. And apparently, his heart is MIA. You don't think Jena had anything to do with this, do you?"

"No," Tim replied. "I got a call from Tessa right before you and Manuel left. She asked Jena about those two guys that attacked your niece. Apparently, Jena was responsible for that, but she didn't say anything about this ordeal. But Jena did mention something rather strange."

"What do you mean by strange?" Manuel asked as he walked up behind his partner, catching the butt end of the conversation.

"Jena was confronted by something supernatural," Tim went on to explain. "She said it looked like a man with demonic-like features. She sensed it was going to attack her while she was in her human form, but when she shifted, it stood down."

"Well, hell," Manuel said. "I don't doubt it. The mere sight of her creature would make the bravest of any man piss himself."

"You think this demonic thing killed Mr. Russo?" Frank asked.

Tim shrugged. "It's definitely a possibility."

Manuel sighed. "Just when I thought things were starting to get back to normal."

"It's never normal in the Breedline world," Drakon said. "And now you two are part of it."

Tim looked to Frank. "How's your niece and her roommate faring?"

"They're pretty shaken up, but considering everything they've been through, especially Carrie, I think they'll be okay after they get some rest. I'll stop by later to check on them."

"It wouldn't hurt if they talked to someone, particularly your niece," Tim said. "After everything that's happened, she could be suffering from shock."

Frank shot Tim a confused look. "I thought you wanted the girls to keep this quiet."

"I do," Tim said, "but I was referring to Dr. Helen Carrington. I can set it up if your niece agrees to see her. Of course, it will be confidential and free of charge."

"Okay." Frank nodded. "I'll talk to her about it. She did ask about those guys that attacked her."

Tim raised an inquisitive brow. "What did you tell her?"

"I didn't give her a definite answer. I just told her she never had to worry about them hurting her or anyone else ever again."

"Good answer, Detective," Tim said. "By the way, I did ask Tessa to find out if Jena picked up your niece's purse. I'll keep you posted."

"Thanks, Tim. I'd appreciate it."

When Manuel's phone dinged, he retrieved it from the inside pocket of his jacket. The second he looked at the screen, he noticed he had a text. "Shit." He rolled his eyes. "It's the Captain. According to this..." He focused on Frank. "...it looks like we've got a long day ahead of us, partner."

Frank groaned. "Knowing the Captain, he'll have us working on this case day and night." Then, as it began to sprinkle, he looked up at the cloud-covered sky. "Great timing. Looks like we're about to get soaked. Why does it have to do this now?"

Manuel glanced up, feeling tiny raindrops against his face. "I believe you'll have to ask the big man upstairs about that one."

"Well, there goes our dinner plans," Frank said. "Our ladies are going to be disappointed."

Manuel extended his hand out to Tim. "Thanks again for helping us out."

"No problem, Detective." Tim shook hands with Manuel and then reached out to Frank. "We're happy to help anytime."

Chapter Six

Nicolas Ratcliff opened his eyes when Jena shifted away from him and onto her side. Then she rolled back over, facing the ceiling. A second later, she flipped over on her stomach. Somehow, during all the tossing and turning, she wiggled out from underneath the covers.

When he slowly tugged the blanket over her body, she snuggled deeper into it and let out a long sigh.

"I didn't mean to wake you," Nicolas whispered.

"You didn't. I was already awake."

"You've tossed and turned almost the entire night, sweetheart." He stroked Jena's arm, wishing he could do something to help clear her mind.

"I know." She took a deep breath and rolled back over, her strong, warrior blue eyes meeting his. "I'm sorry."

"Don't be." He reached for her hand. "You want to talk about it?"

When she shrugged, he said, "You're worried about that girl, aren't you?"

Jena squeezed her eyes shut. Her forehead wrinkled as images of the girl's terrified expression flooded her mind. It was all because of her. The poor girl must have been horrified at what she saw.

"Jena, please. Talk to me."

She lifted her lids and looked into his lavender eyes. "All this," her voice cracked, "wouldn't have happened if it weren't for me."

Nicolas lightly squeezed her hand. "That girl was about to be raped, and maybe killed. You saved her life, honey."

As she lifted higher on her pillow, her long, golden locks fell around her shoulders in total disarray. "But you didn't see the look on her face. She was horrified. And I've created more problems for the Covenant. What if the girl tells someone and this gets out to the public?"

"Trust me. Everything will be okay. That's the least of our problems. What worries me is that *thing* you encountered. Whatever it is, and going by your description, it sounds dangerous."

"Well, it's definitely not human," she said, "or it didn't appear to be. I sensed evil from it, but also something else."

"What do you mean?"

Her brows furrowed. "I'm not entirely sure. It was more like a feeling of intense sorrow. An emotion you get when someone you love dies. Then I sensed something else."

"What's that?"

"Power," Jena said. "A power far greater than mine."

Nicolas looked at her, bewildered. "That's strange. And you said it appeared as though it was coming after you, right? I mean, while you were still in your human form."

When Jena nodded, Nicolas said, "I wonder what it wanted? Do you think it was after blood?"

"I can't be sure, but I'm pretty positive it intended to kill me at first."

"Although," Nicolas began, "it didn't attack you when you shifted."

She shook her head. "It realized then I wasn't human."

"Do you believe this *thing* is hunting humans?"

Jena nodded.

"Tim texted me earlier," Nicolas said, changing the subject.

"What did he say?"

"I was going to wait to tell you, but maybe now is the best time."

"I'm already awake," Jena said, "so tell me."

"The girl you saved is Detective Frank Perkins's niece."

Jena's eyes rounded. "What—"

"Hang on," Nicolas said, giving her hand another squeeze. "Before you get upset, you'll want to hear the rest."

Jena sighed. "Okay. I'm listening."

"Frank is grateful for what you did for his niece. Her name is Carrie Randall. I've worked with Frank on the force for more than fifteen years, and during that time, I've got to know him and his family. Carrie has been more like a daughter to Frank and his wife Missy than anything else. You see, Carrie was Frank's sister's daughter."

"What do you mean by *was*? Did something happen?"

"Carrie's parents were killed in a freak car accident when she was just five years old."

Jena shook her head. "That's awful."

Nicolas regretfully nodded. "It was late, and it had been raining. They had just left Frank's house for a family gathering on Christmas Eve. They hit a deer and the car went off a bridge. By the time first responders arrived, the vehicle had already sunk to the bottom."

"How did Carrie manage to survive?"

"After all these years," Nicolas said, "it remains a mystery. A passing semi stopped when the driver saw her standing by the bridge. When the truck driver asked her what she was doing alone on the side of the road, she told him about the car accident."

"I don't understand." Jena shrugged. "How did she get out of the car?"

"No one really knows. When asked, she said a giant angel saved her. Of course, at her young age, everyone thought it was her imagination and the trauma of losing her family. And the incident gets more bizarre. Carrie was completely dry when the truck driver found her. Not even as much as a drop. It was as though she wasn't even in the car when it went into the river."

"That is odd," Jena said. "Do you believe she really saw an angel?"

"I don't know. It's possible."

"If she did, I wonder why the angel saved Carrie and not her parents?"

"That's a good question," Nicolas said. "I'm sure God has his reasons."

"Did Tim mention anything else?"

Nicolas nodded and told her about the incident with Carrie's boyfriend.

"That poor girl. She must be so traumatized at this point."

"There's more to the story," Nicolas said. "Which brings to mind that unknown *thing* you came in contact with."

"Why is that?"

"Tim said the guy that was murdered had his heart completely ripped from his chest. I don't know any human being capable of such, do you?"

"No," Jena said. "It does sound unusual, and of course, it wasn't me."

"Tim knows you aren't responsible. Tessa talked to him earlier. He also mentioned a meeting here in the Covenant taking place later this morning. They want us to attend." Nicolas reached up and tucked a strand of Jena's hair behind her ear. "Maybe you should try to go back to sleep. You need to rest, honey."

The softness of his touch and the southern drawl in his voice was soothing.

"Maybe it's not sleep I need," Jena said, flirtatiously batting her brows.

He smiled at her, loving the quirky things she sometimes said to him. Jena was his everything. Although Nicolas's life had begun in New Orleans during the eighteenth century, he'd adapted to living as an immortal while the world around him changed and evolved. Now, his life had taken on a new meaning since Jena had come into it. She gave him a sense of belonging and purpose that filled his heart with happiness. He knew without a doubt she was the one.

Before he met her, his life was like a never-ending carousel, spinning out of control. After his older brother, Ashton, suffered a broken heart and committed suicide, he made a deal with Death in exchange for his brother's return. As Death promised, his brother came back, but not as he was. Although they'd been gifted with immortality along with other incredible supernatural abilities, still it came with consequences which could not be undone. His brother had been cursed with the lupine virus and a lust for human blood. Relentlessly, he'd spent years searching for a cure, but regretfully his efforts had proved fruitless. Years later, Ashton was finally set free and now resided in heaven, serving as one of God's battle angels. Unfortunately, despite his brother's freedom, he'd passed the curse on to Jena.

As Nicolas remained lost in thought, Jena tilted her head and studied his face. *God*, she thought. His eyes were breathtaking. The light shade of lavender shimmered against his pale, flawless complexion and the ink-black color of his shoulder-length hair. Not to mention his lips. They were perfectly shaped and kissable. Her eyes trailed lower, below his masculine jaw and past his neck and to his perfectly defined chest. She briefly closed her eyes, feeling as though she was going to come apart by the mere sight of him.

Although Jena had only known Nicolas for a short period, it felt like it had already been a lifetime. It was as if they were fated to be together forever.

Nicolas came back to focus and put his lips on hers. With their mouths locked, she gazed into his half-lidded eyes and whispered, "Nicolas..." Her breathy tone was ripe with surrender. "I need you."

He purred his approval and deepened the kiss. As she gasped, his tongue invaded her mouth and skillfully stroked over her own. Goose bumps prickled over her skin when his hand trailed over her bare shoulder and slowly inched down her arm. Jena closed her eyes, absorbing the feel of his caressing and sensual touch. While his hand worked its way lower, in a matter of seconds, she felt a heat bloom within her that nearly took her over the edge. She arched her back and moaned against his lips.

For a fleeting moment, he released her mouth and then shifted his body so that he was looking down into her eyes from beneath his lush, inky lashes without pressing his weight on top of her. His stare was intense and full of desire. "I love you, Jena." His lavender eyes were dark with need. "I've wanted you from the moment I first saw you."

Before she could reply, he captured her mouth again. Without as much as a thought, she grabbed on to his shoulders, wanting to feel his warm skin and his weight on top of her. He held back for a moment, but then relaxed, realizing what she needed from him, and finally eased his body onto hers.

It wasn't long before Nicolas had Jena undressed, her silk nightgown gone, and her lace panties tossed aside. His body was blazing for her, stimulated by centuries of waiting to be right where he was.

After he had stripped her of what little she had on, he shrugged out of his pajama bottoms and wrapped his arms around her. He gathered her close, so close Jena could hear the rhythm of his heart beating wildly inside his chest.

Jena's hands dug into the strands of his silky hair, her flushed body writhing against the warmth of his flesh. "Please," she pled in a throaty murmur that nearly undid him.

His mouth came down over hers, kissing her as if he'd die if their lips were parted.

As they made love, gasping and panting, their intertwined bodies fit together as though they were made for each other. *Jena was his destiny, and he was hers,* Nicolas thought as they ascended the heights of passion.

When an hour had passed, Jena sighed when she felt his arm around her waist. Although she was more than capable of taking care of herself, lying in Nicolas's arms gave her a sense that no matter what tragic situation she faced, she could survive anything. He enabled the strength she needed to face her fears and be whoever she wanted to be.

Chapter Seven

Although Carrie was desperate for sleep, she couldn't shut her eyes. Every time she tried, her mind kicked up all those horrible images from earlier. Lying in bed, staring up at the ceiling, her thoughts continued to torment her. Her imagination seemed to be getting the best of her, spinning out of control. Tears fell from the corners of her eyes as flashbacks of Kevin's body came to mind. There had been so much blood. It was everywhere. Just thinking about it sent chills up her spine. She huddled beneath the covers like a child afraid of the dark.

Who could have done such a thing? And why Kevin? Then her thoughts went to another place. To the sickening memory of those creeps putting their hands on her, and to the wolfish *thing* that killed them. Whatever it was, it looked like something straight out of a horror flick. Were werewolves real? It didn't seem possible that something like that could exist. She felt like she was losing her mind.

Could that *werewolf thing* be responsible for Kevin's death? "Could it be..." she whispered, swallowing back fear, "...coming for me?"

But morning arrived without incident. When she got dressed and went downstairs, she heard voices coming from the kitchen. Carrie stopped and listened. She clearly recognized her roommate's, but not the other, voice. It sounded like a man. Maybe it was Ryan, she thought.

"Jessica..."

"I'm in the kitchen," Jessica hollered back. "I hope you're dressed. We've got company."

As Carrie started for the entrance to the kitchen, she stopped short when she caught sight of the guy inside. He wasn't Ryan. Although Ryan was easy on the eyes, this guy didn't appear to be your average looking Joe. Going by his profile alone, his attractiveness registered off the charts. His dark, shoulder-length hair—pushed behind his ears— reminded her of the lead actor in the movie, *John Wick,* but with less facial hair. He had a lean muscular build and long legs. For some strange reason, she wondered what color his eyes were.

"Oh, there you are," Jessica said, noticing Carrie standing outside the kitchen.

As the guy faced her, Carrie's body stiffened at his intense blue eyes. It was like they bored deep down into her soul.

"Come meet my *new* friend," Jessica said, motioning Carrie over.

Carrie felt her mouth drop as she looked between her roommate and the handsome stranger. Then a trail of goose bumps prickled over her skin. She could sense something dark and lethal behind the stranger's spectacular eyes.

"Carrie, this is Joseph Parker," Jessica said, grinning like a Cheshire cat.

Joseph smiled, revealing a perfect set of teeth. He stepped forward and extended his hand. "Hello, Carrie." His voice was soft and alluring. "It's a pleasure to meet you."

Carrie nodded hello and instantly took his hand. "It's nice to meet you too, Joseph."

"Mmmm..." the Shadow said, purring inside Joseph's head. *"Carrie looks scrumptious."*

As he released her hand, Carrie tilted her head in question, feeling like she'd seen him somewhere before. "You look familiar. Have we previously met?"

Joseph narrowed his eyes, wondering if she'd spotted him last night in the bar. Surely, she hadn't seen him during the attack, had she?

"Tell her no," the Shadow said.

Joseph shook his head. "I don't believe so."

"He looks so much like Keanu Reeves," Jessica said, still smiling at Carrie. "And he's brought you something." She turned away from Carrie and faced Joseph. "Isn't that right, Joseph?"

"We've come to take your soul," the Shadow muttered.

Carrie looked between her best friend and Joseph, noticing how nervous he appeared. And yes, he certainly looked like the actor Jessica had mentioned. Strangely, he even sounded like him. Then, after a few seconds, he brought his hand forward again. This time, he had a purse in his grasp. "I ah… think this belongs to you."

"Can you believe it, Carrie?" Jessica's eyes lit up. "He found your purse. Isn't that great?"

There was a beat of silence as Carrie seemed lost for words. She couldn't take her eyes off the white handbag. *Impossible*, she thought as flashbacks of the attack came to her in a rush. Finally, she cleared her mind, reached for the purse, and said, "Where did you find it?"

"On Richmond Street," he said. "That's the route I usually ride my bike before work. I spotted it in a ditch. The silver handle caught my attention. Otherwise, I wouldn't have seen it in all those weeds."

"We are good liars."

"But how did you know it belonged to me?"

Joseph tuned out the voice in his head and shot Carrie an apologetic smile. "I looked at your ID."

Carrie unzipped the small handbag and dug inside. When she found her wallet and her cell phone intact, she looked back up at Joseph. "I don't know what to say?"

"How about *thank you*," Jessica said.

"Oh, of course," Carrie said. "You'll have to excuse me. I'm not thinking too clearly this morning. I didn't sleep much last night." She instantly set the purse down on the counter and extended her hand. "Thank you for returning it, Joseph."

He took her hand and lightly squeezed. "You're welcome, Carrie."

Then an awkward silence filled the room.

"Joseph was telling me about his exciting job," Jessica said, breaking the tension. "He's a freelance journalist for the San Francisco Chronicle."

"I like Jessica." The Shadow smacked his lips. *"She looks tasty."*

"Oh, really?" Carrie cocked her head, appearing intrigued. "That's interesting. How long have you been a writer?"

"Basically, since I was a teenager," he said, nervously shoving his hands into the front pockets of his jeans. "The day I read my first mystery novel I knew I wanted to be a writer. That's when I decided to jump into journalism."

With her interest piqued, Carrie said, "So, who's your favorite?"

He shrugged. "As in a writer?"

Carrie nodded.

"I'd have to say, Ernest Hemingway."

"*Liar,*" the Shadow said. "*Stephen King is our favorite.*"

"How so?" Carrie asked.

"Mostly because of his works. Although," Joseph cocked a brow, thinking, "there's one quote he wrote that really stayed with me growing up."

"Tell us," Jessica said with pleading eyes. "We're dying to know."

"*Oh, you'll be dying,*" the Shadow said. "*I promise.*"

"The world breaks everyone," Joseph began, keeping his eyes locked on Carrie's, "and afterward, some are strong at the broken places."

Carrie shivered at the musical lilt of Joseph's voice and the way he pronounced his words. It spread through her, calming her, comforting her somehow. She wanted to know more about this mysterious, handsome man.

"I like it," Carrie said, gazing into his piercing blue eyes. "Would you care for a cup of coffee?"

Joseph checked his watch. "Sure. I have a few minutes, but only if it's no trouble."

"Of course not. I was about to make one myself." She smiled and glanced at her roommate. "How about you, Jess?"

"Oh, no thanks. I'm meeting Ryan across the street at Chloe's Café." She averted her eyes from Carrie and looked to Joseph. "Maybe you two would like to join us?"

"*Make up an excuse,*" the Shadow urged.

"Sorry," Joseph said. "I don't have long. I've got to be somewhere shortly. Maybe another time?"

"Yeah, sure," Jessica said, then turned toward Carrie, flashing her a mischievous grin. "Give Joseph your number so we can plan a double date."

Carrie blushed and shot her roommate a menacing look.

"Or, if you'd like," Joseph said, "maybe just the two of us could go out for dinner sometime."

"Sure," Carrie said, smiling. "That sounds nice. But honestly, I should be the one offering you dinner. You saved me a lot of trouble returning my purse."

"It was no problem," Joseph said. "I'm glad I could help. But I would still like to take you out to dinner. How about tonight? But if that's too short notice—"

"She'd love to," Jessica blurted, batting her brows. "Besides, it is Valentine's Day."

Carrie frowned at Jessica.

"I totally forgot," Joseph said. "If you already have plans, I completely understand."

"No, it's fine," Carrie said. "My plans have recently changed. I'm free tonight."

"You sure? I mean, if you don't want to go, I understand."

"No, no," Carrie said. "I want to go."

"Great." Joseph smiled. "It's a date then."

"Yummy," the Shadow said. *"I can't wait."*

"I better get going," Jessica said. "It was nice meeting you, Joseph."

"Thanks." He waved. "You too."

"Enjoy your coffee," Jessica muttered, winking at Carrie as she turned to leave.

A few minutes later, Carrie poured two cups of coffee.

"How do you take your coffee, Joseph?"

"Just black, please."

"Are you sure?"

When he nodded, she said, "Well, I'm the opposite. I need lots of sugar. I don't know how you drink coffee without it."

She placed the mugs on the table. "Please, make yourself comfortable."

"Thanks." He eased into a chair across from hers.

He watched her take careful sips of her coffee, noticing how lovely her face was. Her bone structure was so delicate, her jaw a graceful arch running from her small ears to her perfectly shaped chin. Her cheek bones were high and tinted with a small amount of blush. Her lips were plump, the bottom fuller than the top, and her beautiful, long, sandy blonde hair was arranged in a ponytail.

He looked at her with curiosity. "So, what do you like to eat?"

"Pretty much anything as long as it's fully cooked," she said, looking up from her mug.

"I take it you're not a big fan of sushi."

She curled her upper lip. "That and oysters."

He chuckled. "I'll make note of that."

"What about you? Is there anything particular you dislike?"

"Nope," he said. "I'll eat pretty much anything."

"And everything," the Shadow muttered. *"Especially pretty young blondes."*

Joseph reached for his coffee. "Aside from disliking sushi and oysters, what do you do? I mean, as in work."

"I'm a substance abuse counselor. I specialize in treating patients who have a chemical dependency on drugs and alcohol."

"Oh, good grief." The Shadow groaned. *"That sounds too much like a shrink. Let's eat her before she tries to get inside our head."*

Joseph raised a brow. "That sounds interesting. How long have you been a counselor?"

"Right after I graduated college and became licensed, I applied at New Hope Foundation in Berkeley. I've been there for three years now."

"That's great," he said, trying his best to sound enthusiastic. "Sounds like you enjoy what you do."

"Yeah." The tone in her voice deflated a little. "Most of it anyway."

"What do you mean by that?"

"Oh, don't get me wrong." She sighed. "I do enjoy helping people. It's just that sometimes the people you work for can turn your passion into something you dread."

"It's your boss, isn't it?"

Carrie's eyes widened. "How did you guess?"

"It's in your eyes, and the tone of your voice when I asked if you enjoyed what you did for a living."

Oh Lord, she thought. *Not only is he handsome and smart, but he's also observant too.*

"I've seen this kind of thing go on where I work," he said. "I'm betting your boss is a female. Am I right?"

She looked at him, puzzled. "Yeah, why do you ask?"

"Isn't it obvious? You're young, pretty, and intelligent. I'm sure your boss is good at what she does, but I'm guessing she's not as young and attractive as you. She's probably a little on the heavy side as well, right?"

When she nodded, he said, "It sounds like she's one of those jealous types and sees you as a threat."

"You really think so?"

"More than likely," he said, chuckling lightly. "Why else would she go out of her way to make you miserable at work? A few women employed at the Chronicle have been let go for this kind of behavior. Believe it or not, one of my male colleagues had something similar with his boss. It was so bad he finally had to go to corporate."

"That's horrible. Did your employers ever do anything about it?"

Joseph nodded. "It took a while, but eventually, they got rid of him."

"Why do some people have to be so immature?" She rolled her eyes. "It's so childish. Why can't everyone just be professional?"

"I wish I had the answers. Although I'm a big believer of karma. Good or bad, whatever you put out there in the world eventually comes back to you."

"Well, that does make sense."

"Trust me," he said. "I've witnessed it myself a time or two."

"Are you saying you've seen bad things happen to bad people?"

"Bad people taste sweeter," the Shadow said. *"Kevin was delicious."*

"Yep." He took a sip of his coffee. "Take my colleague's situation for example. His boss lost his job. A year later, I heard he couldn't find work and lost everything he owned, plus his wife left him. And I'm sure it's just a matter of time before your boss gets her karma."

"Give us the bitch's name and address." The Shadow drew out the s like the warning of a rattler's tail. *"We can take care of her like we did Kevin."*

"Veronica, my boss, clearly deserves her share of karma," Carrie said. "But I never wish ill-will on anyone, not even a jerk like her."

"Verrr-onnn-ic-aaa..." The Shadow purred. *"She sounds succulent."*

"That's because you're a good person, Carrie. You deserve good things."

"Joseph, what the hell are you saying? Remember, she's food."

"Thanks, Joseph." Carrie's eyes brightened, and for some reason, her cheeks flushed. "I'm relieved you found my purse, but I'm also glad I got the chance to meet you. You come across as a genuine guy." She blushed a little. "That's something a girl doesn't easily come by these days."

"Dear God." The Shadow moaned. *"What's with this broad? She's ruining my appetite."*

"It doesn't matter what brought me here," Joseph said, placing his hand over hers. "I'm just glad our paths crossed."

Carrie's heart practically skipped a beat. Was she dreaming? She had to be because guys like him didn't exist in her reality. Or did they? If so, she'd never known one. All the guys she'd ever met were like Kevin or worse. And then she wondered what kind of lover he was. God, she could only imagine. By his caring eyes, the soft tone of his voice, his kissable lips, his perfect skin, and those long legs, he was probably amazing.

"Thanks for the coffee," Joseph said, removing his hand from hers. "I'd love to stay longer and chitchat, but I've got to get going." He quickly took another drink of his coffee and rose from his chair.

"Yeah, me too." Carrie scooted her chair back and pushed to her feet. "I'm already in hot water for calling in late. If I don't make it in before noon, I'll never hear the end of it."

"I'm sorry," he said, looking at her regretfully. "I didn't realize you weren't feeling well. You're not coming down with something, are you?"

"No, I'm fine. Just tired."

"I take it you were up late worried about your purse."

She smiled. "Something like that."

He extended his hand. "It was a pleasure meeting you, Carrie."

She took hold, lightly squeezing. "You too, Joseph."

"I'll pick you up tonight." He slid his hand from hers. "How's six sound?"

"That's perfect."

As he went to turn away, she said, "Wait. Shouldn't we exchange numbers?"

"What are you waiting for? Kill her, Joseph. I'm starving."

He said nothing, just stood there, staring.

"Joseph, are you okay?"

"Do it, Joseph. Do it now."

"Sorry," Joseph said, fixing his gaze toward hers. "Did you say something, Carrie?"

She looked at him perplexed. "Uh, I was just asking if you wanted my number."

"Oh yeah." He grinned, retrieving his phone from his back pocket. "You're not going to give me a fake number, are you?"

"That sounds like something my roommate would do. Besides, you already know where I live, so it's not like I can hide."

They both laughed and exchanged numbers.

As Joseph left Carrie's apartment and got behind the wheel of his Jeep Wrangler, the Shadow said, *"Why didn't you take the girl?"*

"You know I can't be late for my therapy sessions," Joseph said. "I'm still on probation. If my therapist detects any odd behavior, it might raise suspicion. And I don't want to go back to the institute."

"You like her, don't you, Joseph?"

"I think Carrie is a good person. And I've decided not to hurt her."

"Have your fun, Joseph. But don't get too attached. One way or another, you will give her to me."

Chapter Eight

Tim and Tessa anxiously stood in the Covenant's library, waiting for the members of the Covenant to arrive. In addition to the ordeal with Detective Perkins's niece, it was pertinent they discuss the situation concerning the demonic-looking man Jena had encountered.

Tim pulled a chair out for Tessa. "Let's go ahead and take a seat. I have a feeling it's going to be a while before everyone shows up."

"We didn't give them much notice." She sat down and scooted close to the table. "Plus, some of us had to find babysitters."

"It's fine." Tim eased into the chair next to hers. "There's no hurry."

Roman and Lawrence were next to arrive at the meeting. Following behind them were Bull, Justice, and Lena. All five were trained in various military tactics and part of Roman's Special Ops group. They were new to the California Covenant but were already considered part of the Breedline family.

Angie, who was Jena McCain's best friend and had recently bonded with Bull, rushed in and caught up with everyone. "Sorry I'm late. My flight was delayed twice."

Bull reached for her hand. "Don't worry, sweetheart. You're fine. We just got here ourselves." He intertwined his fingers with hers. "I'm just glad you made it. By the way, happy Valentine's Day."

"Aw..." She smiled. "Happy Valentine's Day."

As they approached the table, Angie searched the room. "Where's Jena?"

"Don't worry." Bull lightly squeezed her hand. "I'm sure she will be here with Nicolas shortly."

Angie smiled up at Bull, realizing how much she loved this man. He was a giant compared to the average man and built like a brick house, not to mention sexy as hell. With a common military background, and a soldier of war, Bull was the type of person who stood up for all mankind. His compassion for others spoke volumes for his character. He was genuine and trustworthy, unlike anyone she'd ever met. Although their relationship was new, there was no doubt he was the one for her. They fit good together. *Damn good.*

"Go ahead and take a seat," Tim directed, bringing Angie back to focus. "We'll get started as soon as everyone gets here."

As they settled behind a table that would easily seat thirty people, Drakon came into the room. The beard he'd recently grown out, along with his dark Mohawk, made him look more lethal and menacing than usual. He was big, towering to the height of six-seven, and stronger than all the other men residing in the Covenant. Now that he'd found love again with his beloved Cassie, his life had taken on a whole new meaning, especially after he'd found out he was going to be a father. Before he took a seat next to Roman, he dipped his head in Tessa's direction.

Then Jem Chamberlain and his wife Mia strolled into the room, holding hands, and sat down in the empty chairs next to Drakon. Jem was an IT engineer and the percussionist in the band Chaos. He'd inherited a rare gift from his biological father, Alexander Crest. Not only could he shift into a Breedline wolf, but he could also conjure a portal and turn almost anything to ash with a simple flick of his wrist. To top it off, he was born with the power to heal. Although Mia, a mixed species consisting of a Breedline and a succubus, was considered untrustworthy and dangerous to most full-blooded Breedlines, it didn't matter to Jem. In some cases, especially between bonded mates, true love surpassed all the risks and uncertainties.

Drakon leaned in close to Mia and Jem. "Where's little Evie?"

"She's with Cassie," Mia said. "I guess you had already left your room before we stopped by."

"Sorry I missed her," Drakon said. "I'm sure Cassie was thrilled to babysit for you. She can't wait to be a mother herself."

"With all the practice she's had working in the neonatal unit," Jem said, "and babysitting all the kiddos in the Covenant, she'll make an excellent mom."

Drakon grinned ear to ear. "She already has that motherhood glow about her."

"You ready for fatherhood?"

Drakon nodded at Jem. "Aside from marrying your sister, it's the next best thing that's ever happened to me."

Jem and Mia, along with all the others, smiled at Drakon.

"Where's Jace?" Drakon asked, his eyes focused on Tessa.

"He should be here any minute. He had to make a quick pit stop. He's dropping off the twins at Anna's. She's watching them during the meeting."

"I like Anna," Drakon said. "She fits into the Covenant quite well, wouldn't you say?"

"Absolutely," Tessa said. "I just adore her."

"So does Zeke Rizzo," Drakon pointed out. "Here lately, I've noticed the two spending more time together. Although I'd never put those two together, a nightclub owner with the power to see into someone's past with a simple handshake and a sweet young girl who was raised in a women's convent." He shrugged. "Go figure."

"It is rather odd," Jem said. "I'd never put the two together in a million years. They seem like total opposites."

"You know what they say," Tessa said. "Opposites do attract."

"I can tell you this," Mia said. "Anna has been a godsend to both Jem and I, not to mention my sister Eve. I've never met another person who loves children as much as Anna. It's like clockwork every morning. She stops by our room with my sister's twins, offering to take Evie with them downstairs for breakfast."

Jem nodded. "Since she's been stopping by to take our daughter in the mornings, those few hours Mia and I get alone have been nice."

Mia smiled at Jem. "I agree."

When Jace strolled in, Drakon said, "Well, speak of the devil."

Jace overheard Drakon and waved in his direction. Then his eyes lit up the moment he saw Tessa. Before he settled into the vacant seat next to hers, he leaned over and kissed her on the cheek. "Hey, sweetheart."

Fatherhood had changed Jace, his short temper dialed down a notch. Which was a good thing. Jace, like his twin brother, worked for a prestigious software company and was the lead vocalist and guitarist in their band Chaos. But underneath all that talent and all that long, gorgeous blond hair, and a face just as spectacular, lurked a seven-foot hairy beast that looked like the abominable snowman crossed with a werewolf. When Jace's beast was provoked, everyone, including Drakon, quickly cleared a path. So far, they'd been lucky. The Beast was an asset to the Breedline species, fighting alongside them against the bad guys.

"Thanks for dropping off the boys," Tessa said, placing her hand over Jace's. "Did they take to Anna okay?"

"Oh yeah," Jace said, waving it off like it was nothing. "They clung to her like glue."

"They didn't fuss when you left?"

"Heck no." Jace laughed a little. "Arius and Tidus were there. The second they noticed those two, I became nonexistent. All they cared about was getting to play with their cousins."

Jem leaned back in his chair and crossed his arms. "Anna is going to have her hands full with two sets of twin boys."

"She had help," Jace said. "Eve, Tara, and Manuel's sister Lailah were there."

Jem nodded and Tessa looked relieved.

"I'm proud of everyone," Tim said. "Especially you, Jace. Forgiving Eve and Sebastian proves you have a good heart. And it sets a great example for your sons."

"Thanks, Tim, but it's not always easy," Jace said, a clear smirk in his voice. "Although Sebastian is my half-brother, it sometimes takes everything I have not to kick his ass. I try to keep my distance as much as possible."

"I completely understand," Tim said.

"Speaking of Sebastian," Drakon said. "Is he coming to the meeting?"

Tim shook his head. "I know we're starting to trust him, but I don't think he's ready to be included in our meetings. At some point, we'll see how it works out."

"I have to admit," Tessa said. "Sebastian has made a complete turnaround."

"I commend you, Tessa," Angie spoke out. "After Sebastian kidnapped you, not just once, but twice, you did what most people would never do. You have the biggest heart."

Tessa smiled. "Thank you, Angie."

"I agree," Drakon said. "And it's hard to believe your brother has buddied up with him. I figured if Jace didn't end up killing Sebastian, surely Steven would."

"I'm glad everyone has given Sebastian a second chance," Tessa said. "Forgiveness heals the soul."

"Heals whose soul?" Steven asked as he walked into the room.

"Great timing, buddy," Jace said. "We were just talking about you."

"Oh?" Steven cocked a brow. "What about?"

Jace chuckled. "Everyone is getting all warm and fuzzy about me and you playing nice with Sebastian."

"Is that right?" Steven said. "Since you brought up the subject, Sebastian and I were going to ask if anyone here is interested in a guys' trip."

Jace cocked a brow. "A guys' trip?"

"Yeah, why not?" Steven shrugged. "I thought we'd take the bikes to Arizona for a few days. I've never seen the Grand Canyon."

"Sorry to burst your bubble," Tim interjected. "As much as I like the idea, we'll have to postpone the guys' trip. We've got more pressing issues at hand. That's why Tessa and I called this meeting."

"What guys' trip?"

When everyone turned toward the doorway, Kyle Jones and Casey Barton stood side-by-side with a look of enthusiasm. Kyle, a mechanic and the bass player in the band Chaos, was born a Breedline and bonded with Celina Baldolf. His best friend, Casey, who was a clothing model and the keyboardist in the band Chaos, had recently bonded with Lila Demont. He was born a Breedline but also had inherited the Theriomorph side from his biological parents. Instead of shifting into a Breedline wolf, he transformed into a giant black panther. Although Casey's species was considered a threat to the Breedline, due to a Theriomorph's powers of mind manipulation, the Covenant had graciously accepted him with wide-open arms.

Tim waved them over. "Come have a seat, guys."

The minute they sat down, Kyle said, "So what's this guys' trip I overheard you talking about?"

"I thought it'd be nice if we took a road trip to Arizona for a few days," Steven said. "Then Tim crushed my plans."

"Ah, man." Kyle groaned, averting his eyes from Steven. He looked at Tim with a pitiful expression. "What's so dire that we can't go on a guys' trip?"

"As I was saying," Tim said. "That's what this meeting is about. As soon as everyone gets here, we'll talk."

"Damn," Kyle grumbled. "We never get to have fun."

Tessa focused on her brother. "Is Abbey coming?"

"No, she's with Jonah," Steven said. "He's a little fussy this morning."

"Oh, no," Tessa said. "What's wrong?"

"He's been teething."

Tessa frowned. "Poor little guy."

"Yeah, he's not too happy. He's been up most of the night."

"I bet Abbey is exhausted."

Steven nodded. "She is, but thanks to Kyle's little woman, Abbey is getting a break. Celina volunteered to watch Jonah for a few hours."

"That's my girl," Kyle said, grinning ear to ear.

"Noah seems to really take to her," Steven said. "Celina will make a wonderful mom someday."

"Yep." Kyle nodded. "One of these days."

Alexander Crest stepped into the room with Helen and said, "I hope we're not too late."

"No, you're fine," Tessa said. "Please, have a seat. We're just waiting on Nicolas and Jena."

"We're here," Jena said as she made her way inside with Nicolas trailing behind. "Sorry we're running late." Her eyes roamed over the occupants in the room. "I hope we didn't make you wait too long."

"You're fine," Tim said. "Have a seat and we'll get started."

As Nicolas and Jena sat down in the chairs close to Angie and Bull, Helen said, "What about Detectives Sanchez and Perkins? Shouldn't they be here?"

"Yeah," Kyle blurted. "And what about the Fury?"

"I invited Manuel and Frank," Tim said. "But they couldn't make it. They had to meet up with their superior this morning. Hopefully they'll have some new information on Mr. Russo's murder. I didn't invite the Fury," he added. "Since we don't have much to go on, and this meeting will be quick, I didn't feel the need for them to attend. I'll speak with them later unless anyone feels like they need to be here."

"That's fine by me," Kyle said. "That Apollyon guy makes me nervous."

"Not to mention his sisters, Callisto and Electra," Casey blurted. "It wasn't that long ago they tried to kill us."

"Well, actually," Kyle said. "Electra did break your neck."

"We have to move on and put the past behind us," Tim said. "Besides, if God can give them a second chance, so can we."

"Remember guys," Tessa said. "We are a family of forgiveness."

Casey nodded and Kyle said, "Okay, okay. But don't expect me to buddy up with the guy."

"All I ask is for you to give them a chance," Tessa said. "After all, Apollyon did save Jena."

Jena changed the subject. "Have you heard how Detective Perkins's niece is doing?"

"I spoke to Frank this morning," Tim said, "and he said Carrie seemed to be taking it well. Although, considering everything she's been through, I'm surprised."

"This morning, I received a call from Carrie," Helen said. "Apparently, she took her uncle's advice to get counseling. She's stopping by my office later this week."

"How did she sound?" Tim asked.

"She seemed nervous over the phone," Helen said.

"I don't blame her," Jena said. "I feel responsible for all this."

Nicolas reached for her hand. "It's not your fault, Jena. If it weren't for you, she probably wouldn't be alive."

"He's right, girl," Angie said. "You did what your instincts told you. You saved an innocent life. And those two creeps that attacked her got what was coming."

"I second that," Jace said, nodding at Jena. "Karma is a bitch."

Tessa nodded. "I agree with Angie. Not only did you save Carrie, but more than likely those men would have assaulted other women."

"Those men..." Jena hesitated. "...they were planning on killing her. I couldn't stop the creature within me. It wanted to protect Carrie and destroy her attackers."

"I know you didn't ask for this curse," Tessa said. "None of this is your fault, Jena. I promise we'll help you through this."

Jena smiled a little. "Thank you all for being so supportive."

"I do have one question," Drakon said, focusing on Jena. "And please forgive me if I sound too straightforward. But it's something we have to discuss." When Jena nodded, he went on to say, "How are we going to deal with the remains your creature leaves behind?"

Jena lowered her eyes and shifted nervously in her chair.

"It's okay, Jena," Tim said. "We're not upset with you."

When Jena looked up at Tim, he said, "We just need to come up with a solution. My ears are open to any suggestions."

"I'm not sure what I can do," Jena said, her eyes searching over the room, trying to gauge everyone's reactions. "I don't have a lot of control over the creature inside me once it detects evil."

"We'll all think on it," Tim said. "And maybe we'll come up with a plan. Until then, I want you to contact me when there is another incident. In the meantime..." He paused, his eyes searching every person seated at the table. "...I need to bring up the other issue that Jena has brought to my attention. It appears that Mr. Russo's death may have not been committed by a human but rather something supernatural."

Jace focused on Jena. "Please don't tell me it's another creature like yours."

"It's not like mine," Jena began to explain. "And it doesn't hunt evil. What I saw was evil. It's some sort of demonic entity possessing a man. It looked as though it was going to attack me until he realized I wasn't exactly human."

Jem uncrossed his arms and leaned forward. "How did he know you weren't human?"

"Because I shifted."

"If this thing is indeed evil," Tessa said, "why didn't your creature destroy it? I thought the battle angels said you would hunt down evil."

"There were people nearby," Jena said. "But the guy did speak to me."

Jace looked at Jena curiously. "What did he say?"

"It was rather strange," Jena said. "He addressed himself as the Shadow."

"I think I've encountered this creature before," Roman chimed in.

Everyone focused on Roman with a look of surprise.

"It was a long time ago," Roman said. "I was just a kid."

Jace shook his head. "So, what the hell is this *thing*?"

"I'm pretty positive it's a demon," Roman explained. "When I was ten years old, I witnessed it myself. There was a boy in my neighborhood..." Roman paused, drawing his brows tight. "His name was Joseph Harris. The poor kid didn't have a very good home life. His father was nothing but an abusive drunk. It was evident he beat his wife. On several occasions, we noticed cuts and bruises on her face. My parents tried to help her, but she was too afraid to leave her husband. To make a long story short, one Saturday afternoon, he beat her so bad she died in the hospital the next day. Joseph was only five years old at the time."

"Oh my gosh," Tessa said. "What happened to the boy?"

"Before the ambulance came for Joseph's mother, he shot his father."

"Dang," Jace said, his brows arching high on his forehead. "Joseph was one tough five-year-old. Did his father die?"

"He survived but was later sentenced to twenty years in prison."

"So, what does this demon have to do with the little boy?" Jace asked.

"I'm about to get to that part," Roman explained. "Since Joseph was a minor and there were no other family members to step in, he was placed in foster care. My parents would have offered to take him in, but at the time, my father could barely support our family. Then, a few years later, word got out about him being sent to a mental institute. My parents felt bad for Joseph, so they decided to go see if there was anything they could do. I'll never forget that day. That's when I saw it."

"You mean," Jace reluctantly said, "you saw the Shadow?"

Roman nodded. "I was left alone with Joseph while my parents spoke with his physician. He attacked me, or rather something did. Joseph's face had morphed into something demonic looking. His eyes were like two dark, soulless pits. And it spoke to me, referring to itself as the Shadow."

Jace's eyes rounded. "What happened next?"

"Joseph nearly choked me to death," Roman continued. "Although I was bigger than him, outweighing him by at least fifty pounds, he was much stronger. It was like a demonic presence had taken over his body. Thankfully there were guards close. It took three of them to pull him off."

Tim crossed his arms. "Do you know if Joseph was ever released?"

"I don't know," Roman said. "That was the last time I saw him."

"What about your parents?" Tim asked. "Did they stay in contact?"

Roman shook his head. "After that incident, the institute wouldn't allow him any more visitors."

"What about the institute he was kept in?" Tim asked. "Do you happen to remember the name of that place?"

"It was the Summit Behavioral Institute here in Berkeley."

"Well, going by all the similarities," Tim said, "it appears Joseph could be the person responsible for Kevin Russo's murder."

"We need to find out if Joseph was released," Drakon said. "I'll do some digging."

"Count me in too," Roman added.

Tim nodded. "Thanks, guys. And we also need to find out how to destroy this thing."

"What about the archives?" Tessa asked. "There could be something in there on this particular creature."

"That's a good idea," Tim said. "If Jena cannot destroy it, maybe we'll get lucky enough to find out what will."

"We better get busy," Kyle said. "I'm sure it's just a matter of time before this Shadow thing kills again."

"Looks like we have our work cut out," Tim said. "Let's get to work."

As everyone started to rise from their chairs, Steven said, "I think we should include Sebastian."

"I thought we discussed the situation concerning Sebastian," Tim said.

"Just hear me out for a second," Steven said. "Many of you may not know, but Sebastian is an expert on demonology."

Jace rolled his eyes. "Yeah, whatever."

"No, it's true," Steven said. "During the years he grew up in the private boarding school his stepfather forced him into, he studied demonology. He might be able to speed up the process. Don't you think it's worth a try?"

"All right," Tim agreed. "What do we have to lose."

"I'll ask him," Steven said. "I'm sure he'll be more than willing to help out."

"Great." Jace threw his hands up in defeat. "Just when I thought things couldn't get any worse."

"Remember, honey," Tessa said, "we are a forgiving family."

"I know, I know," Jace said.

"Your parents are babysitting for us tonight," Tessa whispered to Jace, winking. "That gives us some alone time."

"Hmmm..." He arched a brow, smiling. "Things are starting to look up."

Chapter Nine

Joseph pulled into the vacant parking space outside the building where he had an appointment to meet with his therapist. His thoughts were anything but calm. The idea of drudging up all those painful memories of his childhood always made him nervous. He'd spent years burying his past, so digging it back up was difficult. It had taken him a long time to put it to rest.

He imagined himself standing once again in the house he grew up in. Although he had burned it to the ground, he could still remember every detail. From the rancid odor of cigarettes, and liquor, to the hidden bloodstains on the carpet. Eventually, the droplets of blood had gotten too big to cover up. Then an image of his father came to mind, clear as a photograph. He saw the hateful scowl on his face and the sinister look in his eyes. He was evil, straight down to the core. His thoughts shifted to that dreadful day, where he watched his father beat his mother. He could still recall her last words.

"Your father was an abusive drunk," the Shadow whispered into his subconscious. *"But that's in the past. He got what was coming."*

Joseph peered into the rearview mirror at himself. "After what he did to my mother." He snarled his upper lip. "He deserved to die."

"Yesss... And now, his soul belongs to us."

Joseph inhaled a deep breath and held it for a few seconds before he let it out. "Let's get this over with."

He was on autopilot as he got out of the vehicle and made his way across the parking lot. When he walked up to a set of double doors, he stepped aside as a woman with long black hair came through. She kept her eyes forward and hurriedly moved passed him. Although he barely got a glimpse of her face, her perfume lingered. The sweet fragrance reminded him of his mother's. He swallowed the knot that had formed in the back of his throat and pushed his way through the entrance.

On the other side, the small waiting area looked empty. As he moved toward the receptionist's desk, he made eye contact with a pretty redhead who was seated in a chair in the far corner of the room.

"Look at all that red, luscious hair. Mmm... So delectable."

Joseph quickly looked away, ignoring the voice in his head, and trudged forward. When he approached the front desk, a man with a yellow bow tie, and tortoiseshell glasses addressed him. "Good morning. Please sign in and I'll call your name when the doctor is ready to see you."

Joseph nodded and signed in.

It wasn't long after he took a seat he heard his name called. As he got to his feet, he quickly glanced at the redhead. She noticed and smiled at him.

"She likes you, Joseph. You should ask for her number."

Joseph focused on the nurse who stood in the doorway. She greeted him with a smile. "Right this way, Mr. Parker."

Joseph followed her down a long corridor, feeling as if he were going to the gallows. The passageway seemed to go on forever. Moments later, the nurse stopped outside a door and placed a thick binder inside a file holder mounted on the wall. He briefly stared at them, realizing it held all the documented pages of his childhood past. *God...* If only he could make them disappear.

The sound of the door opening suddenly brought him back to focus.

"Please, make yourself comfortable," the nurse said, motioning him inside. "Dr. Mendoza will be with you shortly."

"Mendoza?" Joseph slightly tilted his head, the name sounding oddly familiar. "Where's Dr. Conover?"

"I'm sorry, but Dr. Conover is no longer with us. Dr. Mendoza is taking over all his patients. If there's a problem, we can reschedule you with another therapist."

Joseph shook his head. "No, it's fine."

The nurse nodded and waited outside the doorway while Joseph went inside. As he stepped into the spacious room, a sweet aroma, like French vanilla, invaded his senses. He found it comforting and refreshing.

As soon as the door closed, he sat down in the oversized chair next to a window overlooking the city. The colors of the walls were dusty blue, and across the room, above a desk, was a painting of the beach. Although his nerves were pins and needles, it gave him a sense of calm and relaxation.

"I wonder if the new shrink is a male or a female," the Shadow said. *"I hope it's a female. An attractive female."*

Joseph flinched and looked up when the door sprung open. He felt his mouth go wide when he saw the woman standing in the doorway with his folder in her grasp. She had a dark complexion and long braided hair neatly arranged on top of her head. She wore khakis and a blue pinstriped jacket. She had small gold hoops in each of her earlobes and a pair of reading glasses attached to a lanyard around her neck. Her big brown eyes reminded him of someone from the past.

She came forward with her hand outstretched. "Good morning, Joseph."

Recognizing her soft voice, he slowly rose to his feet and took her hand.

"G-good morning," he said, his heart beating like it was going to burst from his chest.

She smiled. "You do remember me, don't you?"

He quickly bobbed his head. "Y-you're the police officer." He swallowed hard, feeling like his knees were going to buckle. "That helped me." There was a pause. "But how?"

"Please, Joseph," she said, looking at him with kind eyes. "Have a seat and we'll talk."

The Shadow huffed. *"Don't let her get inside your head, Joseph."*

When he settled back into his chair, she walked over to her desk and sat down behind it.

"First, let me reintroduce myself." She placed the file on top of the desk. "My name is Dr. Katie Mendoza. And yes, I was that officer." She raised a speculative brow. "You see, Joseph, that day changed both of our lives. You were just an innocent child, and you didn't deserve what happened to you. When I watched child services take you away, it broke my heart. You lost both your parents at such a young age. Considering the circumstances, it would have been traumatizing for anyone. I'll never forget that look in your eyes. From then on, I knew I wanted to spend the rest of my life helping people."

"Isn't that what police officers do?"

"Of course," she replied. "They do protect and serve others, but I wanted to do more. So, I went back to school and got my degree in psychology. I've been a licensed therapist for fifteen years now."

The blank expression on Joseph's face made her uneasy. She leaned forward. "Joseph, if talking to me makes you uncomfortable, I completely understand. You can reschedule with another therapist—"

"No," he quickly interjected. "I'm fine. Actually…" He released a deep breath. "I'd rather talk with you."

Her eyes lit up. "That's wonderful, Joseph." She straightened her shoulders. "Do you mind if I record our session? Everything will be kept confidential."

When he nodded in agreement, she placed a small recorder on her desk.

"I noticed you changed your last name. It used to be Harris, am I correct?"

"Yes. I wanted a fresh start, so I took my mother's maiden name."

"I see." She nodded slowly, reaching for her glasses. "So, tell me about yourself, Joseph." She focused on his face through a thick pair of lenses. "Reading over your file, it says you're a freelance journalist at the San Francisco Chronicle, true?"

"Not to mention a stone-cold killer."

"Yes." Joseph smiled at her.

"That must be an exciting career. How is that going?"

"I love my job. It's very rewarding."

"I'm glad to hear that. What got you interested in journalism?"

"I don't know." He shrugged. "I guess I've always wanted to be a writer."

"There must have been something that piqued your interest. A certain book or an author maybe?"

"Boring…" the Shadow said around a yawn. *"Kill her, Joseph. Let's just eat her heart and be done with it already."*

Suddenly, Joseph's expression went blank. He looked past Dr. Mendoza and stared off into the distance.

"Joseph, is something wrong?"

As time passed and he didn't answer, she raised her voice, "Joseph…"

He jerked. "I'm sorry. Did you say something?"

"What happened?" She looked at him, concerned. "I lost you there for a minute."

"Sorry. I was just thinking."

"What were you thinking about, Joseph?"

"Eating you," the Shadow replied.

"Oh, nothing really."

"You seemed to be lost in thought. Is there something you want to talk about?"

"Don't fall for her tricks, Joseph. She's playing mind games with you."

"Well, there's this girl I met."

The Shadow groaned. *"Seriously, Joseph?"*

"That doesn't sound like nothing." Dr. Mendoza's voice took on a curious tone. "How did you meet her?"

"I found her purse."

"You found her purse?"

He nodded. "I was out biking early this morning and found a purse on the side of the road."

The Shadow cackled. *"You're such a liar."*

"It had a phone and an ID inside. So, I took it to the owner. She invited me to stay for coffee. We started talking, and then I asked her out. She said yes."

"I'm happy for you, Joseph. When are you going out?"

"Tonight."

"Wonderful." Dr. Mendoza smiled. "And how romantic. Your first date is on Valentine's Day. Are you taking her anywhere special?"

"I thought about Kiraku's, but she doesn't like sushi. So, I decided on Corso's."

"Great choice. She'll love it. The food is delicious. And save room for dessert."

"Don't worry. We'll have plenty of room for more than dessert."

"I was wondering," Joseph said, drowning out the voice in his head. "Could I ask you for some advice?"

"Sure. I'll do my best."

"Should I..." He briefly paused. "...bring her flowers?"

"I'm pretty sure she would appreciate flowers. Especially since it's Valentine's Day."

"Thank you, Dr. Mendoza."

"I'm glad I could help. So, what does this lucky young lady do for a living?"

"She's a substance abuse counselor at the New Hope Foundation."

"Is that so?"

"She helps people." He smiled. "Like you."

"She sounds delightful, Joseph."

The Shadow smacked his lips. *"And delicious."*

"You know, Joseph. After all these years, I've always wondered how things turned out for you. I'd hoped you'd be placed into a home with a loving family. Although it's obvious you've had your share of struggles, it appears you're adjusting quite well. Am I right?"

Joseph shifted nervously in his chair.

"Tell her you're fine."

"Don't worry, Dr. Mendoza. I'm doing fine."

"Are you sure? I mean, if there's something you'd like to talk about, that's what I'm here for."

As silence overtook the room, he felt like an idiot for not saying anything. The fact of the matter was he knew she wanted to bring up his past. But he just didn't have it in him to talk about it, especially that dreadful day.

Finally, she broke the silence. "What about your mother? Would you like to talk about her?"

From out of nowhere, he felt an overwhelming pain in the center of his chest. It was as though his heart was breaking into a million pieces.

"Be cautious, Joseph."

Joseph briefly closed his eyes, remembering the last time he saw his mother. Images of her flashed through his mind. They were so clear, so vivid. Her bruised and swollen face... Her eyes wet with tears and full of regret.

With an overpowering urge to leave, he forced himself to stay and said, "I loved my mother."

"Of course, you did," Dr. Mendoza said. "And I'm sure she loved you dearly."

He quickly lowered his head and bit back tears. He refused to let one tear out.

"Don't give in to weakness," the Shadow said. *"Together, we are strong."*

"Joseph, there's something I'd like to discuss with you. It's about the institute."

He looked back up. His face was stoic. Although his outer appearance seemed calm, his insides were positively screaming. *Oh, God...* He wanted to throw up. He swallowed and nodded instead.

"As I was going over your records, something caught my attention. Your physician, Dr. Manos at the Summit Behavioral Institute, stated you suffered from a lack of empathy and displayed symptoms of schizophrenia at age seven. He mentioned you heard voices, and they told you to do bad things. Do you still hear those voices?"

"Lie, Joseph."

Joseph shook his head.

"Are you sure?" Dr. Mendoza asked.

"Lie better."

"Yes, I'm sure."

"Okay," she said, staring over the rim of her glasses. The look in her eyes said she didn't believe him.

Joseph glanced down at his watch. It was almost noon. God, he prayed the session would soon be over.

"I think that's enough for today, Joseph."

"Finally," the Shadow grumbled.

"I'd like to set up another session in a few weeks."

Joseph took a deep breath. "Yeah, sure."

When Dr. Mendoza rose from her chair, she extended her hand. "It was nice to see you again, Joseph."

He quickly pulled himself up, moved toward the desk, and took hold of her hand. "Thank you, Dr. Mendoza."

"I look forward to our next session. And good luck on your date tonight. I hope you both have a great time."

"Thanks," Joseph said. "Me too."

It hadn't been long after Joseph left when Dr. Mendoza rewound the recording of the session. As she began to listen, she heard something odd in the background. It sounded like a third voice. *No*, she thought. *There must be something wrong with the recording.* Instantly, she hit the stop button and pushed rewind. After a few seconds, she pressed play. She turned up the volume and listened carefully. *Oh, God...* There it was again. She went stiff. Abruptly, the hairs on her arms stood on end. Then she started to tremble from head to foot. Although the voice was muffled and difficult to understand, she was positive she heard the words *"Kill her."*

Chapter Ten

Nearly six hours later, Joseph stood nervously outside the door to Carrie's apartment with one hand behind his back, holding on to a single, long-stemmed rose. Before he reached up to ring the doorbell, he blew out a deep breath and relaxed as best he could. The therapy session from earlier weighed heavily on his mind. Had it been just a coincidence that the officer from years ago was now his therapist? Or could it be some sort of sign? Whatever the case, it had dug up those painful memories he'd buried a long time ago.

"If it makes you feel better, we could eat Dr. Mendoza."

"No," Joseph whispered. "I don't want to hurt her. Besides, I have more sessions to go to. And please, stay out of my head tonight."

"Come on, Joseph. Don't push me out."

Calling on his inner strength, Joseph pressed the doorbell and waited.

As the door swung open, Carrie's roommate greeted him with a smile. "Hey, Joseph."

"Jesssicaaa..." the Shadow said in a sensual, disembodied drawl.

Joseph cleared his throat. "Hi, Jessica. Is Carrie around?"

She nodded and stepped aside. "Carrie..." she called out. "Your date is here."

The minute Carrie came into view, Joseph nearly swallowed his tongue. She was so lovely. Her hair fell loosely past her shoulders in thick, blonde waves. Due to her natural beauty, and her delicate features, she wore a minimal amount of makeup, and the only jewelry she had on was a pair of tiny diamond earrings. As his eyes ventured lower, the little black dress she had on suddenly brought him to attention.

"Yummy..."

Joseph tuned out the voice in his head and gazed into her big, brown eyes. For some odd reason, the color soothed him in a way he could not explain.

"Hello, Carrie," Joseph said, presenting the rose he had behind his back.

"Oh, how lovely," she said, admiring the blood rose that was the size of a grapefruit.

"You look beautiful."

"Why, thank you, Joseph."

He smiled. "You're welcome."

"Please, come in." Carrie motioned him inside. "I'm almost ready. I just need to get my purse and jacket. I won't be but a second."

"Of course." He nodded. "Take your time. There's no hurry."

As he moved past her, Carrie noticed how handsome he looked. God, he smelled wonderful. A hint of lavender, yet manly and unbelievably sexy. He had on black tailored slacks, a matching belt, a long-sleeved dress shirt, and a leather jacket. His square-toed shoes were buffed to a shine, and his shoulder-length hair was neatly pulled back. Despite his good looks, there was something about him. Something dark and mysterious that made her want to know more. He was like a drug, and she found herself becoming addicted.

Moments later, as they made their way to the vehicle, Joseph jogged ahead and waited by the passenger's door. He opened it as she approached. "After you, my dear."

She looked up at him funny. "You're opening the door for me?"

"Of course. Why wouldn't I?"

"I don't know." She shrugged. "I guess I wasn't expecting you to be such a gentleman. You're the first person to ever open a door for me."

He drew his brows tight. "Really?"

"Yeah. I didn't realize chivalry still existed."

"What can I say." Joseph opened the door wider. "I'm an old-fashioned kind of guy."

She ducked inside, and before he closed the door, she looked up at him. "By the way, you look very handsome."

"Thank you, Carrie."

He quickly moved to the driver's side and slid behind the wheel. When he turned on the ignition, he glanced at her and said, "Have you ever eaten at Corso's?"

"No, but I heard the food is fantastic. Is that where you're taking me?"

"Yep. And I was told to save room for their dessert. And since it's technically Valentine's Day, I think we should order some after dinner, preferably something in chocolate."

"Count me in. I love chocolate."

"Well then..." He arched a brow. "...we've definitely got something in common."

As they arrived at the restaurant, the parking lot was full. When Joseph escorted Carrie inside, they were instantly greeted by a female hostess. She had a tall, willowy model's figure and jet-black hair arranged in a long, thick braid. Her green eyes, surrounded by thick, long eyelashes, lingered on Joseph's face. "Welcome to Corso's." Her red-coated lips formed a flirtatious grin. "What is the name of the party?"

"Parker," Joseph said.

"Reservations for two?" she asked as if Carrie was non-existent.

When Joseph nodded, the hostess said, "Please, right this way, Mr. Parker."

She led them to their table that was close to a window overlooking the patio. The view was breathtaking. It had a five-tier granite waterfall surrounded by lights and landscaped with a variety of plants. The sound of rushing water was tranquil, creating a pleasant atmosphere.

Joseph pulled out a chair for Carrie. "Ladies first."

As soon as they were seated, the hostess presented them with menus. "Your server will be with you shortly." She stepped a little closer to Joseph. "Can I get you anything to drink while you wait?"

He looked across the table, waiting for Carrie to speak.

"What kind of white wines do you have?"

As the hostess went over the list, Joseph kept his eyes trained on Carrie's face. Although she wasn't overly pretty, more like the girl next door, she captivated him to no end.

"I'll have a glass of Chardonnay, please," Carrie said.

The hostess faked a smile. "Perfect." She focused on Joseph and cleared her throat. "And for you, sir?"

Joseph didn't take his eyes off Carrie. "I'll have the same, thank you."

"Are you sure?" the hostess asked, trying to get Joseph to look her way. "The Cabernet Sauvignon goes quite well with the Italian."

"The Chardonnay will be fine, thanks."

The hostess took the hint and dipped her head. "Very well. Your waiter will be back with your drinks."

When they were alone, Joseph said, "So, I'm dying to know. How did work go today? Your boss wasn't a jerk to you, was she?"

Carrie sighed. "You really want to know?"

"Uh-oh. That doesn't sound good. If you don't feel like talking about it..."

"No, it's fine," Carrie said, waving it off like it was no big deal. "I guess it wasn't too bad. But I'm probably going to get a tongue-lashing first thing in the morning."

"Why's that?"

"When I showed up late today, it didn't go over too well with her. I was supposed to stay after work to make up my time."

Joseph frowned. "But it's the weekend and Valentine's Day."

"Yeah, well, Veronica doesn't give a hoot about my social life or anyone else's for that matter. Last year, I spent the entire Thanksgiving Day at the office."

"That's ludicrous," Joseph spouted. "What was so important that it couldn't wait?"

"It was over a guy."

He looked at her confused. "A guy?"

She nodded. "A few of our counselors quit right before the holidays and it left us shorthanded. So, we had to find new replacements. They hired Janey Cook and Doug Whitmore. It was obvious my boss was attracted to Doug. She practically made a spectacle of herself. It was rather embarrassing. The entire office felt sorry for the guy. And boy did she pour on the sugar. It's not like her to be nice to anyone, especially her own employees. To make a long story short, he ignored her advances and asked me out."

Joseph chuckled. "I bet she didn't like that."

Carrie shook her head. "Not in the least."

"So, I'm guessing she took it out on you, right?"

"Yep. And I didn't even go out with him. But still, she does everything she can to punish me."

"That's messed up, Carrie. She's harassing you. Don't let her get away with that. You need to report her to upper management."

Carrie sighed. "I can't."

"Why not?"

"Her father is the CEO."

"Damn," Joseph said. "That explains a lot. No wonder she gets away with treating her employees poorly. I'm sorry, Carrie." His brows clenched. "That type of crap unnerves me. It's not right."

"I know." Carrie groaned. "And I've thought about leaving, but I love my job. Other than my boss, all my coworkers are wonderful to work with. I just hate to let one bad person ruin what I've worked so hard for. You know what I mean?"

He reached across the table and placed his hand over hers. "Yes, I know exactly how you feel." His expression softened. "Hang in there. Remember what I said about karma. You reap what you sow."

"*Yesss...*" the Shadow whispered into Joseph's subconscious. "*And we are the reaper.*"

"Thanks for listening," Carrie said, smiling. "Sorry, I didn't mean to be such a Debbie Downer."

"No, you're fine." He lightly squeezed her hand. "You can talk to me about anything."

"I can't wrap my mind around why a guy like you hasn't already been snatched up by now," she said, blushing a little. "You're the nicest guy, Joseph. Any girl would be lucky to date you."

"Well, maybe I just haven't found the right girl."

Carrie's brows lifted. "Maybe."

They were distracted when a male server came over and placed their drinks on the table. "Hi, I'm Gary," he said with a high, feminine pitch. "I'll be your waiter for the evening. Have you had time to look over the menu?"

Joseph removed his hand from Carrie's and reached for his menu. "Could you give us a few more minutes, Gary?"

"Of course. If I may suggest, the Penne Alla Vodka is one of our popular dishes." He used his hands to express his words. "It's one of my favorites. But please, take your time. I'll give you a few minutes to decide."

Joseph nodded. "Thanks, Gary."

As the waiter sauntered off, the Shadow cackled. *"I think Gary is a little light in the loafers."*

Joseph tuned out the Shadow's crude remark. "I think I'll try what Gary suggested." He closed his menu and smiled at Carrie. "It sounds good. What about you?"

"Good choice." Her eyes flipped up to meet his. "I think I'll have the same."

He reached for his glass of wine and before he took a sip he said, "Well, you know what they say?"

She shrugged. "And what's that?"

"Great minds think alike."

"Carrie..." A booming voice drew their attention. "What are *you* doing here?"

When Joseph looked up, his eyes met a pudgy, middle-aged woman wearing a gold-sequined cocktail dress. It reminded him of a disco ball from the '80s. Her bleach-blonde hair and silicone injected lips made her look like a cheap hooker. She hovered over Carrie with a menacing stare.

"Veronica?" Carrie said, stiffening in her chair.

"Now that's what I call a full course meal," the Shadow said. *"I'll have her to go."*

Veronica huffed and flipped her hair back. "Aren't you supposed to be working late?"

"Um..." Carrie stumbled over her words. "I-I had a date."

Joseph instantly got to his feet and extended his hand. "I'm Joseph. It's a pleasure to meet you, Miss...?"

She took hold of his hand. "It's Hernandez. Veronica Hernandez."

He felt like a bug under a microscope as her eyes roamed over his face and ventured lower.

Joseph released her hand. "Are you a friend or a family member of Carrie's?"

"Neither." Veronica snidely remarked. "I'm her boss."

"Oh, I see." He raised a brow. "Well, I'm sure I don't have to tell you how lucky you are to have her as an employee. From what I clearly see, Carrie's dedicated to her work and a great person all around."

Carrie smiled and Veronica said, "Obviously you haven't known her for long."

Joseph frowned and Carrie's smile diminished.

"Actually, I haven't," Joseph said firmly. "But it doesn't take me long to figure out a person's character." Then he glared at Veronica. "I know a bad egg when I see one."

Carrie quickly covered her mouth to keep from laughing out loud.

Veronica smirked. "Is that so?"

Suddenly, Gary appeared to take their order in the nick of time.

"If you don't mind, Miss Hernandez," Joseph said, sitting back down. "I have a lovely date I'd like to get back to."

Veronica's overly plump lips tightened. "Fine." She looked away from Joseph and stared at Carrie with a scowl on her face. "I'll expect to see you first thing in the morning." Her voice dropped deeper. "And don't be late this time."

"But tomorrow is Sunday."

Veronica shrugged at Carrie. "Well then, I guess you better not stay out too late."

"What am I supposed to do on a Sunday?" Carrie asked. "I don't have any patients, and I'm all caught up on my paperwork."

"Oh, don't you worry your pretty little head," Veronica said, thrusting out her hip. "I've got plenty to keep you busy."

Carrie heaved a sigh of relief as Veronica finally stomped off, leaving them in peace.

A few minutes later, after Gary left with their order, Carrie's body shimmered back to life.

"Thank you, Joseph."

"For what?"

"For standing up to my boss. And I have to say..." She arched a brow. "...what you said to her was priceless."

"You're welcome, Carrie." He grinned. "And she had that coming. When you said your boss was a jerk, you were being polite. The word I have in mind is far worse. There's a special place for people who treat others that way."

The Shadow hissed. *"We'll be sending her there soon."*

"No one has ever stood up for me like that. I mean, sure, my family and Jessica have always had my back, but no guy I've dated has ever done something so... nice."

"I'm surprised to hear that," Joseph said, looking at her bewildered. "And to tell you the truth, I'm surprised *you're* single."

"I was dating a guy recently," she hesitantly said. "But it didn't work out."

"I'm sorry to hear that. He must have been nuts to let a girl like you get away."

"Well actually..." She looked down. "...he's dead."

"I'm so sorry, Carrie. What happened?"

Her eyes lifted slowly. "H-he was murdered."

"What?" His eyes rounded. "That's horrible. Was this recently?"

She nodded. "I'm sorry. I probably should have told you."

"No, it's okay, Carrie." His eyes softened. "My God. Were you close?"

"No. We'd only been dating a few months. He wasn't good to me, and there were signs of cheating, but I ignored them. Last night was the last straw. He'd stood me up and it wasn't the first time. That's when I decided to break it off. Then, around three in the morning, he came to my apartment. He was drunk and I refused to answer the door. When he finally gave up, Jessica and I were about to go to bed, and that's when we heard a car alarm going off. We figured he must have passed out in his car, so we went to check. We found him..." She shook her head. "It was awful."

"And he was tasty," the Shadow said. *"The bad ones always taste better."*

A sick taste of guilt welled up inside Joseph. He swallowed, forcing it down and muttered, "I-I—"

He was abruptly cut off when Gary suddenly arrived with their food.

Chapter Eleven

It was getting close to dinner when Tessa decided to call it quits. They all but exhausted themselves searching tirelessly through the library's archives, hoping to find something on the creature who Jena and Roman referred to as the Shadow. They discovered a few things, thanks to Sebastian's expertise in demonology, but nothing on how to destroy it. So far, the only thing they had to go on was it inhabited a vulnerable host, like a child. It preyed on their weaknesses and controlled their mental structure, especially as a motive force. And its main purpose was to gain access to souls. This type of demon was a dark entity with a ravenous appetite. The very root of all evil.

"Please…" Tessa called out, her eyes roaming over the occupants of the room. "Go enjoy the rest of your evening. I'm sure most of you have plans to celebrate Valentine's Day, and some of you have kiddos to pick up. I appreciate all your help."

Drakon came forward. "I'll go check out the Summit Behavioral Institute first thing in the morning. Hopefully, I can get some information on this Joseph Harris. If in fact he was released, it's a possibility he could be the guy we're looking for."

"I'll go with you," Roman said, his eyes focused on Drakon. "Just shoot me a text before you head out."

When Drakon nodded, Tim said, "Count me in as well. Let me know before you two leave. I'll ride with you guys."

"Will do," Drakon said.

"In the meantime," Tessa said, "I'll make sure everyone is informed if anything turns up. Enjoy your evening."

As Tessa stepped out of the room with Jace, she felt overwhelmed and disappointed. She had hoped they'd find something… anything that would explain how to destroy this mysterious Shadow. Although, in the back of her mind, she still hadn't given up on Jena's creature. If they were lucky, she was the one who could destroy it. With her fingers crossed, she said a silent prayer.

Out of nowhere, Tessa felt a stiffness in the base of her neck. As it continued to knot up, she reached her hand around and did her best to rub it.

"Here, babe," Jace said, moving behind her. "Let me take care of that."

Moving her hair aside, he started rubbing her shoulders and worked his way up her neck and then back again.

As his strong hands skillfully massaged over her tense muscles, she relaxed her head slightly forward and released a contented sigh. "That feels amazing, honey."

"Since my parents are keeping the twins overnight," he playfully said, "maybe we should take this somewhere private."

Tessa turned, tilting her head up so she could look up at him. "Is that so?"

He held out his hand. "Shall we?"

She smiled and placed her hand in his. "Lead the way."

As Tessa followed him upstairs, the moment they made their way into their bedroom, her jaw nearly dropped. She couldn't believe her eyes. The room was lit up with candles, soft music was playing in the background, and rose petals, formed in the shape of a heart, covered the satin sheets. And next to the bed, sitting on top of the nightstand, were two glasses of bubbly champagne, a bowl of her favorite berries, and a single, long-stemmed red rose.

"Oh, Jace..." She covered her mouth. "How did you—"

"I already knew you were having my parents pick up the boys," he said, sliding his hands over her shoulders. "So, I wanted to do something special. It's been a while since we had some alone time."

"I love it, honey."

"And I love you, sweetheart," he said, gliding his fingers up her neck to the slender column of her throat and to her jaw. Then he leaned down and pressed his lips to her forehead. "Tessa, you're everything to me."

When she turned to face him, he loved the way she looked at him, like he was her whole world. But in truth, she ruled his. There was nothing he wouldn't do for her. Hell, he'd step in front of a moving train. He'd give her the damn world if she asked for it. Tessa made him want to be a better person. She completed him. Not only did she have a heart of gold, and amazing art skills, she was flat-out gorgeous, for a lack of a better word. She had long, thick mahogany hair, green eyes that sparkled like emeralds, flawless skin, a set of lips to die for. And she was so petite, but tough as nails. Although he was a foot taller than her, she could hold her own. Tessa by no means was a helpless, defenseless woman. She was fearless and her determination was as big as Texas, not to mention the wolf she shifted into. It was twice the size of the ordinary Breedline.

"You make me so happy, Jace." Her trembling voice brought him back to focus. "I love you so much."

As she spoke, she reached for his hand and intertwined her fingers with his.

In that moment, as the song *Thinking Out Loud* by Ed Sheeran started to play, Jace gently took her other hand in his. He pulled her close until their bodies crushed together. "Dance with me, Tessa."

Slowly, they swayed to the romantic tempo.

As the song ended, she rose on her tiptoes with desire in her eyes. "Kiss me, Jace."

He instantly lowered his mouth to hers. His kiss was tender, sending shivers over her skin.

He shook against her as images of them making love consumed his thoughts. He wanted to touch and kiss all of her. His heart thundered in his chest, picturing their bodies tangled in a heated passion.

"Make love to me," she whispered against his lips.

He slowly pulled away. As she gazed into his blue eyes, they burned with desire. His nostrils flared with the effort of his breathing, and when he spoke, his words came out in a rush. "Your wish is my command."

Then he reached out and stroked her cheek with the pad of his thumb, then trailed it over her bottom lip. A few kisses later, they were undressed and under the rose-covered, satin sheets.

"Come here," he softly whispered, taking her against his body.

She gasped at the warmth of his bare skin and the indication of his desire, creating a needy sensation within her.

"I want you, Tessa." His voice was low, a deep rumble in his firm chest.

"I'm all yours."

When his lips touched her neck, she opened her mouth and moaned in anticipation. An instant fire ignited between her thighs, feeling as though she was going to go up in flames. She quickly parted her legs in an invitation to ravish her.

The second he shifted his body over hers and captured her lips, she buried her hands in the long strands of his hair.

He almost lost all control as she wrapped her legs around his hips. In an instant, he threw back his head and gritted his teeth, throbbing with the need to take her. With all the strength he had left, he looked down and gazed into her piercing green eyes.

She smiled up at him, acknowledging that familiar look of desire on his face.

"What are you waiting for," she said in a breathy sigh, her body withering underneath him. "Take me."

* * *

Joseph watched as Carrie took the last bite of her dessert. "So, how was the chocolate cake?"

She eased back into her chair with a contented sigh. "Delicious. Everything tasted fantastic. Thanks for dinner, Joseph."

"You're welcome." He smiled. "Glad you enjoyed."

While sipping wine and waiting for Gary to bring them the bill, Joseph and Carrie easily fell into a conversation. He tuned out the background noise in the restaurant and simply absorbed her every word. She talked a bit about her ex-boyfriend and her past, telling him about how her Uncle Frank and her Aunt Missy had taken her in and practically raised her after the tragic death of her parents. Then she went on to tell him about her friendship with Jessica and Jessica's new boyfriend Ryan. Next was college and how she landed her job.

"I feel like I'm talking your head off," she finally said. "I hope I'm not boring you with all my crazy life stories."

"Not in the least," Joseph said. "As a matter of fact, it's very interesting. It sounds like you've had a rough start, but life turned out well for you."

"What about you?" She slightly tilted her head. "Any serious relationships?"

"I've been out on a few dates. But nothing serious. I guess my work keeps me busy."

"I see. Have you lived here all your life?"

"Yes, I've always lived here in Berkeley. But someday, I'd like to do some traveling and see the world."

Her brows drew together. "You mean, you've never been out of the city?"

"Nope." He sighed. "I guess you could say I'm sort of a homebody."

"Really?" She looked at him bewildered. "I'd figure you as the sightseer type, especially since you're a journalist."

"It's hard to travel," the Shadow said. *"When you're locked up in a loony bin."*

Joseph chuckled, ignoring the voice in his head. "Yeah, you'd think, right?"

"You're kind of a mystery, Joseph. So, does your family live here?"

Suddenly, he got that deer-in-the-headlights look. He stiffened in his chair and looked away, becoming silent, unmoving.

Her question seemed to echo in his head, bringing forth a memory and the smell of blood. And the taste of it.

"She's asking too many questions, Joseph," the Shadow gritted out. *"You need to get rid of her."*

When Joseph didn't answer right away, Carrie reached across the table. "Joseph, are you okay?"

Her voice snapped him back. "Sorry..." He took hold of her hand. "I'm fine."

"Are you sure?"

He nodded even though he wasn't. "Yes, I was just thinking."

"What were you thinking about?"

"Oh nothing," Joseph said, releasing her hand as he relaxed back in his chair. "It's just..." He paused and let out a deep breath. "...sometimes, I lose my train of thought, that's all."

Abruptly, Gary came up to their table. "How was everything?"

Joseph smiled up at him. "The food was great."

"Oh, wonderful," Gary said, placing the check presenter on the table. "I hope you come again soon."

Joseph nodded. "Thank you, Gary."

Moments later, after Joseph took care of the check, he said, "You ready to go?"

When Carrie nodded, he got out of his chair and quickly moved behind hers. As he scooted her chair back, she stood and said, "Thank you, Joseph."

He guided her out of the restaurant and to the parking lot with his hand around her waist. When they approached the vehicle, he opened the passenger's door and helped her inside. After he got behind the wheel and started the engine, he said, "It's still early. Would you care to go somewhere for a drink or better yet, a cup of coffee?"

She turned toward him. "I'd really like to change into something more comfortable. Would you like to stop by my place? I've got plenty of coffee."

"Say yes, Joseph," the Shadow demanded.

"O-okay," he hesitantly said. "Sure."

"It's fine if you don't want—"

"No, no," Joseph said. "Coffee at your place sounds great."

He shifted into drive, and before he accelerated forward, he turned toward Carrie. "Thanks for having dinner with me. I had a great time."

Her eyes lit up. "Me too."

On the way, he felt her eyes on him. He could sense the wheels in her head turning with all sorts of questions. And he knew, sooner or later, he'd have to answer them.

As Joseph brought the Jeep to a stop in the parking lot of her apartment building, Carrie went to reach for the door. He put his hand on her arm to stop her. "Stay put while I get that for you."

Carrie nodded with a slight grin and quickly dropped her eyes as though she was bashful by the way he fussed over her.

Joseph got out and as he opened her door, she said, "You know, a girl could really get used to all this attention."

"Good," he said with his hand out, waiting for her to take hold. "You deserve no less."

"Thanks." She placed her hand in his. "I'll keep that in mind."

As soon as they made their way into the apartment, she locked the door from the inside. While she went to turn on the lights, he stood back and waited.

"You want me to take your jacket?"

"Sure, thanks." He slid it from his broad shoulders and handed it to her.

After she hung it in the coat closet, she gestured toward the sofa. "Please, make yourself comfortable. I'll go start the coffee. If you don't mind, while it's brewing, I'm going to change out of this dress."

"Of course not." He shook his head. "If you'd like, I can make the coffee."

"Are you sure?"

"Go ahead," Joseph said, waving it off like it was nothing. "It's no problem. Besides, I know my way around a kitchen."

"Wow." Her lips curled up. "I really hit the jackpot. I finally met a guy who still believes in chivalry and can also make coffee."

He chuckled. "Lucky you."

"I won't be but a second," Carrie said as she started up the stairs. "The coffee and filters are in the cabinet above the coffee maker."

A few minutes later, Joseph came from the kitchen with two cups of coffee. Carrie was on the couch with her legs tucked under her. She had on pink leggings and an oversized grey sweatshirt that revealed a little shoulder.

"I remembered you liked sugar and cream in yours," Joseph said, extending the cup he'd made for her.

"Oh, thanks." She reached for the cup of coffee. "Please, sit wherever you like."

When he sat down in the wingback chair next to the couch, she said, "I hope you don't mind me putting on something to relax in." She tugged at her top. "Sorry, it's nothing fancy."

"Nah, you're fine. Besides, you'd look good in just about anything."

She smiled and blushed.

"The hell with her clothes. She looks good enough to eat."

"Anyway," Joseph went on to say, overlooking the Shadow's obnoxious comment, "I'm normally a jeans and T-shirt kind of guy. It's all about comfort, right?"

"Absolutely," Carrie said. "Next time we go out, we'll go somewhere casual. I mean... that is... if you want to go out again."

He beamed. "Of course, I do."

"Stop stalling, Joseph. Kill her."

Joseph took a sip of his coffee and disregarded the Shadow's demands.

"Joseph..." Carrie paused and cleared her throat. "...did I say something wrong at the restaurant?"

He looked at her confused. "What do you mean?"

"Well, when I asked you about your family, it looked as though the question made you uncomfortable. I didn't mean to pry. I just wanted to... you know... get to know you better."

"Oh, here we go." The Shadow groaned. *"I warned you, Joseph."*

"No, Carrie. You didn't say anything wrong. It's just that..." He let out a deep breath, thinking if he told her the truth about his parents, it would terrify her. And for some odd reason, he didn't want to scare her off. She made him feel good in a way he'd never felt before. "Talking about my family is hard," he continued, feeling vulnerable and exposed. "Both of my parents are deceased."

Her eyes were apologetic. "I'm so sorry, Joseph. You don't have to talk about it. I probably shouldn't have brought it up."

"It's okay. You didn't know. It was a long time ago."

A sound coming from outside the door suddenly drew their attention. The moment they turned to look, it swung open, and Jessica stepped inside with Ryan following behind her. When Jessica caught sight of them, her brows went up.

"Well, well, well..." She cracked a smile. "Hey, Carrie. Hey, Joseph. I hope we're not interrupting anything."

"Hi, guys," Carrie said. "We were just visiting over coffee. Joseph made a fresh pot if you'd like to join us."

Jessica looked between Ryan and Joseph. "You two haven't met, have you?"

When Ryan shook his head, Joseph got to his feet and extended his hand. "It's nice to meet you. I'm Joseph."

"Hey, Joseph," Ryan said as he took hold of his hand. "I'm Ryan."

"Hmmm..." the Shadow pondered. *"Ryan is keeping secrets."* He chuckled in amusement. *"If only they knew."*

"Thanks for the offer," Jessica said as she moved closer to the sofa. "We're not staying long. I just wanted to change into a pair of jeans before we head over to the club. You guys want to join us?"

Carrie immediately turned toward Joseph to gauge his reaction. She could tell by the look on his face he wasn't interested, and neither was she.

"If it's okay with you," Carrie said, keeping her eyes focused on Joseph, "I'd rather stay in for the night."

"Yeah, me too," Joseph said, glancing at his watch. "Besides, I probably should get going."

"What's the hurry?" Jessica asked. "It's only nine o'clock."

"Carrie has to work tomorrow," Joseph said.

"You've got to be kidding." Jessica furrowed her brows. "On a Sunday?"

"Well, you know the usual punishment." Carrie released a sigh. "I was supposed to stay late tonight, so...?"

Jessica put her hands on her hips. "Your boss is a total bitch."

"I know, I know," Carrie said. "But when your father is the CEO of the company..."

"That's bullshit and you know it, Carrie." Jessica huffed. "Something has got to be done about that woman. I swear, one of these days, she's going to get exactly what she deserves."

"Oh, we can make that happen," the Shadow said. *"Sooner than later."*

"So, Carrie," Ryan said, "if you don't mind me asking, what's the deal with your boss? Why does she have it in for you?"

"It's over a damn man," Jessica blurted before Carrie could answer. "The bitch has been punishing Carrie ever since the new guy at work asked Carrie out on a date."

"That's messed up," Ryan said.

"That's more than messed up," Joseph said, crossing his arms over his chest. "It's morally wrong." He averted his eyes from Ryan and looked to Carrie with a raised brow. "Your boss needs to be reprimanded, or better yet, fired."

Ryan focused on Carrie. "Hey, I've got a friend that's a big shot attorney. I could talk to him. His law firm takes on companies with the same issues. Maybe he could give you some advice."

When Carrie didn't immediately reply, Joseph said, "It's worth a try. What do you have to lose?"

Carrie sighed. "I don't want to take the chance of losing my job."

Jessica groaned. "Jeez, Carrie. Just talk to the guy. It doesn't mean you have to hire him. You're just getting the man's advice."

"Okay." Carrie shrugged. "I guess you're right."

Ryan nodded. "I'll give him a call tomorrow."

"Thanks, Ryan."

"No problem," he said. "Anytime."

"Well, I guess I better be heading out," Joseph said. "It was nice to see you again, Jessica." He looked to Ryan. "And it was a pleasure to meet you."

"Yeah," Ryan said, smiling. "You too, Joseph."

Jessica's lips curled up. "I'm sure we'll see you again soon."

Carrie instantly rose from the sofa and looked up at Joseph. "Please, let me see you out."

As Carrie walked Joseph to the door, Jessica called out, "Hey, Joseph."

When he turned to face Jessica, she went on to say, "If you're free on the last Saturday of the month, say around noonish, we'd love to have you over. Ryan and I are throwing Carrie a party. It's her birthday."

"Oh, sure. I'd love to." Joseph looked away from Jessica and faced Carrie. "That is, if it's okay with you."

"Sorry," Carrie said, her expression apologetic. "I was going to invite you, but it completely slipped my mind. I'd love for you to come."

"It's nothing fancy," Ryan said. "We're just barbequing ribs."

"Count me in," Joseph said. "Do I need to bring anything?"

"If you don't mind, we could use a bottle of rum," Jessica said. "That's Carrie's favorite."

Joseph nodded and then turned toward Carrie with a smile. "I believe I can make that happen."

After they said their good-byes, and Joseph got behind the wheel of his Jeep, the Shadow made a groaning sound. *"What are you doing, Joseph?"*

Joseph closed his eyes and rubbed at his temples, trying his best to suppress the voice inside his head. "Please, not now."

"Sooner or later, you will kill them all."

Chapter Twelve

Lying next to Nicolas in a peaceful slumber, Jena had let her fears of the unknown and all the uncertainties of the future drift away. With the curse weighing on her shoulders, it was as though he was the only solid thing in her life.

Hours later, Jena awoke out of breath, her heart pounding. She instantly sat up in bed. She could hear voices coming from a distance like a beacon calling out to her. A woman was crying for help, begging for her life. Then she heard a small child, desperately pleading.

She felt a painful yearning to go to them, to save them. It was agony suddenly. Every muscle in her body wanted to spring out and run to their rescue.

Without further delay, Jena sprang from the bed and rushed toward the glass doors that led to the balcony. As she looked out, her eyes searching through the darkness, she heard the voices again. For a fleeting moment, Jena froze in place. Her muscles were tense, and her senses on overload. She stood there, taken back by the sounds she was hearing. Somewhere far off, a little girl was screaming for help.

Nicolas woke up to find Jena standing by the balcony doors. Her eyes were fixated on something outside.

"Jena," he called out to her. "Is something wrong?"

Although she registered Nicolas's voice, it seemed miles away. She ignored his efforts and continued to peer out the glass barrier that separated her from the distressed voices beckoning her. And then, a strange and pressing urge called out to her. *Go save them!*

Out of nowhere, her fingernails and toenails began to tingle. She could feel them stretching and elongating until they formed into sharp points. Then the prickle of tiny hairs began to emerge from her shoulders. They grew thicker, spreading to her arms, covering her hands and all ten of her fingers. In a matter of seconds, the hairs completely blanketed every inch of her skin. Her nightgown ripped at the seams as her rib cage contorted and the muscles in her body enlarged, taking on an unnatural form. Her stature lengthened and expanded to gigantic proportions.

Witnessing all the skin-twisting carnage, Nicolas then realized the curse had taken over Jena and there wasn't anything he could do to stop it.

She was completely unrecognizable. Her delicate features and the feminine contours of her body had been replaced with a hideous wolfish beast. Every inch of her pale and flawless complexion was now covered in thick, black fur. It was almost too terrifying to put into words.

Nicolas called out again, attempting to stop Jena as she went to open the doors.

She whirled around and tossed the remnants of her nightgown to the floor. "Don't follow me, Nicolas." Her voice sounded different, guttural. "I must save them before it's too late."

He nodded and watched in silence as she dashed through the opening of the balcony and disappeared into the night.

With one giant leap, Jena dropped from the balcony's ledge and landed on the ground with ease. For only a moment, she waited and listened. Then she heard the voices again. Although she knew better, they seemed close. Their pleas for mercy were loud and clear. It created a raw sensation in the back of her throat, nearly choking her.

She pivoted on the balls of her feet and sprang forward, landing on all fours. At lightning speed, she bounded across the large terrain surrounding the Breedline Covenant. The split second it took her to vault over the wrought iron gates, alarms were sounded. She remained focused and continued her endeavor to get away.

A few minutes later, she came upon a country road with twists and turns. It was dark and desolate, but the voices were louder now, keeping her on track. It wasn't long before the gravel roadway led her to an old, two-story house. It had obviously been neglected for years. The paint on the wood appeared weathered and the grass stood knee-high. Although the place looked abandoned, she noticed a black van parked in the front. The windows were tinted, and the license plate was missing. With the swiftness of a feline, she crept closer to the rickety structure covering the doorway. When she inhaled deeply, a pungent scent flooded her senses. It was the scent of something sinister and evil. The overpowering smell sparked a hunger within and a desire to kill.

Jena's wolfish creature snarled in response, and her muscles coiled.

A woman screaming immediately alerted Jena and brought her head around. They were coming from inside, sounding urgent and panic-stricken. She rose on two feet and in an instant she used the strength in her powerful muscles and bolted toward the entrance. With the force of her new transformation, she charged through like a battering ram, rendering the door into pieces.

Inside was a man tearing at a woman's clothes as though he was about to rape her. She was kicking and screaming, struggling underneath her attacker.

The foul odor emanating from the man angered Jena further. He reeked of cigarettes and cheap whiskey, like he hadn't bathed in days.

Across the room, huddled in the floor, wearing only panties, was a little girl, maybe five at most, her tear-stained eyes rounded in terror. Her hands and feet were bound with rope.

The horrifying images fueled Jena's rage. With incredible speed, she lunged at the man with slashing claws. The force of the impact knocked him off the woman and sent him flying back. His head collided into a wall with a wet crack. Blood pooled beneath him, igniting Jena's bloodlust. She allowed him no time to recover as she pounced on top of him. Now standing on the man's chest, vicious claws dug into his skin, pinning him down. His mouth flew open, and his eyes grew large as he stared into the gapping maw nearing his face.

When Jena's jaws clamped around the man's throat, he bellowed in pain. As sharp canines tore at his flesh, within seconds his screams turned into wet gurgles. The taste of the man's blood intensified Jena's hunger, driving her instincts to go in for the kill. Finally, as she surrendered to the primal impulse of her savage creature, his life ended quickly in a final bright-red arterial spray.

While Jena feasted on the man, the woman scrambled to her feet and rushed to free the little girl. She kept a watchful eye as she feverishly worked at the ropes with shaky hands. A few minutes later, she scooped the child off the floor and into her arms. As she turned to flee, she came upon Jena's creature. Keeping a tight hold on the child, the woman took a few steps back. Her eyes were huge in her battered and bruised face. A face that was frozen with fear.

"Please," she begged with tears staining her cheeks. "Please, don't harm my little girl."

Jena looked into the woman's swollen eyes and then to the frightened child in her arms. Her heart ached for them. She wanted nothing more than to take away their pain and erase this terrifying night from their memories forever.

"I'm not going to harm either of you," Jena said, her voice gravel. "I came to save you."

The woman stared wearily up at Jena. "W-what are you?"

Jena went silent, pondering the woman's question. What was she? The only answer that came to mind was *cursed*. Although she realized if she tried to explain what she was, it would be confusing and seem more terrifying. And to make matters worse, there was a small child present. The poor little girl had already witnessed too much for such young eyes.

"I'm sort of like God's helper. I was created to destroy evil."

The woman slowly nodded, and her shoulders sagged a bit, but she still wore a weary, guarded look that made Jena's heart splinter.

"But..." the woman's lips trembled, "...why do you look like a werewolf?"

Jena heaved out a sigh. "It's a long story."

"You're a good wolf," the little girl said. "You saved my mommy."

Jena's eyes softened. "I'm glad I got to you both in time. There's a van outside." She extended her clawed hand and offered the woman a set of keys. "Please, get to a safe place."

The woman took the keys from Jena and looked to the dead man, who lay mangled and half-eaten. Then she focused her eyes back to Jena. "What about that man? I have no idea who he is. Shouldn't we call the police?"

Jena shook her head. "Forget you ever saw him. I will take care of everything."

When the woman nodded, Jena said, "Do either of you need medical attention?"

"We'll be fine," the woman said. "Thanks to you."

"Can you go with us?" the little girl asked, gazing up at Jena with big brown eyes and freckled, rounded cheeks.

"I'm sorry, sweetheart," Jena regretfully said. "I can't be seen by other people. They wouldn't understand like you. They would be scared."

The little girl looked at Jena utterly fascinated and reached out to her. "I'm not scared of you."

Her remarkable fearlessness took Jena by surprise. Then her wolfish lips curled up as she gently took hold of the girl's tiny hand. "You're a very brave little girl."

"My name is Amy. What's your name?"

"It's nice to meet you, Amy. My name is Jena."

"I like your name." Amy smiled. "It's pretty."

"Thank you, Amy."

"Come on, honey," Amy's mother said. "Let's get you home."

"Wait," Jena said, looking at the woman with pleading eyes. "Will you tell me your name?"

"My name is Martha. Martha Dunlap."

"Martha, do you..." Jena momentarily paused, reluctant to ask. "Do you have a husband or anyone who can help you?"

"No, it's just me and my daughter."

"Martha, you and your daughter are going to need help," Jena said. "I can send someone to check on you. And I promise they are good people. They're my friends. One is also a physician. They helped me when I didn't have anyone. You'd like them, especially the doctor. Her name is Helen Carrington, and she routinely makes house calls."

Martha lowered her head, realizing Jena was right. It wasn't something she couldn't very well deny. And both she and Amy did *need* a doctor.

She lifted her gaze to meet Jena's and saw kindness. The beastly creature looked at her like she was someone who mattered.

"Are your friends like you?" Martha asked.

"No," Jena said. "I'm the last of my kind."

Martha briefly glanced at her daughter, racked by indecision. Then finally, she nodded. "We live at the Adeline Street Apartments. We're upstairs in 10B."

"Thank you, Martha. I will make sure Helen stops by later this morning to check on you and Amy. She will most likely bring someone with her you can trust."

"The neighborhood isn't very safe," Martha said. "How will I know it's your friends?"

"Don't open the door unless they mention my name."

"Thank you for helping us."

As Martha moved toward the broken doorway, Amy looked back and waved. "Bye-bye, Jena."

She waved back. "Good-bye, Amy."

As Jena watched them leave, an unexpected realization hit her suddenly. The creature she was to be for an eternity was not entirely a curse. It was also a gift. It gave her the ability to save innocent lives like little Amy. The thought soothed her heart, giving her a renewed sense of purpose.

* * *

Tessa's eyelids flipped open when she felt a warm hand on her shoulder. Goose bumps prickled over her skin as it slid down her arm, soft and featherlike. She turned her head and came face-to-face with the most gorgeous pair of blue eyes. The color practically glowed. The man they belonged to was even more spectacular. His expression was intense, a combination of desire and admiration.

As she gazed into Jace's amazing baby blues, he glided his fingertips back up her arm and then toward her face. Ever so gently, he smoothed his hand down the side of her cheek and lower to her lips. Using the pad of his thumb, he brushed over her bottom lip. "You're so beautiful, Tessa."

Before she could respond, he leaned in and pressed his mouth to hers. His kiss was tender, and his lips were warm against hers.

When their lips parted, she said, "Thanks for last night, honey. You made my Valentine's Day so special. Everything was perfect, especially the *massage* part."

"You're welcome, sweetheart." He winked at her. "And there's more where that came from."

"Well then," Tessa said, smiling, "I may have to take you up on that offer."

Suddenly, the cell phone on Tessa's nightstand went off. Her attention was alerted by the ringtone, realizing it was Tim Ross calling. She glanced at the clock and noticed it was too early for anyone to be calling on a Sunday.

Jace groaned as she went to reach for it.

"Sorry, babe." She looked at him with apologetic eyes. "This might be important."

He nodded with a pouty lip.

Tessa swiped her phone to answer. "This is Tessa."

There was a long pause of silence, and going by the expression on Tessa's face, whatever was being said on the other end didn't appear good. Before she ended the call, she said, "Okay, we'll meet you downstairs as soon as we get dressed."

"I take it that wasn't good news."

"That was about Jena." Tessa sighed. "There was an incident."

"What kind of incident?"

"Apparently, Jena sensed someone in trouble. She shifted into the creature and went to find them. When Jena followed the voices, it led her to an abandoned two-story house a few miles from here. A man had abducted a woman and her small child. Jena found the man trying to rape the woman, and the child was tied up, witnessing her mother being attacked."

Jace rose from his pillow. "Damn... Are they okay?"

Tessa nodded. "Jena got to them in the nick of time."

"So, where is Jena now?"

"She's in her room resting. According to what Tim told me just now, when Jena came back, she led him, along with Nicolas, Drakon, and Jem to the two-story house. They helped clean up what was left of that man."

"Sounds like they had one hell of a bloody Valentine's. So, why didn't they tell us?"

Tessa shot him a half-smile. "Tim and the others didn't want to ruin our night."

"Well, that was decent of them. I can't say I hate that we missed the cleaning up part." He crinkled his nose in disgust. "But how in the world did Jena get past the security?"

"Tim said the guards sounded the alarms, but Jena was gone before they managed to go after her."

"I wonder why we didn't hear the alarms?"

"I think we had a little too much champagne," Tessa said. "And I have to say, it was rather nice getting some alone time. Since the twins were born, those days are scarce, not to mention a good night's rest."

"I guess you're right," Jace said. "And last night, I slept like a rock."

She leaned over and kissed him. "Come on, honey. Let's get dressed. We're supposed to meet Tim and the others downstairs in the kitchen for breakfast to discuss a few things. And Detectives Sanchez and Perkins are joining us."

"Good." Jace quickly got to his feet. "I'm starving."

As Tessa slipped out of bed to get dressed, Jace took notice of how her silk nightgown clung to her body. Although she was petite, she had curves in all the right places. God, she was beautiful. The sight of her nearly took his breath away.

It took him back to when they'd first met. Most of his life, he'd been a player. He wasn't the settling down type, and it was true enough that he'd enjoyed his share of women. But the moment he laid eyes on Tessa, it blindsided him. He felt powerfully drawn to her in a way he couldn't explain. It was as though they were destined for one another, bound by an unbreakable force. From then on, he was a one-woman man. Tessa was his heart, his beloved, his everything. Hell, according to him, she practically hung the damn moon.

"Hey, Tessa..."

When Tessa turned to Jace, she instantly recognized the look in his eyes. It was the same wicked gleam he gave her last night, right before they made love.

"We don't have time, Jace."

"I just want a little hug," he said, motioning her over.

"You know where this will lead."

He wiggled his brows. "Back to bed, I hope."

"You're incorrigible, you know."

As she got close to him, he put one arm around her waist and tugged her against him. Instantly, he buried his other hand in her hair and crushed his lips to hers. And it wasn't just one little hug, nor a peck on the lips. He kissed her hungrily, so passionately, it ignited a desire she couldn't resist. A few moments later, they were back in bed, tangled in a heat of passion.

Chapter Thirteen

There was something about Kevin Russo's murder that didn't make a bit of sense, Manuel thought as he drove to the Breedline Covenant. Who or *what* had the kind of strength to rip a man's heart completely out of his chest? And for what reason? He'd never seen anything like it in all his years working as a detective.

Of course, he'd never have believed in a million years that there were humans with the ability to shift into wolves. And not your average wolves either. They were as big, if not bigger, than horses. They called themselves Breedlines. Not to mention other supernatural creatures he'd only thought to be a myth or a fairy tale.

Just like Tessa Chamberlain, Detectives Sanchez and Perkins had accidently found themselves smack dab in the middle of this mysterious and unimaginable secret world. A few years back, when Tessa had met and fallen in love with Jace, she too, had never imagined such things like shapeshifting humans, vampire-like creatures, werewolves, and other majestic creatures existed. But believe it or not, they did. Manuel and Frank had seen it with their own eyes.

The Breedline species had, in each state, their own laws and a Covenant. They served as protectors for all mankind against evil beings. Compared to humans, Breedlines had tremendous advantages when it came to health. Their bodies healed fast and were not subject to illnesses or diseases. The only thing that slowed their healing process was silver. It was like their kryptonite. Besides old age, a silver bullet to the brain was the only way to destroy *most* Breedlines. Some, like Jace and his twin brother Jem, were immortal and immune to silver.

Now, the two detectives had somehow found themselves helping the Breedline fight against the dark forces that consistently never seemed to end. And to add to all the madness, he'd recently found out he carried the Breedline DNA. But according to the species, you had to be born with an identical twin for the *wolf thing* to happen. Since the Breedline males shifted on their eighteenth birthday, and

Manuel was already in his fifties, and to his knowledge he'd never produced a tail or howled at the moon, it was evident he wasn't going to transform into a hairy beast anytime soon.

What had baffled Manuel the most was his half-brother's son, Nathan Gage, who—born a Breedline and the owner of several upscale night clubs in the largest metropolitan areas of Northern California—had known about his lineage the whole entire time. But according to the Breedline's True Law, it was imperative their species was kept secret, so Manuel couldn't blame his nephew for not telling him. The day he and Frank were put in jeopardy, the members of the Breedline Covenant revealed the truth and welcomed them into their world.

As Manuel refocused back to Kevin Russo's murder, the only thing that he could come up with was human organ trafficking. To make matters worse, they had nothing to go by, no leads, not even a single drop of evidence at the crime scene.

Instantly, Manuel's gut clenched as his thoughts took him to the worst part of his job. Having to tell someone their loved one had been murdered was something you could never get out of your head. He'd traveled down that road one too many times in the last thirty years he'd spent in homicide. He could still picture all the grief-stricken faces and all the heart-wrenching tears. It was something he knew all too well.

He'd never forget the day his mother had received the news of his sister's murder. It had been years ago, but it still stuck in his head like it was yesterday. That day had changed his life forever. It had been the main reason he'd chosen a career in law enforcement. He took an oath to serve and protect the innocent, and that's exactly what he'd promised his mother before she passed. Dealing with complete strangers was one thing, but when it happened in your own home, that was another.

"So, you think the Covenant has a lead on Mr. Russo's case?"

Manuel briefly glanced at his partner. "Let's hope the hell they do. So far, we've got nothing to go on."

Frank sighed. "Right now, anything would be better than nothing."

"How's your niece?" Manuel asked, changing the subject.

"Carrie seems to be doing all right, considering what all she's been through. And as a matter of fact, according to my wife, Carrie has met someone."

"Really?" Manuel cocked a brow. "When did this happen?"

"Remember when she lost her purse?"

When Manuel nodded, Frank went on to say, "Apparently, some guy found it. He got Carrie's address from her ID and took it to her. I guess they somehow hit it off by what Missy said when she talked to Carrie the other day. He asked her out on a date."

"It sounds like things are turning up for her," Manuel said. "After everything she's had to endure, she deserves some good luck for a change."

"I agree. That poor girl has had her share of hardships."

"Have you met this guy?"

Frank shook his head. "Not yet. But her roommate has, and she seems to approve."

"Are you going to run a background check on him?"

"Nah," Frank said. "I think I'll give Carrie the benefit of the doubt this time. She seems to really like the guy, and going by what she described to my wife, so far he's a true gentleman. She said it's the first time a guy has opened a car door for her."

"That's rare these days," Manuel said, "especially with the younger generation. What's this guy do for a living?"

"He's a writer, I think."

"Well, at least this one's got a job and doesn't live off his parents like her last boyfriend. Speaking of Mr. Russo, how's Carrie handling his death?"

"She seems to be taking it fairly well," Frank said. "I think meeting someone new has helped. Besides, I have to say, Kevin Russo wasn't exactly the nicest guy. He was nothing more than a spoiled brat and he treated Carrie like she was beneath him."

"You can thank his parents for that," Manuel said, smirking. "Hell, what do you expect when you buy your adult kid a car that costs more than I make on a year's salary. And that doesn't include the penthouse they were paying for.

That's what's wrong with all these kids nowadays. They never learn the meaning of hard-earned money. Instead of making them work for it, their parents just keep doling out the cash."

"Amen to that," Frank said. "I'm just grateful my parents taught me the value of a dollar so I could pass it on. It's discouraging that in today's times a lot of parents don't teach their children good work ethics. I think Missy and I did a decent job raising Carrie. That young lady is one hard worker. We're so proud of her. She was so young when her parents died. After Missy and I took her in, we've always considered her our own. Since we couldn't have kids, Carrie was like a blessing." Then he chuckled. "Listen to us go on. We sound like a couple of old coots."

"Have you looked in the mirror lately?" Manuel grunted. "We're not exactly spring chickens."

Suddenly, out of nowhere, a red sports car cut in front of them.

"*Shit!*" Manuel gritted his teeth as he slammed the brakes. As soon as he flipped on the flashing lights, the driver instantly pumped his brakes.

"Probably one of those little rich bastards," Manuel said as he sped up and rode the guy's bumper.

"Maybe we ought to pull him over and give him a few driving lessons," Frank said. "And a big old fat ticket."

"Today is that guy's lucky day," Manuel said as he drove past the sports car, who had pulled off on the side of the road, obviously expecting a ticket. "We've got more pressing issues to deal with."

"Whatever you say," Frank said. "But if it had been me, I would have pulled that guy over and given him a good old-fashioned tongue-lashing."

"Yeah, yeah." Manuel grumbled, switching off the flashing lights, then stomped on the accelerator. "Let's just focus on our task ahead. I'm dying to know why Tim Ross asked us to stop by the Covenant so early."

"Didn't he say why in the message he left you?"

"He invited us over for breakfast and mentioned they had a situation last night they wanted to discuss."

Frank tilted his head. "I wonder if this has anything to do with Jena?"

"Who knows. Although I'm hoping they found some information on whoever murdered Kevin Russo."

"Maybe this time we'll catch a break."

"Well, keep your fingers crossed," Manuel said. "Considering our luck lately, we're going to need all the help we can get."

Chapter Fourteen

A half hour later, Tessa and Jace finally made their way downstairs. Before they stepped into the kitchen, whatever was cooking on the inside instantly invaded their senses and ignited Jace's appetite.

As he pushed through the set of double doors and held one side open for Tessa, they were surprised to see the kitchen already packed. With the exception of Jena and Nicolas, everyone else in the Covenant were gathered around the table.

Tessa noticed Alexander Crest—Jace and Jem's biological father—sitting close to Helen with his arm around her. It warmed her heart to see them in love, and it made her wonder when they were finally going to tie the knot.

Settled in the chairs across from them were Cassie and her husband Drakon. They were facing each other, and by the looks on their faces, Tessa could tell how much they loved one another. And if she had to bet, the two were most likely talking about baby things. Cassie was moving along in her pregnancy, and they were excited to have a family of their own.

Alongside the pregnant couple sat Mia and her husband Jem. Nestled in Jem's lap was their daughter, Evie. She was the spitting image of her mother but with Jem's gorgeous blond hair and blue eyes. Everyone in the Covenant adored her, especially all her cousins and Tim and Angel's little girl, Natalie.

At the far end of the table, sitting next to Alexander, were Eve and Sebastian. Their twin boys, Arius and Tidus, sat in highchairs nearby. Both boys had dark curly hair and golden eyes like their father. They were eating biscuits with jelly, although most of the strawberry jam covered their faces.

Next to Helen sat Abbey and her husband, Steven, who was holding their son, Jonah. The rest of the Breedline crew were engaged in conversation, chatting and laughing. Although Tessa enjoyed every minute she had alone with her husband, all the voices inside the crowded room made her feel at home. The only thing missing were their twin boys. The thought made her want to call Jace's adoptive parents, but she decided to be patient and let them have more time with their grandbabies. Besides, they had been practically begging to keep the boys overnight, and she wasn't the type to say no to her in-laws. John and Sarah were wonderful people and took excellent care of little Jem and Jax.

Jace rubbed his stomach. "Is that bacon and eggs I smell?"

Tim rose from his chair and motioned them over. "Please, come join us."

Tessa smiled at Tim and then at Angel, who was seated next to him. Their daughter, Natalie, was in a highchair close by, drinking out of a pink sippy cup. The cat, Buddy, was nestled on the floor beneath her highchair. Although the black feline belonged to Jace, he mostly stayed close to the little girl. Two seats were empty at the far side of the couple, and Jace went to pull out a chair for Tessa.

Tessa settled in her seat. "Sorry we're running late."

"You're fine." Tim smiled, realizing it had been a while since Tessa and Jace had time alone. Besides, he knew all too well what it was like chasing after a toddler, and they had double the trouble.

"As a matter of fact," Tim said, "we're still waiting on the detectives to arrive. They should be here shortly."

Jace took a seat next to Tessa and said, "They better get here soon. I'm starving."

"Someone better feed him," Kyle chimed in. "We all might end up on the menu."

"Careful, Kyle," Casey warned. "Remember the last time Jace got pissed off."

"Whatever," Jace groaned, rolling his eyes.

Mia held up a plate of biscuits. "Help yourself, Jace. Maybe this will tide you over until the detectives get here."

"They're delicious," Drakon piped in. "I've already had two."

"Me too," Lawrence said around a mouthful.

Roman grinned at Lawrence. "They must be good since that's your third one."

Lawrence merely smirked at Roman.

"Thanks, Mia." Jace reached for a biscuit. "You're a life-saver."

When Jace stuffed the entire thing in his mouth, Tessa shook her head, clearly annoyed by his caveman manners. Just as she was about to say something, Bruce Carmichael popped his head inside and said, "Detectives Manuel Sanchez an' Frank Perkins have arrived." He spoke with a thick, Scottish accent. "Should ah escort them in?"

"Of course," Tessa said. "Thank you, Bruce."

He nodded and ushered the two detectives into the kitchen.

"Make yourself comfortable, Detectives," Tim said, easing back into his chair. "You too, Bruce. And I hope you guys brought your appetite. The ladies made quite the spread."

"Thank ye, Mr. Ross," Bruce said.

"That goes for me too," Manuel said. "Thanks for having us over. Everything looks delicious."

"Thanks for inviting us," Frank said, eyeballing all the platters of food. "You ladies out did yourselves."

"You're welcome," Angel spoke out. "Please, have a seat and dig in."

"After we eat," Tim said, looking between the two detectives, "we'll meet in the library to talk in private."

Manuel nodded. "Sounds like a plan."

Not long after everyone finished eating, the women stayed back to clean up, except for Tessa and Helen, while the group of men escorted the two detectives to the library.

The moment everyone gathered around the seating area, Manuel said, "I hope what you have to say has something to do with Mr. Russo's case."

"I'm sorry, Detective," Tim regretfully said. "This is about Jena. But I promise, we're still working on that issue."

"I had a feeling this was about Jena." Manuel exhaled a deep breath. "So, what's going on?"

After Tim explained the situation concerning the woman and her daughter, including the man who kidnapped them, everyone at the table went speechless.

Finally, Manuel said, "I take it there's not much left of the kidnapper."

Tim shook his head. "His remains are in our morgue. We cremated what was left of him."

"What about that abandoned house?" Frank asked.

"Don't worry, Detective," Drakon said. "We made sure everything was taken care of."

Manuel arched a brow. "Are you saying all the evidence has been destroyed?"

"What would you have us do?" Drakon asked. "We already know the details, unless you want us to notify the authorities so they can waste taxpayers' money on an investigation."

"Okay, okay." Manuel held up a hand. "I get your point. The last thing we need is for this to get out."

"I know covering up evidence isn't the best option," Tim said. "But in this case, we had no other choice."

Tessa nodded. "I agree."

"What about an ID?" Manuel asked. "Do we know the assailant's identity?"

Tim placed what looked to be a man's billfold on the table. "We found the guy's wallet. Peter Ferguson was the name listed on his driver's license."

Manuel pointed to the wallet. "May I see that?"

"Of course." Tim slid it down to Manuel.

When Manuel got a look at the photo on the driver's license, his brows went up.

"Is that who I think it is?" Frank asked.

Manuel looked up at Frank. "It sure the *hell* is."

"Are you going to clue in the rest of us?" Jace asked.

"Jena just solved a big case," Manuel said. "We've been working on this for over two years."

Jace shrugged. "What case are you talking about?"

"He's talking about the Ferguson case," Frank said. "The guy Jena took out was a notorious rapist and a serial killer. We just haven't been able to catch the guy. He's responsible for the death of fifteen women. And those are just the ones we found his DNA on. It's possible there's more."

"I've heard about this on the news," Jem said. "He's nicknamed Slippery Pete."

Frank nodded. "That's him all right. Every time we'd get a lead on the guy, he somehow managed to slip through the cracks."

"Well, I guess Jena solved your problems," Jace said. "Ol' Slippery Pete won't be able to put his hands on another woman ever again."

"You said that right," Kyle blurted. "I'm betting the guy didn't even have a limb left after Jena's creature got a hold of him."

"Actually, she did leave one arm," Drakon pointed out.

"Serves the bastard right," Jace said. "If I'd caught the guy, he'd be lucky to have a head left."

"Okay, guys," Tim firmly stated. "I think we get the picture."

"What about the woman and her child?" Frank asked. "Are they okay?"

"They survived, thanks to Jena," Tim said. "And she got the woman's name and address. Miss Martha Dunlap lives at the Adeline Street Apartments."

"Good lord," Jace muttered. "What's she doing raising a kid in that area? It's in a real bad location. Those apartments are overrun with drug dealers."

Tim averted his eyes from Jace and looked to Helen with concern. "If you don't mind, we'd like you to go check on Martha and her daughter. Jena promised we'd make sure they had a medical examination. By what Jena said, and the low-income housing, I take it they don't have the funds to pay for medical expenses."

"Of course," Helen said. "I'd be more than happy to offer my services."

"Helen shouldn't go alone," Alexander said. "I'll go with her."

"Thank you, Alexander," Tim said. "I was planning on going, but since you're volunteering, I will go on ahead to the institute with Drakon and Roman."

Manuel looked at Tim, befuddled. "What institute?"

"The Summit Behavioral Institute," Tim replied. "It has something to do with Kevin Russo's murder. We're not sure, but we may have a lead."

"What kind of lead?"

"How 'bout you and Frank go with us," Tim said to Manuel. "We'll give you the details on the way. Plus, your badges might help us get the information we're looking for."

"If this will get us closer to finding the perpetrator," Manuel said, "we'll definitely do all we can."

"Sorry to change the subject," Jem said. "But just as a precaution, I think it's a good idea if I go with Helen and Alexander. Jace was right about that apartment complex. It's really bad."

Tim nodded. "Thanks, Jem."

"I'd like to go too," a voice came from the doorway.

When everyone turned to look, they saw Jena with the door slightly propped open and Nicolas standing behind her.

Tim rose from his chair and motioned them inside. "Please, join us."

As they approached the table, Nicolas settled Jena in a chair next to Tim and then sat down on the opposite side of her.

"Are you sure you want to go along?" Tim asked, looking between Jena and Nicolas. "It would mean giving up your true identity to Miss Dunlap and her daughter."

"Yes, I'm sure," Jena said. "I want to reassure them. To let them know someone cares."

"Jena, you saved their lives," Tessa said. "I'm sure Miss Dunlap realizes that. I don't think it's in your best interest to reveal who you are."

"I know. But it would mean a lot to me if I could visit Martha and her daughter. I want them to see me as I truly am, and not the scary monster they witnessed."

"I'll only agree to this if you promise you'll keep the Covenant a secret."

Jena dipped her head. "I give you my word, Tessa."

Chapter Fifteen

When Jem parked the vehicle at the Adeline Street Apartments, Helen's brows drew together as she took in the condition of the rundown building. There were bars covering the outside windows of each unit and some were cracked while others were busted out completely. By the overgrown weeds surrounding the brick structure and trash littering the parking lot, it was obviously poorly managed. The place didn't even look livable or safe by any means.

"Jace was right," Helen said. "This is definitely not a good environment to raise a child."

Jem nodded in agreement and cut the engine to the SUV.

"Poor little Amy," Jena said, peering out of the backseat window. "There's got to be something we can do to help them."

"I may know someone who can help," Nicolas said.

Jena faced him. "You do?"

"There's an organization that helps single mothers. They provide housing and other provisions along with financial assistance for anyone who qualifies. I can get in contact with the person in charge if Miss Dunlap agrees to it."

Jena reached for Nicolas's hand. "Thank you, honey."

He smiled. "You're welcome, sweetheart."

The moment a red Mustang pulled into the space next to them, the loud music blasting from inside drew their attention. The dark-tinted windows made it impossible to see the occupants within. Then everything went quiet as two men emerged from the vehicle, along with a thick cloud of cigarette smoke. The one behind the wheel had on a black hoodie with an image of a marijuana leaf on the front and the passenger wore a Yankees ball cap with a black satchel strapped over his shoulder.

Before Jem and the others got out of the SUV, they waited until the men went into the apartment complex. As soon as they were out of sight, Jem said, "Remember the plan, ladies." He looked to the passenger's seat at Helen and then toward the backseat at Jena. "You two stay close behind us. The minute we find apartment 10B, I'll knock, and we'll go from there."

Helen nodded and Jena said, "Martha won't answer the door unless my name is mentioned."

"Okay, good," Jem said. "If she asks who it is, you can announce yourself."

Moments later, as they made their way upstairs, it wasn't long before they located Martha's apartment. After Jem knocked, they waited for what seemed like several minutes before they heard a woman's voice.

"Who is it?"

When Jem nodded at Jena, giving her the OK to answer, she said, "Martha, it's Jena."

Finally, the door slowly cracked open. Behind a deadbolt chain, a thin-faced woman with swollen and bruised eyes looked directly at the pretty young woman with long, blonde hair standing outside her door. She seemed confused by Jena's human appearance, remembering the wolfish creature who had saved her and her little girl.

"Jena?" the woman said, her voice laced with bewilderment. "Is that..." She was hesitant, tilting her head. "...really you?"

Although Jena could barely make out the woman's features through the tiny opening, she instantly recognized her. The scared look in her eyes and her battered face was a dead giveaway.

"Yes, Martha," Jena said, smiling. "It's me, Jena. I'm the one who helped you last night. And I brought along some friends. Remember, I promised I'd bring a doctor for you and Amy."

There was a hint of relief that shadowed Martha's face before uncertainty crept back in. It was as though she was grappling with the decision to unlock the door.

"I give you my word," Jena said. "No one is going to harm you or your daughter. We're here to help."

After a few moments, Martha finally slid the deadbolt chain to unlock the door. Slowly, she cracked the door wider, but not all the way.

And then, a little girl's freckled face suddenly appeared from behind Martha. She had on a flowery nightgown and her long, auburn hair was arranged in pigtails. Her mouth was smeared with what looked to be grape jelly and she had a worn-out, stuffed cloth doll in her hand that looked handmade. She immediately tucked one arm around her mother's leg, anchoring herself close.

Jena crouched down. "Hi, Amy."

The little girl gave a deer-in-the-headlights look as she glanced up at her mother with big brown eyes and then back to Jena. Then finally, her gaze flickered warily up at the other people crowded outside the door. The giant man with light blue eyes and long, pale-blond hair made her flinch back in fear.

"It's all right, Amy. They're my friends." Jena averted her eyes from the frightened child and looked up at Alexander, realizing how intimidating he must appear to her. He towered to the height of at least six-five with broad shoulders and a menacing stare. He reminded Jena of the character on the Netflix series, *The Witcher*. When Jena focused her eyes back on Amy, she said, "I told them what a brave little girl you are."

With wide eyes, Amy edged more firmly behind her mother and swiped at her jelly-covered mouth with the back of her hand.

"What's their names?"

Jena smiled at the child and then looked back up at Alexander with a slight nod. He came forward and got down on one knee.

"My name is Alexander Crest." His voice was deep but gentle. "I'm very pleased to meet you, Amy." He looked up at Jem who stood beside him. "And that's my son, Jem Chamberlain."

"Hello, Amy," Jem said, waving at the little girl, who looked up at him with a curious expression on her face. "It's nice to meet you."

Helen leaned over. "Hi, Amy. My name is Helen Carrington, and I'm a doctor."

When Helen noticed Amy eyeballing the stethoscope that was around her neck with fascination, she said, "Amy, would you like to listen to your heartbeat?"

She answered by bobbing her head up and down.

"And this is my best friend, Nicolas Ratcliff," Jena said, drawing back Amy's attention. "He's a policeman."

She shifted her gaze toward a man who came forward and stood close to Jena. He had ink-black, shoulder-length hair and purplish-colored eyes. He smiled down at her. "Hello, sweetheart." His voice had a thick, southern accent and sounded funny to Amy.

She bashfully hid her face and let out a giggle.

Nicolas bent down and pointed to the doll. "Who do you have there?"

Amy held up the old, tattered doll by its flimsy arm. "This is my friend Maisie."

"Maisie is a lovely name," Nicolas said, smiling. "Did you pick it out?"

Amy nodded. "Uh-huh."

Jena inched closer. "Amy, do you remember the good wolf named Jena who saved your Mommy?"

Amy's eyes went big on her small face. "Jena is my friend," she said with a smile in her voice.

"Well..." Jena briefly paused, trying to find the right words to say. "That was me. I'm Jena."

As Amy moved closer, her eyes searched over Jena's face. A few seconds later, it was like a light bulb had suddenly gone off. Her recognition was almost instantaneous. She jumped up and down with excitement stamped all over her sticky face.

"Mama! Mama!" Amy squealed. "It's Jena! Hurry, let them in!"

Before Martha managed to step aside, Amy darted past her with her tiny hand outstretched.

The second Jena took hold, Amy tugged her forward. "Hurry, Jena. And bring your friends. Come meet my new kitty-cat."

As Jena and the others hurriedly followed her into the apartment, Amy rushed over to a shabby couch riddled with holes. Lying on top of one of the armrests was a scraggly, long-haired tabby. Amy quickly set her doll down and scooped the feline into her arms.

It went limp and meowed when she held it up for Jena to see.

Jena knelt on the worn and ratty carpet, smiling at Amy. "What's the kitty's name?"

"I named her Alley Cat because Mommy found her in the alley eating out of the trash. You can pet her. She likes wolves."

"Uh... okay," Jena said, surprised by Amy's statement, not sure what to reply. "That's good to know."

While Jena was introduced to the family pet, Helen strode over to where Martha stood and extended her hand. "It's a pleasure to meet you, Miss Dunlap. I'm Dr. Helen Carrington."

Martha tentatively took Helen's hand. "It's Martha, and thank you for coming, Dr. Carrington."

"Please," Helen said, releasing Martha's hand. "You can call me Helen. And if you don't mind..." Helen glanced over her shoulder at Amy. "...is there somewhere private where we can talk?"

"We only have one bedroom," Martha reluctantly replied. "Will that be okay?"

"Of course." Helen nodded. "That will do just fine."

As Martha took Helen to the back room, the guys crowded in the small living room. Alexander noticed how warm and muggy it was. Then he realized there was no air conditioning. The windows, the ones which weren't already busted out, were wide open to allow some air to get in. It was gut-wrenching to imagine them living here. And by how malnourished Martha appeared, it was obvious she was struggling to survive.

"We can't just leave them here," he whispered to Nicolas and Jem. "This place is not suitable for anyone, much less a small child."

"And it's definitely not safe," Nicolas said, keeping his voice low. "You saw those two guys that pulled up next to us. I've been a detective for most of my life. I recognize a drug dealer when I see one, and those two immediately set off my radar."

Jem nodded. "I agree. What do you propose we do?"

"It will take at least a week or two to get them assistance," Nicolas said. "And hopefully there's an opening to get them housing."

Alexander exhaled a heavy sigh. "There's no way I'm walking away, leaving that precious little girl in this rathole another day."

"So where can we take them?" Jem shrugged. "You heard what Tessa said. She didn't want Jena involving the Covenant."

"I have more than enough room," Nicolas said. "Martha and Amy are welcome to stay at my cabin as long as they want. Besides, I mostly stay with Jena in the Covenant."

"That's very generous of you," Alexander said, patting Nicolas on the shoulder. "Now all we have to do is convince Martha and get them packed up and ready to go."

"You think she'll agree to let us help her?" Jem asked.

Nicolas shook his head. "I don't know, but there's only one way to find out."

"Yeah," Jem said. "And after what Martha has been through, she might not be so trusting."

"I say we bring it up with Jena," Alexander said. "Amy seems crazy about her. Maybe if Jena asks Martha, she'll agree to it."

"Good idea," Nicolas said. "I'll ask Jena."

As Nicolas started to make his way over to talk to Jena, Amy ran up to him, stopping him in his tracks.

"Jena said my mommy and I could come sleep over at your cabin." Amy held up the cat. "And Alley Cat too!"

Nicolas smiled at Amy, and when he lifted his gaze to meet Jena's, her expression was one of sympathy.

"I think that's a wonderful idea," Nicolas said, then focused back on Amy. "How about we go tell your mommy?"

Then, to Nicolas's surprise, Amy quickly put the cat down and wrapped her arms around his legs.

"Thank you, Mr. policeman." She squeezed tighter.

Tears gathered in Nicolas's eyes. "You're welcome, sweetheart."

Chapter Sixteen

So far, Drakon—after a sleepless night of searching—had finally stumbled upon some crucial information dealing with the Summit Behavioral Institute. Although he'd dug up a list of patients, it frustrated the hell out of him that there was nothing on a Joseph Harris, or anyone going by that first name.

As he dug deeper, he uncovered something peculiar. He found a file listed as classified. Using his computer geek skills and the Covenant's decryption software, he broke through the encrypted files and opened them. What he'd managed to come across was completely shocking. The institute was using mental patients as guinea pigs. They were mixing human and animal DNA in the hopes of advancing medical research for a pharmaceutical drug company called Adam & Eve Pharmaceuticals, A&E

And then Drakon uncovered financial records. Payments were being made to the institute by A&E and another private facility outside Berkeley, California.

Right after the morning meeting, and ensuring Helen had enough backup while she went on a house call in a well-known drug district, Drakon met up with Tim, Roman, and Detectives Manuel Sanchez and Frank Perkins to go over what he'd discovered.

"This stuff is classified information," Drakon began to explain. "And it took me hours to crack through the institute's encrypted files. A&E and another unknown facility is paying them to experiment on their own patients."

"Son of a—" Manuel grumbled under his breath. "Did you manage to get the names of those patients?"

"I printed out the list," Drakon said, reaching into his back pocket. "These patients are separated from the others." He handed Manuel a folded piece of paper. "They're being held in some type of secret ward in the institute."

"And probably against their will," Frank piped in.

Drakon nodded. "Most likely."

"Did you find anything on this Joseph Harris guy?" Manuel asked.

Drakon shook his head. "No, not a damn thing."

"Well, that's not surprising." Manuel sighed. "That would be too easy. Although the institute could have him listed anonymously."

"It's possible," Drakon said.

Tim looked between the two detectives. "So where do we go from here?"

"Before we do anything, we'll need a search warrant," Manuel said, roaming over the names listed on the printout Drakon had given him.

"How long is that going to take?" asked Roman.

"About the same amount of time it will take us to get to the institute," Manuel said, focusing on the list.

"How's that possible?" Roman asked, looking at Manuel, wondering how he was going to get a judge to authorize a warrant that quick.

"Because..." Manuel began, lifting his gaze to meet Roman's, "one of the patients listed here is Judge Weaver's granddaughter. She turned up missing a few weeks ago. According to the law, that gives us probable cause."

Tim grimaced. "How old is this girl?"

"She just turned eighteen," Manuel replied. "Her name is Susan Hill. She was planning to go to Princeton right after she finished her senior year."

"Well..." Drakon shrugged. "What are we doing standing around? Let's go shut this place down and bring Miss Hill back to her grandmother."

"Then let's do it," Manuel said, tossing the car keys to Frank. "You're driving, partner."

The moment Tim, Roman, and Drakon made it to the institute, they parked their SUV alongside the two detectives' unmarked car, who'd arrived just moments earlier.

"You guys hang back while Frank and I go in," Manuel said, handing Tim a two-way radio. "We'll holler if we run into any trouble."

"Wait," Roman said, looking between the two detectives. "Didn't you call in for backup?"

"That's what you guys are here for," Frank said. "Depending on what we're going up against, and what's lurking behind those doors, things might get a little ugly, if you catch my meaning."

"He's right," Manuel said. "It would be a waste of time calling the precinct for backup. If indeed they're experimenting with patients, we might encounter something supernatural. And that's where you guys come in."

Drakon nodded and Roman said, "We got your back, Detectives."

"You think we're enough?" Tim asked. "The Covenant is only a phone call away. I can have Tessa send others."

"It wouldn't hurt to give her a call," Manuel said. "But for now, keep them on standby. At least they'll be aware of the situation if things go south."

Tim held up the handheld transceiver. "Keep us informed."

Manuel dipped his head. "You can count on it."

As soon as both detectives started for the entrance to the institute, Tim quickly phoned Tessa and gave her a heads-up. The second he ended the call, he closed his eyes and rubbed his forehead wearily. He was worried Manuel and Frank were getting in way over their heads even though they'd proved themselves capable of getting the job done. Although this wasn't just their average criminals they were dealing with. They might very well encounter whatever was being created to profit A&E Pharmaceuticals. And he suspected the government also had a hand in this.

"I'm not sure this is such a good idea," Drakon spoke out, drawing Tim's attention.

Tim faced Drakon. "What do you mean?"

"I don't know." Drakon shook his head. "After uncovering all that stuff, I have a bad feeling. Are you sure they should be going in alone? I mean, this is some serious shit."

"Did we have a choice?"

"Not really, but when did that ever stop us?"

Tim cocked a brow. "You have a point. And I have a hunch the government is involved."

Roman leaned in from the backseat. "The government could be the private facility helping fund all this research."

"Yeah," Drakon said, his jaw visibly clenched. "That's what I was thinking."

Tim put a restraining hand on Drakon's arm, worried he'd say *screw it* and charge into the institute. "Let's not overreact just yet. We'll give the detectives a few more minutes." Tim checked his watch. "If we don't hear anything in the next twenty minutes, we'll go in."

As they waited in ready silence, it seemed an hour had passed according to Tim. Although, by his watch, it had only been ten minutes. And he wasn't the only one edgy and restless. Drakon and Roman were a bundle of nerves.

"How long has it been?" Roman blurted, breaking the silence.

As if on cue, Frank's voice suddenly came over the two-way radio. "We need backup. Over. I repeat. We need you guys."

"Shit," Tim muttered under his breath. He put the handheld transceiver up to his mouth. "Copy that, Detective. We're on our way."

Tim glanced between Drakon and Roman. "Let's do this."

The minute everyone piled out of the vehicle, they sprinted double time to institute's front entrance.

As Drakon burst through the doors first, Tim and Roman charged in behind him. All three came to a screeching halt when they noticed the staff on the floor, huddled together in the corner. They looked scared out of their minds.

When they heard screams and gun fire, they shot past everyone and ran down a corridor toward an open door where the sounds were coming from.

They immediately stopped dead in their tracks at the sight before them. There was blood everywhere. It looked like someone had painted the walls with it.

"What the *hell* happened here?" Roman sputtered.

Tim reached for the two-way radio clipped to his belt and pressed the push-to-talk button. "Frank, where the hell are you guys?"

"We're on the east side of the building," Frank said, sounding out of breath. *"Come quick and you better get prepared. By that, I mean you better shift."*

Tim blew out a deep breath. "Can you tell me what we're up against?"

"*Hell, it's hard to describe,*" Frank said. "*It's a hybrid wolf of some kind. The damn thing is as big as a house.*"

"Ah shit," Drakon said, rolling his eyes. "Ask Frank if he has any idea where it's at."

Tim nodded at Drakon. "Frank, do you have the subject's location?"

"*It's on the lower level. We've got ourselves barricaded, but we're not sure how long it will last. If this thing figures out where we are, it won't take much for it to get in.*"

"Stay put and give us a few minutes," Tim said. "We're headed that way."

"*Copy that,*" Frank said. "*But it might be a good time to ask Tessa for backup. Jace's beast might be the only thing that can go toe to toe with this thing.*"

"Affirmative," Tim said. "We'll contact Tessa. Until then, hang tight."

* * *

By the time Carrie arrived at work, she noticed how bare the parking lot was. *Of course,* she thought, rolling her eyes. *Who works on a Sunday?*

"Damn it, Veronica." She groaned. "Why do you have to be such a jerk?"

She swallowed back her pride and reached to open the door. A dinging sound coming from her purse suddenly caught her by surprise. As she reached inside to retrieve her phone, she noticed there was a text from Joseph.

Are you allowed a lunch break?

Carrie's lips instantly curled up. She texted back a laughing emoji and typed, *the warden allows me an hour every day.*

Her phone dinged with another text. *LOL. Pick you up at noon?*

Sounds great. Where are we going?

Her phone dinged. *You choose the place.*

How's Augie's Deli sound?

He texted a hungry emoji face and added, *Perfect! Can't wait!*

After she texted him a thumbs-up emoji, she put her phone back inside her purse and opened her door to get out, wearing a smile.

The second Carrie exited her Volkswagen Beetle, a sporty black Mercedes pulled up alongside her. She immediately recognized her boss's expensive car and grumbled under her breath.

Although Carrie was ready to get the day over with, she stood there and waited as Veronica got out of her car.

She lifted her designer sunglasses and glared at Carrie underneath a thick layer of blue eyeshadow. "Well, I'm surprised you made it in," she snidely remarked. Then she glanced at her watch and added, "And on time too."

"Good morning to you too, Miss Hernandez."

Veronica arched a brow. "Looks like someone's in a mood. What's a matter?" She smirked at Carrie. "Did your Valentine's date go sour?"

"As a matter of fact," Carrie said, "I had a wonderful time. Joseph is a great guy."

"Is that so?" Veronica asked, tilting her head. "You know, I was surprised to see you out on a date."

Carrie shrugged. "Why's that?"

"Wasn't your boyfriend murdered recently? It's not like it's a big secret. It was all over the news."

"Kevin was my ex-boyfriend," Carrie said. "And yes, his life was taken tragically. But if you don't mind, I'd like to keep my personal life private."

"Fine." Veronica huffed. "But it sounds a little odd to be dating someone else so soon. Just saying."

Carrie rolled her eyes, and before she started for the front entrance, Veronica called out, "Hold up, Carrie. I've got a few boxes of files in my trunk that need brought to my office. I'll need you to take care of those." Then she tossed Carrie her car keys. "Make sure you lock up when you're done."

"Wait a minute," Carrie said, stopping Veronica before she walked away. "They're not patient files, are they?"

Veronica shrugged one shoulder. "Yeah, why?"

"When did we start taking our patient's files home? Doesn't that violate HIPAA?"

"Honestly Carrie. Are we really going to go there?"

"But I was just—"

"Stop undermining my authority," Veronica interjected. "I don't pay you to question my judgement. Just keep your mouth shut and do your damn job. And hurry up with those boxes," she added as she turned away, flipping her hair. "You keep flapping your jaw and we'll be here all day."

Finally, after Carrie set down the last of the four boxes, she said, "This is the last one."

"Good." Veronica sneered. "Now you can file them."

"I don't understand." Carrie looked at her, perplexed. "Isn't that your assistant's job?"

"Yes," Veronica replied with a spiteful pitch in her voice. "But for today, you're taking her place."

"But—"

"Please, don't argue with me," Veronica snapped, cutting Carrie off. "I don't have the patience today. Just do what I ask for once. Besides, do you really think I enjoy being here, Carrie? You wouldn't be here in the first place if you hadn't been late Saturday morning."

"Miss Hernandez, did you ever consider the reason why I was late?"

"You said it was personal."

"It was," Carrie said. "I was attacked and almost raped by two men. And after I managed to get away, later that night me and my roommate found Kevin's body in the parking lot of my apartment building."

A moment of silence cropped up between them. Then Veronica muttered, "Oh..." She visibly swallowed. "You should have called in sick that day."

"This is why I didn't call in sick." Carrie threw her hands up in defeat. "I was afraid you'd make me work through the entire weekend to make up my hours. I'm not some hourly factory worker, for Pete's sake. I'm a licensed substance abuse counselor, and a damn good one at that."

"How dare you take that tone with me," Veronica said through gritted teeth. "Remember who you're talking to. And if you think I buy all that garbage, Miss Randall, think again. Now, if you don't mind, I'd like some coffee before you start filing."

Carrie's jaw dropped, completely astounded by Veronica's harsh words. She'd never met anyone so cruel, so heartless. She wanted nothing more than to tell her boss to go to hell, but instead, she said, "If you'll excuse me…" She bit back tears. "I need to use the ladies' room."

As Carrie turned to leave, Veronica said, "Don't forget about my coffee. I take it with cream and sugar."

The day seemed to painfully tick away at a snail's pace. Carrie spent most of it filing and fetching coffee while her boss talked on the phone. She could tell by Veronica's flirtatious voice whoever was on the other end didn't have anything to do with work. Nevertheless, Carrie did whatever she had to do to get through the day.

A long exhale escaped Carrie's lips the moment she looked at the clock and saw it was almost noon. *Thank goodness,* she thought. *At least my day isn't completely ruined.*

"Carrie," Veronica called out. "I need you to go pick up my lunch. I called in an order at Ike's Sandwich Shop."

"Why don't you just have Ike's deliver? It's not far from here."

Veronica snarled her upper lip. "Because I told you to go pick it up."

"It'll take a while," Carrie said. "I've got a lunch date. But I can stop by and get it on my way back."

"Oh?" Veronica cocked a brow. "Is this that Joseph fella or someone else?"

"It's Joseph. The same guy you met last night."

"Yes, I remember. The tall handsome guy with a bit of an attitude. So, what does he do for a living?" She lightly snickered. "Or does this guy even have a job?"

Carrie tried her best to ignore Veronica's insults. "He's a freelance journalist for the Chronicle."

"Well, well, well," Veronica said in a dragged-out fashion. "Lucky you. Seems like you landed someone with not only looks, but brains. Tell me…" A wicked smile curved her lips. "…is he any good in the sack?"

Carrie furrowed her brows. "This conversation is making me uncomfortable and it's inappropriate."

"Oh, come on, Carrie. Don't be such a stick in the mud. You take everything way too serious."

"I take my job very serious, Miss Hernandez. I think there's a time and place for personal business and this is not one of them."

"Okay, okay," Veronica said, waving it off. "Forget I said anything. Go have fun on your little lunch date. I'll call Ike's back and have them deliver my food." She rose from her chair and sauntered across the room toward a mirror. "And don't worry about coming back. You can finish this up first thing Monday morning."

"What about you?"

"I'm leaving as soon as I have lunch." Veronica averted her eyes from the mirror and looked over her shoulder at Carrie. "I've got a date this evening."

It seemed like five minutes beyond infinity that Veronica went on and on, bragging about the man she'd met. As soon as Veronica finally shut her pie-hole, Carrie scurried out of the office, shot through security, and exited the building in less than two minutes. When she saw a black Jeep pull into the parking lot and park by her car, she waved in Joseph's direction.

Before she reached for the door handle, she took a deep breath. As the anxiety eased off a bit, she proceeded to open the door. A voice calling out stopped her hand midway.

"Wait, let me get that for you."

Carrie looked up as Joseph got out of the driver's side and hurried over to open her door.

"You don't have to do that," she said, looking over her shoulder at him with the biggest grin on her face. "I can open my own door."

"I know." He smiled back at her. "But I enjoy it."

After she climbed inside, he closed the passenger's door and got back behind the wheel.

"I'm starving." He put the Jeep in reverse. "How about you?"

"I'm famished."

"Good." He wiggled his brows. "I like a girl with a healthy appetite."

She smiled up at him as he shifted in drive and tore out of the parking lot.

When they arrived at Augie's Deli and ordered their food, Joseph sat down in the chair across from Carrie and reached for her hand. "Is something wrong, Carrie?" He kept his voice low. "You look a little upset."

She sighed. "I'm sorry, Joseph. I don't mean to ruin our lunch date."

"No, no," he quickly replied, lightly squeezing her tense hand. "You're not ruining anything. You wanna talk about it?"

"It's just hard for me to talk about."

"It's your boss again, isn't it?"

"It's time to take care of Miss Veronica," the Shadow whispered into Joseph's subconscious. *"I'm starving, and I'm losing my patience, Joseph."*

Carrie closed her eyes, and when they reopened, the heartache shining in them nearly sent Joseph over the edge.

"Listen to me, Carrie. You can trust me."

She shook herself and forced a smile. "It's nothing I can't handle myself. Let's talk about you. How's your day so far?"

"Are you sure you don't want to talk about it?" His eyes met hers steadily. "I've been told I'm a good listener."

"What?" the Shadow said. *"You never listen to anything I say."*

Carrie stared at him for a long moment, as if she was debating what to tell him. "Well, after today, I've decided to give that attorney a call. My boss has overstepped the boundaries."

"Good for you, Carrie. I think you're making the right decision."

The sincerity and encouragement in Joseph's voice lifted some of the weight off her shoulders.

"Me too. And you're right. You are a good listener. Thanks, Joseph."

"She's wasting her time," the Shadow said. *"After we get done with Miss Veronica, her problems will be solved indefinitely. Instead of an attorney, she'll need her boss's dental records to identify what's left of her body."*

Chapter Seventeen

While Jena and the guys kept little Amy occupied, Helen took Martha in the back bedroom to examine her injuries.

As Martha sat down on the bed, Helen reached for the stethoscope around her neck, noticing how fragile and thin she looked.

She peered at Martha over her glasses. "Martha, when was the last time you had a meal?"

"I tried to eat yesterday," Martha said as tears immediately swirled. She bit her lip to keep the moan of despair from escaping. "But I can't keep anything down."

Helen's face twisted in sympathy. "Is there something you're not telling me?"

Martha lowered her head and nodded.

"You can trust me, Martha." Helen placed her hand on her shoulder. "Please, let me help you."

Martha slowly lifted her chin. "I have cancer," she said around the catch in her throat. "It started in my colon and has spread to my kidneys."

Helen's heart nearly seized. "I'm so sorry, Martha." She looked at her with compassion. "Do you mind if I ask you a few questions?"

As Martha dipped her head, Helen said, "How long have you known?"

"I found out four months ago."

"What did the doctors say about treatment?"

"It's too far advanced," Martha choked out. "Stage four. And I don't have medical insurance, so..."

For a split second, a memory flooded Helen's mind like random pictures from her childhood past. They were images of her adoptive little sister and how she died at such a young age. Although Helen was only seven years old at the time, everything about Hanna's death was still so clear: hospital beds, needles, and all the chemo treatments. In an awful mental snapshot, she saw her sister's bald head, sickly pale skin, and a tiny, frail body who didn't look like the flourishing person she was before. Near the end, Hanna was completely unrecognizable.

"Martha," Helen said soothingly, tossing the dreadful memory aside. "Does Amy know?"

"No," she said with sorrow burning brightly in her eyes. "She's too young to understand."

Helen sighed then squatted beside Martha. "Do you have a plan for Amy? I mean, if—"

"If I die?" Martha said as Helen's voice trailed off.

When Helen reluctantly nodded, Martha went on to say, "Amy's father died in a car accident when she was just a baby, and his family isn't what you'd call responsible caretakers. I never knew my biological parents. I was given up for adoption and went from one foster family to another. My childhood wasn't exactly good. So basically, it's just the two of us, and I'm not sure how much time I have left."

Deciding to step in, Helen said, "If I offered, would you let me help you and Amy?"

"I don't understand," Martha said, furrowing her brows. "Why would you do that? You don't even know us."

"Because, Martha, I know what it's like to go through something tragic. And you and your daughter are going to need help."

"I-I don't have anything to give you in return."

"I'm not asking for anything, except for your trust."

Emotion knotted Martha's throat and tears burned her eyelids. Unable to speak, she simply reached out to Helen and took her hand in hers.

When Helen was done with Martha's examination, she said, "You've got some severe bruising, but nothing seems to be broken. But you're going to have to take it easy for the next several days. I'd like to have you come into my office as soon as possible so I can do some more tests."

"But I can't," Martha protested. "I have no means to pay you. And I have nothing of value. Everything I own can fit in one suitcase."

"All you need to worry about is getting some rest," Helen said. "Let me worry about all the other stuff." She patted Martha's hand. "I'll go check on Amy while you take a few minutes to dry your tears."

Martha sighed but nodded her agreement. "Thank you, Helen."

"You're welcome, Martha."

As Helen walked out of the room, the woman's illness plagued her mind. How long did she have and who would care for little Amy when the time came? That was the million-dollar question. Then her thoughts suddenly went to Steven and the rare gift he possessed. She wondered if he could heal Martha's illness. If not, maybe Jem could use his powers of healing.

She felt some of the tension ease at the sound of Amy's laughter. It instantly brought her mind around. The minute she stepped into the living room where the others gathered, Alexander came forward.

"How is she?" he asked, noticing the grim expression on Helen's face.

Reluctantly, Helen kept her voice low and told him everything about Martha's condition.

Alexander stared at her for a moment and then shook his head. "My God..." He gasped. "What do you suggest?"

"I want to help them," Helen said. "They shouldn't stay here one more day. Martha needs medical attention as soon as possible. I'm going to have them stay at my place so I can keep her in my care. I have the extra room, and besides, they have nowhere else to go and no family they can turn to. It will give us the opportunity to prepare Amy for her mother's illness."

"Did Martha agree to let us help her?"

Helen nodded. "She knows time is wearing thin, leaving her no alternative."

"What about Steven?" Alexander asked. "Do you think he could heal Martha?"

"The thought came to mind," Helen said. "And I also considered Jem. I'll discuss the possibilities with the others as soon as we get back to the Covenant. This just might be our last option. Although there are risks involved, I'm afraid if we don't try, Martha won't survive much longer."

Alexander smiled at Helen and reached for her hand. "Have I told you lately how much I love you?"

"Every day," she said, smiling back. "But I never tire of hearing it."

He brought her hand up to his lips and lightly kissed it. "I love you, sweetheart."

"I love you too."

"Speaking of Martha and Amy," Alexander said, "Nicolas has offered his cabin to them. And Amy seems quite thrilled with his invitation."

"That's very kind of Nicolas," Helen said. "I'll bring it up with Martha, but I don't see any reason why she'd turn either offer down. At this point, what options does she have?"

A few minutes later, after Martha dried her tears, she pushed herself to her feet. Her entire body ached, feeling like one giant bruise. And that wasn't the worst of it. Nausea welled in her stomach as though she was going to be sick. Instead, she swallowed it back and forced herself forward.

As she padded down the small hallway, she stopped and peeked into the room where Amy and the others were. Everyone was focused on her daughter, smiling and listening as she kept up a constant stream of chatter over her excitement of getting to sleep over at the policemen's house and play in his backyard with her cat. She mentioned Jena more than once, reminding her how much Alley Cat loves wolves. It brought a smile to her face.

And then she thought how wonderful it must be to be part of such a loving family. Everyone in Jena's circle seemed tight knit. Was it fate that brought them together or just a coincidence? Although she had never been a big believer of fate, maybe this was God's way of taking care of her daughter. After all, who'd believe there were such things as werewolves? Never in her wildest dreams would she have imagined one would save her and her daughter's lives. All the fiction horror movies portrayed them as savage killers, not saviors. It was then she realized Jena was not a coincidence. It was God who had sent her.

Suddenly, tears burned the edges of her eyes and she quickly blinked them away, not wanting to worry her daughter. Not when she had something to look forward to. In fact, everything was moving in the right direction. Perhaps this was the answer to her prayers. Finally, she'd found a loving family for Amy.

Martha glanced up to see Helen motioning her to come in. After wiping her eyes, she went into the living room to join the others.

"Look, Amy," Alexander said, glancing between Martha and Amy. "Your mama is back. Why don't you tell her the good news?"

Amy's eyes lit up when she saw her mother.

"Mama! Mama!" she said with enthusiasm, running toward her. "Pack some clothes! Mr. Policeman said we could come to his house for a sleepover! And Alley Cat too!"

Martha smiled, delighted by Amy's excitement.

"That's wonderful news, sweetheart," she said, lightly ruffling Amy's hair. "Go on ahead and start packing some of your things. I'll be in there in a minute to help you."

"Okay, Mama," Amy said, smiling.

As soon as Amy left the room, Martha roamed over the faces standing before her. They all looked so very sincere. And sympathetic.

"How can I ever thank you enough?" she said with tears in her eyes.

Jena came forward and gathered Martha's hands in hers. "We want to do this for you and Amy. You'll have our entire family behind you."

"You've been through a lot," Alexander said, his voice somber. "And I can tell you're a strong person. You're a true warrior, Martha. Think about what you've done so far and everything you've endured. I have faith you can do anything if you put your mind to it."

"And you won't have to do it alone," Jem added.

"Our point is that everyone needs help at one time or another," Nicolas said. "I've had my share of fears and issues to work through." He looked at Jena and then to the others. "I wouldn't know where I'd be if it weren't for everyone in this room." He refocused his eyes back on Martha. "This is a group of good people I'm proud to call my family. And just like me, you'll learn to appreciate what family—or at least this family—is all about."

Emotion filled Martha's heart until tears streamed down her cheeks. She had no idea what to say or if she could even speak at all. She bit her lip, desperate to hold back the sobs that welled in her throat.

"It's okay, Martha," Helen said. "You've taken far too much on your shoulders, and now it's time to let someone take care of you. Cry all you want. You've earned the right."

The moment Martha started to sob, Jena, Helen, Alexander, Nicolas, and Jem gathered around her. As they all embraced her in loving arms, she wept and let the joyous moment invade her soul.

* * *

When Tim ended the call with Tessa—urging her to send backup—he was out of his clothes within seconds. Thick, dark hair sprouted all over him, covering him from head to toe. His face lost all recognition as it began to twist and elongate. His mouth protruded until it took the shape of a wolf's muzzle with long curving fangs. While he continued to transform into his Breedline wolf, Drakon too, felt his own impending changes coming on fast. His gut spasmed and his skin sizzled.

With no time to spare, Drakon toed out of his boots, stripped off his shirt, and hurriedly removed his pants. Instantaneously, wiry hair poured out of his scalp and trailed down his broad shoulders. Like wildfire, it spread over his entire body, blanketing his skin with a shiny coat of black fur.

Drakon was down on all fours before he even willed it, growling, and snarling like a rabid dog. Although he'd been born a Breedline, an incident from his past had changed him. Instead of converting into a Breedline wolf, he was something entirely other. Most thought it to be a curse, but according to Drakon, he believed otherwise. His rogue wolf was massive, twice the size of an average Breedline. And the immense strength it bestowed had its benefits, especially in situations like the one they were about to face.

As his body began to expand, he could feel his skin reshaping and his bones reforming. It was an exquisite sensation, like being reborn. The moment his transformation was achieved, he felt his throat open with a howl. Instead of giving in to his primal instincts, he remained silent, waiting for his comrades to complete their transitions.

Roman was the last to shift. Grabbing the hem of his shirt, he quickly pulled it over his head and tossed it aside. He took in a deep breath and slowly exhaled, trying to focus on the task ahead. Realizing time was of the essence, he gritted his teeth and brought forth his Adalwolf. His transformation came on strong and fast-moving. Roman's pants ripped at the seams as his frame expanded and grew twice the size. His features mutated beyond what he'd looked like just moments before. He still resembled somewhat a man but crossed with a wolfish beast. His skin took on a luminous, grayish sheen and his eyes sparkled like diamonds. He stood on two feet, every bulging muscle in his body taut with a boiling rage.

The sound of an animal's thunderous roar echoing in the near distance quickly sent their adrenaline racing. They knew a hybrid wolf when they heard one. And going by the pitch of the thing, it was obviously big. As it grew louder, they realized it was moving in their direction fast.

Readying themselves for battle, Tim bared his sharp teeth, and Drakon pawed at the ground, while Roman stood firm, clawed hands twitching at his sides.

Then, out of nowhere, a giant furry creature leaped from out of the shadows. It came at them so fast they had no time to think. Acting on pure instinct, Roman lunged forward with slashing claws and sliced at the creature's throat. Blood sprayed like a crimson geyser, coating Roman and the whitewashed walls behind him.

The wolfish hybrid collapsed onto the floor, convulsing with spasms as its life drained in a pool of red. When it finally went limp, Manuel burst into the room. He was too focused on the giant creature lying on the floor, covered in its own blood, to register Tim's, Drakon's, and Roman's presence.

The sound of several footsteps drawing near made the detective look up. He sagged in relief, realizing it was Jace and Tessa. As they came up to the dead creature, Jace's jaw nearly dropped. "Damn," he said in stunned disbelief. "It looks like you didn't need our help after all."

"Is everyone okay?" Tessa asked, looking at the detective, and then to Roman, Drakon, and Tim, who were all three still in their transitional states.

"We're fine," Roman said, his voice guttural. Then he pointed to the lifeless creature as it began to transform. It was as if the impending changes took on a will of their own. In a matter of seconds, its furry hide started to shrink and disappear. It wasn't long before human features took the place of the hairy beast.

Manuel knelt next to the body of a young man. He was now completely naked, his throat cut so deep his head was nearly severed.

"Damn shame," Manuel said, releasing a sigh. "He doesn't even look old enough to be of age." And then he looked up at Tessa with his brows furrowed. "Why isn't he healing?"

"I don't know, Detective," Tessa said. "It's obvious he's not a Breedline, so whatever he's been mutated with, it must not have healing abilities."

"How in the hell did all this happen?" Jace asked.

"The minute my partner and I entered the institute," Manuel said, "we heard screams coming from inside. Immediately, we rushed in and followed where it was coming from. As soon as we made it to the lower level, we found some of the staff. They'd been torn to pieces. Before we could manage to see if there were any survivors..." He paused and pointed to the dead man's body. "...that poor young man came after us. Fortunately, we were able to get away. We barricaded ourselves in what looked to be some sort of lab. That's when we called for backup. For a minute, Frank and I thought we were goners. It wouldn't have been long before that thing broke down the door. For some reason it stopped." He looked between Drakon and Tim, and then at Roman's humongous stature. "I guess it sensed you guys when you shifted into your..." He shrugged, thinking of the right words to describe their supernatural forms. "Well, you know what I'm trying to say."

"I'm just glad everyone is okay," Tessa said. "We did find a few staff members as we came in. They were huddled against the wall, terrified. I told them we were here to help and to stay put."

"We saw them too," Roman said. "But when we heard screams and gunfire, we didn't take the time to ask questions."

Manuel looked to Drakon's rogue wolf. "If it hadn't been for Drakon digging up all that stuff on the institute, that thing would have escaped, and who knows how many other casualties there would have been."

In response, Drakon raised his wolfish head and snorted.

"Wait a minute," Jace said, his eyes searching for Frank. "Where's your partner?"

"We split up. Frank's looking for Judge Weaver's granddaughter."

Jace shrugged. "Who's—"

The detective held up a hand as Frank's voice suddenly came over his earpiece. He covered it so he could hear more clearly. "Frank..." He raised his voice. "Can you repeat that?"

After a few moments, the detective's eyes rounded. "Stay put, partner. I'm headed your way."

"What's going on?" Roman asked. "Did Frank find the missing girl?"

"Yeah," Manuel said. "And it doesn't sound good. Frank said she's incoherent like she's been drugged. He's also apprehended one of the institute's physicians. We're going to have to call this one in. Thanks to you guys, I think we've got this covered from here on."

"Are you sure you don't need any help?" Tessa asked. "Maybe one of us should stick around until your backup arrives. Jace and I could stay while Roman, Drakon, and Tim make their way back to the Covenant."

"Thanks, Tessa," Manuel said. "I appreciate your offer, but I think it's best if you're not involved. When my Captain arrives, he'll want to know why you guys are here."

Tessa nodded in agreement. "Let us know if you run into any trouble."

At the sound of approaching sirens, Roman shifted back to his human form and retrieved his, Drakon's, and Tim's clothes. After a quick transformation, they got dressed and exited the institute along with Tessa and Jace.

As soon as Manuel made it down to the institute's lower level in search of his partner, his heart nearly plummeted when he pushed his way through a door. It led into what was supposedly a laboratory, but it looked more like a torture chamber. Lying next to a stainless-steel table were various types of surgical instruments with sharp-pointed ends.

In the far corner of the room, sitting in a chair, was a young woman with long brown hair and skin as pale as a corpse's. Her vacant eyes were fixated on the wall, staring pointedly at nothing. By the bruised coloring under her lids and her bony cheeks, she appeared half-starved. But still, he recognized her. It was Judge Weaver's granddaughter.

"According to what I got out of Dr. SeGovia," Frank said, standing a few feet from the girl, "Miss Hill has been drugged for days. She has no idea I'm even here. And she's not the only one like this. I found the rest of the patients. They're all locked up down here. This whole lower level is like a dungeon from hell. I've got an ambulance on the way."

"Son of a..." Manuel grumbled under his breath. "Where's the rest of the staff?"

"Most of them were killed in the attack. Somehow, that *thing* that went after us got loose and wreaked havoc on its captors. Please tell me our backup took care of it."

Manuel nodded. "It's taken care of. Roman took it out."

"Well, I guess we didn't need Jace's beast after all," Frank said. "Is everyone in one piece?"

"They're fine. I told them to take off before the cavalry arrives. So, where's this physician you were talking about?"

"I've got him handcuffed to a chair in the other room," Frank said. "He says he's ready to make a deal."

"What deal?"

"He said he'd give up the name of the pharmaceutical company who's paying them to do the research if we put in a good word for him," Frank explained. "He's aware he'll lose his license over this, but he's hoping for a reduced sentence if he talks."

"He's not getting off that easily. Besides, we already know it's A&E Pharmaceuticals."

"I know," Frank said. "But Dr. SeGovia doesn't."

"What about the other private facility that's been paying them? You know, the one Drakon mentioned that was outside of Berkeley."

"I've already questioned him about that," Frank pointed out. "He claims he doesn't know. But another physician here does. I believe his name is Dr. Leonard Manos. Apparently today is his day off."

"Is that so?" Manuel said, cocking an eyebrow. "Well then, I think it's time we go visit Dr. Manos and bring him in for questioning."

"What about Dr. SeGovia?"

"Wait till Captain gets here," Manuel suggested, smirking. "We'll let him *deal* with the good ol' doc."

Chapter Eighteen

Jena watched from the bedroom doorway as Amy sat on the floor packing the clothes her mother had made for her doll. Her brow was creased in concentration, and she nibbled at her bottom lip, carefully placing the tiny scraps of material one by one inside a plastic bag.

Then, out of nowhere, a strange feeling came over Jena. The hairs on the back of her neck stood on end and goose bumps trailed down her arms. It was like a warning of some kind. Seconds later, an odor invaded her nostrils. As she drew it in deeper, it became all too familiar. It was an overwhelming stench of evil.

And when she heard voices, they seemed like whispers from far away. As she listened more carefully, they grew louder, seemingly closer, but she was unable to recognize them. She looked back at the others inside the apartment and listened. But all she could hear was chatter and meaningless words as Helen and the guys helped Martha gather her things.

Suddenly, her fingernails began to tingle. When she brought her hand up to her face, it was covered in tiny, black hairs and her nails were longer. For one second, she felt an uncontrollable desire to shift. *No,* she thought. *It cannot be.* She covered her mouth. *Why is this happening now?*

Jena was so overcome with panic she could barely draw in a breath. She simply stood froze in place, unable to move, fearing the worst. *Is someone in danger?*

Without warning, she felt the weight of a hand on her shoulder. She immediately flinched and spun around.

"I'm sorry," Nicolas said as he looked into Jena's rounded eyes, noticing the sheer-panic in them. "Is something wrong?"

"I-I think," she choked the words out, "something bad is going to happen." Her voice was a little guttural, roughened. "I can sense—"

"I'm ready!" Amy said, rousing Jena and Nicolas' attention.

When they turned around, Amy was standing before them with a satisfied smile on her face. She had a little bag in one hand and her flimsy doll in the other.

"I've got all Maisie's clothes packed," Amy said, looking between Jena and Nicolas. "I'm ready to go to your house, Mr. Policeman."

Nicolas quickly knelt in front of Amy. "Very good." He held out his hand. "Let me take those so you go wrangle up your kitty cat. You wouldn't want to forget her."

"Okay," Amy said, handing over the plastic bag and the doll to Nicolas.

As Amy went to gather up her cat, Nicolas silently waved at Jem and Alexander, motioning them over. By the grim expression on his face, they knew something was wrong.

Jena frowned and looked to the apartment door. The chain to the lock was unattached and the deadbolt was in the unlocked position. Then a pungent, nauseating smell hit her like a ton of bricks. The powerful odor of evil overrode her senses until it was almost suffocating.

"*Oh, God, no,*" she said silently.

Everything seemed to move in slow motion. The door instantly flew open. At that very moment Amy came running across the room, her long pigtails flowing behind her, and her cat tucked securely in her arms. "I found Alley Cat," she called out.

"No!" Jena screamed.

The sequence played out in a series of only a few seconds that seemed to last an eternity: Nicolas looking at Jena as she darted forward with her arms outstretched, shouting a warning. Amy running in their direction, her face lit up with joy. Two men charging through the front door with guns drawn.

The blast of a gun echoed like the crack of lightning. The sound sent the cat fleeing from Amy's arms with a high-pitched screech. Jena lunged for Amy, trying to shield her tiny body with hers, but sadly, she didn't make it in time. Amy was struck in the back. The bullet came out the other side, bursting through her chest. Jena caught her as she fell, her own heart screaming in agony.

As Jena dropped to her knees with Amy's limp and bloodied body cradled in her arms, Nicolas suddenly vanished. Right into thin air.

It was like magic. One moment Nicolas was standing in bedroom doorway, the next there was nothing but air where he had been. When he reappeared, he stood behind the shooters. A bone-cracking sound came next. The guy wearing a black hoodie dropped to the floor with his neck twisted at an unnatural angle.

The other guy with a Yankees ball cap barely registered Nicolas's movement. With unbelievable speed, he shoved his fist straight through the guy's backside. For a moment, the guy went stiff, looking down at the hand protruding from his chest. With his mouth agape, he fell forward, dropping to the floor like a stone.

As everyone gathered around Jena, time seemed to shift back into full speed. But to Jena, everything still moved at the pace of a snail. Martha knelt in front of her, reaching for Amy, her eyes drenched in tears. Her mouth was moving, but Jena couldn't hear what she was saying. Helen looked at her, trying to tell her something, but whatever it was, it didn't register in Jena's brain. It was as if the volume in her ears had been turned all the way down. She felt powerless, completely incoherent, holding little Amy in her arms. Then suddenly, Helen's voice rang loud and clear. It was like someone had cranked up the volume, snapping her back to focus.

"Jena..." Helen said, placing a hand on the side of Jena's face. "Did you hear what I said?"

"What?"

Helen raised her voice. "Put Amy down so I can look at her injury."

Instantly, Jena obeyed Helen's orders and gently lowered Amy onto the floor.

"No!" Martha cried out, caressing Amy's hair. "Please God, not my baby!"

The buttons on Amy's pajama top scattered across the floor as Helen ripped it open down the middle. There was so much blood. Helen tried to stop it, but it was too late. The bullet had severed a main artery in Amy's heart.

"I can't save her," Helen said. Then she lifted her gaze to meet Jem's. "But *you* can."

His eyes grew weary and before he could utter a single word, Helen said, "You can do this, Jem. You've done this before, and you can do it again."

"W-what?" Martha asked, sobbing. "Y-you can save my little girl?"

Jem averted his eyes from Helen and looked to Martha. He could see the sorrow and desperation etched into every groove of her face. His eyes softened with compassion. Then he focused back on Helen.

"But..." Jem began, worry stamped all over his face. "Amy is human. What if—"

"It doesn't matter," Helen said. "You have to try. It's the only way."

"Do it, Jem," Jena said, releasing a strangled breath. "Please..."

Alexander placed his hand on Jem's shoulder. "Have faith, son. I know you can save her."

"He's right, Jem," Nicolas said as he knelt next to Martha. "Use the gift God gave you."

Martha reached out to Jem and grasped his hand. "I don't know what you are or how you can do this." Tears streamed down her cheeks. "But I'm begging you. Please help my daughter. She's too young to die."

Jem lightly squeezed her hand. "I promise I'll do everything I can to save her."

Martha released his hand and covered her mouth. "Oh, thank God."

Jem gently lifted Amy off the floor, cradled her close, and rose to his feet. She looked so small, so fragile in his arms. He took a shuddering breath as he peered into her freckled face. Her eyes were closed, and her skin was already pale.

He closed his eyes and blocked out everything around him: the loud music echoing from the apartment upstairs, the sound of his own heartbeat pounding in his ears, and even Amy's cat gathered by his feet.

As death closed in, Jem knew he had not a moment to spare. With all the strength and perseverance he could muster, he concentrated on a pathway of healing.

And then, to everyone's surprise, Jem's body began to glow. The brilliance of the light surrounding him swept over Amy, completely enveloping her like a blanket.

"Listen to my voice, Amy," Jem whispered. "Let it guide you back to the light."

In the silence, he waited, praying she would hear him.

Suddenly, her long eyelashes started to flutter.

"That's it, Amy." Jem held her tighter. "You can do it. Open your eyes, sweetheart."

Everyone quickly gathered and hovered in silence, waiting for Amy to open her eyes.

When her lids slowly lifted, the light sheathing her body dissipated. She looked up at Jem and smiled. Although her vision blurred a little, she could still make out the image looking down at her. She could see he had tears in his eyes and his body shimmered with sparkles of light.

Martha stood there staring at her daughter, disbelief evident in her gaze.

"Welcome back, sweetheart," Jem said.

"Are you..." Amy's eyes were big on her small face. "...an Angel?"

"No, Amy." Jem smiled. "I'm not an Angel. Besides, Angels have wings."

Her eyes curiously roamed over his shoulders until she finally realized there were no wings attached to his backside. Then she reached out and placed her hand on the side of his face. "Did you know you're covered in pixie dust?"

"Pixie dust?" Jem raised an inquisitive brow. "I wonder how that happened?"

"It was Tinker Bell," Amy said, giggling.

"Tinker Bell?"

"Yeah," Amy said. "Don't you know who Tinker Bell is?"

"Um..." Jem paused, thinking. "Isn't that Peter Pan's friend?"

Amy nodded and Jem smiled.

A few seconds later, Amy lifted her head, her eyes searching for her mother. "Mama?"

"I'm right here, sweetheart," Martha said, looking over Amy, amazed by the miracle staring back at her. There were no words to explain what she'd just witnessed. It was as though she'd imagined everything. A few minutes ago, her daughter was fighting for her life, and now, somehow, she'd been magically healed.

"Don't cry, Mama," Amy said, drawing Martha back to focus.

Amy's sweet, concerned voice nearly broke Martha's heart. She reached out and gently tucked a loose strand of her hair behind her ear. "These are happy tears, honey."

"I love you, Mama."

Martha reached tentatively for Amy, taking her from Jem. "Oh, darling. I love you too."

Amy's arms went around her mother's neck, hugging her tightly. When she pulled back, she said, "Where's Alley Cat?"

"She's right here," Jena said as she bent down to pick up the cat. A few moments later, she held up the furry feline for Amy to see. "She's all safe and sound."

Amy's eyes brightened. "There you are." She giggled. "You silly cat."

With Amy secure in her slender arms, Martha looked up at Jem and silently mouthed, *Thank you.*

He dipped his head. "You're welcome."

* * *

When Joseph pulled into the New Hope Foundation parking lot, he parked beside Carrie's Volkswagen Beetle. After he turned off the ignition, he reached for his seat belt and... froze with his hand on the clip, fixating his eyes on something outside, seemingly far off into the distance.

"Which one will it be, Joseph?" the Shadow's words echoed into his subconscious. *"Sweet Carrie or her bitchy boss? Decide before I do it for you."*

Carrie turned toward him, noticing he was in some sort of trance. "Joseph?"

He closed his eyes, drowning out his surroundings. God, he'd give anything to be normal. To make his own decisions, to live his life by his own rules, to think for himself.

"Without me," the Shadow said, *"you are weak and pitiful. I give you strength and courage to survive in this cruel world. You are nothing without me, Joseph."*

"Joseph..." Carrie raised her voice. "Is something wrong?"

He rubbed his eyes and finally said, "It's nothing."

"Are you sure?"

"Yeah." He shrugged it off and faked a smile. "I was just thinking."

"About what?"

"Nothing really." He unfastened his seat belt and reached for the door handle. "Just work stuff, that's all."

He went around the front of the Jeep and opened her door. She smiled the moment he held out his hand, waiting for her to take hold.

As she put her hand in his and stepped out of the vehicle, her body instantly came up against his. Instead of moving out of her way, he stood there, looking down at her. He knew he should take a step back, but he felt he couldn't. Something about her kept him there. It was like she held him under a spell of some kind.

Unexpectedly, his hands went to the base of her neck. He lowered his head and hovered close to her lips.

"Don't do it, Joseph. You're letting your emotions take control."

Ignoring the voice in his head, he was bound and determined to kiss her, even if it killed him to do so. The need to touch her nearly drove him mad.

Carrie stared up into Joseph's blue eyes, her shoulders slumping in defeat, anticipating his touch. She was lost in his hypnotizing gaze.

Unable to stop himself, he closed the distance between them and gently pressed his lips to hers. As his tongue invaded her mouth, she grabbed his shoulders and pulled him closer. She quivered on shaky legs as she kissed him back. Then he changed the kiss, going in deep and sensual, exploring every inch of her mouth.

"Carrie..." A sharp voice called out.

Instantly, Joseph flinched and pulled away. He looked up while Carrie took a moment to catch her breath.

Carrie turned, and when she saw her boss, she said, "Veronica—"

Veronica stared at them with a hateful glare. "Carrie, what the hell do you think you're doing?"

"I... uh..." Carrie muttered, profoundly tongue-tied.

"What's your problem?" Joseph gritted out. "For crying out loud, we're just kissing good-bye."

"I say we pick the bitchy boss," the Shadow said. *"She's had it coming for way too long."*

Veronica came forward and stood with her hands on her hips. "Well, well, well," she said with a smug look on her face. "That's one hell of a smart mouth you got there, Mr. Parker. You might want to be mindful of how you use your words. I mean, you wouldn't want to piss off the wrong person."

"I'm going to enjoy killing this one. Slow and very painful."

"Excuse me?" Joseph asked, furrowing his brows. "Did you just threaten me?"

Carrie took hold of Joseph's hand. "Please..." She kept her voice low. "It's not worth it. Just let it go."

"Speak up, Carrie," Veronica said, flipping her long hair back. "I didn't quite hear you."

Carrie quickly let go of Joseph's hand and focused her eyes on Veronica. "It-it's just that I don't want anyone getting worked up over nothing."

Veronica cocked a brow. "Is that so?"

"I know public displays of affection are against company policy," Carrie said. "But it was just a simple kiss. And it's not like it happened in the office."

"A simple kiss my ass," Veronica said. "He practically had his entire tongue crammed down the back of your throat."

"I promise," Carrie said. "I won't let it happen again."

"You can bet your ass it won't." Veronica huffed. "Mr. Parker will no longer be permitted on the company's premises."

Joseph frowned. "Are *you* serious?"

"Oh, believe me, Mr. Parker. I'm dead serious."

"You'll be dead all right. Sooner than you think."

"By whose authority?" Joseph asked. "You don't own this company."

"Let me ask you this, Mr. Parker. Do you like your job at the Chronicle?"

"What the hell is that supposed to mean?"

"It means," Veronica smirked, "I can have you terminated with one phone call."

"You're deranged." He snarled his upper lip. "And that's a polite way of describing someone like you."

"Oh really?" Veronica pursed her lips. "We'll just see about that, now won't we."

"Go ahead," Joseph said, brushing it off like it was nothing. "If it makes you feel better, get me fired. I could give a shit."

Veronica's mouth fell open, but Joseph ignored her reaction and looked down at Carrie as she took hold of his hand again.

"I'm so sorry, Joseph. This is all my fault."

"This is not your fault, Carrie." He squeezed her hand. "None of it is. And I'm not going to stand by while this woman, who doesn't deserve to breathe the same air as you, much less have you as an employee, continues to treat you like a doormat. Do you understand?"

Carrie nodded as tears gathered in her eyes.

Before Joseph had the chance to tell Carrie's boss exactly what he thought of her, the sound of tires squealing took him by surprise. When he turned to look, he saw the back of Veronica's Mercedes as it tore out of the parking lot.

"The nerve of that woman," Joseph said, shaking his head.

"What about your job? Do you really think she'll try to get you fired?"

Joseph wrapped his arm around her waist. "Come on." He pulled her close. "Don't worry about it. I'm sure she's more bark than bite."

"You really think so?"

"Look at this face." Joseph grinned ear-to-ear. "Does it look like I'm worried?"

"Oh, Joseph." A smile curved over Carrie's lips. "What am I going to do with you?"

He leaned over a little and puckered his lips. "How 'bout another kiss?"

Carrie rose on her tiptoes and lightly pressed her lips to his.

"I'll call you later tonight," he said, opening her car door.

"You're still coming to my party, right?"

"Are you kidding? I wouldn't miss it for the world."

Moments later, as Carrie got in her car and drove away, Joseph hung back in the parking lot. As he sat behind the wheel, he pondered the situation with Carrie's boss.

"You're overthinking this, Joseph. You know what to do."

Chapter Nineteen

When Jem arrived back at the Covenant, Mia welcomed him home with one arm wrapped around his waist and the other anchored to their daughter.

"It's my favorite two girls," Jem said, pressing his lips to Mia's and then to his daughter's chubby cheek.

Evie cracked a little smile and settled back against her mother's chest.

Jem held out his arms. "Come to Daddy."

The second Evie reached for him, Mia made the exchange, gently depositing her in Jem's arms. He tightened his hold, securing her more firmly to his chest and planted a kiss on top of her head that was thick with blonde curls.

Evie stared up at him from underneath her long, dark lashes with the biggest grin on her face.

When he tickled her belly, she squirmed in his arms and giggled.

"So, how's Martha and her daughter Amy doing?" Mia asked.

Jem averted his eyes from Evie and looked to Mia with a weary expression.

"Let's sit down," Jem said, gesturing to the dining area. "There's some good news and some *not so* good news."

Mia sighed. "Oh dear."

The moment they sat down, Jem told Mia about Martha's condition and what had happened with Amy.

Mia listened to his every word in stunned silence. When he got to the part where he used his gift to heal Amy, Mia's distressed features shifted to one of relief.

"Thank goodness Amy is okay," Mia said. "You did a wonderful thing, honey."

"If I hadn't been there—"

"But you were," Mia said, reaching for his hand.

Jem nodded in silence and lightly squeezed Mia's hand.

"What about those men who broke into Martha's apartment? Did they get away?"

Jem shook his head. "Nicolas took care of them."

"You mean, he arrested them?"

"No," Jem said. "They were carted off in body bags."

"Oh," Mia said, grimacing. "So, where are Martha and Amy going to stay?"

"We gave Martha the choice to stay with either Helen or Nicolas," Jem said. "But since Nicolas has a cabin in the country and lots of space, she thought it would be better suited for Amy."

"I'm glad they're at a safe place," Mia said. Then she looked at Jem with a clear question stamped on her face. "Are you going to try and heal Martha's cancer?"

"When Tessa and the others get back, we're going to discuss our options."

"Hopefully Tessa will agree to it," Mia said, her voice concerned. Granted, she knew Tessa had a big heart when it came to helping others, but the thought of Martha dying and leaving Amy behind bothered her. It bothered her a lot.

"Don't worry, honey. No one is going to let Martha die. Besides, between Steven and I, surely one of us can heal her."

Mia nodded, some of the worry easing from her mind.

Suddenly, Evie let out a squeal of delight and then stretched her little arms outward as Jace and Tessa walked into the room.

"Come here, you little rascal," Jace said, rushing over to Evie.

Jem hoisted Evie up. "What is it about you, brother?" He looked up at Jace with his brows furrowed. "Every time you come into a room where there's kiddos, they all seem to flock to you."

Jace's expression split into a goofy, idiotic grin. "What can I say?" He scooped Evie into his arms, squeezing her gently. "I'm a fun guy to be around."

Jem rolled his eyes and Mia said, "She adores you, Jace."

"It's the tickle monster she loves," Jace said, playfully growling as he tickled Evie's bare feet.

She instantly broke out into laughter and excitedly kicked her feet.

Finally, as Jace sat down across from Jem and Mia, Evie quietly nestled against his chest.

Jace noticed Evie rubbing her eyes. "You sleepy, baby girl?"

She yawned broadly, burrowing more deeply into his lap.

He secured her in his arms then focused his attention on Tessa as she sat down beside him.

"Looks like someone is ready for a nap," Tessa said, keeping her voice low.

"You want me to take her?" Mia asked.

"Nah," Jace whispered. "She's perfectly fine."

Mia nodded. "So, is everyone okay?" She looked between Tessa and Jace. "I mean, I heard there was an incident at the institute and you two went to help."

"Fortunately," Tessa began, "they didn't need our help after all. Tim and the others had everything under control. And of course, both Detectives Sanchez and Perkins are fine. But there were some casualties. One of the institute's experiments got loose and killed some of the staff."

"That's awful," Mia said. "What was it?"

"It looked like some kind of mutated hybrid wolf," Jace said. "Although when it confronted Roman after he shifted into his Adalwolf, the thing didn't last long."

"What about the missing girl?" Jem asked. "Did the detectives find her?"

"Yes." Tessa nodded. "We don't know all the details yet, but going by what Detective Sanchez said, it appears she'd been drugged for several days. And they did locate the other patients along with one of the physicians."

Jem shook his head, completely baffled by what Tessa had told them. "Did the detectives manage to get any information on Joseph Harris?"

"As soon as we pulled up to the Covenant," Tessa said, "I got a call from Detective Sanchez. He said the physician they apprehended was willing to give them all the information he had. Not about Joseph Harris, but regarding another physician who knows some information on the other facility that's been funding the institute's research. They're hoping this physician might also have files on this Harris guy."

"Yeah," Jace said. "If we're lucky. So far, that guy seems to be turning into a mysterious phantom."

"At least they managed to shut down the institute," Mia said. Then her brows creased. "Where's Drakon, Tim, and Roman?"

"They're upstairs getting cleaned up," Jace said. "Things got a little bloody. If you catch my meaning."

"I get it." Mia crinkled her nose. "You don't have to go into details."

"So, how are you doing, Jem?" Tessa asked. "I talked to Helen as soon as I got off the phone with Detective Sanchez. She told me about what happened with Amy."

"Oh, I'm fine." His lips formed a half-smile. "Just glad I was there."

"So am I," Tessa said, smiling back. "You did a good thing saving that little girl. And if it weren't for you, I wouldn't be here today."

"Well, don't thank me," Jem said. "Thank the big guy upstairs."

Tessa nodded in agreement. "I thank God every day for all his blessings."

"Speaking of blessings," Mia said, changing the subject. "Are you going to agree to let Jem heal Martha's cancer?"

"Of course," Tessa said. "Jace and I are planning to leave here in a few minutes to drive out to Nicolas's place. We wanted to stop here first to check on the twins. We're meeting Helen there to discuss the situation. After we talk to Martha, I'm sure she won't dismiss our offer."

"If Jem can't heal Martha's cancer," Mia said, "will you ask your brother for help?"

Tessa nodded. "I'm sure Steven will be more than willing to help out in any way he can."

"Thank you, Tessa," Mia said. "The thought of that little girl being left without a mother breaks my heart. I know firsthand how that feels."

"I promise to do everything I can to keep that from happening," Tessa said, moving to her feet. "I guess we should head that way." She looked to Jace. "You ready to go?"

Jace looked down at Evie, who was sound asleep, cuddled into his lap with one hand on his chest and her thumb tucked between her lips.

"I hate to move her," Jace said. "She looks so peaceful."

"Then let her be," Jem said. "I can go with Tessa."

Jace looked at Jem. "You sure?"

"Yeah." Jem nodded. "Besides, I'd like to check on Amy and talk to Martha." He looked up at Tessa. "Only if it's okay with you."

Tessa smiled. "It's fine with me."

"Thanks, brother," Jem said as he leaned forward and then lightly bumped knuckles with Jace. "Take care of my girls."

"I will," Jace said. "You take care of *my* girl."

"Will do." Then Jem leaned over and kissed Mia. "I'll be back soon, honey."

Before Jem left with Tessa, he took one more glance into the room, taking pride in the sight of his twin brother holding his little girl. The image brought a smile to his face.

* * *

Joseph remained in the vacant parking lot of Carrie's employment, staring out into the far distance. Through the dark-tinted windows of his Jeep, he watched as the sky grew dreary and gray. And his mind was as dismal and gloomy as the clouds above: a complete whirlwind, filled with dread and turmoil. But it was also full of emotions he hadn't felt in years: empathy, compassion, and... *love.*

He'd thought, prayed, that after he avenged his mother's death, he would start to feel normal again, but that wasn't the case. He had evil inside of him. An evil derived from the deepest pits of hell.

The voice in his head continued to taunt him, to control him, and to use him to do its evil bidding. The Shadow's continuous urges to kill were taking a toll, not only on his body, but his mental state as well. He couldn't help but wonder if his life would finally come to some sort of normalcy, or was he doomed to live the remainder like a puppet on a string. And was he truly at fault for all the killings he was forced into? The horrifying thought rolled around in his mind, sickening him to the core.

165

He closed eyes. *No,* he thought. *It's not my fault.*

"*Stop whining, Joseph,*" the Shadow said. "*And get moving. My patience is wearing thin.*"

Joseph's lids flipped open. "Please..." He looked to the rearview mirror at himself. "I don't want to do this anymore."

The Shadow laughed. "*You wouldn't last a day without me. You can't even make it through the morning without my help. How else do you think you're able to get out of bed? Without me, you'd be a pathetic loser... a detriment on society... nothing but an empty vessel, aimlessly wandering around in a brainless meatsuit. Can you honestly imagine what your life would be?*"

The Shadow continued to rant, "*Think, Joseph. Who do you think encouraged you to pull that trigger after your father murdered your mother? You were but a mere frightened child with no one to protect you. I gave you that power. And who gave you the strength to survive and overcome all those years in the mental institute? I provided you with those cunning skills. You'd still be in there if it wasn't for me.*"

Joseph frowned and looked away, gripping the steering wheel until his knuckles went white. The inner core of him couldn't bear how weak and powerless the Shadow's words made him feel. Then, out of nowhere, something inside of him took over. All at once, a tremendous emotion boiled in his gut and grew until he felt he was going to explode. It was a rage he'd never felt before. With a sudden surge, he curled up a fist and punched out the driver's windshield.

Just as his anger was getting away from him, the Shadow's voice whispered into his mind, "*Look at me, Joseph.*"

As Joseph stared out of the broken window, continuing to ignore the Shadow, he braced himself for the repercussions of his actions.

After a few moments of silence, the Shadow raised his voice. "*I said, look at me, Joseph.*"

He swallowed back the pain burning in his hand and slowly turned toward the rearview mirror. He froze as he looked at the repulsive reflection staring back at him and heard himself wince. He rubbed his eyes, not sure if what he was looking at was real or just a figment of his imagination. He was completely unrecognizable, his handsome features replaced by something demonic. His eyes were two dark pits, and his mouth displayed rows and rows of sharp, jagged teeth.

"My God..." Joseph gasped, his voice no longer the same.

His first thought was to get out and run, but instead, he opened his mouth and said, "What's happening to me?"

"Take a closer look in the mirror," the Shadow said, his taunting voice echoing in Joseph's mind. *"This is who you really are."*

Joseph kept his eyes forward although he wanted nothing more than to look away from the horror staring back at him.

"Tell me, Joseph, do you like what you see?"

"Please..." Tears raced to his eyes. "No more. I'm begging you."

"The girl is changing you, Joseph. She's making you weak. We need to get rid of her."

"No." Joseph shook his head. "Carrie has nothing to do with—"

Joseph flinched at the booming voice, coming from the broken window. "What the hell are you still doing here?"

The moment he turned to meet Carrie's boss face-to-face, her eyes instantly bulged in horror.

"Kill her, Joseph."

The second Veronica opened her mouth to scream, Joseph's only thought was to save Carrie. And then painful memories flashed before his eyes like random images in a photobook. He thought of the brutal death of his mother at the hands of his father. Pictured the years of abuse and deterioration etched into every groove of her face. Recalled the last words she'd spoken. Remembered the loneliness and isolation that consumed him. And in the center of all his recollections, he felt a dark presence taking form and inhabiting his body, using him for the sole purpose of evil.

"If you want Carrie to live, kill Veronica."

He snapped back to focus as Veronica's scream blared into his ears like the sound of a trumpet. And her wide, horrified gaze was locked onto his dark-pitted eyes.

The moment she turned and took off at a dead run he went after her. As she got to her car and reached for the door, he grabbed a fistful of her hair.

When she started to scream, he yanked her head back and clamped his free hand over her mouth. Although his strength overrode her ability to get away, she squirmed against his hold and screamed into the palm of his hand.

"Now finish her off, Joseph."

As Joseph stood there with his hand over Veronica's mouth, a part of him wanted to end her life, to shut her up for good. Besides, what choice did he have? His hand was being forced to pick between two lives: a woman with a spiteful heart or the woman he loved. Even though he did not want to kill again, Carrie was worth the sacrifice.

But when Veronica started to sob, something inside of him shifted. His pulse throbbed and his heart raced. It was rather strange and mystifying. Then a chill came over him, tingling all over the surface of his skin. Joseph was bewildered, lost suddenly, and unable to choose between life or death. It was as though he was stuck in limbo. And then he thought of his mother again. He pictured how she looked right before her death. The painful and terrified expression on her tear-stained face swirled together with the woman's he was about to kill.

"What are you waiting for, Joseph? End her rotten life!"

"I cannot," Joseph said.

"I can force you. My blood courses through your veins."

Joseph gritted his teeth. "And so does mine."

Without saying another word, Joseph released Veronica's hair and placed a firm hand on her shoulder. After a few seconds that seemed to last forever, he finally said, "If I remove my other hand, promise me you won't scream."

She quickly nodded against his hand.

While he silently waited for her to collect herself, it wasn't long before her sobs diminished to soft puffs of air. Then slowly, he lowered his hand and took hold of her arm. Right away, her shoulders tensed when he turned her around to face him. But to her relief, the horrid image of what she'd witnessed only moments ago was no longer present.

Her legs shook uncontrollably until her knees threatened to give out. The second they started to buckle, Joseph tightened his grip and held her steady.

"It's okay," he said in a gentle voice. "I'm not going to hurt you."

Veronica closed her eyes and bit at her bottom lip, holding her tears at bay. With all the strength she could muster, she lifted her lids. And to her surprise, Joseph's eyes were wet with tears.

Out of nowhere, an unexplainable emotion came over her as she peered into the tortured depths of his blue eyes. It was so overwhelming, a pain of a different kind, like having part of your soul ripped out.

"Oh my God..." She gasped. "What's happened to you?"

Shame instantly crowded into his eyes. "It-it's..." He lowered his head. "It's hard to explain."

"Please," Veronica said as she reached out and cupped his chin. "Look at me, Joseph."

Joseph could feel her staring holes through him as he lifted his gaze like she was trying to figure him out.

"I'm sorry, Joseph."

His jaw nearly hit the ground. "What did you say?"

"I'm sorry for what I said to you earlier," Veronica said. "And I'm sorry for how I've treated Carrie."

Chill bumps prickled his skin. *What the heck?* For some odd reason, the science fiction horror film *Invasion of the Body Snatchers* suddenly came to Joseph's mind. It was like Veronica had somehow magically transformed into someone nice. And she seemed a little forgetful. The previous incident between them appeared completely removed from her memory. *But how can it be?*

As he opened his mouth to speak, she held up a halting hand. "I promise, first thing in the morning, I'm going to apologize to Carrie. You have my word. From now on, things are going to be different."

"Oh, you can count on that," the Shadow said. *"There will be retribution."*

The Shadow started to laugh, lightly at first, then louder, until Joseph's ears hurt from the pitch of the sinister, murderous glee.

Chapter Twenty

As soon as Jem and Tessa arrived at their destination, they got out of the vehicle and walked toward Nicolas's place, a cozy two-story cabin that butted against a lake. It was breathtaking, and apparently well kept. It had a rustic look, with an exterior made from cedar, stone, and brick cladding. Going by the size of the thing, it had to be at least three thousand square feet, if not bigger.

The cabin was surrounded by acres of trees that stretched across a grassland as far as the eye could see. It was already getting hot, but the cool breeze from the lake was refreshing and made it tolerable to be outside.

Before they left the Covenant, Tessa decided to bring along her and Jace's twin boys, Jax and little Jem. She thought it would be good for them to take on an adventure and experience what nature had to offer. And hopefully, Amy would enjoy having playmates for the day.

With Jax tucked securely in his arms, Jem looked in Tessa's direction and said, "Man, this place is spectacular." He inhaled deeply, taking in the distinctive smell of fresh country air. "I'd love to have a place like this."

"You and me both," Tessa said as she repositioned little Jem over her hip. "The boys would love it here, especially the lake."

Jem nodded. "I'll have to bring Evie for a visit. She loves the water."

A few moments later, they were greeted at the door by Nicolas. He motioned them inside. "Please, come on in," he said, his voice laced with a southern drawl. "Everyone is gathered on the back patio."

"Thank you, Nicolas," Tessa said, moving inside with Jem following in behind her. "I hope you don't mind me bringing the boys along."

"Of course not." He smiled. "I'm glad you brought them. Amy will be thrilled to have someone to play with."

Tessa smiled and Jem said, "This place is like a slice of heaven." He looked up at the cathedral ceiling, noticing the chandelier made of deer antlers and then back to Nicolas. "How long have you had this place?"

"Believe it or not..." Nicolas cocked a brow. "...I've owned this property for more than a century. Of course, I've made a few upgrades since then. There's about seven hundred acres here."

"You're giving away your age, Nicolas," Tessa said. "Although you don't look a day over twenty."

He chuckled. "That's about the only good thing immortality has to offer."

As soon as Nicolas led them through the opening to a sliding glass door and onto the patio, Amy rushed forward, smiling at the twins. "Hi, my name is Amy." She looked between Jem and Tessa. "Can they play with me?"

"You betcha, sweetheart," Jem said. "This is Jax." Then he looked to Tessa and the toddler in her arms. "And that's his twin brother, little Jem and their Mama, Miss Tessa."

Amy looked up at the little boy and then back to Jem with a puzzled look on her face. "How come that baby has the same name as you?"

"His daddy is my twin brother," Jem said. "He named him after me."

She grinned, appearing satisfied with his explanation.

When Jem lowered Jax to his feet, he watched in fascination as Amy got on her knees and wrapped her arms around him. The second Amy pulled away from Jax, he reached out and tugged at one of her long pigtails.

"I'm sorry, Amy," Tessa said. "Jax is just very curious."

"It's okay." Amy smiled. "He didn't hurt me."

"Do you like chocolate chip cookies, Amy?" Tessa asked.

Her eyes brightened. "I love chocolate chip cookies!"

What little kid didn't, Tessa thought. And then she recalled the trauma Amy had gone through when her and her mother had been kidnapped by a serial killer. It nearly gutted her. No child should be subjected to such evil. It made Tessa want to weep, but she couldn't show it. At least not in front of Amy.

"But first," Tessa said, "we better ask your mommy if it's okay."

"Okay," Amy bashfully said, her thumb automatically going to her mouth.

Amy quickly looked up when she felt a hand on her shoulder. Her eyes lit up when she saw it was her mother.

"It's okay, sweetheart," Martha said. "You can have a cookie."

Amy lowered her thumb from her mouth and offered her mother a tentative smile. Then she looked up at Tessa. "Miss Tessa, Mama said it's okay."

"One chocolate chip cookie coming right up," Tessa said as she reached into the bag that was strapped over her shoulder. When she brought her hand out, she had a plastic baggie full of cookies the size of cup saucers.

Amy's eyes rounded and the twins clapped their hands.

Martha stood back and smiled as Amy took to Tessa and the others so easily. It all seemed too good to be true, but she was grateful to have met such good, caring people.

Jem watched as Amy stuffed a piece of cookie into her mouth, her eyes glittering with joy, savoring the chocolate treat.

"Amy, do you mind if I steal your mama for a moment?" Jem asked.

She nodded with her cheeks stuffed full.

"Enjoy your cookie, sweetheart." Jem chuckled, ruffling her hair. "And save one for me."

Jem and Martha moved to a comfortable area on the other side of the covered patio so they could speak in private.

"I'm glad you came," Martha said, sitting across from Jem. "I don't think I thanked you enough for saving my daughter. If you hadn't been there—"

"It's okay, Martha. I'm just glad she's okay, and that's all that matters."

"What you did was a miracle," Martha said, her voice laced with tears. "Amy is everything to me. She's all I have."

Jem scooted his chair close to Martha's and leaned forward. "I came by to see how Amy was doing, but I also wanted to talk to you about something important."

Martha nodded. "Nothing's wrong, is there?"

"No," Jem said. Then he hesitated for a moment. "Helen told me about your condition, and I'd like to help. That is, if you agree to let me."

"You mean..." Her eyes rounded. "With my cancer?"

"Yes, Martha. I think I can heal you, or at least I'd like to try. But you must realize, my gift is new to me. There's a chance it could be dangerous. So, it's all up to you."

Suddenly, tears streamed down Martha's cheeks. And before she managed to utter a single word, he reached out and took hold of her hand.

Although they only sat there for a few minutes, it felt like time stood still. Martha sat in silence, trying her best to comprehend the offer Jem had presented to her. Finally, she said, "I would like more than anything to try. But how is this possible? I mean, how can you..."

"Heal people?" Jem said.

When she nodded, Jem went on to say, "It's hard to explain and I know you're confused, considering everything you've been through. Especially all the bizarre things you've witnessed in the last few days. But all I can tell you is... this gift I have... it's something I was born with. Can you accept that answer?"

Martha smiled. "Absolutely."

Jem lightly squeezed her hand. "Thank you, Martha."

As Martha started to pull her hand away, Jem tightened his hold. "Would you like to do this now?"

She looked at him surprised. "Really?"

"Why not? Aren't you ready to rid yourself of all the pain and finally start living?"

"More than anything." She blinked more tears. "What do I need to do?"

"Just close your eyes, Martha. Let me do all the rest."

As soon as Martha closed her eyes, Jem shut his and focused on nothing but healing. It wasn't long before a warm sensation crept through his body and surrounded hers like a ray of sunshine.

At once, the effects of Jem's healing energy poured into Martha. Slowly, the pain magically lifted from her body. It was like something she'd only hoped to imagine. She felt renewed and somehow free.

The moment Jem sensed strength in Martha that hadn't been there before, he released her hand. "Martha, you can open your eyes now."

When she lifted her lids, she stared at him with an open mouth. She closed it and reopened it several times but not a word came out. Then her expression softened, and her eyes glistened with tears.

"Thank you. I'll never forget what you've done for me and my daughter."

"It was my pleasure, Martha."

Then a small voice said, "Did you take away my mama's sickness?"

Jem's brows lifted when he turned to see Amy standing next to him. Her eyes were full of wonder and her lips covered with chocolate.

"Yes, sweetheart." Jem smiled. "Your mama is much better now."

Amy extended her hand. "I saved you the biggest cookie."

"Why, thank you." Jem graciously accepted the cookie Amy offered him. "That is the biggest cookie I've ever seen."

Amy patted his cheeks with her sticky hands. "You and Jena are my bestest friends."

"Well then," Jem said, taken back by the little girl's words, "I consider that a real honor. What did I do to deserve that?"

"You saved us, silly," she said with a giggle, and then looked toward her mother. "Isn't that right, Mama?"

More tears gathered in Martha's eyes. For a moment she remained silent, clearly overwhelmed by what Amy had said. She should have realized her daughter was more observant than she gave her credit for. After all, Amy was brighter than the average five-year-old.

Amy looked worried when her mother didn't answer right away. She hurried over and climbed into her lap, putting her little hand to her mother's cheek.

"Don't cry, Mama." Amy wiped at her mother's tears. "It'll be okay." Amy looked to Jem for approval. "Won't it, Jem?"

"Most definitely, sweetheart," he said, looking between Amy and Martha with a genuine expression on his face.

Slowly, Jem reached out for Martha's hand and then he reached for Amy's, linking them all together. "You can count on me and everyone here. We're your family now."

Martha smiled and Amy launched herself from her mother's lap and into Jem's arms. His heart melted as she wrapped her arms around him, squeezing tightly. If he hadn't already been solidly attached to this little girl, that would have sealed the deal.

Chapter Twenty-One

Later that night, after a quick shower, Joseph was ready to call it a night. He flopped down on his bed and propped himself against a mountain of pillows. As he stared at the ceiling, he couldn't shut his eyes without thinking of the incident with Carrie's boss. He was worried. Did Veronica really forget what had happened earlier, or was she faking it? He feared her unexplained loss of memory and her odd behavior was just an attempt to mislead him so she could escape. If so, would she expose his secret? The thought was almost too much to bear.

He turned to look when his phone on the nightstand vibrated. He grabbed it and instantly saw it was Carrie calling. And then he noticed the time. *Dang!* It was already after nine o'clock. He'd let the day slip by, forgetting to call her.

He quickly swiped to answer. "Hello, Carrie."

"Hi, Joseph. I hope I'm not calling too late."

"Absolutely not. I'm still up. And I'm so sorry. I completely forgot to call you."

"It's okay. You don't have to apologize. I was just getting worried, that's all."

"You were worried?"

"Of course." Concern brimmed in her voice. "I mean, after what happened with my boss today, I figured maybe you were ready to throw in the towel."

"What are you talking about?"

"I thought you might not want to see me anymore."

"Are you kidding me?" He lightly chuckled. "It's going to take more than a little feud with your boss to chase me off."

"Really?"

"Absolutely."

"So, you're still coming to my birthday party?"

"Heck yeah. I'm looking forward to it."

"Oh, good." She sighed into the phone. "It wouldn't be the same without you."

"I wouldn't miss it for the world."

"You're already in bed, aren't you?"

"How'd you know?"

"It's your voice. You sound exhausted."

"Sorry." He fought back a yawn. "I guess I haven't been getting enough sleep lately."

"Why's that?"

"Maybe it's because I've had a *certain* person on my mind."

"Oh?"

"Yeah." He smiled against the phone. "And her name rhymes with Harry."

"Well then..." She laughed. "Maybe this *Harry* person should stop calling you so late."

"For crying out loud," the Shadow said, his distorted voice thundering in Joseph's head. *"Tell her good-bye already."*

Joseph closed his eyes and forced the Shadow's voice out of his mind.

After a few moments of silence, Carrie said, "Joseph, are you still there?"

"Sorry." His eyes popped back open. "I was just thinking. You want to have lunch one day this week?"

"Sure. I'd like that."

"Great. I'll talk to you tomorrow. And Carrie..."

"Yes..."

"I'm glad you called."

"Get some sleep, Joseph."

"Good night, Carrie."

When he ended the call, he closed his eyes with Carrie on his mind and didn't sleep at all.

The following morning, Joseph filled a travel mug with coffee, preparing to meet his therapist before he dropped off his Jeep to get the window repaired, then start his day at the Chronicle. Although his mind was focused on Carrie's boss, worried she'd remember their little incident from yesterday, he was still able to go through his everyday rituals like clockwork. Wake up, eat breakfast, exercise, shower, and get dressed.

The minute he climbed into his Jeep and fastened his seatbelt, his thoughts took him to a different place. It was something he didn't want to think about.

"You can't ignore the inevitable for long, Joseph. Soon, you will kill for me."

"I can't." Joseph swallowed a gasp. "I won't do this anymore."

"You have no choice, Joseph."

As Joseph grappled with the Shadow's demands, a quick moment of conscious awareness took hold. And that's when he decided what he had to do. He had no other choice but to stop seeing Carrie. The decision to break it off with her brought on a painful feeling in the center of his chest. He felt like his heart was splintering in half, but it was the right thing to do. It was the only way to keep Carrie and everyone around her safe.

"You're too weak, Joseph. You'll never go through with it. The girl has you wrapped around her little finger. You cannot resist her."

Joseph shook his head. "I can do this."

"That sounds like a challenge. I accept."

Joseph calmed himself by rubbing his face. *Dammit.* He hadn't expected things to come down to this. But if it was a challenge the Shadow wanted, then that's what he'd get.

A half hour later, Joseph stared at the floor with his mind focused on Carrie, waiting to be escorted inside the room where he had an appointment to meet with his therapist.

The nurse opened the door and called out, "Mr. Parker, Dr. Mendoza is ready to see you now."

Joseph lifted his chin and smiled when Dr. Mendoza greeted him with her hand outstretched.

"It's good to see you again, Joseph."

He took hold of her hand. "Thank you, Dr. Mendoza."

She released his hand and motioned him inside. "Shall we get started?"

Joseph nodded, and as he stepped into the spacious room, a familiar scent invaded his senses. He shut his eyes and inhaled the smell of French vanilla deep into his nostrils. Instantly, it soothed some of the anxiety that had been weighing on his shoulders. The second he reopened his lids, he spotted the artwork that hung above Dr. Mendoza's desk. The painting of the beach with a breathtaking view of the ocean somehow comforted him in a way he could not explain. It was as if he could hear the waves rolling onto the sandy beach and peacefully fading away.

He averted his eyes from the painting when he heard her say, "Please, make yourself comfortable."

As he sat down in an oversized chair, she settled in behind her desk and placed a small recorder in front of her.

"Joseph, do you mind if I ask you something concerning our last recorded session?"

When he nodded, she went on to say, "Remember when I asked if you still heard the voices? The ones you heard as a child."

"Yes," Joseph said, swallowing hard.

"Were you being honest when you said you no longer heard them?"

"I told you she didn't believe you. You should have been more convincing."

"Yes, Dr. Mendoza." Joseph furrowed his brows. "Why would you think otherwise?"

"After our last session, I reviewed the recording and discovered something rather strange."

Joseph nervously shifted in his chair. "What do you mean by *strange?*"

"I heard another voice mixed into our conversation."

"Impossible," the Shadow said.

"But how can that be?" Joseph looked puzzled. "We were the only ones in the room."

"We've got to get rid of her. She's asking too many questions."

"I know this all sounds a bit bizarre," she said. "Believe me, I thought I was hearing things at first. But after reviewing it closer, I'm positive there's a third person on the recording. And what it said was unsettling." She released a deep breath. "Please, Joseph, I'd like you to listen for yourself."

"If she shares this with anyone, they'll put you back in the looney bin."

Out of nowhere, an uncontrollable fear came over Joseph, so powerful, his hands started to shake, and his forehead beaded with sweat. He leaned forward and placed his face into the palms of his hands.

"Joseph?" Dr. Mendoza rose from her chair. "Is something wrong?"

Her voice suddenly snapped him out of his trance. Numbly, he looked up, his sapphire eyes shifting to hers. "Uh... okay." His reply was barely audible. "I mean..." He raised his voice. "Yeah, I'll listen to it."

"Are you sure you're okay?" Her eyes roamed over his pale face. "You don't look so well."

He just stared at her. He felt his mouth go wide, working as if he were trying to say something, but the words would not come.

"Joseph..."

He exhaled a deep breath and shook himself back to focus. "C-can we do this another time?" His voice cracked. "I'm suddenly not feeling well."

"Of course. Is there anything I can do?"

"No. I'll be fine." He stood up. "I-I just need some rest. Haven't been sleeping well, that's all."

"But Joseph—"

He headed for the door. "Thank you, Dr. Mendoza. I'll see you later—I'll reschedule."

After rushing out, Joseph hurried down the hallway, and as he shot past the receptionist, he heard him say, "Mr. Parker, don't forget to make—"

The receptionist's voice trailed off as Joseph pushed through the door and made his way outside. A few seconds later, he found himself in the parking lot, bent over, retching up his entire breakfast.

* * *

Manuel groaned when his alarm went off with the most annoying sound. He stretched over toward the nightstand and quickly silenced it. His head felt like he'd been on a bender from hell. And not because he'd been drinking. He'd been up most the night, along with his partner, working a homicide case.

A few hours after Manuel and his partner discovered the Summit Behavioral Institute's connection with an illegal research operation—along with the Breedline Covenant's help—they apprehended most of the staff who were involved. That is, the ones they found alive. And fortunately, during the raid, they recovered the patients, along with Judge Weaver's granddaughter, who had been abducted and used as guinea pigs, mixing their DNA with animals for the sole purpose of science.

While the detectives interrogated a physician at the institute, he willingly gave up one of his colleagues, Dr. Leonard Manos, who was hired by A&E Pharmaceuticals and another unknown facility outside of Berkeley to do the unethical research. But before the detectives got the opportunity to arrest Dr. Manos and haul his ass into the precinct for questioning, a body was discovered inside a burning vehicle parked outside a nightclub, registered in the physician's name.

By the time they arrived at the crime scene, the area was surrounded by police cruisers and blocked off with yellow tape. Finally, when the fire was extinguished and the scene was safe to enter, the coroner went in and did her thing. Soon after, the victim's charred remains were taken to the crime lab for identification. Although evidence was destroyed in the fire, it was undeniably a hired hit. Apparently, someone was afraid Dr. Manos would divulge incriminating evidence against the unknown facility involved with A&E Pharmaceuticals and the Summit Behavioral Institute.

During his time as a homicide detective, Manuel found that investigating murders was nothing out of the ordinary. It was just part of the job. And he'd seen his share of dead bodies over the last thirty years. Some of them gruesome and in unimaginable conditions. But this? This kind of death was overkill. The bastard who was responsible was nothing but a spineless coward, hiding behind a big corporation with a disposable income. *Blood money.*

As Manuel pulled himself upright, he hung his legs off the bed. Before he got to his feet, the smell of smoke and burned metal invaded his senses. He sniffed at the T-shirt he'd worn underneath the button-down collar from last night and instantly recoiled in reaction to the unpleasant smell. With one swift motion, he grabbed the hem of his shirt, yanked it over his head and tossed it to the floor. It landed on top of his miniature French bulldog, who was sleeping on a padded crate next to his bed. When the dog let out a yelp, he said, "Sorry ol' girl."

Finally, as he pushed himself upright, the room tilted a little. He closed his eyes until he felt steady on his feet. As soon as he lifted his lids, his phone went off.

"For crying out loud," he grumbled. "What now?"

He retrieved his phone off the nightstand and instantly recognized the number on the caller ID. Then he exhaled a breath and answered. "This better be important."

"Good morning to you too, Detective," Frank said. "Sounds like you're in a mood."

"Hell, Perkins," Manuel barked into the phone, "we've been up half the night." He glanced at the alarm clock. "It's hard to focus with only two hours of sleep."

"I hear ya, partner. I'm already on my second cup of coffee."

Manuel yawned. "So, what's the urgency?"

"I may have a lead on this Joseph Harris guy."

Manuel straightened his shoulders. "What kind of lead?"

"I did some digging into the department's crime reports. There was an arrest record on a Joe Harris back in 2001. He was sentenced to twenty years for beating his wife to death. And according to the file, they had a five-year-old son named Joseph."

"You think this is our guy?"

"I know it is," Frank said. "He was placed in foster care and then landed in the Summit Behavioral Institute just like Roman said."

"We already know all this, so how is it going to help us track him down?"

"Hold on, Detective," Frank said. "I'm getting to that part. You remember Officer Katie Mendoza?"

"Yeah." Manuel nodded against the phone. "She was one helluva police officer. Too bad she left the precinct. If I'm not mistaken, didn't she go off to study psychology or something?"

"Yep. And she was the first officer at the crime scene when Mr. Harris killed his wife."

"You think Katie might have some useful information?"

"It's worth a try," Frank said. "What do we have to lose?"

"I'm guessing you already know where Katie is, am I right?"

"She's a therapist at the Jones Therapy Clinic, right here in Berkeley."

"After I get my shit together," Manuel said, "I'll meet you at the precinct. Give me an hour."

Before Frank got a word out, Manuel abruptly said, "On second thought. Make that two. It'll take me a while to wash off all the crud from last night. My lungs are probably corroded from all the smoke. And then I'll need time to consume large amounts of coffee."

Frank laughed. "Don't take too long. Remember, we're supposed to meet up with the captain later this morning to go over the details he got out of Dr. SeGovia on A&E Pharmaceuticals. And going by what information he discovered, along with what Drakon dug up, we've got enough evidence to get a search warrant."

"Yeah," Manuel said. "And hopefully, we won't run into what we encountered at the Summit Behavioral Institute. Captain will have a damn stroke if we come up against anything supernatural. The last situation we dealt with 'bout done him in."

"You're right," Frank said. "Not to mention all the freakin' reporters. Can you imagine if this gets leaked out to the press?"

"I don't even want to think about it."

"You and me both," Frank said.

"I'll shoot you a text before I head out."

"Sounds good. I'll see you later, partner."

When Manuel ended the call, he briefly shut his eyes. *If only I had a few more hours of sleep, then I might feel like a human again.*

As soon as he started a fresh pot of coffee, he grabbed a quick shower and shaved. A half hour later, he was dressed and ready for a shitload of caffeine.

In the middle of his first cup, he heard a knock at the door. Ira went into full-blown bark mode and rushed toward the door, her nails clipping across the hardwood floor.

"Who in the hell?" He groaned as he walked over to the door and put his eye up to the peephole. When he saw the person standing outside his apartment, a smile stretched across his face. Quickly, he flipped the locks and threw open the door. Ira barreled between his legs only to melt into a puddle of wagging tail and excited whimpers.

"Kathryn..." Manuel's smile broadened. "What a surprise."

Kathryn bent down and reached out to pet the dog. "Well, hello, Ira," she said, looking up at Manuel with a smile. After a few moments of petting Ira, she stood straight and held out a covered Styrofoam cup. "I heard about the fire." Her expression grew sympathetic. "I thought maybe you could use a little caffeine to start off your day."

He eyeballed the cup in her hand. "You mean, you came all the way here just to bring me coffee?"

"Sure. Why not?"

"Wow..." He reached for the coffee and motioned her in. "I feel pretty damn special."

She laughed a little. "You are special. Isn't that right, Ira."

The dog jumped up and down as Kathryn made her way inside.

"Please..." He gestured toward the tiny kitchen. "...make yourself comfortable. I just made a fresh pot if you'd like to join me before I head to the precinct."

"Thanks. I'd love to."

While she settled into a chair, he poured her a cup. "Would you like cream or sugar?"

"Both please."

It wasn't long before they fell into conversation, starting with his grueling night and then to her long shift in the ER.

Kathryn was employed at the Bates Hospital, where they'd met for the first time. She'd been the nurse on duty the last time he'd been rushed to the hospital for a gunshot wound. Fortunately for him, it turned out to be just a graze. Although the attraction between them was instantaneous, it was Helen Carrington who had officially hooked them up.

Six months had passed since their first date, but with their busy schedules, it was hard to find free time to spend together. And it didn't help with Manuel's standoffish personality. He wasn't the type to easily share his feelings.

When an awkward silence cropped up between them, Kathryn finally built up the courage to say, "Manuel, how come you've never tried to kiss me?"

Manuel stiffened in his chair. "I—"

"Don't you find me attractive?"

"Of course," he finally said. "It's just that... well... I don't know?" He shrugged. "Would you like me to kiss you?"

"Yes, I would." Her eyes softened. "I'd like that very much."

He cocked a brow. "Right now?"

"Now is as good a time as any, don't you think?"

Without so much as a single word, he shot out of his chair like a torpedo. In the blink of an eye, he was upon her. It all happened so fast. It was as though an alien had temporarily taken over his body. When he took her by the arm and tugged her out of her chair and against his body, the element of surprise shocked her into complete surrender. Overwhelmed by his boldness, she gasped as he dug his hand into the long strands of her blonde hair and crushed his lips against hers.

He kissed her long and passionately, his tongue going in, so teasing... so demanding. She shivered at the feel of his warm palm as it slowly traveled down her neck and to the small of her back.

What seemed like an eternity, his kiss ended in a matter of a few minutes when he finally pulled from their embrace. "Well..." He wiggled his brows. "How was that?"

The smile she gave him was radiant. "That was *unexpected*, but wonderful all the same."

He smiled back. "Good, because there's more where that came from."

"Mmm..." she purred. "I'm definitely looking forward to it."

Chapter Twenty-Two

While Nicolas stayed back at the cabin, making sure Martha and Amy were settled in, Jena was up and dressed bright and early, preparing for a long morning run. Before she headed out, she packed a few essentials in a fanny pack with a water bottle holder and strapped it around her waist.

Slipping out the front door before anyone inside the Covenant was up and about, she was off, pounding down the driveway toward the security building. After she checked in with the guards, they gave her clearance and opened the gates.

As she started off, loving the feel of the fresh air and the morning breeze against her skin, it wasn't long before she fell into a fast stride. She felt so carefree. So invincible.

In fact, her legs never felt stronger. She'd always been a fast runner, but now that she was immortal, everything about her transition gave her an overwhelming amount of strength, along with heightened senses and being insusceptible to any illness or disease. It was as though she was indestructible.

Ten miles later, she found herself close to Stinson Beach. The ocean breeze and the sounds of the waves rolling onto the sand and fading away drew her onward. A few miles later, she jogged past vacation rentals, shops, restaurants, and small crowds of people as they mingled about. As she approached a nearby café, she decided to stop for brunch and relax on the outdoor patio it had to offer.

After she finished eating, she merely sat back and observed all the people as they gathered underneath the covered patio. The atmosphere was soothing and calming, with acoustic music playing in the background. There were smiling faces and cheerful conversations everywhere she turned. *Why couldn't life always be this easy?* she thought.

Then two men came in and sat down at the table across from hers. They looked out of place. Instantly, as the hairs on her arms stood on end, she sensed danger.

One of them had on a black ball cap. He wore it low on his forehead, making it difficult to see his face. He was tall and lanky. The other guy was bald and large boned. He wore dark sunglasses, and his brows were drawn tight, appearing angry.

There was something suspicious and decidedly off about them, the way they kept glancing in her direction and then back at one another. It was as though they were plotting something malicious. And they reeked of pure evil. The stench created an uneasy feeling deep down in her gut.

On instinct, the creature within her stirred. She felt a sudden prickling on the surface of her skin. Jena's eyes rounded when she peered down at her hands. They were covered in tiny black hairs, and she could feel them spreading.

Please, God... She closed her eyes, squeezing them tightly. *Don't let me shift in front of all these people.*

Then the moment she lifted her lids, the tiny hairs were gone. It was as though they magically willed themselves back into her pores all on their own.

Jena breathed out a sigh of relief. *Thank you, God.*

Focusing back on her stalkers, she calmly watched as a waitress came up to their table and took their order. As soon as she sauntered off, the bald guy got up and left. His buddy continued to periodically look over at her.

They were obviously up to no good, Jena thought. And by the way they kept staring, it had something to do with her. But what?

A few minutes later, the bald guy came back to the table and sat down across from his buddy. Jena kept her eyes peeled for the slightest move.

It wasn't long before the waitress brought the two guys their food. That's when Jena decided to leave.

If those thugs have a lick of sense, she thought to herself as she made her way through the exit, *they'll choose their next course of action wisely. Following me will lead them down a path they'd wished they hadn't taken.*

As Jena moved through the crowd of people, a familiar scent of evil stopped her in her tracks. The second she inhaled the intrusive odor into her nasal cavity, it thickened and surrounded her like a veil of fog. Her muscles quickly tensed, and her heart raced. She stood there, caught by the unpleasant smell, but utterly unable to define where it was coming from.

Finally, she realized someone was closing in from behind. When she turned to look, she expected to see the two men from the café, but to her surprise, it was two women. And they looked identical. For a moment, Jena thought she was seeing double. Their hair was the color of fire, and their eyes were dark, seething. They were tall, taller than Jena and had a body builder's physique. By the harsh expression on their faces, they looked to do her harm.

Well, according to Jena, they could try. Fortunately, nothing could kill her. And by what she'd learned, her only kryptonite was her own species. One bite was all it took. But as far as she knew, she was the last of her kind.

Jena squared her shoulders when one of the women took a few steps closer. Her twin was right on her heels.

"I don't know what the hell you two want," Jena said, standing her ground. "But take my advice, ladies. You *don't* want no part of me."

The closest redhead placed her open hand, as big as a catcher's mitt, on Jena's chest and tried to shove her backward, but Jena didn't budge.

A few onlookers gathered around, whispering among themselves and pointing.

"I'm only going tell you once more." Jena raised her voice, "Turn around and leave."

Both women eyeballed Jena with a menacing glare. The time it took the brave redhead to draw back her fist, Jena struck her square in the face before she even registered her movement.

The other woman looked between Jena and her doppelganger—who was lying on the ground unconscious and bleeding—with bewilderment stamped all over her face. Then she came at Jena in a snarling rage. Before she knew what hit her, Jena used all her strength and head-butted her right in the face. Jena's attacker recoiled in pain and reached for her bloody nose.

"I warned you," Jena said, anticipating the woman's next move. "Had enough?"

The redheaded attacker curled her upper lip and wiped at her nose with the back of her hand. "Is that all you got?" she said with a hateful scowl on her face.

"What are you waiting for?" Jena said, motioning the woman onward. "Come and get some."

As soon as the woman charged forward, Jena landed a round kick to her jaw. The impact knocked her out cold. In a split second, she crumbled to the ground and the small crowd of people cheered.

One side of Jena's mouth curved up into a half-smile, and when she turned to leave, a blinding pain caught her from behind. In a matter of seconds, it was as though her entire body was lit on fire. Realizing she'd been hit with a tranquilizer, she reached for the back of her neck.

No, she feverishly thought, refusing to give up.

She gritted her teeth and quickly removed the dart. As soon as she started forward, she was hit again. This time, her vision clouded, and her body weakened. She immediately felt disorientated, her surroundings dizzying. Instantaneously, panic set in. Then she heard faint voices around her and the sounds of people fleeing to get away. With the last bit of her strength, she fought to remain conscious.

As she swayed on her feet, a strong arm snaked around her to prevent her fall.

"Sorry, Miss McCain," a male's voice whispered into her ear. "But I can't have you shifting into your creature."

Despite her blurry vision, she could still see the face of the person staring down at her. It was the angry-looking bald guy from the café.

"I have to say," he finally said, smiling in amusement, "you put up one helluva fight. You took out two of my best girls."

"What do you..." Jena released a strangled breath, "...want with me?"

"It's not me who wants you. My associates and I were just hired to capture you."

"Then who?"

"If you cooperate, all your questions will be answered in due time. But if you give me trouble..." His smile faded. "...I can promise you, Miss McCain. Things will get very unpleasant."

His promising words sent chills through her body.

"Do we have an understanding?"

She forced back the obnoxious reply that hovered on her lips and slowly nodded.

He smirked. "Smart decision."

Seconds later, Jena's sight began to fade. Although she was too drugged to make out her surroundings, her hearing seemed to be working.

"We're running out of time." Jena heard another man say. "It won't be long before someone calls the cops. You get the girl out of here while I take care of the twins."

"You sure you can handle the both of them?"

"Yeah," the other man said, slightly chuckling. "They definitely had their asses handed to them, but they seem to be coming around."

"All right," the bald guy said. "I'll meet you back at the lab. Dr. Michaels is expecting us to deliver Miss McCain within the hour."

As Jena went limp in the bald guy's arms, he lifted her off her feet and carried her away.

* * *

When Joseph checked his watch and saw he had only a few hours until lunch, he scribbled his last edit on a piece about a car fire near a high-end nightclub on Durant Avenue.

A tip came in early this morning that the incident was thought to be a hired hit. Although the victim had been burned beyond recognition and the police remained tight-lipped, word still traveled. According to the club's owner and the registration on the vehicle, the unidentified victim was thought to be the head physician at the Summit Behavioral Institute. And that wasn't the only angle he had to go on. His informant had more pressing information on the institute. Apparently, it had been recently shut down due to an illegal research operation with a big pharmaceutical company. Going by his source's details, the institute was getting paid to experiment on their own patients. But there were two missing pieces of the story. The name of the pharmaceutical company and the type of experiments the institute was doing. But for some reason, deep down, his intuition told him Adam and Eve Pharmaceuticals was somehow involved.

With all the violent crimes, drug trafficking, and prostitution in the city, there was plenty of news to keep him busy. Although he'd been holding out for the perfect article that would lead to a promotion. So far, he was just a beat reporter, but he had dreams of becoming more, and this story might just get him there.

Finally, Joseph put the article aside and focused on his computer screen. He pulled up a file he'd been researching on demonic possession. His fingers flew over the keyboard, typing a rash of words in hopes it would lead him in the right direction. He was desperate to find something—anything— that would free him from the unruly and insufferable voice inside his head.

"Hard at work, Parker?"

Joseph quickly changed screens and looked up. "Hey, boss." He faked a grin. "Just finishing up some proofreading."

"I heard you got a big lead on that car fire."

"Yeah," Joseph said. "I got lucky. I happen to know a guy who is kin to the club owner."

"It never hurts to know the right people."

Joseph nodded in agreement. "It sure doesn't."

"Keep this up, Parker, and it might just get you promoted."

"Thanks, Mr. Johnson." He smiled for real this time. "Will do."

As soon as his boss walked away, Joseph heard his phone ding. He reached for it and noticed he had a text from Carrie. His eyes widened the second he unlocked his phone and read her message.

We need to talk ASAP. Are you free for lunch?

Shit! He wondered if Carrie had talked to her boss. If so, did Veronica tell her about their confrontation and what she'd seen? Unfortunately, there was only one way to find out.

Sure, he texted back, adding a smiley emoji. *Where would you like to eat?*

How 'bout Zach's?

Sounds great. Want me to pick you up?

I'll meet you there.

Uh-oh, he thought. *Does she know?* Desperate to dig for answers, he texted her back, *Carrie, are you okay?*

Can't talk. Boss nearby. See you at noon.

He texted back a thumbs-up emoji and sank back into his chair. Seconds later, his phone started to ring. He almost answered it, thinking it was Carrie, but when he looked at the caller ID, he saw it was his therapist. *Dammit.* He ignored the call and let it go to voicemail. Besides, he had a pretty good idea why Dr. Mendoza was calling. He'd left this morning's session in such a hurry he'd forgotten to reschedule his next appointment. The thought of going back made him sick to his stomach. Whatever was on that recording she had, he didn't want to face it, much less talk about it. He'd rather pretend it didn't exist and deal with his problems on his own. Although he knew he had no other choice. Sooner or later, he'd have to reschedule.

"Kill the doctor. Then your problem will be solved."

Joseph ignored the voice inside his head and brought up the file he'd been working on. He clicked on the search engine and typed: *Names of demons.* Instantly, he deleted it, thinking of a better word. Instead, he typed: *Shadow demon.*

God, he cringed at the image that popped up. It was hideous, reminding him of the Spirit of Vengeance possessing Nicolas Cage's character in the movie *Ghost Rider,* minus all the flames of fire it wielded. And then a horrid thought came to him. *Is* this *what's inside of me?*

"No," the Shadow said. *"I'm much more handsome."*

"Hey, Parker, got plans for lunch?"

Joseph flinched. "Jeez..." He heaved out a deep breath the second he looked up and saw his coworker leaning over his desk. "Stewart, you're one sneaky bastard."

"Sorry, man," Stewart said, holding up his hands. "Didn't mean to startle you. What's got you all jumpy? Too much caffeine?"

Joseph shut off his computer and rose from his chair. "Yeah, I guess." He shrugged. "Between that and not getting enough sleep."

"You too, huh?" Stewart arched a brow. "I think everyone around here is on edge, stressed over that new position that's up for grabs."

"You mean the lead reporter position?"

"Yeah," Stewart said. "Don't tell me you're not interested."

"Eh..." Joseph waved it off. "I'm not getting my hopes up. But I can't say I'd hate the thought of landing that gig. That job comes with a lot of opportunities."

"Well, good luck, Parker. I don't know anyone at the Chronicle who deserves it more than you."

"Thanks, Stewart. You too."

"So, you got plans for lunch? I thought we'd check out that new café on Montclair Boulevard."

Joseph brought his wrist up, and when he saw what time it was, he groaned. "Ah, crap. It's almost noon. Sorry, buddy." He dug in his pocket for his keys. "I've got to get going. I made a lunch date with Carrie." He started off down the hall. "Maybe next time. It'll be my treat," he hollered on his way out of the newsroom, waving over his shoulder.

Stewart waved back. "I'll take you up on that."

Shortly after, as Joseph arrived at Zach's, he noticed Carrie's Volkswagen Beetle parked in front. Fortunately, it wasn't too packed and there was an opening next to hers. He wheeled into the vacant parking space, put it in park and hustled to get inside.

The moment he spotted her sitting at a table in the back, she looked up from the menu and waved him over. As he approached her, his nerves were on pins and needles. But before he could get a word out, she said, "Hurry, sit down. I can't wait to tell you what happened at work today."

Joseph sat down, holding his breath.

"Veronica actually apologized to me this morning," Carrie said. "She said I deserved more respect and a big raise."

His mouth opened with the longest sigh. *Thank God.* Then he reached across the table and placed his hand over hers. "That's wonderful." His eyes softened. "Congratulations, Carrie."

"Thanks, Joseph." She intertwined her fingers with his. "But I wonder what caused her to have such a change of heart.

I mean, you should have heard her. She was practically on her hands and knees begging for forgiveness. Do you think it has anything to do with you?"

His eyes rounded for a moment. "W-what makes you think that?"

"Well." Carrie shrugged. "You're probably the first person who's ever stood up to her. Maybe it had some weird effect on her. You know, opened her eyes to her own bad behavior."

"Who knows. But whatever the case, I'm just glad you're finally getting treated the way you deserve. And now you can look forward to going to work instead of dreading it."

"Yeah, you're right." She smiled and squeezed his hand a little. "I think this is the best thing that's happened to me in a long time, aside from meeting you."

Her kind and sentimental words warmed his heart. How in the hell was he going to find the courage to let her go? The mere thought nearly tore him into a million pieces.

"You're pathetic, Joseph. I knew you didn't have the balls to go through with it."

Joseph shut out the voice and simply smiled at Carrie. "Come now," he said, changing the subject. "This calls for a celebration. How 'bout dinner tonight? I'll take you anywhere you want to go."

Her eyes lit up. "I'd love to. How about the place you took me on Valentine's Day?"

"Sounds perfect," he said, regretting what he had to do. "Now, what do you say we order some food?" He released his hand from hers and reached for the menu. "I'm starving."

Chapter Twenty-Three

Manuel left his apartment in a good mood. As he got behind the wheel of his unmarked car, he couldn't seem to take his mind off Kathryn, especially after what they'd just shared. He was on cloud nine, feeling like a teenager all over again. Today was officially their first kiss.

Before he switched on the ignition, he closed his eyes and pictured her face. Without a doubt, Kathryn Hobbs was flat-out gorgeous. She had long, silky blonde hair, piercing blue eyes, skin that smelled like blooming roses, lips deliciously soft, not to mention a figure to die for. It all seemed too good to be true. He almost felt like pinching himself to make sure he wasn't dreaming.

The males at the hospital she worked at, and some females for that matter, were all goo-goo eyes for her, and Manuel had to give her props. She never mixed business with pleasure. She took her job seriously and kept everything professional. He'd witnessed her expertise firsthand. Kathryn was a damn good nurse. Besides, by now, everyone at the hospital realized she was hands off. Occasionally, during lunch, he'd pop in for a visit. And by the way he looked at her, it was clear to all the guys and gals she was taken. Plus, he had a pretty good idea his badge and gun had something to do with it. To some, a shield and a weapon looked intimidating.

A half hour later, he pulled into the precinct and parked his car near the front entrance. As soon as he set foot in the building, he noticed his partner standing outside their captain's office, waving him over. Frank was dressed in his normal attire: tan slacks, dress shirt, and a matching tie. And along with his neatly pressed and tidy outfit, he wore a classic crew cut. Frank was the type who everyone got along with. It took a lot to get under his skin, but when he got mad, you'd be the first to know. On occasion, he'd bend the rules a bit, especially if it came to helping others. He would give the shirt off his back for just about anyone. But in most cases, he did things by the book. And no matter what, he was willing to do whatever it took to bring justice to those who deserved it.

Manuel, on the other hand, sported more of a rugged look. Nothing fancy, just blue jeans, a button-down shirt, and a pair of worn-out cowboy boots. On chilly mornings and late-night crime investigations, he always wore the same old leather jacket he'd had for years. Manuel wasn't always easy to get along with. He was slow-to-warm-up-to, hot-headed and had a smart mouth that usually got him a tongue-lashing from his captain. Although he resembled the handsome Spanish actor, Antonio Banderas, his hairdo favored James Dean's. He kept it cut short in the back with longer lengths on top, styled in a sweep-back. When it came to getting things done, he made no bones about it. Manuel was old school. And he'd fight dirty if that's what it took. He was in his fifties, but still, he could give a young man a run for his money. During his years boxing, he'd developed an iron-jaw and one helluva mean left hook. Aside from his tough exterior, Manuel always fought for the people he cared about, the innocents, and for justice.

As Manuel strode up to where his partner was waiting, he held up a halting hand. "I know, I know. I'm late. You don't have to ride my ass."

"What the hell took you so long?" Frank asked, a hint of frustration in his voice. "You were supposed to be here an hour ago. The captain's 'bout ready to tear you a new one, if you catch my drift."

"Cut me some slack. I have a good excuse."

"Yeah?" Frank cocked a brow, his eyes roaming over Manuel's face. "Does it have anything to do with that lipstick stain?"

"Huh?" Manuel looked at Frank puzzled. "What are you talking about?"

"I'm talking about the red lipstick you're wearing." Frank chuckled. "I have to say, that color really suits you. It goes great with your outfit."

"Shit." Manuel grumbled and quickly wiped at his mouth with the back of his hand. "Thanks smart-ass."

Frank's lips curved up. "Sounds like someone finally got the nerve to make a move. I didn't think you had it in you, Detective."

"Ah, shut your pie-hole, already," Manuel shot back. "And stop busting my balls."

"Come on, partner." Frank gestured to their captain's door. "Ladies first."

Manuel rolled his eyes and reached for the door. The second he opened it, a booming voice came from inside. "It's about damn time."

"Sorry, Cap." Manuel slumped his shoulders. "Got caught in traffic."

"Traffic my ass," Captain Hodge gritted out. "Cut the shit, Detective. You know I don't have patience for lame excuses or tardiness. We've got a ton of work to do on this case. Are you ready or not?"

Frank stood beside Manuel wide-eyed as though he was anticipating an ass chewing next.

"I'm all eyes and ears, Cap," Manuel said.

"Listen, we've all been up half the damn night," Captain Hodge said. "I know you're exhausted. Hell, I've already went through a whole pot of coffee. And neither of us are exactly spring chickens. But crime never stops, and we've got to stay on top of this. If we sit around on our asses, something's liable to get overlooked. We can't let that happen. We owe justice to those innocent people who were taken against their will, especially Judge Weaver's granddaughter. That poor young girl will probably never be the same. What was done to her and the others goes beyond reason." He looked between the two detectives with a stern but wholehearted expression. "So, are we ready to find the bastards who are responsible and put them where they belong?"

Manuel and Frank answered in unison, "Yes, Captain."

"All right then. Let's get cracking. Right before you two decided to stroll in, I received a call from the coroner."

Abruptly, there was a knock at the door. When they turned to look, the door cracked open.

"Captain..." Detective Palmer said as he stuck his face inside. "We've got a report on a kidnapping in broad daylight right outside Parkside Café, located at Stinson Beach."

Captain Hodge rose from his chair and cursed under his breath. "All right." He motioned the detective inside. "Give us the rundown."

Detective Palmer pushed through the door. "A young woman in her twenties, blonde, about five-nine. Witnesses said she had an altercation with two other women. Apparently after she knocked them unconscious, two men intervened and took the girl against her will."

"Do we have an ID on the girl?" the captain asked.

The detective shook his head. "As far as we know, she was alone. Witnesses said she and the two men dined at the Parkside Café right before the incident. There's a good chance we might be able to get a visual from the café's video footage."

Captain Hodge averted his eyes from the detective and focused on Manuel and Frank. "I want you two on this. But as soon as you're done, haul your asses back. The coroner got a positive ID on the victim from the car fire. Turns out it was that physician from the Summit Behavioral Institute."

"Dr. Leonard Manos?" Manuel asked.

When his captain nodded, Frank said, "Damn. There goes our lead suspect."

"Tell me about it," Captain Hodge said. "Although there's a positive side to all this madness. Judge Weaver came through on that search warrant for A&E Pharmaceuticals."

"Sorry, Cap," Manuel said. "But if you've got a search warrant, shouldn't that be our top priority? I mean, there's plenty of qualified guys here in the precinct you can send to investigate that kidnapping."

"I said Judge Weaver approved it," the captain said. "I didn't say I had it in my hands just yet. Besides, we're not dealing with your average criminals here. A&E is a multi-million-dollar industry. You can bet your asses they'll be prepared for a search warrant. This is going to take some time and planning. And we're not going in unprepared. So be ready, Detectives. The feds are helping us with this one. They should arrive this afternoon."

"Great." Manuel groaned. "That's just what we need. Someone to tell us how to do our jobs."

"Sorry, guys," Captain Hodge said. "But you know how it goes. This investigation went up the ladder and now my hands are tied. We have no choice but to work together on this one."

Before Manuel got the chance to reply, Frank said, "Don't worry, Captain. We've got this."

Captain Hodge nodded at Frank, and then looked toward Manuel. "All right, Detectives. That's all for now. We'll catch up as soon as you return."

Without a word, Manuel walked out of the captain's office and started down the hall at a fast pace. Frank quickly caught up to him and walked alongside him. "Come on, partner. It's not the captain's fault. You know if it was up to him, he'd let us handle this case on our own."

Manuel heaved out a deep breath. "I know. But still, I hate dealing with the Bureau. You know they're not going to let us do things our way. Solving this case with all their red tape bullshit will take forever. And now we'll have to put off searching for Joseph Harris. I was really hoping we'd get a jump on that guy."

"I hear you, partner," Frank said, releasing a sigh. "But we'll get to him soon enough. After it's all said and done, what really matters is we give justice to those innocent people at the institute. How we get it done is the least of our problems."

Manuel stopped as they reached the exit. He turned toward Frank. "You're right. And come hell or high water, we're not only going to solve that case, we're going to find that missing girl. Then we'll get back to this Harris guy."

Frank clapped a hand over Manuel's shoulder. "Now that's the partner I know."

A half hour later, the detectives pulled into the parking lot of the Parkside Café and parked next to a police cruiser. As soon as they got out, two of Berkeley's finest greeted them. After gathering all the details, the detectives decided to question the manager at the café and check out the video footage. If they were lucky, they just might get a visual on the young woman who had been taken, and better yet, the perpetrators involved.

It wasn't long before the manager, Mr. Jilani—a middle-aged, balding, short Italian—pulled up the video recording from earlier. The second the image of the young woman came into view, the manager said, "That's her." He paused the video and pointed toward the two men sitting across from her. "And those are the two men who took her."

Manuel and Frank instantly recognized the woman. It was Jena McCain. Instantaneously, they faced one another wide-eyed.

"Shit," Manuel silently mouthed.

"I was coming in for the day when I spotted one of them carrying her away," Mr. Jilani said. "The young woman looked unconscious, so I decided to call the police."

Manuel focused on the manager. "What about the two women that were said to be involved? Did you happen to get a look at them?"

"I saw them leave with the other guy. Both women looked identical, like they were twins or something. They were tall and muscular. And they had long, red hair. It wasn't a natural color. More like a dyed job."

"Did you see what kind of vehicle they left in?" Frank asked.

"The bald guy who took the girl got in a white box truck. The other three drove off in a black panel van."

Manuel crossed his arms. "You didn't happen to catch the license on either of those, did you?"

"Sorry, Detectives." Mr. Jilani shook his head. "I wish I had more information, but that's all I have."

"You've been very helpful, Mr. Jilani," Frank said. "Do you think you could identify those two women if you saw them again?"

"Are you kidding? Those two stuck out like a sore thumb. They looked like a couple of female wrestlers."

"We're going to need you to come down to the station to make a statement and look at some mug shots," Frank said. "It's possible you might be able to identify those two women if you come across their photos."

"Of course. I'll do whatever I can to help."

"And we're going to need that video recording as evidence," Manuel said.

"Yeah, sure. Like I said, whatever I can do to help."

The minute the detectives got what they needed and made it back to the vehicle, Manuel took Frank aside. "Something tells me this has to do with A&E Pharmaceuticals. Why else would someone drug Jena and take her against her will?"

Frank dragged a hand over his short-trimmed hair. "If you're right on this, we've got to inform the Breedline Covenant. And God..." He sighed. "When Nicolas finds out, all hell will break loose."

"Yeah." Manuel blew out a deep breath. "Things are about to get personal, and bloody."

Chapter Twenty-Four

Jena was desperate to open her eyes. As much as she fought to open them, she found it useless. It was as though her lids were stitched shut. *Am I dreaming or dying?* She'd never expected death to feel like this. So quiet, so lonely. "Nicolas..."

She was struggling against the silence, fighting to overcome the darkness that was fast closing in. It wasn't long before she slipped into a dream.

Underneath the light of a pale moon, surrounded by a thick layer of fog, she ran so fast her feet barely touched the ground. With long strides, she continued to make her way toward an old cemetery. It seemed so familiar somehow, but she couldn't understand why.

As she approached the entrance, the wrought-iron gates were wide open as if they were inviting her to enter. She jogged past row after row of graves with cracked and worn headstones. Some of the stones were simple rectangles, others had rounded shoulders, and a few had flowers arranged over the tops. And that's when she heard a noise. It was the sound of twigs snapping underfoot. With her heart stuck in her throat, she instantly stopped in her tracks. She could hear the rhythm of heavy breathing coming from behind. She could almost feel the warm breaths on the back of her neck.

The moment she turned to look, she was caught by surprise and knocked to the ground. She closed her eyes as terror and pain exploded within her. Lying there on her back in the wet, soggy grass, among all the dead bodies buried deep below, she suddenly felt trapped. When she lifted her lids, a shadowy figure stared down at her. It was so dark she couldn't tell if it was a man, or a woman, but by the weight pinning her down, it was surely a man. She immediately feared for her life. When she opened her mouth to scream, a large hand silenced her.

A man stood above Jena and watched her. By the rolling of her eyes underneath her closed lids, and the whimper that escaped her lips, he realized she was dreaming. Although it sounded more like a nightmare. And he wondered who Nicolas was.

Her eyes bulged as the man drew his face closer. Although she couldn't place a name, his features seemed vaguely familiar. He had stringy dark hair that hung past his shoulders in a tangled mess and a scar on his ugly face. Her stomach churned at the strong odor that wafted from his rank breath and the ungodly smell of his cologne. As she struggled under his weight, his hands shot out and seized her wrists. All the things Jena had heard about rape feverishly rushed through her mind. Thinking fast, she let out a visceral scream.

He quickly released one of her wrists and slapped her hard across the face.

Jena squeezed her eyes shut and cried out in pain. In an instant, she tasted blood.

When he forced her legs apart and reached down to unzip the front of his pants, she suddenly caught an overwhelming scent. Not the sickening smell of his breath, but a stench of evil. The permeating odor mixed with his cheap cologne nearly made her gag. Within seconds, her skin crawled with a wild sensation. She felt a tickling of tiny hairs as they erupted from every pore. And her fingernails expanded with long, sharp claws. She could even feel her gums throbbing with a raw sense of power until her teeth lengthened, forming into sharp points.

Before the man freed himself from his jockey shorts, Jena lunged at his jugular like a rabid dog. In utter shock, he gripped desperately at his throat and opened his mouth with a wet, gurgling gasp. As he toppled over on his back, she quickly moved to her feet. She stood over him, staring into his horrified gaze, and spoke in a deep, distorted voice. "When I finish my run, I'm coming back..." She arrogantly grinned, her ivory fangs shining under the light of the full moon. "...to eat you."

"Miss McCain..."

Then she heard an unfamiliar voice from somewhere. Was she still dreaming? It was calling out to her as though it was coming from a faraway distance.

When Jena finally regained consciousness and opened her eyes, an image of a man suddenly came into view. He was looming over her with an enthusiastic expression in his steely blue eyes. The surgical mask he had on kept his features hidden, but she could tell he was older by the creases on his forehead and wrinkles etched in the corners of his eyes.

She struggled to move her arms and legs, but unfortunately, they wouldn't budge. She'd been secured with metal clamps to some sort of platform. Even her head was bound to the unholy contraption. The only thing she could move was her mouth. And it was as dry as sandpaper. So dry, her tongue stuck to the roof of her mouth. She was so angry she wanted to slap that look off his face.

Finally, she couldn't stand the weight of his stare and managed to get her tongue to work. "Who-who..." Her words slurred. "...are you?"

The moment he tore off his mask, his expression changed. The lines on his forehead deepened and he looked over her face with a clinical eye. It made her uncomfortable, like she was a bug under a microscope. She noticed his features had a slightly Latin American cast and he appeared to be in his fifties or perhaps older. His short-trimmed hair was coal-black with flecks of gray. By the white lab coat he wore, and the stethoscope draped around his neck, he was obviously a physician of some kind.

"I don't believe we've been formally introduced." He grinned perfectly white teeth. "My name is Dr. Henry Michaels."

"What the hell do you want with me?"

"Calm down, Miss McCain." He held up a hand. "I'm not going to harm you. I just want to learn about *what* you are."

"I don't know what you're talking about."

"Oh, come now." He cocked a brow. "You can drop the act. I already know all about the Breedline species and your little secret."

She snarled her upper lip. "You have no idea what you're dealing with."

"On the contrary, I know quite a bit. The only thing that has me stumped is how you bring on your creature. Are you able to shift of your own free will or does the full moon bring forth the change?"

She kept silent and fixed her eyes on his calculating stare, swearing to God Almighty she'd take her secret to the grave.

"Stop with all the bullshit," she finally said. "I want to know the truth." Her voice grew insistent. "Tell me the real reason why you've brought me here."

The physician's eyes grew shadowed and suddenly he looked angered by her demanding words. And there was also a coldness to his expression. The look of a madman. Then he released a deep breath and lightly patted her on the shoulder.

"I'll leave you to think about your next choice of words, Miss McCain." As he turned to leave, he paused and added, "There's one more thing you should know. My *patience* only goes so far." He heavily emphasized the word *patience*. "When I return, I'll expect an answer to my questions."

At the sound of the door closing, Jena shut her eyes and squeezed them tight. She was so angry. And what was more irritating, she couldn't shift. Whatever her kidnappers had given her must be affecting her ability to sense evil. It was the only explanation she could come up with. She couldn't even smell it. Surely by now she would have picked up the scent. The physician should have reeked of it, but there had been nothing.

If only she knew where she was. *Focus, Jena. You've got to focus.*

But if they didn't intend to do her harm, and had no intention of killing her, what did they ultimately want? *Are they going to experiment on me? Use me as a guinea pig?* That was Jena's worst fear. And how did the physician find out about her and the Breedline? Someone had to have leaked out the information. And it had to be someone close to the Covenant. Maybe whoever gave them up was being threatened in some way.

Jena pondered for several moments until she couldn't think anymore and blanked out her mind. She took a deep breath and tried to shake off the effects of the drugs. She prayed it would pass soon. Her creature was the only chance she had if she ever planned on getting out of here. Wherever *here* was.

She opened her eyes as panic quickly set in. What if this was permanent? What if she'd lost her ability to shift? *No,* she thought. *That can't happen.* She'd been cursed. And to her knowledge, nothing could lift the curse once you had a taste of human blood. Although her fate had been sealed, and her life had been completely turned upside down, she would continue to fulfill her promise. God had tasked her with an important purpose: to protect innocent people and destroy evil. That was her destiny.

Anger and then determination coursed through her veins. Jena sucked in air through her nose and slowly released it. *Calm down. You've got to come up with a plan. Somehow, you've got to find a way out of this place.*

Her adrenaline suddenly kicked in when she heard the creak of a door opening. She swallowed and remained quiet, straining to hear even the slightest noise. As soon as she heard footsteps creeping along the floor, fear gripped her throat until she could barely draw in a breath.

They were getting closer and closer. In anticipation, her eyes frantically moved side-to-side. She was desperate to catch a glimpse before they came up on her. And then a face appeared.

Instantly, Jena flinched and let out a surprised gasp.

It was a woman. A woman with long, dark hair. She had it pulled back, away from her pale face. Her features were lovely, but excessively thin. The sharp angles of her face appeared frail and weak. Although her dark eyes had a pinpoint look to them, they also radiated kindness. She reminded Jena of an angel. A guardian angel. The thought eased her in a strange way.

"Shhh..." the woman whispered, holding a finger to her lips. "Don't be afraid." Her voice was soft and as caring as her eyes. "My name is Fiona. And I'm here to help you."

"Who are these people?" Jena kept her voice low. "And what do they want with me?"

"I don't have time to explain." Fiona started working at the restraints that bound Jena's arms. "But trust me, they will never let you go. And I can't bear the thought if something bad happened to you."

As soon as Fiona freed Jena's arms and legs, she went to work on the metal clamp strapped over her forehead. The moment Jena felt completely free of the restricting device, she raised her head so that her gaze met Fiona's.

Jena slowly pulled herself up. "Thank you, Fiona."

The woman's features quickly brightened and then shifted into seriousness. "There's not much time." She offered Jena a small handgun and motioned toward the door. "Quickly, you must hurry."

Jena looked down at the gun in her hand and then back up at Fiona. "What about you? Aren't you coming with me?"

"There are others." Fiona looked between Jena and the door. "I cannot leave them behind."

"I promise you," Jena said as she hurried to her feet. "If I manage to get out of here, I will come back for you. And I'll bring help."

The dark-haired woman nodded a silent understanding. "I've sent the guard posted outside your door for a nurse. You've got at least eight to ten minutes before he returns. As you step out the door, take a left. Keep going until you come to an exit. That door will lead you to a stairwell. When you get to the bottom, there's a manhole. Once you open it, there's a secret underground passageway that will lead you to safety."

"Do you know where this passageway ends up?"

"It will take you an hour to get there," Fiona pointed out. "But eventually, it will lead you to the Berkeley Fire Trails. You're going to need a flashlight to guide you through the tunnels and provisions for the journey. As you climb down into the manhole, you'll find a small rucksack with those things. It's the best I could do in such short notice."

Jena opened the door, and before she rushed out, she glanced back at Fiona and smiled. Seconds later, she followed Fiona's instructions, realizing she only had moments before it was discovered she'd escaped. Finally, as she made it to the exit, her pulse suddenly leapt into her throat at the sound of oncoming footsteps. And then she heard a voice call out, "Stop!"

On instinct, Jena spun around and aimed the gun.

Dr. Michaels quickly raised his hands and took a few steps back. "Miss McCain, there's no way out of here, so put the weapon down."

She shook her head. "No way, asshole. Either you stay back, or I swear... I'll shoot you."

His Adam's apple bobbed as he swallowed. "Come now." He took a step forward. "Let's talk about this."

"I'm warning you." Jena raised her voice. "Stay back!"

He lowered his arms and then took another step. Jena squeezed the trigger, sending him to his knees with his hand over his left arm.

He looked up at her completely shocked. "Y-you shot me."

"Well?" She shrugged. "I warned you." *Dumbass.*

When she turned and fled through the exit, she heard the physician cursing in anger.

* * *

As Nicolas gathered firewood outside his cabin, an unsettling feeling suddenly came over him. It left him light-headed and somewhat sick to his stomach. The second he became unsteady on his feet, he dropped the wood plank he had in his hand and propped himself against a tree. He lowered his head, trying to regain his bearings, and took a long, shuddering breath. And then it hit him. Something was wrong. He quickly lifted his chin and stared blankly at his surroundings. Rage and confusion swirled inside his head, clouding his thinking. *Oh God... Jena...*

Everything inside screamed at him that she was in danger. In a panic, he turned in a rapid circle. When he came to a stop, he gathered himself and instantly reached into the back pocket of his pants to retrieve his phone. As soon as he brought up the caller ID and found Jena's number, he quickly hit send. The second it started to ring, he said a silent prayer. *Please God... I'm begging you. Please let her answer.*

He let it ring until finally it went to her voicemail. After the beep, he left a message. "Please, Jena. Call me as soon as you get this. Something doesn't feel right." He let out a ragged breath. "I just need to know that you're all right. Anyway, call me. I love you."

It wasn't but a few seconds after he ended the call, his phone went off. Thinking it was Jena, a sense of relief quickly took hold. But when he looked at the caller ID and saw that instead it was Tim Ross calling, his heart sank.

Nicolas swiped to answer. "Tim..." His voice sounded desperate. "Have you seen Jena?"

There was a brief period of silence on the other end. Finally, Tim reluctantly said, "Nicolas, there's something I need to tell you."

Oh God. "It's about Jena, isn't it?"

He held his breath and waited for Tim's answer, praying he was wrong and Jena was okay.

"I'm sorry, Nicolas. She's been taken."

"Taken? But how? Who...?"

"I just got off the phone with Detective Sanchez," Tim said. "They have a witness at the Parkside Café at Stinson Beach who stated she was approached by two women. Soon after, they had a physical confrontation. Jena was successful at taking them down, but then two men tranquilized and abducted her. Both Detectives Sanchez and Perkins have a pretty good idea A&E Pharmaceuticals are involved."

"Dammit, I'm two hours away," Nicolas said. "I'm heading there right now. And I swear if anyone even lays a hand on her—"

"Trust me, buddy," Tim said. "I completely understand. As we speak, Manuel and his partner are working on this. By the time you arrive, they should be here, and hopefully they'll have a lead on Jena's abductors. And I promise, as God as my witness, we're going to get her back."

It wasn't long after the detectives arrived at the Breedline Covenant that Nicolas burst into the room where they were gathered with Tim, Drakon, and Roman.

Nicolas's eyes nervously roamed over the group of men. "What did you find out?"

Manuel stepped forward. "The manager at the Parkside Café who witnessed Jena being taken identified the women that were involved."

Nicolas looked at the detective in question. "Who are they?"

"Karina and Kian Adams," Manuel said. "They're identical twins. Thirty-four years of age. I searched their names through our database and found out they were picked up and brought in on battery charges a few years ago. Going by the details in their file, they roughed up a guy in a bar. Apparently, they beat 'im pretty bad. The guy nearly died. Got six months in county for it. At the time, they were working as bounty hunters for Bad Boy Bails."

Nicolas shrugged. "How's that going to help us locate Jena?"

"Well, according to what we found on Bad Boy Bails, it's owned by a guy named Sam Michaels. He's the brother of a Dr. Henry Michaels, who happens to be employed at A&E Pharmaceuticals."

Nicolas frowned at Manuel. "You think this is somehow all connected to the Summit Behavioral Institute and what they were getting paid to do to their patients?"

Manuel nodded and Frank said, "Unfortunately, we do. Somehow, they found out about Jena."

Nicolas looked like he'd just swallowed a rock. Drakon and Roman exchanged *what-the-hell* looks. And Tim remained quiet, but the shocked look on his face said without words what he was thinking.

"But how is that possible?" Nicolas looked at the detectives in disbelief. "Someone in the Covenant had to have leaked it out. There's no one else that knows about her curse."

"I hate to admit it," Frank said. "But I think you're right. Someone inside the Covenant must be selling out information."

"Or they're being threatened," Manuel suggested.

"We'll deal with that situation in due time," Tim said. "Right now, our main concern is Jena. What about the two men that were involved? Did you discover their identity?"

"We got a visual off the video footage at the café," Manuel said. "We didn't find them in our database, but we managed to identify them through facial recognition."

Nicolas's eyes narrowed. "What's their names?"

"Adrian García and Maximum Pierce," Manuel said. "And they're both ex-military. They were given a dishonorable discharge for manslaughter. They served ten years in a military prison. As soon as they were released, they relocated here. I'm not a betting man, but if I was, I'd put my money on Dr. Michaels. My gut instincts tell me all four that were involved with Jena's kidnapping were hired by this SOB through his brother's connections."

Nicolas looked at Tim and then quickly back at Manuel. "So why in the hell are we still standing around? If these guys were hired by this physician, shouldn't we be looking for Jena at A&E?"

"It's not going to be that easy," Manuel said. "The FBI are now involved. And not only with the Summit Behavioral Institute, but A&E as well."

"I don't give a shit about the feds," Nicolas said. "If you think I'm going to wait around while God knows what those bastards are doing to Jena, you can think again."

Tim moved next to Nicolas and placed a reassuring hand on his shoulder. "I promise, Nicolas. We're not going to take the backseat on this. But let's take a minute to think this through." Then he averted his eyes from Nicolas and looked between the two detectives. "What are our options? Surely you don't suggest we wait around for the FBI to make a move, do you? I mean, if we're dealing with what we came up against at the institute, not even the pros are equipped to handle something of this magnitude."

"You're right about that," Manuel said. "There's no way our guys or the Bureau for that matter can handle this kind of situation. Like it or not, we've got no alternative. Somehow, we'll have to come up with one helluva plan."

"I suggest we start with Bad Boy Bails," Frank said.

"You know if the owner is involved," Drakon piped in, "he's not going to willingly give up information that may implicate himself or his brother."

"That's why you always come prepared," Manuel said, arching a brow. "Before we left the precinct, we did some checking up on Mr. Sam Michaels and his so-called bail-bond company. We got a tip that he has two illegals helping his bondsmen apprehend defendants who skip out on their bail. According to the courts and the state of California, that's a definite no-no. All bondsmen must be a U.S. citizen. If our findings are true, the company's license can be suspended or revoked. And without a license, Bad Boy Bails won't be doing any more business."

"How are you going to get this Sam guy to come clean?" Nicolas asked. "It's not likely he'll admit to breaking the law."

"We never come empty handed," Manuel said. "Let's just say our tipster came with a video which has some incriminating footage that won't look good if it's brought before a judge."

"I get it." Roman smirked. "You guys are going to use this as leverage, am I right?"

Manuel's lips curved up. "You're learning fast, kid."

"While you guys are out grilling this guy," Nicolas said, "what are we supposed to do in the meantime?"

"Look," Frank said, "we're all concerned for Jena. And I promise, we're going to do everything we can to get her back. Let us get some information and then we'll go from there. But I have a feeling Jena can take care of herself. She's about the bravest person I know."

"Yeah." Roman nodded in agreement. "And I bet right about now, she's kicking ass and taking names."

"They're right, Nicolas," Drakon said. "Your girl is a force not to be reckoned with."

"I do have to say," Nicolas said, smiling a little, "Jena can definitely hold her own."

"And that's before she shifts into the creature," Manuel said. "I'm sure by now whoever's working for A&E, has already had their asses handed to them. I wouldn't be surprised if anyone there is still breathing. She's probably on her way back as we speak."

Nicolas sighed. "God, I hope so."

Chapter Twenty-Five

The second Jena made it down the stairwell, the sound of alarms going off caught her by surprise and panic instantly set in. "Shit!"

I've got to hurry, she fretted anxiously. *Soon, they'll send guards. Or perhaps something far worse.* And then ghastly images flashed before her. It was of the unholy experiments she'd heard about from some of the members of the Breedline. What they'd discovered at the Summit Behavioral Institute sent shivers up her spine. *Is the institute and Dr. Michaels somehow connected?* She shuddered at the thought.

Jena quickly cleared her mind and approached the manhole, which looked to be cast iron, weighing at least a hundred pounds or more. *Oh great,* she thought as she knelt in front of the round cover that led to her freedom. *This is going to take a miracle to get open.*

She looked up and searched over the small space, hoping to find a crowbar or an object with the capability to pry open the lid. Going by the small, circular keyholes on each side, it was obviously the proper way to get it open. If only she could find something small but sturdy enough to fit inside.

Finally, her eyes pinpointed a metal bar lying on the floor alongside the wall. It appeared to be a hook of some kind. *Voilà! It might just work!*

As she rushed over and went to pick it up, she paused and looked over her shoulder when she heard the pounding of several heavy footsteps. They seemed to be coming from above and moving in her direction. With no time to spare, she grabbed hold of the hook and quickly made her way back to the manhole. Keeping her back straight, she slightly bent her knees and inserted the hook, using it as a lever to pop open the lid. Pushing down with all her strength, she managed to pry it up and maneuver the thing off to the side.

She released a ragged breath. "Thank you, sweet Jesus."

It wasn't long before she made her way inside the dark opening and climbed down the narrow, rusting ladder. As soon as her feet touched the ground, she felt a sense of relief. Before she took off through the dark and dreary passageway, she picked up the small rucksack lying at the bottom of the step Fiona had stashed for her. Quickly, she unzipped it and dug her hand inside. Her lips curved up the minute she identified the contents. Not only did Fiona pack a flashlight and a bottle of water, she left an extra clip for the Ruger 9mm and a silver dagger.

After Jena tucked the blade into a side pocket of the rucksack, she hurriedly passed her arms through the two straps and positioned it over her back. With one hand gripping the weapon, she extended the other and used the flashlight to brighten the path ahead. There was a musky, farmyard odor in the air. As she began her journey through the humid underground chamber, it was like a hidden cave beneath the world, stretching on for miles into the darkness.

As she traveled onward, about a mile into the tunnel, distant noises, more like nails clawing, came out of nowhere. The wicked sounds echoed off the concrete walls. She stopped to listen in ready silence with her trigger finger positioned alongside the barrel. Nerves on edge, she slowly turned around, raised the gun, and waited.

Suddenly, an ominous growl came from behind, raising the hairs on the back of her neck. *Shit!* She instantly realized what it was. As the growling grew louder, pounding footsteps, like the sound of an onrushing bull, started closing in. On instinct, she spun around with the flashlight facing forward and aimed the gun. She gasped at what she saw and prayed like hell the bullets were tipped with real silver.

A massive creature, covered in dark, matted hair and with glowing eyes, charged at her so fast she barely had time to discharge her weapon. As soon as the blast made contact, striking the hairy beast between the eyes, blood sprayed and coated the back wall. It immediately skidded to a halt and collapsed to the ground. Within seconds, the hairs covering its hideous form began to dissipate as though the pores were somehow magically willing them back inside. As the transformation continued, it wasn't long before its beastly features reshaped into the form of a man. His complexion was dark, and he looked to be no older than seventeen or eighteen. At once, she felt somewhat of a pang of regret. Staring into his dead, glassy eyes, she noticed he had a steel collar around his neck and wondered how this stranger came to be. Was he some sort of research project, forced into captivity, or was it by choice?

At last, Jena sagged her shoulders and released the breath she hadn't realized she'd been holding. She inhaled deeply, filling her lungs, and before she had the chance to exhale, something big and immense rammed into her backside. Instantaneously, the force of the impact propelled both the flashlight and the gun from her hands. Thinking fast, she threw her arms out to brace herself against the fall. It seemed like an eternity she fell, until finally she hit the hard surface below, knocking the breath out of her.

As Jena struggled to regain her bearings, an unpleasant odor, like the smell of rotting meat, instantly assailed her senses. The moment she looked from the corner of her eye, she caught a glimpse of a hideous monster. It hovered above her, baring its sharp-pointed teeth. Foam dripped from its black, wolfish lips in anticipation of her raw, human flesh. When the ghastly thing opened its jaws, Jena quickly sprang into action. In one fluid motion, she reached for the rucksack and snatched the dagger from the outside pocket. Gripping it firmly, she rolled onto her side and drew back her arm. As she plunged the blade deep into the creature's skull, it let out a whimper and instantly toppled over. In the wake of its death, Jena watched as it started to revert to a human form. And to her surprise, it took the shape of a young woman. She wore the same type of collar as the young man.

Jena regarded the dead girl with sympathy as she retrieved the blade and then rose to her feet. With the bloody dagger in her trembling hand, she wondered how many more of these things were down here. Shifting back to focus, she tucked away the blade and gathered her weapon and the only light source she had. As she shined the flashlight ahead, she advanced cautiously down the tunnel.

It wasn't but a few minutes later, she heard footsteps again. They were moving toward her, and going by the sequence, it was more than one person. Then the redheaded twins she'd encountered earlier at the beach stepped from the shadows like two lionesses stalking their prey. Their eyes glowed in the darkness as they came at her looking to wreak havoc and vengeance. Although they were clearly unarmed, Jena's odds were still outnumbered, and she did not underestimate her approaching enemies. Instead of taking the easy road and shooting them outright, she took out the first attacker with the butt of the gun, then delivered a side kick to the woman's doppelganger. The unexpected blunt force knocked the woman off balance and sent her tumbling backward.

Jena moved next to the redhead who was still conscious and trained the gun at her head. "I want some answers," she gritted out. "And I want them now. What is this place and who hired you?"

The woman smirked at Jena from behind her gun. "You don't scare me."

"I guess we're going to have to work on that, now aren't we?" Jena said, shifting the gun toward the other woman, who lay unconscious with her arms and legs sprawled out and blood trickling down her temple.

The woman's frosty gaze fell upon her sister and then she looked back at Jena nervously.

"Don't worry," Jena remarked dryly. "Your sister will live. But if you don't give me answers, I can change that in a heartbeat."

"Adam and Eve Pharmaceuticals," the woman said. "My sister and I were hired by the head physician."

"You mean, Dr. Michaels?"

When the woman nodded, Jena said, "And what about the two men at the beach who sedated me? How are they involved?"

"We were all hired by Dr. Michaels."

"Why did he hire you?" Jena continued to grill the woman. "What does he want with me?"

"We're bounty hunters." The redhead glared at Jena. "Besides, isn't it obvious why? You saw those two hideous things. They're Dr. Michaels's test projects. He wants your DNA for an important research project he's working on."

"What kind of project?" Jena demanded, directing the gun back at the redhead. "Tell me what you know?"

The woman ignored Jena's implied threat and pushed herself upright. "I was paid a lot of money to bring you in alive. And the more I think about it, it would've been easier just to kill you instead." A seedy grin stretched across her face. "Sorry to disappoint you, but that's all I know."

Jena scowled at the redhead's mockery and squeezed the trigger. The bullet struck the ground next to the woman's hand, wiping the grin off her face. She flinched and instantly recoiled in shock. "Son of a—" She looked up at Jena wide-eyed. "Are you insane?"

"If you don't tell me everything you know," Jena said, "the next one goes between your eyes."

"All right already." She held up her hands. "We were told you had some kind of supernatural abilities and that we were to sedate you so you couldn't use them to get away."

"Uh-huh," Jena said, waving the gun. "I'm listening."

"The people who work here," the redhead said, "they're getting paid to seek out individuals like you to create a new species. I heard them talking about something called the Breedline."

"Who is paying Dr. Michaels?"

"I don't know." The woman shook her head. "I'm guessing it's the government."

"What else did you hear about the Breedline? How'd they discover them?"

"You're one of them." The woman cringed in fear. "Aren't you?"

"I'm asking the questions here," Jena said, her tone firm. "Keep talking."

"That's all I know. I swear."

"What kind of side effects does the tranquilizers they used on me have?" asked Jena.

"Dr. Michaels supplied it. He said it would keep your abilities contained for at least a day."

Thank God, Jena thought. *It isn't permanent.*

"Get up." Jena kept the gun poised at the redhead. "Let's go. On your feet."

As the redhead slowly got to her feet, she said, "Where are you taking me?"

"You're going to lead me out of here. And if you try anything stupid, I won't hesitate to put a bullet in the back of your head."

"What about my sister?"

"She'll be fine right where she's at. I'm sure she'll eventually come around." Jena pointed the gun in the direction ahead. "Get moving."

* * *

The moment the two detectives arrived at Bad Boy Bails, they didn't waste time as they hurried inside and asked the receptionist to speak with the owner.

She gestured toward the seating area. "Make yourselves comfortable, Detectives. He's with a client, but I'll let him know you're here."

Frank gave her a polite smile and nodded. When he sat down, he reached toward the stack of magazines lying on the table next to his chair. Manuel, on the other hand, remained on his feet with his arms crossed and a frown on his face.

When the receptionist returned, she sat behind her desk and purposely met Frank with a half-lidded, smoky desire. She was practically undressing him with her eyes.

Frank was an old-fashioned guy, and he wasn't used to another woman's attention besides his wife's, so it didn't take long for his face to turn three shades of red. In response to the receptionist's obvious flirtation, he quickly looked down at the magazine he had in his hand and started flipping through the pages.

Manuel was oblivious to what had transpired, too angry over having to wait. Patience was not one of his strongest characteristics. Not even on his best day.

Thirty minutes later, they were still waiting. Frank glanced up at his partner, lifting one eyebrow as he checked his watch. Manuel shook his head, appearing as though he was a breath away from barging into the owner's office and choking the life right out of the SOB.

Every now and then, Frank caught his partner's eye—who was steaming at this point, looking as though he'd swallowed a lemon—and gave him a shake of his head and silently mouthed *patience,* praying Manuel would cool down before he took matters into his own hands.

Just as Manuel opened his mouth, preparing to say something to the receptionist—a smart-ass remark, no doubt—a tall man with a dark goatee came into the waiting area and greeted them. "Sorry to keep you waiting, Detectives. Welcome to Bad Boy Bails." He extended his hand to Manuel. "What can I help you with?"

Manuel ignored the guy's outstretched hand and cut to the chase. "Are you Sam Michaels?"

The guy smirked and lowered his hand. "Yes. I'm the owner. Is there some kind of problem?"

Before Manuel got the chance to reply, Frank shot over and extended his hand. "I'm Detective Perkins and this is my partner, Detective Sanchez."

When Sam took hold of his hand, Frank said, "Is there some place private where we can talk, Mr. Michaels?"

"Uh, sure." Sam pulled his hand away and directed them toward his office. "Please, right this way."

As soon as Sam ushered them inside, he motioned toward the empty chairs across from his desk. "Please, make yourselves comfortable. Would either of you care for a cup of coffee?"

Manuel waved it off with a shake of his head, and Frank said, "I'm good. Thank you."

"Suit yourselves," Sam said as he poured himself a cup and then plopped down in his oversized chair. After he took a slow, careful sip, he leaned forward and rested his elbows on top of his desk. "So, tell me, gentlemen..." He cocked a brow. "...what brings you two here? Got someone you need tracked down? I'll assure you. We're good at what we do."

"I'm sure you are," Manuel said. "We're here to ask you a few questions. And of course, this is off the record."

"Okay," Sam said, his expression appearing curious. "What's this about?"

"Your former employees, Karina and Kian Adams," Manuel said. "Can you tell me the last time you had contact with either one?"

"Uh…" Sam visibly swallowed. "It's been a few years. Why?"

"They're both connected to a kidnapping which occurred late this morning," Manuel said. "We've got a witness who identified them. They confronted the female victim outside Parkside Café. You know, the one at Stinson Beach?"

When Sam nodded, Manuel went to say, "Well, it soon escalated into a physical confrontation. And believe it or not, the victim rendered both women unconscious. Soon after, two men, who we later discovered as Adrian García and Maximum Pierce, sedated the young woman, and took her by force."

"Sorry to hear that." Sam stiffened in his chair. "But like I said, I haven't seen the Adams twins in a few years. I had to let them go after they got into some trouble and lost their license."

"What about the two guys?" Frank asked. "Have you ever heard of them?"

"Can't say I have." Sam shrugged. "I wish I could be more helpful."

"Oh, I think you can," Manuel said, his tone smug.

"How so?"

"Have you heard of a pharmaceutical company called Adam & Eve?"

"Yeah, why?"

"Correct me if I'm wrong," Manuel said, "but isn't your brother, Henry, the head physician there?"

Sam looked at Manuel frustrated. "What's my brother have to do with anything?"

"Adam & Eve Pharmaceuticals is under an investigation," Manuel replied. "We have reason to believe they're linked to a mental institute who has been recently shut down for performing illegal experimentations on their patients, along with kidnapping charges. One of the physicians there gave us some incriminating information that connects the research to A&E. Going by the files we found, they were paying the institute."

"Are you saying my brother is involved with all this?"

Manuel rose to his feet. "Cut the innocent act, Mr. Michaels. We know you're somehow linked to those Adams twins and the kidnapping. I'm thinking you gave your brother their contact information so he could hire them to track down the victim."

Sam glared at Manuel. "You don't have jack shit on me."

"Maybe not with the kidnapping," Frank said. "But we do have some interesting footage of some of your so-called bondsmen."

Sam shot out of his chair. "What the hell is this, some kind of threat?"

"Calm down, Mr. Michaels," Frank said. "We're just trying to find a missing woman. And time is of the essence. But remember, this is still off the record. You cooperate with us, and I'm sure we can come up with a solution before your business gets shut down."

"What do you mean shut down?" Sam asked, pointing at what looked to be a flash drive in Frank's hand. "What the hell is that?"

"We know about your illegal employees," Manuel said. "And I know a judge that would love nothing more than to shut your business down. You feel me?"

Sam huffed. "All right, all right. But I had nothing to do with that woman getting kidnapped. All I did was give my brother Karina and Kian's last known contact info. Henry told me he was trying to track down a former colleague of his. He said the guy owed him money. When I offered him my help, he flat out refused, saying he preferred the Adams twins. I told him they didn't work for me anymore and hadn't in over two years. But he insisted, so I gave him the information in the files I kept on them. I had no idea they were even still living here. Hell, last I heard, those two fled the country."

"Are you sure that's all you know?" Manuel pinned Sam with an inquisitive stare. "Something tells me you're not giving us everything."

"I swear. That's all I know."

"Okay." Manuel slowly nodded. "But if we find out you're holding back anything that could be crucial in finding this missing girl, I'll personally deliver that flash drive to Judge Weaver myself. And just so you know, solving this case is high on her list. Besides, in your type of business, I'm sure you know her reputation quite well. She's not the type of judge that shows much leniency when it comes to criminals or illegal immigrants."

"Yeah," Sam reluctantly said. "I get your meaning."

Before the two detectives walked out the door, Manuel turned to say, "From here on, make sure your business stays on the up-and-up. If I find out you're still breaking the law, you'll be in the hot seat with Judge Weaver. Do I make myself clear?"

"I hear ya, Detective." Sam narrowed his eyes. "Loud and clear."

Manuel dipped his head and Frank said, "Good day, Mr. Michaels."

Chapter Twenty-Six

As Jena and the redhead made their way through the tunnel, the distant sounds of dogs barking startled them. In unison, they stopped in their tracks and turned to look.

"How much further?" Jena asked, keeping her voice low and the weapon trained on the woman.

"There's an exit port not far from here. We should be there in less than twenty minutes."

Jena gave her a slight nod. "Hey, you wouldn't happen to have a cell phone, would you?"

"It won't do you any good. There's no service down here."

"Let's keep moving." Jena waved the flashlight ahead. "And as soon as we get to the surface, I'll be using that phone of yours."

The redhead shrugged. "Whatever."

"Oh, by the way," Jena said, "what's your name?"

The woman briefly turned and fixed her dark eyes on Jena. "What do you care?"

"I don't. But humor me anyway."

"It's Kian. Kian Adams."

"And your sister?"

"What does her name matter?"

Jena furrowed her brow. "You know, you have a bit of an attitude problem. Remember who has the gun. Just answer the question."

"Fine." Kian grumbled. "Her name is Karina."

"Ah..." Jena arched a brow. "That figures."

"Why do you say that?"

"Because..." Jena lightly chuckled. "Parents who have twins always come up with matching names."

"So? What's wrong with that?"

"Nothing," Jena said. "Just makes me appreciate being an only child."

"You know if they catch you," Kian said, "they'll most likely kill you."

"Well, they better bring on their A-game then."

"Aren't you afraid?"

Jena tilted her head. "Of what?"

"Dying."

"That's impossible for me," Jena said. "Seeing that I'm immortal and all."

Kian came to a halt and looked over her shoulder, her eyes wide. "How is that even possible?"

The sound of dogs barking grew closer.

"Come on," Jena said. "We don't have time for chitchat. Let's pick up the pace."

When they finally came to a dead end, Jena trained the flashlight toward a ladder that led to an opening above.

"Well, this is it," Kian said. "If you climb to the top, it should lead you to your freedom."

"You first." Jena directed Kian toward the narrow, rusted ladder. "Get climbing."

"Oh hell, no. You're not taking me with you."

Jena raised her voice a little. "I said, get climbing."

Kian rolled her eyes and groaned as she made her way to the ladder. The second she climbed onto the first step, she looked back at Jena. "If you let me go, I'll give you the names of some very important people."

"What are you talking about?"

"There are people in higher positions," Kian said. "People in charge of Dr. Michaels research."

"I thought you said you didn't know anything else."

"You don't understand," Kian said. "These people will stop at nothing to get what they want. My sister and I took this job because we were desperate for the cash. We had no idea what we were getting ourselves into. When they find out you escaped and took me with you, they'll think I talked. And before they can get to me, they'll kill my sister."

"You know I can't just let you go."

"Please…" Kian's voice took on a pleading tone as she craftily tried to trick Jena into letting her go. "Karina is the only family I have."

Right, Jena thought. She didn't believe a word of it.

"Dr. Michaels hired bounty hunters to bring me in, and I don't believe for one minute he gave you or the others the names of the masterminds behind all this." Jena pointed the

Ruger in Kian's direction. "So, get your ass in gear before I pump you full of lead."

Kian angrily shifted around, cursing under her breath, and began to climb her way up to the opening. When her pace slowed, Jena tapped on the railing from a few steps below and hollered, "Pick it up."

Kian cursed again and climbed faster until finally she managed to get to the top. The minute she pushed her way through the opening, she instantly brought her hand up to shield her eyes from the evening sun.

As Jena maneuvered herself to the top and rose to her feet, the warmth from the golden rays felt good against her face. The time it took her to survey their surroundings, she finally breathed a sigh of relief, realizing where they were.

"I take it you know where we are, right?"

Jena nodded and pointed toward the west. "Let's keep moving in that direction."

"So, where are we going?"

"To a safe place," Jena said, thinking of her beloved Nicolas and everyone at the Breedline Covenant. "Where I belong."

Before they started off, Jena tucked the flashlight into her rucksack and extended her hand out to Kian. "I'll be using that cell phone of yours. I'm sure you've got service now."

With a smirk, she reached into her back pocket and retrieved her phone. "Knock yourself out," Kian said, placing it into the palm of Jena's hand.

"And the security code to access it?"

Kian snarled her upper lip. "It's 0926Karina."

"Thanks." Jena typed in the code to unlock the phone. "So why 0926? What's the significance?"

"It's mine and Karina's birth date."

Jena smiled at Kian's response and quickly dialed Nicolas's number, praying he'd answer. And to her surprise, he picked up on the first ring. "Hello..." His voice was shaky but there was a thread of hope infused in it.

She smiled against the phone. "Nicolas... It's me. Jena."

"Thank God." He blew out his breath. "Where are you, sweetheart?"

"I'm at the Berkeley Fire Trails."

"Are you okay?"

"Don't worry, Nicolas. I'm fine."

Her words made his shoulders sag with relief. And as much as he wanted to get his hands on her kidnappers, he willed himself to quell the fury that burned within him. For Jena, he would try his best to remain calm.

"Sweetheart..." He briefly hesitated, keeping his tone even. "How did you manage to get away?"

"It was an angel. My guardian angel came to my rescue."

"What are you talking about, Jena?"

"It's a long story." Jena laughed a little. "But if it weren't for the kind woman who set me free, I wouldn't be here talking to you now. I'd still be strapped to a table and most likely someone's research project. And now, she needs our help. We have to go back and save her."

"I promise, sweetheart. We'll do everything we can to help her."

"There's one more thing," Jena said. "The phone I'm using belongs to one of my kidnappers. I've got her in my custody as we speak."

"Her?" Nicolas asked. "Are you talking about one of the Adams twins?"

"How'd you know?"

"Detectives Sanchez and Perkins were called to the crime scene right after you were taken. The manager of the Parkside Café called it in and helped them identify the two women. We know they're linked to A&E Pharmaceuticals."

"That's where I was held captive. A physician named Henry Michaels is responsible for all this."

"You keep moving, sweetheart. It's only two hours till dusk. I'm on my way."

"I'll see you soon. I love you, Nicolas."

"I love you too."

* * *

A few moments after Joseph and Carrie arrived at Corso's and were escorted to their table, an awkward silence cropped

228

up between them. Joseph seemed miles away as he sat there looking down, staring blankly at his menu.

Carrie reached out and slightly nudged his hand. "You seem quiet tonight."

"Are you going to break it off before or after dinner?" the Shadow spoke into Joseph's mind, distracting him from Carrie. *"I'd wait until after. Who knows? Maybe if you play your cards right, things may end up at her place."*

When Joseph didn't respond, Carrie raised her voice a little. "Joseph, is something wrong?"

Joseph ignored the voice in his head and looked up. "I'm sorry, Carrie. Did you say something?"

Carrie smiled. "I was just asking why you're being so quiet this evening. It seems like you've got a lot on your mind."

"Oh, it's nothing really." He smiled back at her. "Just a work thing, that's all."

"You want to talk about it?"

He chuckled. "I'd bore you to tears."

"Oh, come on." Carrie lightly patted his hand. "Nothing you could say would bore me. Besides, you've heard all about my job, in addition to all the drama with my boss. Heaven knows you've experienced Veronica's bad behavior more than anyone should. So, it's only fair you get to unload on me. And I'd love to hear more about what you do."

"You sure?"

Her smile broadened. "Absolutely."

"Okay," he said, shrugging one of his shoulders. "There's a new position for the lead reporter coming up soon and I'm thinking of applying for it. I mean, I'm not getting my hopes up or anything, but still, I think I have as good a chance as any."

"That's wonderful, Joseph." Carrie's eyes brightened. "I think you should definitely go for it."

"Really?"

"Of course. Don't you think you deserve it?"

The Shadow cackled. *"A straitjacket, maybe, but not lead reporter. Unless we kill all the other applicants."*

Joseph shut out the Shadow's crude remark and said, "Well, there is this article I've been working on. And so far, my boss seems to be really impressed with it. He even mentioned that it could lead to a promotion."

"That's very exciting, Joseph. Sounds to me like you already landed the position."

"Well, I wouldn't put money on it, but at least I've got a shot at it."

"So, tell me." She leaned in closer. "I'm dying to know. What's this article about?"

"Technically, I'm not supposed to say anything. It's kind of classified."

"Oh please," Carrie pleaded. "At least give me something."

"We'll give you something, all right. And I promise, dying will be at the top of the list."

"I don't know," Joseph said playfully. "This is top secret stuff. I'm not so sure if you can be trusted. If this gets leaked out—"

"Come on." She groaned. "Stop messing around. You know I wouldn't tell a soul."

"Okay." Joseph grinned. "But only if you promise to keep it a secret."

"I promise." Carrie put her thumb and forefinger together and moved them along her closed lips, making a show of zipping them tight. "My lips are sealed."

"Remember that car fire a few days ago? You know, the one outside that nightclub on Durant Avenue?"

"You mean Gemini's Gentlemen Club?"

Joseph nodded. "Well, I'm working that story."

Carrie's eyes rounded. "Are you serious?"

"Yeah." He leaned in close, keeping his voice low. "And I happen to know a guy who is a family member with the club owner. What's even better, this guy is one of my informants and he's giving me all the details. Of course, he's practically charging me an arm and a leg, but it's top-secret information that only the police have and they're keeping all this tight-lipped."

"Do you think this is enough to get you promoted?"

"There are still a few details I'm lacking," Joseph said. "But even if I don't get those, I think what I have could make the front page."

"Wow, this must be some juicy stuff. So, did you discover who was in that car fire?"

"You can't say a word, but according to my guy, it was the head physician at the Summit Behavioral Institute."

"Oh my gosh." Carrie gasped. "Are you saying it was Dr. Leonard Manos?"

"Yeah, why?" Joseph asked. "Did you know him?"

She nodded. "We refer some of our patients to Dr. Manos. He's one of the leading psychiatrists in the nation. Who would do such a thing?"

"He may have been the leading psychiatrist, but apparently he wasn't what you'd call ethical. Dr. Manos, along with the institute he worked for, was getting paid to do some sort of illegal research on their patients."

"What?" Carrie furrowed her brows. "I can't believe it. Are you sure?"

"I'm sorry, but I'm pretty positive. The institute was shut down a few days ago."

"That's horrible," Carrie said. "Do you know who was paying them?"

Joseph sighed. "That's the part I'm still trying to find out, along with the type of research the institute was getting paid to do. Although I have a hunch Adam and Eve Pharmaceuticals might be involved, but I don't have anything to back it up."

"Maybe I can do some digging of my own," Carrie suggested.

"What do you mean?"

"My Uncle Frank is a detective. I could ask him."

"No." Joseph shook his head. "I don't want you getting involved. Plus, your uncle is not going to give you any information. He could lose his badge over that."

"Yeah, I guess you're right. And I wouldn't want him to jeopardize his job."

Joseph reached for Carrie's hand and lightly gave it a squeeze. "Thanks for the offer, though."

When she smiled, he pulled his hand back. "Hey, let's change the subject and enjoy our evening. Remember, Carrie, we're supposed to be celebrating your big raise."

At that moment, a female waitress approached their table. Before she said a word, she stared down at Joseph in stunned disbelief. She was practically drooling over him, looking lost for words. "Oh my gosh," she finally said. "Has anyone ever said you look like that actor—"

"Keanu Reeves," Carrie interjected before the waitress could get the words out.

The waitress took her eyes off Joseph and looked toward Carrie. "Yeah," she drawled, bobbing her head. "Doesn't he, though?"

"Come on now." Joseph chuckled, drawing Carrie and the waitress's attention. "Don't you think you're over exaggerating just a bit?"

"No way," the waitress said. "You could be his twin when he played in the *Matrix,* except for your hair."

Joseph's eyebrows drew together. "What about my hair?"

"Oh nothing." The waitress shook her head. "It's just, yours is longer. More like Keanu's hair when he starred in the *John Wick* sequels."

"*Okaaay...*" Joseph said, rolling his eyes.

"Listen to you talk..." The waitress beamed, cocking her head. "You even sound like him. It's like I'm actually meeting the real celebrity."

"Well, in that case," Joseph said, "is it possible to get our food order in?"

"Oh, I'm so sorry." The waitress let out a giggle that ended with a snort. "I guess I got carried away. It's just that I'm such a big fan of Mr. Reeves. So, what can I get you, or do you need a few more minutes to decide?"

Joseph looked pointedly at Carrie. "You ready, or do you need more time?"

"No, I'm ready to order. I'll have the Shrimp Verde with a glass of Pinot Grigio."

"Fantastic." Then the waitress turned to Joseph. "And for you, sir?"

"*How 'bout your beating heart?*" the Shadow said, using an upper-class British accent. "*Served with some fava beans and a nice Chianti.*"

"I'll have the Creamy Pesto Shrimp. And make that two glasses of Pinot Grigio, please."

The waitress nodded at Joseph. "Coming right up."

When she sauntered off, Joseph looked at Carrie. "Tell me the truth. Are you just dating me because I look like a movie star?"

She laughed. "Just when I thought my secret was safe."

"Really, Carrie." Joseph's expression grew serious. "Why *are* you dating me?"

"You don't seriously think I'm dating you because of your looks, do you?"

"No. I've seen myself in the mirror." He smiled. "But I would like to know why such a beautiful, talented, and intelligent woman finds me appealing."

"Don't you see, silly." She reached for his hand. "You make me smile. You make me laugh." She intertwined her fingers with his. "And more importantly, you make me happy."

At that moment, Joseph caught his breath. God, he'd never expected to hear that word from anyone, especially someone like Carrie. Happy. He made her *happy*.

"Joseph, did I say something wrong?"

He swallowed the knot that had formed in the back of his throat. "Absolutely not." His voice dropped until it was almost a purr. "You said everything right, Carrie. As a matter of fact, you couldn't have said anything more perfect. And you..." He swallowed again. "You make *me* happy."

"Loser," the Shadow gritted out. *"I knew you wouldn't go through with it. Admit it, Joseph. You're completely pussywhipped."*

Chapter Twenty-Seven

After a relaxing evening, Joseph and Carrie exited the restaurant and headed toward the parking lot holding hands. Before they made it to Carrie's Volkswagen Beetle, she tugged at his arm. "Wait…" She nervously gazed into his blue eyes. "I know it's a workday tomorrow, but would you care for some coffee?"

"Say yes, Joseph."

"Are you sure it's not too late?" Joseph checked his watch. "I mean, it's almost eight o'clock."

"It's not too late for me," Carrie said.

"Do it," the Shadow continued to encourage Joseph. *"You know you can't resist her."*

"Uh, sure," Joseph said. "I'd love to. I've heard of this little café that's open twenty-four hours. It's not far from here, and my coworkers are always raving about the coffee."

"Oh." Carrie's voice sounded conflicted. "I was thinking of my place, but if you'd rather go there—"

"No," Joseph quickly replied. "Your place sounds fine. But are you sure your roommate won't mind? I wouldn't want to intrude on a work night."

"Oh, don't worry about Jessica," Carrie said. "She's been staying at Ryan's place lately. And besides, she never goes to bed before two in the morning. Not even on weekdays. I don't know how she does it. That girl can survive on just a few hours of sleep."

"That's crazy." Joseph chuckled. "I'd never be able to get through the next day."

"Yeah," Carrie said. "Me neither. Jess has been like this since we were kids. I think it's just in her nature. She's like the pink Energizer Bunny. You know, the one on that Duracell battery commercial?"

Joseph laughed again. "I can sense that about her. And she seems like a good friend to you."

"She's the best," Carrie said.

Joseph smiled. "So, I guess I'll meet you back at your place?"

"Sounds great." Carrie's eyes brightened. Then she released his hand. "I'll see you in a few."

As Carrie reached out to open her car door, she halted her hand and quickly looked up when she heard the degrading sounds of a man's catcalls. They were coming from somewhere in her proximity. Her eyes darted around, searching the shadows of the parking lot and to the front entrance of the restaurant. But there were too many people to make out where it was coming from. And then it immediately took her back to the incident of when she was attacked. As the horrifying memories flashed through her mind, pungent odors—a combination of cigarette smoke and dirty armpits—suddenly invaded her senses. In sheer panic, her eyes rounded, and she began to shake uncontrollably. Instantaneously, her body flooded with fear and her heart pounded as though it was going to beat straight out of her chest.

"Carrie..." Joseph called out to her, noticing her odd behavior. "Is everything okay?"

When she didn't answer, he moved next to her. The moment he placed his hand on her shoulder, she flinched and let out a yelp.

As soon as she spun around, Joseph said, "I'm sorry, Carrie. I didn't mean to startle you."

"Oh, Joseph, I'm..." She helplessly shook her head. "I'm so embarrassed. I haven't felt so terrified since..." She covered her mouth with her hand, holding back the sobs that lingered in the back of her throat.

"It's okay." He pulled her close. "I promise, there's absolutely nothing to be embarrassed about."

No matter how hard she tried to hold still, her body trembled in his embrace.

"My God, you're shaking." He lightly squeezed her. "Carrie, did something happen?"

His question brought her to tears. While she cried, he held her against his chest, cradling her in his arms.

When she finally stopped sobbing, he pulled back and gently wiped her tears. "Please, Carrie. Talk to me."

"Something terrible happened," she finally said. "Before I met you."

His eyebrows drew together. "Do you want to talk about it?"

When she nodded, more tears streamed down her cheeks.

"Let's go. I'm driving you home."

"But Joseph—"

"It's fine, Carrie. Don't worry. I'll pick you up in the morning before work and bring you back to your car."

She smiled up at him. "Are you sure?"

"Of course." He smiled back. "I'd do anything for you, Carrie. And whatever this is, no matter what, I want you to know I'm here for you."

"Thank you, Joseph. That means everything."

"Come on." He took hold of her hand. "Let's get you home."

As Joseph held the passenger's door open for Carrie, she took one more look around the parking lot before she got inside his car. Everything seemed quiet, except for the pounding of her heart.

On his way around to the driver's side, Carrie settled in, buckled her seatbelt, and leaned back against the seat. Once Joseph got behind the wheel, he reached out and stroked her cheek with his thumb. "Everything is going to be all right, Carrie. You're safe with me."

"You're getting good at this, Joseph. I think she's starting to trust you."

Carrie looked at him with soft eyes. "You make me feel safe, Joseph."

He forced the voice from his mind and thought about what he had to do to keep her safe. The thought of continuing to put her in danger literally turned his stomach. He hated lying to her. And Carrie deserved more than what he could give her. She deserved someone normal. Someone who wouldn't hurt her.

The drive to Carrie's place didn't take long. It almost seemed to go by in a flash. As Joseph brought the Jeep to a stop in front of her apartment building, she yawned and unbuckled her seatbelt. The second she reached for the door, he put his hand on her arm. "You wait right here. Let me get that for you."

She smiled at him and nodded in silence.

It wasn't long before they made it to the door to her apartment. She seemed nervous as she unlocked it and stepped inside. Joseph followed in behind her and waited as she secured the lock.

She switched on a light and faced him. "You still want some coffee, don't you?"

"How about you sit down while I make the coffee. Remember..." He winked. "I'm a man that knows his way around a kitchen."

"But you made it last time."

"I don't mind, Carrie." He placed his hand on her arm. "Besides, I enjoy making you coffee."

"You're so sweet, Joseph." She smoothed her hand over his. "Thank you."

"You're welcome." He forced his hand from hers, letting it fall to his side. "One cup of coffee with sugar and cream coming right up."

While they sipped coffee, Joseph listened to Carrie—although he already knew—as she confided in him about the two men who attacked her. Even though he didn't know her at the time, and he'd witnessed the incident, it was still painful to hear her tell her side of the story. He felt so damn guilty. He cursed to himself, thinking she should slap him for what he'd done. That same night Carrie was assaulted, she'd also been a target for the Shadow. What was worse, he'd planned on killing her. If it weren't for the wolfish creature interfering and killing those men, God knows what might have happened to Carrie.

All this time, he'd been lying to her. And if she knew half the things he'd done, she'd be mortified. Now, here he was, pretending to be someone he wasn't. He wanted to tell her the truth, he really did. But he couldn't bear the thought. Because the truth would terrify her, and she would hate him.

Almost an hour later, they managed to polish off the entire pot of coffee. When she finished telling him about her horrific incident, there was an awkward silence in the room.

"I didn't make you feel uncomfortable, did I?" Carrie looked at him nervously. "I just wanted to... you know... tell you what happened."

Joseph frowned. "No, Carrie. Nothing you could say would make me feel uncomfortable. I'm glad you told me. It's just that I'm..." He swallowed hard. "I'm so angry with myself."

"Why should you be angry with yourself?"

"Because..." He sucked in a breath. "I didn't help you."

Her eyes grew sympathetic. "Don't feel bad. You weren't even there."

Without saying a word, he got up and sat down next to her. "I'm so sorry, Carrie." He shifted her body, so she was nestled in the croak of his arm. "Please forgive me."

The pain in his voice cut through her like a knife. She tilted her head and looked up at him, her expression confused. "I don't understand. Why would I need to forgive you?"

There was a pause like what she'd asked him didn't register.

"Joseph?" Her hand trembled as she reached out and placed it on the side of his face. "What's wrong?"

"Carrie, I won't ever hurt you. I promise."

"I know you would never hurt me." She pegged him with a hard stare. "But why in the world would you say such a thing?"

What are you doing, Joseph? You had her eating out of the palm of your hand.

"Close your eyes for me."

His words surprised her. "What?"

"Please, Carrie."

In anticipation, she lowered her lids for him.

Then Joseph tilted his head to one side and gently put his lips to hers. When Carrie's mouth opened with a gasp, his tongue slipped inside and stroked against hers.

Her heart soared, sensing his arousal the moment he let out a low moan. It wasn't long before the passion between them intensified.

As his kiss deepened, images swam in her head. Images of him undressing her, touching her, caressing her.

"Please..." She murmured against his lips, her mind imagining the feel of his weight on top of her. "I want—" Her voice trailed off the moment his lips moved to the crevice of her neck. The warmth and softness of his breath gave her goose bumps, creating a needy sensation deep down in her core.

"Joseph, I—"

"Say it, Carrie."

She released a breathy sigh. "I want you, Joseph."

Carrie couldn't believe how fast he moved. One second, he was holding her in his arms, trailing kisses down her slender neck. The next he had her on the floor, underneath him. When he lowered his weight on top of her, she could feel his arousal probing through the fly of his jeans.

Carrie's breath heaved out of her lungs in a heated rush.

"Do it, Joseph. Kill her."

Without a warning, Joseph's skin began to tingle, itching so badly he could barely stay still. He could almost feel the Shadow scratching from within, trying to claw its way out.

Oh, God, Joseph thought. *I can't let it take control. If the Shadow takes over...*

Concern for Carrie's life sent his heart into overdrive that only made the situation worse. He quickly turned away from her. When he inhaled a deep breath and released it, the sound of his breathing changed. It was as though there were two people breathing inside of his body. And that's when the shaking started. It began in his arms and worked its way down his spine.

Carrie noticed his strange breathing and the way his body jerked like he was on the verge of having a seizure. "Joseph, are you okay?"

When he turned to face her, she screamed at the horror staring back at her. His eyes were as black as coal and his features demonic.

Joseph jumped to his feet, shielding his face, and stumbled back against the wall.

Carrie shot upright and scooted back. "W-what..." Her voice trembled. "Are you?"

Joseph wished there was some way of taking the fear from her, taking it into himself.

"Fear is power," the Shadow said. *"And it's so much more appetizing."*

"Please," Joseph said, his voice raspy and distorted. "Forgive me, Carrie. I don't mean to scare you."

"No more secrets, Joseph. I want to know the truth."

"What are you waiting for? Kill her now!"

"I promise." Joseph peeked between his fingers. "You don't want to know. I just can't—"

"Can't what?" Carrie slowly rose to her feet. "You think I can't handle the truth, Joseph? You have no idea what I can and cannot handle." She swallowed back tears. "I've seen things that would tip the ordinary person to the brink of insanity."

He shook his head. "No, Carrie. I just can't tell you."

"Why?" She took a few steps forward. "What are you afraid of? I know you, Joseph. You would never hurt me."

"Do it, Joseph."

"Please, Carrie." He continued to shield his face. "Don't come any closer."

"Talk to me, Joseph."

He pointed toward the lamp. "Could you please shut that light off?"

Carrie kept her eyes locked on Joseph as she moved toward the lamp. The second she reached up and switched it off, the room instantly darkened. Thank goodness she'd thought to light a candle earlier. Otherwise, they'd be standing in total darkness.

Suddenly, Joseph fell to his knees, gasping in pain.

Carrie couldn't make sense of what was happening, but going by his sudden surge of agony, she knew he was suffering. And there was no way she was going to let him go through this, whatever it was, all alone.

"What's wrong, Joseph?" She reached for him. "Is there something I can do?"

When he shook his head, she lowered her hand and took a step back.

After a few moments of silence, he rose to his feet and dropped his hands, revealing his face. To her relief, his eyes were no longer black. Although they were wary, somehow the blue color had been magically restored, along with his handsome features, no longer a demonic mask of horror.

"Are you okay?"

Joseph's body appeared tense, as if he were prepared to bolt, but he kept his feet planted where he stood.

"Listen, Carrie. I really should go."

Her eyes narrowed. "Why?"

"You're not safe with me here."

"I don't believe it, Joseph. Not even for a minute. If you were going to hurt me, you would've already done so."

Ah, hell, Joseph thought. She was too good for him. She really was.

"You have to believe me, Carrie. Don't you see? I'm no good for you."

"Yes, you are. Regardless of what you think, I know you're a good person." Her eyes pleaded. "Just let me help you."

He closed his eyes and let his head fall back. Here was this beautiful woman, who was so fearless, who'd just seen something so terrifying, and now she was offering to help him.

She moved closer and offered her hand to him. "Will you let me help you?"

Joseph opened his eyes and looked forward. When he took hold of her hand, he placed it over his heart. "Thank you, Carrie. But I can't let you do that. It's too risky."

"What are you saying, Joseph?"

"I just can't..." He choked back tears. "...see you anymore. You need to let me go, Carrie. You're not safe around me."

"No, Joseph." She feverishly shook her head. "Please, you don't mean that. Whatever is causing you pain, you can tell me. Together, we can fight this."

"You can't help me." He tugged his hand away from hers. "Not with this. No one can."

"But Joseph—"

"I've been lying to you, Carrie."

Her eyes rounded. "What?"

"When I was five years old, I watched my father beat my mother to death. I tried to help her." He swallowed back more tears. "And when he was sent to prison, I was placed in foster care. I went from one family to another. No one wanted me. There's something wrong. Something evil inside my head. A voice. It makes me do horrible things. And I can't stop it. I've been in a mental institute for most of my life. The day I was released, I went to search for my father. I found out he'd done his time and moved back into the house where he murdered my mother. I wanted to make him pay for what he'd done. The voice told me to..."

"Shut up, Joseph."

"What did you do, Joseph?"

"I-I..." He drew in a deep breath and then exhaled. "I killed him. Then I burned down the house with my father's body inside."

Carrie instantly covered her mouth and stared at Joseph with a stunned look on her face. When she finally lowered her hand, she cautiously said, "Is this voice telling you to hurt me?"

Joseph slowly nodded. "It wants me to kill you."

"Traitor," the Shadow gritted out.

"So, what's stopping you? Why haven't you killed me?"

"Because I—"

"Tell me." She raised her voice. "Why, Joseph?"

"Because I love you, Carrie."

Chapter Twenty-Eight

Jena sat in the passenger's seat as Nicolas pulled into the Covenant's drive. In the backseat next to Tim, Kian sat with her wrists and ankles in restraints. As soon as the vehicle came to a stop, the two detectives parked their unmarked car beside them.

Before Jena got out of the vehicle, Angie came running toward her door with a worried look on her face. The second Jena exited the vehicle, Angie tugged her into a tight embrace. "Jesus, girl. You had me worried sick. Are you okay?"

Jena chuckled. "Well, I'm still in one piece."

When Angie pulled back, she caught a glimpse of Manuel and his partner. They were guiding someone from out of the backseat. Her brows instantly drew together when a tall redhead stepped out. She was shackled in chains. Her broad shoulders and muscular physique reminded Angie of a female wrestler.

"Who the *hell* is that?"

"One of my kidnappers," Jena said.

"What the—" Angie started to go after the redhead.

Jena quickly put her hand on Angie's shoulder. "Hold on, girl. You're too late. I already gave her a beatdown."

Angie took her eyes off the redhead and looked Jena square in the eyes. "Are you for real?"

"Yep." Jena grinned. "And her twin sister too. Come to mention it, I kicked their asses twice."

Angie's eyes rounded. "Really?"

"Actually, I knocked them both out the first time around," Jena explained. "Then her sister again. But this one..." She jabbed a thumb in Kian's direction. "...I kept her conscious so she could help guide me out of that hellhole. And when I say hellhole, I mean that literally. I had to travel in a filthy underground tunnel for almost an hour. Not to mention all the unexpected surprises I came across."

Angie cocked a brow. "Surprises?"

"I don't mean the good kind either," Jena said. "I was attacked by what looked to be an experiment gone wrong.

Believe it or not, there's actually creatures uglier than the one I shift into."

"I swear, Jena..." Angie shook her head. "...you never cease to amaze me. And I think I like this new you. You're one little badass."

Jena laughed again.

Tim came forward and said, "Jena, we need to gather inside. Before we make our next move, you'll need to give us a rundown on the situation with A&E Pharmaceuticals and this Dr. Henry Michaels. Anything you know will be helpful."

"Kian will be more beneficial than me," Jena pointed out. "That is..." She rolled her eyes. "...if you can get her to talk. Or tell the truth, for that matter."

When they stepped inside the Covenant, Tessa greeted them at the door, looking at Jena with a soft expression. "Welcome back, Jena." She reached out to hug her. "Are you okay?"

"Thank you, Tessa." Jena hugged her back. "Don't worry. I'm just fine."

"Well now that we have you back safe and sound," Tessa said, pulling away from Jena, "everyone is waiting in the library to discuss the situation at hand." Then she looked toward the tall, muscular redhead who was standing between Manuel and Frank. When Tessa moved closer, the woman scowled at her, but Tessa could see the fear behind her tough exterior.

"This is Miss Kian Adams," Manuel said. "Her and her sister Karina were involved with Jena's abduction."

"Miss Adams," Tessa said, pegging Kian with a hard stare, "My name is Tessa Chamberlain. This is my home and my family. And I'm very protective of both. I'll only tell you this once. If you disrespect either of them, I promise you'll not enjoy the grave repercussions of your actions. Do I make myself clear?"

With her lip curled in distaste, Kian nodded an understanding.

"Good," Tessa said. "Now that we're clear, let's go meet with the others and discuss a few things. And by the way, Detectives," she said, looking between Manuel and Frank, "you'll be happy to know we discovered some interesting information regarding this mysterious Shadow."

"That's good to hear," Manuel said. "We need all the help we can get. As soon as we deal with this situation, we'll be ready to get back to solving that mystery. And there's a possibility my partner and I may have a lead on this Joseph Harris guy."

Tessa nodded. "It'll definitely stay on our list of priorities."

The moment everyone gathered into the library and settled around the table with the rest of the Breedline members, Jena told them everything she knew about Adam and Eve Pharmaceuticals. Which wasn't much. When she was done, Kian came clean and told them everything she knew, including about Dr. Michaels. But not before she tried to make a deal with the two detectives. Although they refused to let her and her twin sister off the hook, they did agree to help get her sister safely out of A&E Pharmaceuticals when they went in to make an arrest. Both women had no other choice but to face punishment for their crimes.

"So, what's our plan?" Jace asked, cutting into the conversation. "And we still haven't found out who outed us to that psycho physician at A&E. My gut feeling points to Sebastian."

"That's why we're all here," Tim said. "And to answer your question regarding the person responsible for revealing our species to Dr. Michaels, that still remains a mystery. But I don't believe Sebastian had anything to do with it."

"I agree with Tim," Tessa said. "It has to be someone who has no close ties here."

"You mean like an outsider?" Roman asked.

Tessa nodded. "It's definitely someone we're not close to. Maybe someone from another Covenant."

"Whoever it is," Tim said, "they'll eventually get caught and brought before the council. And I promise, there will be no leniency. Now, let's get back to the topic at hand." He looked between Manuel and Frank. "What do you suggest, Detectives?"

"We're going to have to notify our captain," Frank said. "We've got no other choice. The feds are involved with this case."

"Are you sure that's a wise decision?" Tim asked. "Think about it, guys. You heard what Jena came up against at A&E Pharmaceuticals. There's a good chance there's more of those creatures. And no amount of police force can deal with something of that magnitude."

"Tim is right," Tessa said. "If you get the police involved, there will be innocent lives at risk."

"Are you proposing we handle this ordeal ourselves?" Manuel asked.

"I don't see the problem," Drakon said. "We took care of the situation at the Summit Behavioral Institute, so why not A&E?"

"Okay," Manuel said, releasing a sigh. "You've made your point. So, I guess that means you guys are stuck with this too. But that doesn't mean my partner and I are sitting this one out. We're going to do our part."

"Don't worry, Detective," Tessa said. "We're going to need both of you. Besides, I think we all make a great team, don't you think?"

Manuel nodded and Frank said, "I completely agree. If it weren't for the Breedline, humans would probably be extinct by now. God created you for a good reason. You all make a difference in this world."

"Thank you, Frank," Tessa said, smiling. "We're glad we have the ability to make a difference."

"How are we going to go about all this?" Drakon asked, directing the group back to the main topic. "Go in with guns-a-blazing, or do we have a better plan of action?"

"If I were you," Kian said, drawing everyone's attention, "I'd use A&E's underground passageway."

"I don't know if that's such a good idea," Jena said, focusing on Kian. "I mean, think about it. Now that I know about the tunnel, and they have knowledge of the Breedline, don't you think they'll be expecting me to bring reinforcements? I'm sure as we speak Dr. Michaels is preparing his men and those creatures for an attack. Especially after what I did to him."

"What are you talking about?" Kian asked, looking at Jena, perplexed. "What *did* you *do* to Dr. Michaels?"

One corner of Jena's mouth lifted. "I shot him."

"What the..." Manuel's eyes rounded. "You shot him?"

"Don't worry," Jena said. "He was still alive when I left him. Besides, I did warn him beforehand."

"Atta girl," Jace said, giving Jena a thumbs-up. "Serves the sucker right."

Roman nodded an approval. "You go, girl."

Jena beamed at Jace's and Roman's outbursts of praise, but soon her smile turned upside down when Kian said, "Dr. Michaels will be gunning for you now. Especially when he discovers his kids."

"What kids?" asked Jena.

"Oh, did I forget to mention that part?" Kian's eyes glittered with mischief. "Well, silly me."

"Stop messing around." Jena glared at Kian. "What are you talking about?"

"Those creatures you killed in the tunnel were Dr. Michaels's flesh and blood."

Jena's face grew pale. "Are you saying they were his children?"

Kian winked. "Bingo."

"Ah shit." Jace grumbled. "We better get ready for an all-out war."

"But that doesn't make any sense," Jena said. "Dr. Michaels would have to be insane to experiment on his own children."

"You hit the nail on the head," Kian said. "He *is* insane, but very rich. He's got more than enough dollars to pay someone to replace his dead kids. Hell, for the right amount of cash, I'd even consider it."

Angie pointed at Kian. "I've had about enough of your mouth. Shut it!"

"Okay, everyone," Tim said, taking charge of the room. "Let's use our brains first and save our fists when it matters.

Time is getting away from us. And we've got to come up with a strategy."

Jace smirked. "And it better be a damn good one too."

* * *

Joseph's words took Carrie's breath away, nearly bringing her to her knees. Her breath was rising in her chest, threatening to explode from her throat. As tears gathered in her eyes, she stared at him for what seemed an eternity. It took everything she had to muster the courage to speak. Finally, she opened her mouth and said, "You *love* me?"

"Of course, I do," he said. "I think I fell in love with you the moment I saw you."

"Liar," the Shadow said. *"You wanted to kill her."*

From out of nowhere, an intense pain exploded in Joseph's head. He instantly dropped to his knees again, gasping into the palms of his hands. The throbbing started at his temples, working its way down to the back of his neck and to the base of his spine.

Carrie immediately reached for Joseph, every instinct screaming at her that something was terribly wrong. "Joseph..." She placed a comforting hand on his shoulder. "What's happening?"

"If it weren't for that meddling angel," the Shadow grumbled, *"Carrie would have died on that bridge along with her parents years ago."*

Joseph concentrated on making the pain go away. With the last bit of strength, he tried to block it out.

"I love you, Joseph," Carrie whispered. "Did you hear me?" She raised her voice. "I love you, Joseph Parker."

Her words slammed into him with the force of a freight train. Joseph lowered his hands and slowly rose to his feet. He turned toward Carrie, who wore a look of worry all over her pretty face. And then he simply shook his head as if he couldn't wrap his brain around the idea that someone like her could love someone like him.

"You can't..." His voice cracked. "You can't love me, Carrie."

"The hell I can't."

"I'm a monster, Carrie. If only you knew..."

"Knew what, Joseph?"

When he didn't answer, she said, "Please tell me. I want to know everything."

"I was there the night you were attacked."

"I don't understand." She slowly shook her head. "How can that be?"

"When you left the bar, I followed you."

"But..." Carrie's words trailed off as she instantly thought back on that night. She briefly closed her eyes, remembering the details of that horrible incident. Then images flashed inside her head. Images of those two men dragging her to that abandoned building. Their dirty hands were all over her, tearing at her clothes, threatening to kill her. Then out of nowhere, something came from the shadows. It was a wolfish creature of some kind. It viciously killed her attackers and saved her life. Then she recalled Joseph returning her purse the following morning. She'd lost it the night of the assault. He'd told her he found it alongside the road and got her address from her ID. That's when the pieces of the puzzle suddenly started to come together. She snapped back with a gasp and opened her eyes. "It was you." Her voice trembled. "You're the creature, aren't you? The one who saved me."

"No, Carrie." He regretfully shook his head. "That wasn't me. I did not save you."

"But, if it wasn't you, then why—"

"Why didn't I help you?" His words came out painfully. "I was going to stop those men, Carrie. I was going to kill them. But not because I wanted to save you."

"Then why?"

The Shadow was annoyed by Carrie's questions. She was relentless, an irritating nag, driving him to kill her even more.

"Because I wanted to kill *you*."

Carrie backed away from him and wrapped her arms around herself. "Joseph, did *you* want to kill me that night or was it the voice inside your head?"

"*We* wanted to kill you, Carrie. But then after—"

"*Joseph, I'm warning you.*"

"After what?" Carrie persisted.

"I don't know." Joseph shrugged. "It's hard to explain. But when I'm around you, I feel different. I've never felt this way about anyone before. You make me feel..."

"Feel what?"

"Like I have something to look forward to. You give me a reason to live."

Carrie almost smiled. And then she reminded herself that they were alone, and that he'd admitted to killing his own father, in addition to the voice inside his head encouraging him to kill her.

"I feel the same about you, Joseph," she said, silently battling with her emotions and justifying her true feelings, realizing she was in love with a killer. "This is the first time I've ever felt this way. And when I said, I love you, I meant it."

"You won't after you realize everything I've done."

Shut up, Joseph.

Carrie looked at him confused. "What do you mean by that?"

"I'm responsible for your ex-boyfriend's death."

"What?" She cocked her head to the side as if she'd heard him wrong.

"I'm sorry, Carrie. I killed Kevin."

Good lord. He was serious.

"No..." A stream of panic threaded through her body. "That can't be true."

"Please believe me, Carrie. That's why you're not safe around me."

She covered her ears. "No... No... Please, God, no."

He reached for her. "Carrie, wait..."

She quickly backed away. "I think you should go."

"I'm sorry, Carrie."

"Leave." She pointed to the door. "Please."

Joseph merely stood there, staring at her with his mouth slightly agape. For a moment it seemed like he was going to say something, but then he nodded and went for the door. He strode outside and jogged toward the parking lot.

On impulse, Carrie shot through the open door, calling after him. When she got to the parking lot, she stopped and looked for his Jeep. It was still there, but Joseph was nowhere in sight. "Joseph?"

It was a long while before Carrie finally gave up and went back inside.

Chapter Twenty-Nine

The members of the Breedline Covenant, along with Manuel and Frank, finally devised a plan. They all decided to take Kian's advice and enter A&E Pharmaceuticals through the underground tunnel. It wasn't the best plan of action, but it was all they had. And there was no way they were involving the police. Humans would be weak and defenseless with the kind of monsters they were about to face.

An hour later, they parked a half mile from the underground passageway to go over the details before they traveled further.

Drakon slid out from behind the wheel of the Hummer and Tim exited from the passenger's side. While Roman, Jace, and Jem all piled out from the backseat, Drakon went to the trunk and popped it open. Inside, lying in the far corner, was a large duffel bag. He quickly grabbed it and strapped it over his shoulder. As soon as Drakon and the others approached the detectives' car, they waited for them to get out. Nicolas and Jena emerged from the car's backseat soon after. The rest of the Breedline crew hung back at the Covenant on standby.

"Okay, guys," Tim said while everyone gathered around. "We do this smart." He pointedly looked in Jace's direction. "No one goes in all gung-ho."

Jace rolled his eyes. "Why do I get the feeling you're preaching to me?"

"Come on, Jace," Drakon said. "Do we really need to explain?"

"Yeah, brother." Jem crossed his arms, staring at Jace with a raised brow. "Try to maintain an even temper. We don't need the Beast rearing its ugly head unless it's necessary."

"Well," Jace said with a clear smirk in his voice, "you might be praying for the Beast when it's all said and done."

Roman clapped a hand over Jace's shoulder. "I know I'm thankful for the ugly SOB. That Beast of yours has saved my sorry ass a time or two."

"If at all possible," Tim continued on, "let's just get this done without casualties."

"Good luck with all that," Jena interjected into the conversation. "Trust me, if we come up against the same creatures as I did, we're not going to be able to talk ourselves out of a fight. Those things are nothing like us. You can't reason with them. They were created for one thing only, and that's to kill."

Tim released a deep breath. "I do realize we may have no other choice. Whatever it takes, we've got to shut this place down. And if that means taking out a few of Dr. Michaels's experiments, then so be it."

"I second that," Jace said. "Let's get this shit done."

When Drakon slapped a Glock against Jace's stomach, he flinched and quickly grabbed hold. "What the hell is this for?" He grumbled, frowning at Drakon. "Since when do I need a weapon?"

"Since now," Drakon said, a seriousness etched in the tone of his voice. "By what Jena explained, silver is like kryptonite to those things. We need to be prepared for whatever we're likely to encounter. So, you've got about fifteen rounds of silver in your grasp, buddy." He raised his other hand and flashed a weapon of his own. "You never know. It just might come in handy." His eyes roamed over each person in the group. "And I brought enough to put in each of your hands, along with some extra clothes. You know..." He shrugged. "In case we shift and shred the ones we're wearing." Then he focused on Jena. "That goes for you too. Cassie helped me pack a couple of things for you."

"Thanks, Drakon," Jena said. "And he's right. We should all take precautions and arm ourselves."

Nicolas turned toward Jena with a look of approval. "Like Angie said earlier..." He smiled broadly. "...Jena, you're definitely one little badass."

She winked at Nicolas. "You better believe it."

"Just remember," Tim said, "silver is also deadly to some of us. So don't get sloppy. Make sure you aim your weapon in the right direction. One bullet to the brain, and it's lights out, permanently."

As soon as everyone armed themselves, making sure their weapons were locked and loaded, something caught Jena's attention. Out of nowhere, the surface of her skin tingled. The second she took a big whiff of air, her stomach churned in protest. It was an all-too-familiar scent—a perforating strong stench of evil. The worst she'd ever smelled.

Jena instantly stopped in her tracks and turned her head. The distinctive odor was coming from behind, igniting her senses along with her intuition. She quickly raised her hand, alerting the others to hold up. They immediately halted their movement and waited in silence, readying themselves for action.

As seconds ticked by, tension crackled in the air. Tired of waiting, and with his usual lack of patience, Jace swore under his breath, then blatantly called out, "Psst... Hey, Jena—"

Jem shoved at him. "Dammit, Jace."

"What?" Jace said with a shrug.

Jem huffed out a deep breath and shook his head.

While the two brothers quietly bickered in the background, Jena's senses sharpened even further. She picked up on more than one set of footsteps, and they were moving in their direction. Up ahead in the darkness, in the wooded area, she saw the silhouettes of what looked to be several wolfish fiends and glowing eyes. As they crept closer, their putrid scent was so thick it rose like smoke in her nostrils. Jena found she could barely breathe. It almost made her gag. Then her skin began to crawl with a wild sensation. The creature within her was itching to be released. Already she could feel tiny hairs prickling all over. She tried to keep from shifting, to stay human long enough to warn the others. *Hold on. Stay in control.*

Jena finally spoke out, keeping her voice low. "Hey, guys." She pointed toward a thicket of trees. "Get ready. We've got company." Her voice became rough, gritty. "And I don't mean the good kind."

"Ah, shit," Jem said as he maneuvered in front of Manuel and Frank, using his body as a protective shield.

Jace grinned so wide, his teeth flashed. "Let's rock an' roll."

"Calm down, Jace," Drakon said in a mock-scolding voice. "Don't—"

An unearthly howl cut him off, followed by the sound of twigs snapping underfoot.

Jace leveled his eyes at Drakon and whispered, "Are you so sure about that, buddy?"

Before Drakon could reply, a chorus of howls flooded his ears, and he had a pretty good idea *what* they were coming from.

The change in Jena grew stronger and had now taken full control. She'd never felt the urgency to kill her enemies like this before. It was spreading inside her like wildfire. Deep in the pit of her gut the desire rose, surprising in its intensity. She was ravenous for their demon souls. And then a voice within called out to her. *Evil creatures! Destroy them all!*

In a matter of seconds, dark hair erupted from every pore and spread all over Jena's body. Before it was too late, she shrugged out of her shoes and stripped down to her undergarments. Everyone, except for Nicolas, looked away.

Jena's arms and legs lengthened and grew, rendering her bra and panties into bits and pieces. Then, acting on pure instinct, a monstrous roar came out of her, echoing throughout the woodland and beyond.

Nicolas stood back and watched, his eyes wide and full of fascination. How delicate and vulnerable she had seemed only moments ago, and now his beloved stood like a magnificent, giant beast.

Jena's dramatic transition caused a chain reaction within some of the others. Drakon was the first. Quickly, he stuffed his weapon into the duffel bag and set it on the ground. Then he toed off his boots and stripped down to his jockey shorts. Seconds later, he dropped to his knees and looked up at the dark, star-filled sky with a deep-throated growl. At warp speed, thick black hair poured out of his scalp and trailed down his broad shoulders. Within seconds, it covered his entire body. The muscles beneath his skin stretched and converted beyond its shape. It was as if something inside was trying to break free. The skin-twisting carnage seemed to have no end, until finally, a gigantic, prehistoric-looking wolf appeared in his place.

Tim's transformation hit him hard. It was almost painful. He could feel the change rising fast, burning with a raw power. His muscles began to expand, splitting his clothes at the seams. Thinking fast, he hurriedly got undressed just as his limbs started to transform into the shape of an animal. When he fell to his hands and knees, he gritted his teeth, holding back the howl that hovered in the back of his throat. Dark wiry hair erupted from the top of his head, spreading wildly over every inch of his body. It wasn't long before he mutated into a huge Breedline wolf. It was twice the size of any average wolf, if not bigger.

Jace looked between Drakon and Tim in amusement as they stood on all fours. *And they were the ones lecturing me,* he thought.

Suddenly, lurking from out of the shadows came several hulking creatures with dark, matted fur and elongated snouts. Their long, protruding canines reminded Jace of Drakon's rogue wolf. As they stalked closer, he noticed they had some sort of metal contraption attached to them. It resembled a dog's collar with strange electrical wires. And that's when he began to question Jena's theory. Could silver really kill those things? With the Glock in his grasp, he pondered whether to bring forth his Beast or just go ahead and start plugging them full of holes. But before he made up his mind, one of the creatures—the largest of the mix—charged forward, snapping its jaws.

That's when Jena made her move. She lunged at the creature with lightning speed, pinioning it to the ground. In a matter of seconds, she had its wolflike head between her massive jaws. When she bit down, its skull split open with a loud cracking sound.

Jace and his comrades-in-arms merely watched in amazement as Jena tossed the lifeless creature aside like it was nothing more than a flimsy doll.

While she ripped into the throat of another unholy beast, Nicolas vanished into thin air. It was like magic. When he reappeared, he was standing behind one of the creatures who was about to attack Jena from the rear. In the blink of an eye, he quickly wrapped his arms around the creature's neck. As it struggled to get free, he tightened his grip. Sounds of bones breaking filled the air. The moment Nicolas let go, its limp carcass collapsed to the ground in a heap.

A sudden fury rose from deep within Roman as he witnessed the bloody scene right before his own eyes. Anger pumped the Adalwolf blood through his body, infusing him with a burst of fiery rage. His body expanded and grew twice its size. Powerful muscles bulged atop his chest and claws jutted from his hands and feet. Instantly, Roman was no longer human. A hybrid of some kind. Half-man and half-wolf. With all the strength he could muster, he grabbed one of the four-legged creatures by the torso and flipped it on its back. It fought like hell to get up, but Roman was a force beyond the other creature. He twisted its neck at such an unnatural angle, nearly severing the thing's head.

It seemed every person present—except for Jace and Jem, who maintained Manuel's and Frank's safety—were engaging in war.

Amid all the chaos surrounding them, Drakon and Tim fought against the remaining savage beasts with unbelievable strength and agility. It wasn't long before the howls of their enemies turned into defeated whimpers, until finally there was nothing but dead silence.

That's when Jena noticed something odd. The creatures—who were no longer moving, much less breathing—did not shift back to their human bodies. They remained in their ghastly wolf-like forms.

Jace clapped. "That was freakin' awesome, guys." His outburst drew everyone's attention. "And just think, you did it without my Beast."

"Don't get too comfortable," Manuel spoke out. "We're not done yet. I'm sure there's more of those things where we're going."

"Then what are we waiting for?" Jace said as he grabbed the duffel bag Drakon had brought. Then he stuffed the weapons and clothes that were strung out and slung it over his shoulder. "Sooner we get this over with, the better."

"I don't understand?" Jena's voice was rough, almost as deep as a man's. "The creatures..." She slightly tilted her head, staring down at the fallen beasts. "They didn't shift back."

Jem came forward and stood next to Jena. "You mean back to their human forms?"

"Yes."

"Did the creatures you encountered earlier in the tunnel shift back?"

She nodded at Jem.

Frank glanced over all the dead and dismembered beasts. "Maybe it's better this way."

"Not for their families," Manuel said. "In this condition, we'll never be able to identify who they were."

"There's nothing we can do now," Jem said, looking between the two detectives. "But I promise, we'll come back and give them all a proper burial. For now, we need to get on the move."

It didn't take long before they came upon the opening of the underground passageway. By what Jena had experienced, once they climbed down, it would take approximately an hour to get to their destination. But eventually, it would lead them straight into the heart of Adam and Eve Pharmaceuticals.

Frank shuddered as he stared down into the dark hole. The thought of running into more of those hideous creatures created an uneasy feeling. "Maybe if we're lucky," he said, "those things back there were the last of their kind."

"Don't fret it, Detective," Jace said. "We've got your back."

Frank's breath hitched as Tim trotted up to him and pawed at the ground. Shortly after, Drakon—who was far bigger and more terrifying than Tim's Breedline wolf—slid in next to Manuel with a low growl.

Acknowledging the tense expression on Frank, Jace reached out and gave him a comforting pat on the back. "Aren't you glad we're on your side?"

Frank nodded. "Definitely."

"We better get moving," Nicolas said. "You guys want me to lead the way?"

"Be my guest," Jace said, motioning for Nicolas to move ahead.

Jena peered down into the dark pit that seemed to go on for miles. When she lifted her head, she gave Nicolas a slight nod. As soon as he shined a flashlight in the opening and started to make his way down into the narrow cavity, Jena climbed in after him.

The minute Roman stepped up, readying himself to go next, he started to shift back into his human form. By the time he completely transformed, he stood barefoot, shirtless, and his pants were split down the seams.

"Damn, buddy." Jace eyeballed Roman's ripped jeans. "Looks like you're literally hanging by a thread."

"Tell me about it." Roman exhaled an aggravated sigh. "But at least I still have my pants."

Jace chuckled. "Barely."

Roman rolled his eyes and began to climb his way down.

"Okay, Detectives," Jace said. "You're up next."

Manuel slowly lowered himself onto the steep stairwell and started to climb downward on shaky legs, cursing under his breath.

Jace looked down at Manuel. "You're not afraid of heights are you, Detective?"

Manuel glanced up with a snarl on his face. "Smartass."

Jace laughed and proceeded to help Frank.

As Frank descended lower, Jem followed in behind, leaving Jace with Drakon and Tim.

"Well, guys." Jace looked back at Tim and Drakon. "Better shift back. There's no way you'll make it down those stairs in your current condition." He tossed the duffel bag that held their clothes and weapons. It landed with a thud between Drakon's humongous paws. "Let's go." He snapped his fingers. "Time is ticking."

About midway into the dark and musty tunnel, the coppery scent of blood filled the air. As Jena and her companions continued onward, the distinct odor grew thicker. So thick she could almost taste it. That's when she recognized her surroundings. This was the place where she'd been attacked by those two creatures. The same ones she'd killed, although their bodies were nowhere in sight. Obviously, they'd been removed.

She stopped and closed her eyes, recalling those dreadful images. What she'd discovered after they'd shifted back to their human forms tore at her heart. They looked so young. Clearly no older than seventeen or eighteen, if not younger. Their youthful faces would forever haunt her memory. And according to Kian, they were Dr. Michaels's children. The physician had to be out of his mind. How could anyone experiment on their own children? What he'd turned them into went against the laws of nature. The circumstances made her feel somewhat guilty, regretting what she'd done. As she lifted her lids, her dark eyes flashed with helpless frustration.

The others, who were following her lead, came to an abrupt halt and cautiously waited.

Nicolas approached her, noticing the tortured expression on her wolfish face. "Is something wrong, Jena?"

Forget about it, Jena mentally told herself. She had to keep her mind focused. She hadn't the power to turn back time. Besides, those creatures had tried to kill her, leaving her no choice but to defend herself. Jena cleared her thoughts, and without a word, she answered Nicolas with a shake of her head. When she moved past him, Nicolas silently motioned to the others. Weapons ready, they trudged warily through the desolate passageway and followed close behind.

A few rats scurried along the path, and their beady, glittering eyes twinkled in the darkness like a string of Christmas lights. When one of the beady-eyed rodents shot between Manuel's feet, he nearly jumped out of his skin. "Son of a—" He caught his breath. "Dammit..." He gritted his teeth. "I *hate* rats."

Jace snickered and Frank had to bite his lip to keep from laughing out loud.

Manuel looked between the two and smirked. "Ha-ha-ha," he mocked. "Very funny." He snarled his upper lip. "Smartasses."

Jena's senses were on high alert, realizing they weren't far from the facility. She kept a close eye ahead, half expecting more creatures to burst from the shadows. But to her relief, nothing but empty shadows and the smell of rotting earth surrounded them. It seemed too easy. Way too easy.

Finally, as they neared the end of the tunnel, Jena stopped and threw up a hand, bringing the others to a standstill. Nicolas followed her gaze to the open manhole. She nodded, confirming her suspicions, and said, "They're baiting us."

Drakon gripped his semi-automatic as he moved next to Jena and looked up. "You're right about that. There's no way they'd leave the opening exposed. It's definitely a trap." Then, out of the corner of his eye, he spotted something shiny. As Drakon turned to get a closer look, he saw something glistening under the light coming from the circular opening above.

There, almost invisible to the untrained eye, was a metal object on the wall in the far corner.

"What is it?" Jace asked as Drakon's eyes zeroed in, trying to decipher what it was.

Drakon held up a halting hand. Then, with curiosity gleaming in his deep blue eyes, he reached into the back pocket of his jeans and retrieved a portable light. As soon as he aimed it forward, the bright beam swallowed up the darkness, revealing what looked to be a door. He noticed the metal exterior was so corroded it was a miracle the rusted hinges hadn't given away.

He instantly turned toward the others. "It's a door."

Chapter Thirty

After a while, Carrie finally gave up on Joseph. She went upstairs to her bedroom and turned on the TV. Paying no attention to what was on the screen, she sat by the window and stared out for at least an hour, waiting for him to come back for his Jeep. Had he taken an Uber? Surely, he wouldn't have walked back at this hour. It was already after eleven and his apartment was at least ten miles from here.

She lay down across the bed and buried her face in her arms. Instantly, her eyes welled up with tears. Before they spilled onto the sheets, she quickly wiped them away. She wanted nothing more than to fall asleep—a sleep so deep it would qualify as a coma—and forget everything that had happened between her and Joseph. But her mind betrayed her, and her thoughts kept wandering. Carrie recalled every strange and frightening sequence of the evening. Bits and pieces of images flashed inside her head like the pictures of a moving photo book. It was of Joseph's handsome face. His mesmerizing blue eyes. Eyes filled with empathy and compassion. It was as though they could see into her soul. Then his features shifted. They were darker now. Sinister. Terrifying. *Evil.* She saw hell in his eyes. They were like two soulless pits.

The images swirled together on an endless loop, flipping back and forth. He went from alluring to unsightly. Attractive, and then to hideous, like Dr. Jekyll and Mr. Hyde.

Suddenly, the images of Joseph were replaced by her dead ex-boyfriend. The whole thing had been a nightmare. And she'd already been through hell. The grisly state of his body would be permanently embedded in her memory. There was so much blood... *Oh, God. It was everywhere.* Thinking about it made her body rigid with fear. The fact that Kevin had been murdered in cold blood—his heart completely ripped from his chest—was so hard to swallow. But when Joseph had confessed to committing the crime, it had left her feeling broken. Her heart felt shattered into a million pieces.

Her mind was a whirlwind. *Should I contact the police?* Maybe it was best to talk to her Uncle Frank since he was a detective. No, she thought. *I can't do that to Joseph. He'll go to jail, and it wasn't really his fault, was it?* He'd told her about the voice in his head. It had been controlling him since childhood, making him do these horrible things. Joseph was a good person. She was sure of it. There was no way he was capable of murder. But the voice, it wanted to kill her too. Was she in danger? *Please, God. What should I do?*

The guilt was more than she could endure—the doubts, the decisions, the regrets, replaying the terrifying images of Joseph's demonic features and the things he'd told her. It all seemed so surreal. *Why is this happening to me? And how am I supposed to deal with this?*

Then her whole body recoiled from the dreadful reality of it all, and for several agonizing moments all she could do was lie there, her mind torn between right and wrong.

As her heart thudded in her ears, beating at a wild tempo, she put her hands over her ears and squeezed her eyes tight. Thinking too much was painful to her now. And the slightest thing just might send her over the edge.

"Make it stop," she cried out, her body curling into a ball. "Please, God. Make it stop."

Finally, Carrie broke. She covered her face, and as she started to sob into her hands, it was like a dam breaking in slow motion.

A knock at the door startled her, followed by her roommate's voice. "Carrie, are you okay?"

Carrie swallowed back tears. "Y-yes." She stared at the door and sniffled, praying her roommate wouldn't come in. "I'm fine, Jessica."

"Are you sure? I thought I heard you crying."

"Sorry." Carrie wiped her eyes. "It must have been the TV. I didn't mean to wake you. I thought you were staying at Ryan's tonight."

"No." Jessica's voice muffled on the other side of the door. "He had to work an early shift at the hospital, so I decided to sleep in my bed tonight."

For a moment silence settled between them.

"Carrie, are you sure you're all right? I could have sworn I heard you—"

"I'm sure, Jess."

"Okay then." There was an awkward pause. "Well, I guess I'll see you in the morning."

Carrie cleared her throat. "Good night, Jess."

And then something flickered in the back of Carrie's mind. *Oh, damn. My car.* It was still at the restaurant.

She quickly called out, "Hey, Jess."

"Yeah..."

"Can you give me a ride to Corso's in the morning?"

"Corso's?"

"Uh, yeah." Carrie sighed. "That's where I left my car."

"What? Why'd you leave your car at Corso's?"

"It's a long story. And it's getting late. I'll tell you about it in the morning."

"Uh, okay. G'night, Carrie."

"Night, Jess."

Exhausted beyond reason and with a weary sigh, Carrie burrowed deep into the purple goose-down comforter her aunt and uncle had given her. It was her favorite color and had been a Christmas gift. The second she laid her head down, she closed her eyes. As she slipped into a deep sleep, her eyes moved underneath her lids. She was dreaming now. Although it was more like a memory than a dream.

Carrie was herself at the tender age of five, sitting in the backseat of her parents' Honda Accord, cuddling her new doll. It was Christmas and she'd gotten exactly what she'd asked Santa for. A Baby Alive Doll. She talked, sucked a pacifier, and sang a discordant version of "Twinkle, Twinkle, Little Star."

After spending the holiday at her Uncle Frank and her Aunt Missy's house, they were on their way home. It had been raining most of the day. Although her uncle thought it safer for them to spend the night and leave in the morning, her father decided against it, saying the roads were fine. If only it had been so.

By the time they'd left, it was already sundown, but the rain had subsided.

Through the dark-tinted window, she stared up at the star-filled sky. They reminded her of the tiny twinkling lights on her aunt and uncle's Christmas tree. This year, they'd put up a real one, decorated with handmade ornaments, string popcorn, and traditional candy canes. For the tree topper, nestled snugly in place, was a plastic, blond-headed boy angel. She could still smell the sharp, woody, and refreshing fragrance that wafted from the pine needles.

Then her mother turned toward the back seat and faced her with a smile. "How are you doing back there, sweetheart?"

"I'm okay, Mama."

"Do you still like the gift Santa brought you?"

She snuggled the doll closer and nodded.

"Have you named her yet?"

She bobbed her head and answered, "Dot."

Her mother tilted her head a little. "Why Dot?"

She pointed at the white polka dots on the doll's pink dress.

Her mother smiled, raising a brow. "Oh, I see. I like it."

She cracked a smile, and it quickly turned into a yawn.

"Close your eyes, sweetheart," her mother said. "Get some rest. We'll be home soon."

A few minutes later, she closed her eyes and let her head fall back against the car seat. The hum of the motor mixed with the sound of the windshield wipers made her drift off. She was in a pleasant state where everything seemed warm and safe.

Suddenly, her eyes sprung open at the sound of her mother's scream. Her father didn't see the deer standing in the middle of the road. When he hit the brakes, metal crunched, and glass exploded. The collision jolted her body against the seatbelt, whipping her head forward in a surprised startle. The force of the impact jarred the doll loose. It shot out of her arms like a bullet and crashed into the back of the front seat. The second it made contact, it started to sing the recorded little melody.

She extended her hand, grabbing for the doll. It slipped through her little fingers and toppled to the floor.

The tires screeched and the car skidded across the wet asphalt and began to spin. Whirling around in circles, she could see the snow off in the distance, spinning and swirling until she felt dizzy. Her surroundings were nothing but a white blur.

Everything seemed as though it moved in slow motion. She watched as her mother tried desperately to reach toward the backseat, her eyes wide and panic stricken.

"Carrie—" Her mother's words were cut off as her head slammed into the window.

"Mommy!"

The Honda careened off the road and smacked into the side of a bridge. The moment it flipped over the railing and hit the water, the world around her darkened as if it had swallowed her whole.

Like in a dream where you could fly, she felt weightless and floaty. Then a gentle voice whispered, "You're okay." It sounded like a woman's voice, but she wasn't sure if it was her mother's. It drifted in a soft echo. "I've got you now."

"Mama?" her little voice called out. "Is that you, Mama?"

When there was no answer, she struggled and strained to lift her lids, but they wouldn't open. They felt so heavy. It was as though they'd been glued shut. "Mama..." Her voice was urgent, panicked. "Mama, where are you?"

A pair of arms enveloped her like a warm embrace, cradling her with tenderness, and a calmness instantly took hold.

"It's okay," the woman said. "Open your eyes, sweet child."

As if waking from a night terror, her eyes shot open, and her mouth parted with a gasp. The darkness around her slowly dissipated, and she glimpsed into the face of a stranger. It was a woman. And she was very pretty. Although her vision was a little blurry, she could sense a kindness in the woman's features. Her hair was the color of fire, and fell over her shoulders in long, thick waves. She stared into the stranger's eyes—eyes that sparkled like green emeralds—and wondered who she was.

"Who-who are you?" she asked the redheaded woman with odd markings on her arms.

"My name is Lailah."

And then her eyes rounded as immense black wings shot from Lailah's back. Bright flames blazed at the feathery tips.

Was Lailah an angel? "Are you an angel?" she said out loud, her eyes wide on her small face.

Lailah smiled with a graceful nod. "I am the angel of holy fire. God sent me here to save you."

Her brows bunched. "Huh?" she said, looking at the angel, confused.

"Don't you remember?" Lailah asked, setting her down on the side of the road. "Your car..." The giant angel hesitated for a moment as she got down on her knees and faced her. "It went into the lake, and—"

"Mommy!" she cried out. Tears spilled from her eyes. "Where's my mommy and daddy?"

"Shhh," Lailah whispered. Her voice was soothing, easing all her worries in a way she could not explain. "It's going to be okay, Carrie."

"B-but..." She blinked the remaining tears away. "How do you know my name?"

Lailah smiled again. "God told me."

"You can talk to *God*?"

"Yes."

"What does *God* look like?"

"I do not know." Lailah shrugged. "I have not seen him, only heard his voice."

"Why not? Don't you live in heaven with him?"

"Well..." Lailah tilted her head. "Kind of. I, along with all the other battle angels, live close to heaven."

"What's a battle angel?"

"A battle angel is like God's special warriors," Lailah explained. "We watch over heaven's gate, keeping everyone safe."

"Who else lives in heaven?"

Lailah smiled. "Good people."

"Is my mommy and daddy in heaven now?"

"Yes, sweetheart. They are with God."

"What about Jesus? Isn't he there?"

"Yes."

"I want to go too. Will you please take me there?"

"You cannot go there just yet."

"But..." Her bottom lip pouted. "Why can't I?"

"You are very special, Carrie. God needs your help."

"What does he need my help for?"

"I do not know." Lailah shook her head. "But I'm sure it's something very important."

"After that, then can I go? I want to be with my mommy and daddy."

Lailah silently nodded and then averted her eyes at something on the ground. She went to reach for it. Seconds later, she brought her hand back.

"Dot..." Her eyes brightened. "You found my doll!"

"There you go, sweetheart." Lailah placed the flimsy doll in her arms. "She's good as new."

She wrapped her arms around the doll. "Oh, Dot..." She squeezed it tight. "I thought I'd lost you."

"Take good care of her." Lailah rose, towering above her. "And stay here." The angel's eyes grew serious. "Promise me, Carrie."

"I promise."

"There's a big truck coming," Lailah said. "The nice man driving it will stop and help you. Tell him about the car accident."

"K.'" Her shoulders sagged. "Are you going back to guard heaven?"

"Yes, Carrie."

"Will you come back to visit me?"

"I do not know." Lailah extended her fiery wings. "Maybe someday."

With the doll tucked snugly under her arm, she watched as the angel took flight. Before she completely disappeared into the star-filled sky, she waved. "Bye-bye, Lailah."

The sound of a woman screaming brought Carrie's eyes open. She sat up in bed, her sleepy eyes searching the room. But to her relief, it was just the television. There was a woman being chased by a large man wearing a hockey mask and an axe in his hand. She sighed, realizing she'd fallen asleep with the TV on. When she reached for the remote and clicked the *off* button, there was nothing but silence now. Her mind drifted back to the dream. And it had been more than just a dream. It was a childhood memory. *Had Lailah been real?*

As she grew up, she'd cast the thought aside, believing the angel had been a figment of her imagination. That she'd created Lailah in her mind as a coping mechanism. After the car accident, she went to live with her Uncle Frank and Aunt Missy. The child therapist they'd taken her to see, said it was her way of dealing with the death of her parents. But now, she wasn't so sure. Besides, after all the strange things she'd witnessed—the wolfish creature who had saved her life and the recent revelation that Joseph was possessed by something demonic, *or whatever the hell it was*—she couldn't refute the fact that the angel might very well have been real. And then she remembered what Lailah had told her so long ago. That God needed her help.

"But..." she whispered. "Help with what?"

Chapter Thirty-One

A sharp voice filtered through the small group like the crack of a whip. "Have our guests arrived?"

Two guards turned rapidly, stiffening with fear.

"Yes, Dr. Michaels," a stalky guard said as he nervously rose from behind a desk and approached the physician. "The Breedline found the door. It won't be long now."

"Excellent," the physician said, the skin around his mouth peeling back in a devilish grin. The deep lines on his forehead and the crow's-feet around his dark eyes told his age, along with the abundance of gray mixed in with his coal-black hair. "They're in for a bit of a surprise." He let out a little chuckle, but it sounded more like a mad cackle.

There was a slight shift in the air, and then a tall, lanky man stepped into the room. He moved toward the guard's desk without so much as a word. His eyes were fixated on a large monitor that displayed several images of the underground tunnel. He stood there staring in suspended silence, watching the camera images. They captured a huge male with a dark, short-trimmed Mohawk, leading the way. Two tall, blond, long-haired men, who looked identical, followed close behind the Mohawked guy. A wolfish creature—the woman who'd been cursed—crept behind the two blond-headed twins. Four other men, of which one he recognized and another who he sensed was something other than a Breedline, tailed the others. The remaining two were obviously human. He could always pick out a human among his kind. It was something about their weaknesses, their vulnerability, and their eyes. Their eyes were the windows to their souls. He could sense they were good people, and with the exception of the two humans, they were very powerful.

He continued to watch as the group cautiously traveled down a dark corridor. Some of them were packing weapons, and others had portable lights guiding their way. They were all oblivious to what lay ahead. A trap waiting to be sprung, and hopefully, one they could not easily escape. He needed them. He was desperate for their help.

When he finally averted his eyes from the cameras and focused them on Dr. Michaels, he remained silent, his expression unreadable. His bloodred eyes were unnatural, almost hypnotizing, and somewhat terrifying. The color blazed like fire. Although he looked a bit sickly, his skin as pale as a corpse's, his features were still handsome. The perfect contours of his face were both regal and masculine, resembling the Greek statue of Michelangelo's David. The veins beneath his pasty skin looked like a roadmap of tiny webs of purples and blues. His long, pale-blond hair was pulled away from his frosty face and tied back with a strip of white silk. The getup he wore accentuated his thinness and gave off an iconic Jim Morrison fashion and an old blue-blooded aristocrat vibe: tight black breeches, white collared shirt with cuffed sleeves, and a pair of black leather Italian riding boots. The combination teetered between a vampire and a rock musician all rolled into one.

The vampirish-looking man didn't waste time with pleasantries. A snarl protruded over his plump upper lip, revealing an ivory tip of a fang. "The Breedline are quite persistent." His tone was snobbish, seemingly cruel. "They have no idea what *real* monsters are made of."

"Indeed," the physician said, clasping his hands behind his back. "Indeed, they do not."

"There are humans among the Breedline," the pale-faced man said. "Why?"

"They are the two detectives involved with shutting down the Summit Behavioral Institute."

"And how did they learn of us?"

"I can assure you," the physician quickly replied, "they know nothing of you. But somehow..." He paused, releasing a sigh. "...they managed to hack into the institute's system and retrieved some of my files."

The pale-faced man looked annoyed, his eyes appearing darker. "I do not want the two humans harmed, nor the Breedline for that matter."

There was a beat of silence, as if the physician was weighing his words. "I have no intentions of harming any of them," he lied. "They will be released as soon as I get what I need."

"And what of the cursed woman?" the pale-faced man asked, his bloodred eyes lit with interest. "Do you plan to keep her alive as well?"

"Of course." The physician nodded, knowing deep down his words were untrue, all the while, feeling the stare of haunting eyes upon him.

"Oh?" The pale-faced man's eyebrow shot up. "She killed your children, did she not?"

A spark of grief crossed the physician's face, but it quickly passed. "Yes, it's true," he said, regretting his decision to send them into the underground tunnel, knowing they were unstable. "She killed my LaToya and Abraham." He paused and swallowed, his Adam's apple visibly bobbing. "But it was in self-defense, so I have no ill will toward Miss McCain. And of course, she will not be harmed," he lied again. "It's pertinent that she remains alive."

"And what purpose will she serve you?"

A slow smile seeped onto the physician's face. "She has a rare gift. The immortal creature within her will benefit my research."

The pale-faced man stepped closer, seeming to loom over Dr. Michaels. His crawling, bloodred gaze slid over the physician in questionable doubt. "How so?"

Dr. Michaels unclasped his hands and leaned forward, arching a brow. "Ah, good question, Lenny. My dear *old* friend."

He emphasized the word *old* because, in fact, the physician's pale-faced friend was indeed old. Eighteenth-century old. Although his youthful appearance oddly suggested otherwise. He looked to be in his late twenties. Leonard Saxon III, or *Lenny* for short, was born on October 21, 1805, during the war between Britain and France. Living most of his life in England, it wasn't until the passing of his parents in 1830, due to the major influenza epidemic, that he left his homestead and established a new life in America.

It was an exciting time, where railroad building marked history, the year Emily Dickinson was born, and when he met Augustus Rutherford II.

Lenny, being an only child, grew rather fond of Augustus in such a short time. He was like a brother to Lenny. An older brother. They'd crossed paths a month after Lenny settled in Manhattan, New York, and found work as a saloon keeper and bartender at McFarley's Old Ale House. He'd acquired the trade from his father, growing up in the little rundown tavern they'd owned back in England. His father taught him everything about bartending: mixing cocktails, including some of his own concoctions, and sometimes while juggling bottles, cups, and mixers. After his parents' death, the business had already begun to fail, and when he was forced to sell, it barely brought enough to pay for the trip to America and suitable lodging. He'd rented a room above the saloon where he'd befriended the owner, Mr. Jaime McFarley, who emigrated from Ireland in the early 1800s.

A year into Lenny and August's—*short for Augustus*—friendship, he offered him a rather peculiar proposition. He'd asked Lenny to quit his job at the saloon and come to live with him and his fraternal twin sister, Athena.

At first, Lenny wasn't sure if this was such a good idea. He'd always been hardworking, and never one to take hand-outs. His parents had brought him up with morals, integrity, and good work ethics. But now, he had no close ties to family back in England, or close friends for that matter. So, with much deliberation, he finally made the decision to accept August's proposal, although he did not leave his employment. Rather, not right away. Besides, August and Athena came from money. Old money. A fortune passed down over multiple generations. And they had more than enough room in their luxurious mansion to accommodate him and at least twenty or more. This new life in America was starting to take off in a direction he hadn't expected.

The two siblings lived an extremely comfortable and elegant lifestyle. Lenny hadn't the privilege of such lavish things in an upper-class world. He didn't grow up exactly poor either. His family never went without food, clothing, or shelter, but by no means were they wealthy.

After a few years, Athena and Lenny's friendship eventually evolved. Their fondness for one another grew and developed into something more. As their passion blossomed, so did his friendship with August. The three of them were practically inseparable.

It wasn't until the fall of 1833 when things took a turn in the opposite direction. Ongoing reports of mutilated bodies of men and women were discovered in the Hudson River. Their throats had been torn and their hearts gone missing. The findings also claimed that all the victims had been completely drained of their blood. Just when things couldn't get any worse, the unimaginable happened. Weeks later, August and Athena introduced Lenny to a mysterious and secret underground group they'd kept hidden. That's when he learned the meaning of vampirism and all the vampires in Manhattan. *But that's entirely another story.*

"Long story short," the physician continued, his eyes bulging with a hint of madness, "I believe Miss McCain's blood contains the antidote you've been looking for."

Lenny's expression was one of shock, his jaw nearly hitting the floor. "You're serious?"

"Dead ser—" The physician hesitated, acknowledging the fact that his *old* friend was no longer among the living, and he might not appreciate his choice of words. "Yes, indeed. But I'll need more time to perfect it. If there's a slightest defect, it will not work."

"How long?"

"As soon as I retrieve a sample of Miss McCain's blood," the physician said. "It should be ready to test on the *others* within the next twenty-four hours."

The tips of Lenny's fangs appeared as a smile emerged on his pale face. "Perrrfect," he said in a dragged-out fashion, looking at the physician the way you'd look at someone who you knew without a doubt was lying. "Until then, I'll be waiting, *Henry.*"

"Yes, of course." The physician dipped his head. "Anything for you." His voice cracked, struggling to say the words, "My dear old friend."

As Lenny reached for the door, he paused and looked over his shoulder. "A little reminder, Henry..." A smile touched the corner of his mouth, and for a moment he said nothing, just stared at the physician with a menacing gaze. "If you betray me in any form or fashion," Lenny finally said in a tone with the intention of inflicting pain, "I will drain every ounce of blood in your body. Do you understand?"

The physician's eyes rounded in alarm. "B-but, Lenny..." He hesitated, feeling the rhythm of his heart as it thundered inside his chest. "What would make you think I'd betray you?"

Lenny turned to face him and flashed a smile so wide his fangs showed like ivory pins. "Have you forgotten, Henry? I not only have the ability to sense when someone is lying, I can smell it a mile away." His smile faded. "And you reek of deception."

Smug bastard! Dr. Michaels swallowed back his nerves. "You must be mistaken, my friend." His hands fisted at his sides. "My intentions are good, I assure you." He faked a grin. "I'm here to assist your needs."

As silence filled the room, Lenny's gaze dropped to the physician's throat. He could see the thick, blue vein throbbing with each beat of his betrayer's heart. When his eyes trailed back up to meet the eyes of a liar, he said, "And what of *your* needs, Henry?"

"Uhh..." the physician stuttered his words, "...m-my needs? I'm afraid I don't understand."

"What do you strive to gain out of all this?" Lenny waved his hand toward the camera's monitor. "Surely, you're not doing all this just to find a cure for me, your mother, and my companions. I've been alive for over two hundred years, so don't think I'm so easily fooled. I suspect there's something you're not telling me. Something that has to do with what the Breedline discovered at the Summit Behavioral Institute." He made a distasteful face. "And those detestable creatures you've created."

The physician's mouth bobbed like a fish out of water. "I-I—"

Sensing Lenny's rising anger, the guards nearly tripped over one another as they cleared the room.

Moving in warp speed, Lenny was on the physician, hovering over him with a calculating stare, so close he could almost taste his lies. "I do not trust anyone who experiments on their own flesh and blood. You should have kept that to yourself, *Henry.* So, tell me..." His bloodred eyes blazed like fire. "What is it you truly desire?"

Don't look into his eyes... Don't look into his eyes... Don't look—

The physician tried to pull his eyes away, but they would not obey. Instead, he found himself trapped in Lenny's hypnotic gaze. The vampire's eyes held a kind of power no one could resist, and staring into them Henry felt compelled to reveal everything he'd kept secret. Then, as he began to spill his guts, he spoke each word as if he were vomiting the truth.

"I-I want to create..." He gasped, struggling to get the words out. "A new species. Stronger than any Breedline. And far more powerful."

Lenny stared at the physician with daggers in his eyes. "Why?"

"F-fame..." Henry said, trying to resist Lenny's spellbinding gaze, but he'd lost the battle before it started. "And f-fortune."

"I knew I should have killed you long ago," Lenny said through gritted teeth as he took hold of the physician's throat, clenching it with an iron grip. "And you're no friend of mine. You never were. I always resented the way you discarded your mother like she was nothing but a mere servant. She deserves a son far better than you have proven."

"P-please..." Henry looked up at him with pleading eyes, gasping for air. "H-have mercy."

Lenny squeezed tighter, relishing the panicked expression on the physician's face, his bulging eyes, and the cords straining in his neck. "You're nothing but a pathetic worm. One that doesn't deserve to breathe air."

The physician began to choke, struggling to get air into his lungs. The room began to swim, and tiny specks of light flickered, blurring his vision. Before his legs went out from under him, Lenny held him steady and drew him closer. So close he could smell the vampire's coppery breath. *Oh, God... He's going to kill me.*

The second Lenny loosened his grip, Henry sucked in a deep lungful of air.

"I'm not going to kill you," Lenny said as though he read the physician's mind. "Not just yet anyway." He smirked. "You still have work to do. And I need that antidote."

Henry bobbed his head up and down, continuing his endeavor to get air into his lungs. Finally, he cleared his dry throat and rasped out, "Yes. Yes. The... antidote."

Chapter Thirty-Two

As Drakon placed his hand on the silver doorknob, he paused and looked over his shoulder, eyeballing the others. "Stay close and be on alert. We could still be walking into a trap."

There was a clicking sound as Manuel racked the slide of his semi-automatic. Then came a similar noise as his partner chambered a round in his weapon.

The moment everyone nodded a silent understanding, Drakon opened the door and poised the flashlight ahead. Then he cautiously stepped inside the dark entrance, with his free hand palming the Glock and his eyes on alert. A strange noise, like the sound of wings flapping, halted his movement. It was so abrupt, Jace slammed into the back of him with an "*oof.*"

"Shit," Jace grunted, feeling as though he'd face-planted a brick wall.

Drakon held up a hand. "Hang tight. I hear something up ahead."

Jace sighed. "I don't hear—"

"Shhh..." Drakon cut him off. "Listen."

Jace stood listening, his head slightly tilted, one eyebrow cocked, wondering what the hell Drakon had heard. He couldn't make out a thing.

After a few minutes had passed and nothing made a peep, Jena slowly crept forward. "I don't hear anything," she said, trying to keep her guttural voice low.

Jace looked to Jena. "That's what *I* said."

"What exactly did you hear?" Tim asked.

"I'm not sure." Drakon shook his head. "But it sounded like a bird or something. I could have sworn I heard wings flapping."

"Maybe it was just your mind playing tricks on you," Jace said. "This place does give me the creeps." He felt a shiver work its way up his spine. "It reminds me of Dracula's dungeon."

"Or it was a bat," Frank pointed out.

"A bat?" Manuel frantically looked up.

Jace lightly chuckled. "You're not afraid of bats are you, Detective?"

Manuel shot Jace a dirty look. "Oh shut up, Chamberlain."

Jace laughed again. A little louder this time.

Drakon finally shrugged it off, figuring Jace was right and it was just his imagination. "Come on." He motioned to the others. "Let's keep moving. And you." He eyeballed Jace. "Not so close this time. Capeesh?"

"Yeah, yeah." Jace rolled his eyes. "Whatever."

As the group made their way down the dark underground maze beneath Adam and Eve Pharmaceuticals, they kept their eyes peeled and their ears on high alert for the slightest noise, preparing themselves for anything.

They'd only traveled a short distance when this time they all heard a sound.

Flap, flap, flap.

Drakon halted and the others stopped behind him and listened.

The strange noise came again—a flapping sound—raising the hairs on the back of Manuel's neck.

"It's coming from over there, I think," whispered Manuel, pointing toward a dark corner on the concrete wall. Although it was impossible to tell for sure, considering how dark it was.

Then the noise stopped.

"Well, hell," Drakon said, releasing an aggravated sigh. "Let's just keep moving. Whatever is making that noise doesn't seem to be a threat. If it was, it would have already made a move."

They continued further, readying themselves for something to spring out, when Drakon stopped again. "I see something." He aimed the flashlight up high. "Over there."

The others looked to where Drakon shined the light, and in the distance, perched on the ceiling, were hundreds, if not thousands, of tiny glowing eyes. Bats' eyes. As they blinked, it was like a string of twinkling Christmas lights all bunched in a cluster.

Manuel didn't move, his eyes stunned. And terrified.

"Holy shit," Jace muttered. "Now that's a lot of freakin' bats."

Jem peered around Jace's back. "Where'd they all come from?"

"Hell, if I know." Drakon shook his head. "But I'm guessing this is their nesting area."

"Nesting area?" Manuel asked. His low voice held a blend of distaste and worry. "What in the hell is that supposed to mean?"

"It means where they roost and sleep during the day," Frank chimed in. "This is kinda like a cave where predators can't get to them. They're nocturnal, so this place provides a perfect dark shelter. They only hunt during the night."

Manuel's brows pinched together. "And what exactly do they hunt?"

"Don't worry, partner." Frank smiled, clapping a hand over Manuel's shoulder. "They only forage on bugs."

Manuel blew out a sigh of relief. "You mean, they're not bloodsuckers?"

Frank chuckled and shook his head.

Jace bared his teeth and flashed them at Manuel. "I vant to suck your blood," he said, mimicking a Bela Lugosi voice. "Bleh, bleh, bleh."

Without saying a word, Jem frowned at his twin brother.

"Laugh it up, Chamberlain," Manuel said, obviously irritated. "I hope one of those flying rats swoop down and bites you square on the ass."

"Now, guys..." Nicolas stepped between Jace and Manuel with a cocked brow. "Play nice."

"Ah, come on, Detective," Roman said as he gathered close. "Don't get so uptight. You know Jace is just joking around."

"I'm just messing with you, man," Jace said, offering Manuel a fist pump.

After a few moments of silence, Jace inched his knuckles closer. "Come on, Detective. Don't leave me hanging."

"All right, then." Manuel bumped knuckles with him. "Just give me a break. I have a phobia when it comes to heights and creepy and crawly things. And I don't know what's worse." He visibly shivered. "Rats or bats?"

"Okay." Jace dipped his head. "Point taken."

"There's one good thing about those beady-eyed creatures," Drakon said.

"And what's that?" Manuel asked.

"They had to get in from somewhere. And that means there's an opening in the direction we're heading. They couldn't've came from where we entered. Unless bats can open doors."

"Good point," Tim said. "Let's continue on, and hopefully it's not far from here."

"I sure hope those bats don't get all stirred up," Jace said, pointedly looking at Manuel with a goofy grin. "Just saying."

Manuel narrowed his eyes and grumbled something under his breath.

As soon as the group moved forward, the bats started to stir. Then, all at once, their wings furiously began to flap in unison. The second the colony took flight, squeaking in protest, it was like a swarm of angry birds.

Drakon instantly ducked. "Everyone, get down!"

Most of the others followed Drakon's warning and ducked for cover. Jena on the other hand, didn't seem to be bothered by the winged creatures. She stood there and watched in fascination as they flapped their tiny wings and circled her. Then, in a matter of seconds, they swooped back up and flew away, seemingly heading in the direction they were going. It wasn't long before the winged creatures disappeared into the darkness.

"All right," Drakon said. "They're gone. Let's get a move on." He pointed the flashlight ahead. "This has to lead somewhere."

Manuel's nerves were pins and needles, his heart pounding in his ears, but now that the bats were out of sight, he slowly started to unwind. As they headed toward an unknown destination, a dark figure suddenly appeared in the distance. Instinctively, Manuel put his hand on his holster.

The dark figure just stood there. It was hard to tell, but it looked to be a man. Drakon shined the flashlight toward his face, capturing a tall, lanky man with hair the color of ash. The long strands were pulled back, revealing pale skin and haunting features. Then he slowly began walking toward them with his hands clasped behind his back.

No one moved, just stood there watching him. Waiting.

Jena sniffed the air, but there was nothing. No scent of evil.

Drakon finally called out, "Whoever you are, stop right there." He kept the flashlight steady, trying to get a better look at the stranger's face. "I'm warning you. Don't come any closer."

The lone figure came to an abrupt halt. "Please..." He held up a hand, shielding his face from the blinding light. "I mean you no harm."

"Who are you?" Drakon asked.

"My name is Leonard," the man said, slightly bowing his head. The words rolled off his tongue like silk. He sounded English. "Leonard Saxon III. But please, call me Lenny."

"*Lenny*," Nicolas whispered.

Drakon turned to Nicolas. "You know him?"

"Yes." Nicolas nodded. "We go way back."

Drakon raised a speculative brow. "Like how far back?"

"A century or two," Nicolas replied, sending the hairs on Drakon's neck on full salute.

"Nicolas Ratcliff..." Lenny began, his voice etched with bewilderment. "Is that *really* you, my long-lost friend?"

"Yes." Nicolas stepped forward and raised his voice. "It is I, Nicolas."

"Ah, splendid," Lenny said. His satiny voice glittered with excitement. "It's wonderful to see you again, my friend. Might I come a little closer? It's been too long since we last spoke. And there's something very important I'd like to ask one of your..." He briefly paused to look at Jena. "...companions."

"Please." Nicolas held up a hand. "Wait there a moment. Let me speak with my friends."

"Of course." Lenny smiled. "Please, take your time."

While Lenny waited for permission to approach, Nicolas looked toward the others. "I can assure you, he's not a threat." He kept his voice low. "Lenny and I go way back. Almost a few centuries back. You must understand, living forever isn't always what it's cracked up to be. After I was made immortal,

I stopped aging and eventually had to say good-bye to family and friends before my unusual youth aroused suspicion. I met Lenny when I left New Orleans and moved to Manhattan. We immediately became good friends. He was very kind to me and understood my situation due to his own immortality."

Jace leaned in close. "If he's immortal, what the hell is he?"

"A vampire," Nicolas simply said.

Jace instantly looked toward Lenny and then back at Nicolas, his jaw nearly hitting the floor. Finally, he managed to say, "Are you freakin' kidding me?"

"I know what you're thinking," Nicolas said. "But if you give me a moment, I can explain. Lenny is not what you think. He's a vampire, yes, but he doesn't kill people. There are different types of vampires. Lenny's kind has always been peaceful. He was created by a Daywalker."

"Daywalker?" Jace blurted, shrugging his shoulders. "Are you saying vampires can actually walk in the daylight?"

"Some of them." Nicolas's eyes roamed over the others and then back to Jace. "Daywalkers are the first vampires in existence. They were born into vampirism, not turned. They are what you call True Bloods. There are other peaceful vampires like Lenny's kind, except they're not True Bloods. They're hybrids, created when a Daywalker turns a human. And each group has their own special uniqueness about them. Nevertheless, they all have one thing in common."

"Let me take a wild guess." Jace smirked. "They all drink blood?"

"Yes," Nicolas replied. "They need it to survive."

"Well, what do you think he wants?" Jace persisted. "And did you see the way he looked at Jena?"

"I don't know." Nicolas averted his eyes from Jace and looked to Jena with a soft expression. "And yes, I noticed."

"You mentioned something about each group having a special uniqueness," Jem said, bringing Nicolas back to focus. "What exactly can they do?"

"Hybrids are a bit like Daywalkers," Nicolas began to explain. "They're both immortal and have superior strength and speed, heightened senses, and they can perceive deception, and they also have the gift of persuasion. Daywalkers are the only vampires that can survive daylight, produce offspring, possess the power of levitation, and the ability to shift into bats."

"Aha," Jace said. "So those bats we came across were actually vampires."

"It's possible." Nicolas arched a brow. "Or they could have just been regular bats."

"And what about the other kind?" Manuel asked, staring at Nicolas with avid curiosity. "I mean, the bloodthirsty killer kind."

"Unfortunately, Detective, there are still a few of those left. They are known as Biters."

"Huh?" Jace asked. "What the hell are *Biters*?"

"It's a term the True Bloods have always used," Nicolas said. "They are brutal killers and true enemies to the Daywalkers and the hybrids. They evolved by mistake. A defect that was created by mixing the DNA of a hybrid and a succubus. Rather nasty and downright malicious individuals if you ask me."

"How do you mean?" Jace asked.

"Biters are all females. They use their sexual physicality, seduction, and hypnotic abilities to lure in their victims."

"What else can these *Biters* do?" Manuel asked.

"They are bloodthirsty immortal beings with superior strength and speed. But there are things they can do that the others cannot. Biters are very clever when it comes to hypnotizing their victims. Since they're all female, they have a greater power of persuasion than Daywalkers or hybrids, and they can communicate with one another telepathically. It's like their subconscious is linked to one another somehow. And their bloodlust for humans, especially males, is insatiable."

"If these Biters are all females," Frank said, "then how do they multiply?"

"With venom," Nicolas explained. "Only True Bloods can produce offspring. If a Biter decides to turn a human, and they only choose females, they bite their victim and secrete a contagious venom. Shortly after, the body will slip into a comatose state until the venom takes over. In less than twenty-four hours, they will be transformed, but not fully. The new vampire must drink human blood to complete the transformation."

"Why do they only turn females?" Jena asked.

"It's just in their nature to seek females," Nicolas said. "They view males as the weaker sex and only use them for food."

Manuel sighed, rubbing at his temples, thinking he'd stepped into a world that didn't make sense. "I feel like I'm in the *Bizarro World* again."

Nicolas lightly chuckled. "I completely understand."

"What if their victims don't drink blood?" Frank asked. "Will they turn back human again?"

Nicolas shook his head. "They will die of starvation. But if their maker is killed before they ingest human blood, they will eventually go back to their human form. The same is true if a Daywalker or hybrid turns a human."

"Do they only drink human blood?" Jem asked. "What about our blood?"

"Biters do prefer human blood," Nicolas explained. "But if they're hungry enough, they'll feed off anything. Although their venom and hypnotic abilities hold no power over the Breedline or other supernatural beings."

"Un-freaking-believable." Jace slowly shook his head. "How is it we never heard of them?"

"We have," Tim interjected. "At least our ancestors have. According to our archives, they went extinct many years ago."

"Your ancestors were fooled into believing it was true," Nicolas said. "Since the Breedline were true enemies with the vampires, their feud went on for many generations. I witnessed the last battle between your kind and the vampires during the Civil War. The vampires, including True Bloods, were believed to be soulless. In the eyes of your ancestors, they were evil, an abomination. And correct me if I'm wrong, but what I've learned over the years the Breedline were created for the sole purpose of protecting mankind. Am I right?"

When Tim and a few of the others nodded, Nicolas went on to say, "Well, that's exactly what they did, just as you still do today. They protected humans. And back then, vampires were their biggest rivals. Although the war they fought was with the Biters. The Daywalkers and the hybrids remained peaceful, promising to only take sustenance from animals. So, your ancestors left them alone, but only if they promised to never turn a human again."

"What about the Biters?" Tim asked. "If our ancestors thought they'd destroyed them all, how did they remain undetected all these years?"

"The ones who survived went secretly underground for years," Nicolas continued. "They only came out to feed off the homeless, drifters, prostitutes, or whoever they thought wouldn't be missed. And when it was believed that all vampires were nonexistent, the Breedline eventually stopped searching for them."

"So now they're all out and in the open?" Jace asked.

"The Daywalkers and the hybrids keep to themselves," Nicolas said. "They're very discreet. The last thing they want is to draw attention to themselves. They do not want their identity known."

"And what about the others?" Manuel asked. "I mean, the Biters. Are they out of hiding?"

Nicolas shrugged. "I do not know."

Tim cleared his throat. "Let's see what your friend has to say. I'm curious to find out why he's here and what he wants. And I'm hoping he's not assisting Dr. Michaels."

"Well," Nicolas's gaze flickered to Lenny, "he's waiting. Let's go find out."

"Wait a minute." Jace stopped Nicolas by putting a hand over his shoulder. "Before we go talk to this guy, I want to know how you kill one of those bloodsuckers."

"There are only three things that can kill a vampire: sunlight, except for Daywalkers, since they are invulnerable to the sun, but starvation and beheading will kill them all."

"What happened to the wooden stake to the heart?" Jace asked. "And holy water, crosses, or silver?"

"That's all just a myth," Nicolas replied. "Except silver. It's not fatal, but it will temporarily stun them for a few minutes."

"So," Jace said, jabbing a thumb in Lenny's direction, "if your friend over there starts some shit, you're saying since there's no sunlight down here, we'll have to lop off his head to kill the bastard?"

"Since he's a hybrid, yes," Nicolas said. "Beheading will destroy his kind."

Jace was liking Nicolas more and more. He deviously smiled at him. "Good. To. Know."

Chapter Thirty-Three

As Nicolas and the others approached, a smile stretched across Lenny's mouth, and for a moment, he said nothing, just stared up at Jena's wolfish creature with those piercing, bloodred eyes. He was fascinated and intrigued by her distinctive features. Although Jena was indeed captivating, she was also the most terrifying creature he'd ever laid eyes on. Then, before Nicolas could utter a single word, Lenny quickly averted his eyes and looked to Nicolas with an extended hand.

"Nicolas Ratcliff..." His voice was cultured, satiny, laced with a distinguished tone. "It's very nice to see you again. How have you been all these years, my dear friend?"

Nicolas took hold of Lenny's hand, noticing how frail and pallid his face appeared. Paler than he remembered. So pale he could see the blue, webbed veins beneath his skin.

"Fine, thank you." Nicolas dipped his head, his southern accent once more defining him. "And you?"

"Ah..." Lenny smiled again, flashing his ivory fangs. "I've seen better days, but please, let's discuss the matter shortly. First, I'd very much like to meet your interesting group of companions."

Lenny released Nicolas's hand and looked to the group crowding him. "Once again, let me introduce myself," he said with a bow. "My name is Leonard Saxon III, but please, call me Lenny."

Tim stepped forward before Nicolas had the chance to introduce everyone. "I don't mean to come across as rude," he said, "but I have a few questions to get out of the way before we start a formal introduction."

Lenny nodded. "Of course." He showed his palms, shrugging. "Mister...?"

"It's Ross. Tim Ross."

"Ah, yes." His smile flashed brighter. "How may I be of service, Mr. Tim Ross?"

"Nicolas has explained a bit of your history and the friendship you two share," Tim began, "and we are aware that you're a vampire. Although that's not what concerns me."

"Oh?" Lenny raised a brow. "How fascinating, considering you're a Breedline. But please do tell, Mr. Ross. What are you concerned about?"

Tim cleared his throat. "I'm most interested in the reason why you're here? Are you affiliated with Adam and Eve Pharmaceuticals or Dr. Henry Michaels?"

Lenny straightened, his brow arching further. "Yes, I'm aware of the physician you speak of. And you can rest assured. I am not affiliated with this dreadful establishment, nor am I in cahoots with the insidious doctor and all his unethical research. He is simply helping me find an antidote."

"An antidote?" Tim asked. "For what?"

"For my companions and I." Lenny's smile faded. "You see, Mr. Ross, I have been undead for more than two centuries. I'm sure Nicolas has explained the details." He looked at Nicolas with a friendly smile and then back at Tim. "There are not many of my kind left. Our race is dying."

"Dying?" Nicolas exclaimed, his face a mask of shock. "But how can this be?"

"A virus," Lenny said. "A vampire virus of sorts." His tone was downcast. "And one we cannot heal from. I do not know where it originated from, but it's slowly taking its toll, until I'm afraid, we haven't much time."

Nicolas's heart sank. "Athena and Augustus." He gasped. "Are they—"

"They're still alive." Lenny visibly swallowed. "But time is running out."

"I'm so sorry, Lenny. Is there anything we can do?"

"Yes. That's why I'm—"

"I don't mean to sound unsympathetic," Tim cut in, "but I need to ask you a very important question, Lenny."

Lenny's bloodred gaze flickered to Tim. "Of course."

"How did you find out about Dr. Michaels?"

"Through his mother, Miss Fiona."

Jena's blood turned thick. "Fiona..." Her mind reeled. "Are you saying Dr. Michaels is Fiona's son?"

"Yes," Lenny said. "Miss Fiona is the one who brought me and my companions here."

"But how can that be?" Jena tilted her wolfish head. "Fiona doesn't look old enough—"

"Miss Fiona is a vampire," Lenny abruptly said. "She lived as a housekeeper for my companions for years. In 1965, she was at her death bed after giving birth to Henry, so I turned her. Granted, our kind had promised your ancestors we'd never again turn another human, but I couldn't bear the thought of the babe growing up without a mother. To make matters worse, Fiona had already a toddler to tend to. And the father, *the rotten bastard*, fled the moment he learned of her pregnancy. Anyway, after I turned her, she was very grateful for what I had done and vowed someday that she would find a way to repay me for saving her life. As time passed, her son Henry grew up, and with financial help from my companions, he went off to study medicine. Although he kept in contact with Fiona over the years, I believe he only did it for the money. Henry was a very cruel and selfish child, and I see things haven't changed. I guess he takes after his father." Lenny sighed. "Then when the virus began and continued to worsen, Fiona contacted Henry. Since he's a well-established and highly esteemed physician, she hoped he could find a cure. What better way for him to pay back my companions for their kind charity, wouldn't you say? Anyway, that's when he sent for us. We've only been here a short time."

"Is Fiona okay?" Jena's guttural voice was reluctant.

"Miss Fiona is like me," Lenny said, "not as ill as the others, but time is not on our side." He looked at Jena with a quizzical expression. "May I ask how you know her?"

"Fiona was the one who freed me."

Everyone was speechless and Lenny continued to look confused.

"Freed you?" Lenny shrugged. "From where?"

"Here!" Jena said. "Dr. Michaels had me kidnapped." Her words came out angry. "Apparently, he wanted me for some type of research. Most likely, the same thing that he's done to his own children. But before he could get his paws on me, Fiona came to my rescue and set me free."

Nicolas glanced at Lenny. His bloodred gaze appeared duller now. He looked dispirited, like something weighed heavily on his mind.

"That's why we're here," Nicolas spoke out, grasping Lenny's attention. "To put an end to the physician's madness and to shut this place down. I'm not sure if you realize, but the things he's done goes beyond madness. Not only has he turned his own flesh and blood into monsters, but he's also used his own patients for ungodly experimentations. We've been forced to kill them in self-defense. And I know you, Lenny. You're not the kind of person who would turn a blind eye to such atrocity."

"Yes." Lenny sighed, looking pain-stricken. "I was recently made aware of the doctor's detestable behavior. And I promise, he will be punished for his crimes, but—"

"I believe we'll be in charge of that," Manuel interjected, flashing his badge. "My partner and I are here to arrest Dr. Michaels."

"I'm sorry," Lenny said, "but I don't believe we've had the pleasure."

"I'm Detective Sanchez, and this is my partner," he said, gesturing at Frank, "Detective Perkins. Dr. Henry Michaels is wanted by the FBI. We've got a warrant for his arrest."

Lenny's brows drew together. "I'm sorry, Detective Sanchez, but I cannot let that happen. If you arrest Dr. Michaels, my companions and I will surely perish. He is the only one who can produce the antidote." He averted his eyes from the Detective and looked up at Jena. "This is why I've come to meet you, Miss McCain. My life, Fiona's, and my loved ones, and what's left of my species, rest solely in your hands."

"I don't understand?" Jena shook her head. "What does this have to do with me?"

Lenny tried to figure out where to begin. "Your blood," he said. "Or might I say the blood of the immortal creature you bestow. It has the power to cure the virus. And we need Dr. Michaels. He's the only person who can test the antibodies in your blood to ensure its sustainability."

"There has to be more to this," Jena said, her tone firm, feeling a surge of resentment. She thought of all the questions the mad physician demanded to know about her creature. "I believe Dr. Michaels has alternative plans for me other than your cure."

"I'm sorry, Miss McCain." Lenny lowered his eyes, regretting his decision to ever put his trust in Henry. There was no doubt the doctor was insane. He lifted his gaze to meet hers. "After everything that's come to light, I believe you may be right."

Jena opened her mouth, but Nicolas cut her off, his eyes blazing with anger. "There's no way I'm letting that madman get his hands on Jena. I won't allow it."

Lenny's eyes went wide, sensing a strong protectiveness in Nicolas. "You're in love with her, aren't you?"

"I—" Nicolas paused, turning a soft gaze to Jena. "I am." He smiled at her, then returned his eyes to Lenny. "Jena is my beloved."

Hearing Nicolas's words made Jena's heart race.

Lenny closed his eyes and for a moment was lost in thought. He was thinking of his beloved Athena. His mind traveled back, taking him down a road of better times. He smiled to himself as images of her came to mind. She was breathtaking, and petite, no more than five feet tall. Her hair flowed past her small hips like blazing fire, although she kept the long, auburn strands mostly swept up into a twisted braid. The sapphire shade of her eyes, surrounded by thick lashes, captivated him to no end. And the crimson color of her full lips emphasized the porcelain whiteness of her flawless skin. Then a long-ago memory crashed back to him. Their first kiss. He remembered it like it was yesterday. Her lips were so soft against his. As soft as rose petals. That was the day he'd given over his heart and his soul.

Their love had been ageless, but now, time was quickly ticking away. And years of burying his own kind had taken its toll. As time went on and the virus spread, he seemed increasingly obsessed with losing Athena and her fraternal twin brother, and his best friend, Augustus. That's when he began to do something he hadn't in decades. He began to bargain with God.

The moment Lenny shook the memory away and reopened his eyes, he said, "You're right, Nicolas. And I don't blame you. But please, put yourself in my place for just an instant. What if it was your beloved who was dying and there was a chance you could save her?"

When Nicolas stood silent, Lenny turned away and focused on Jena with pleading eyes. "I'm begging you, Miss McCain. We haven't much time. Please, you must save my Athena."

Jena mulled this over. "So, if I agree to help..." She paused and threw up a hand when Detective Sanchez opened his mouth to voice his opinion. Manuel was getting impatient. He wanted to arrest the physician, not make a deal. "Will you give me your word you'll cooperate with the Detectives and help them apprehend Dr. Michaels so he can be locked up where he belongs?"

"And Jena's not to be left alone with that bastard," Nicolas spouted. "Not for a second."

Lenny's shoulders instantly sagged. Then he straightened and dipped his head. "I give you my word."

"I don't get it," Jace spoke out. "What is it about Jena's blood that can heal this so-called vampire virus?"

Lenny arched a brow. "That's a good question, Mister...?"

"It's Chamberlain, but you can call me Jace."

"Although I don't know the scientific reasons," Lenny said, "I do know that Miss McCain's blood contains great power. I suppose it has to do with the curse of the immortal creature within her. According to what Henry had explained, the creature has the ability to detect and destroy evil souls."

"But how did Dr. Michaels get access to this kind of information?" Jena questioned. "Only the Breedline Covenant has knowledge of this."

Lenny shook his head. "I do not know. Possibly through torture."

"Torture?" Jena shook her head. "What do you mean?"

"Instead of paying attention to what Dr. Michaels was doing, I focused my sights solely on my companions and a cure. I believe he's tortured some of your people into giving him information. I assume that's how he found out. Unless you have a traitor among your kind."

"Well, that wouldn't surprise me," Jace said, rolling his eyes. "And it wouldn't be the first time."

"Let's not jump to conclusions," Tim said. "Besides, what's done is done. There's nothing we can do about it now. And by the way, since we're working together, I'd like to officially introduce the others you haven't met."

As Jena stood back while Tim introduced Lenny to the others, it became harder to believe she'd agreed to all this. Some part of her thought she might very well be walking straight into a trap and taking the others with her. The other part of her—the gut feeling part—felt she was doing the right thing. Jena knew she'd never forgive herself if she didn't do everything she could to save Fiona. If it hadn't been for her, there was a big possibility she'd still be strapped to that examination table. And God only knew what would have become of her. What she really wanted to do was tear Dr. Michaels limb from limb.

"Okay," Drakon said, his deep voice bringing Jena back to focus. "So, what's our plan?"

"Before we assemble our next move," Tim said, directing his question to Lenny, "where can we find Dr. Michaels in this godforsaken place?"

"I have him secured."

"What do you mean by that?" Tim asked.

"I caught him in a lie before I came looking for you. So, I placed him in a secure room where he cannot do any further harm."

Nicolas narrowed his gaze toward Lenny. "How did you know we were down here?"

Lenny pointed to an area on the ceiling behind the others. "There's security cameras down here."

When everyone turned to look in the direction Lenny was pointing, he went on to say, "Henry's guards knew the exact moment you entered through the tunnels. They were planning a trap, that is, until I intervened.”

“What about his guards?” Drakon asked. “Are they going to give us trouble?”

“No.” Lenny’s lips curled up. “They are terrified of me. Besides, I have the gift of persuasion, so they won’t be a problem.”

Chapter Thirty-Four

As Lenny and the others neared the entrance to the facility, Jena raised her chin, nostrils flaring. The overwhelming scent of evil surrounded her. Then she cocked her wolfish head, listening to something the others couldn't hear. "Dammit." Her eyes steamed with rage. "Fiona's in danger."

Instantly, Manuel looked to Frank, his heart hammering, and nodded a silent understanding. Then, in unison, they whipped their guns from their holsters and kept pace with Lenny and Jena as they made their way inside.

The serious expressions on their faces alerted Drakon. And when he saw the two detectives reach for their weapons, he knew there was no time for questions. Quickly, he motioned toward the others and took off after Manuel and Frank. It wasn't long before Jace, Jem, Nicolas, Roman, and Tim caught up with Drakon.

The minute they strode through the opening, they came upon the bodies of two security guards. They lay dead in pools of their own blood.

Lenny stood staring in utter disbelief. Then his eyes filled with anger.

"What the—" Jace spouted as he stepped in behind Drakon, taking in the gruesome scene. Going by the amount of blood coating the floor and the bodies, it appeared something very sharp had gone to work on their throats.

On instinct, the detectives raised their weapons, readying themselves as they cautiously surveyed the room.

Moments later, after finding the area vacant, sounds of scuffling seemingly coming from the next room alerted their attention. Then a faint muffled cry made the hairs on Lenny's neck stand on end.

"Fiona," he whispered, slowly inching toward a set of double doors. Earlier, Lenny had locked Henry behind those doors with two guards posted outside. Unfortunately, it had been the same two guards they'd just found dead.

Jena also heard the cries and moved alongside Lenny. She looked at him through narrowed eyes and gestured to the door. "Dr. Michaels has Fiona in there, doesn't he?"

He nodded, briefly closing his eyes, trying to erase the thought of Henry hurting his own mother. But at this point, he'd come to realize the physician had gone completely mad.

Suddenly, the doors burst open as Jena kicked with all her strength. The first thing they saw was Fiona, her eyes wide with terror. She was locked in the arms of her own son who held a knife to her throat.

Henry's feral eyes shot forward, his gaze impaling Jena. In a split second, he recognized the wolfish creature who stood in the broken doorway. He instantly snarled his upper lip as flashbacks of her shooting him came to mind.

"Let her go," Jena said, releasing a growl.

Manuel aimed his Glock, finger on the trigger. "Put the weapon down, Dr. Michaels!"

Frank stood alongside his partner, his weapon drawn, still not believing his eyes. He couldn't tell if the physician was even cognizant by the crazed look on his face but then saw a flicker of recognition as he opened his mouth to speak.

"She must pay for her betrayal," Henry said, glancing between the two detectives, his lips curled back in a malicious sneer.

"Please, Henry." Fiona pleaded around her sobs. "Stop this madness."

"Shut up, Mother."

"Listen to me, Henry," Lenny said, taking a step closer, his hypnotizing gaze blazing like fire.

"Stop right there," Henry warned, placing the edge of the blade up against the main artery of Fiona's neck. "No tricks, or I swear..." He glared at Lenny. "I'll slit her throat from one end to the other. And you know as well as I do, my dear old friend, she doesn't possess the power to heal in her weakened state."

Frank slowly lowered his weapon. "It's all right, Dr. Michaels. Just take it easy." His voice was calm, but inside he was a bundle of nerves, fearing the mad physician was on the verge of snapping. "What do you say we talk this through?" He took a step closer. "There's no reason why anyone needs to get hurt."

"Get back!" Henry raised his voice. "I'm warning you!"

Fiona gasped as Henry dug the blade into her skin just enough to draw a few droplets of blood.

"Okay, okay," Frank said, taking a cautious step back. "Just take a breather, Dr. Michaels." He slowly raised a hand. "Please, calm down."

"I'm done listening to you." Jena stalked closer. "Let Fiona go or—"

"Or what?" Henry cut her off. "You'll kill me?" He laughed, his gaze moving from Jena to Lenny. The deranged look in his eyes made the hairs on Lenny's neck prickle. "If I die," he said with a cocked eyebrow, "you'll never get that antidote."

Lenny stared at him in fury, realizing Henry was toying with him and in the pit of his gut, he knew there wasn't much time. And without the antidote, his kind, and Fiona for that matter, were doomed.

"I'd listen to Miss McCain," Manuel spoke out, keeping his gun trained on the physician. "Let your mother go. If you kill her, I'll make damn sure you never see the light of day. Look around. The odds are stacked against you. Face it, Dr. Michaels. You're outnumbered."

"Outnumbered?" Henry smirked. "What makes you think I'm outnumbered? I think you've underestimated me, Detective." He looked to Lenny, his eyes glittering with insanity. "Surely, you didn't think I wouldn't be prepared for your little group of visitors, did you?"

"You've gone mad, Henry." Lenny's voice held a blend of anger and impatience. "There's no one here to defend you. The rest of your guards, the ones you haven't killed, have fled."

"Is that so?" Henry said, his face shifting into a mask of amusement. "Well, about that..." His eyes trailed away, appearing to look past them. Then he called out, "Ladies."

Suddenly, Jena caught a scent. It was the distinct pungent odor of evil and death. As it grew stronger, it invaded her senses enticingly. Then came a voice. A voice calling from within, raising her wolf hairs as she listened closely. *Evil creatures. Destroy them all!*

Distant giggling suddenly filtered from behind.

Everyone turned and faced the empty doorway that led into a dark corridor. For a few brief moments they waited, listening in silence.

"I thought I heard laughter," Jace said.

"You did," Lenny replied. "I also heard it."

The putrid scent of rotting flesh hit Jena. She instantly recoiled and looked at Lenny, then at the others. By the foul expressions on their faces, it was clear they smelled it too.

Jace covered his nose and muttered, "It smells like something died in here."

Then, out of nowhere, several dark figures emerged from the shadows. As they moved closer, gliding across the floor like haunting phantoms, their pale but youthful faces finally came into view.

Jena peeled back her wolfish lips and uttered a low, menacing growl, keeping her eyes trained on the vampirish creatures.

"What the hell?" Jace's booming voice halted the strange group of girls.

"They're Biters," Lenny hesitantly said.

They all wore sleeveless dresses made of black chiffon, possessing a style between vintage and a gothic-chic fashion that accentuated their pale-white skin. Their bloodred eyes flared with hunger as they roamed over the occupants before them. There were at least a dozen, ranging between the ages of sixteen to eighteen, all similar with coal-black hair that hung past their shoulders in a tangled mess. As they peeled back their red-coated lips, strings of saliva dripped from their sharp-pointed teeth.

"What have you done, Henry?" Lenny said, his voice trembling with outrage.

Henry started to laugh. "There is nothing more dangerous than a group of Biters that hasn't fed in days."

The thirsty teens, hissing like cobras, slowly stalked closer and closer.

Jena was in a rage. She stood her ground, claws fully extended, ready to spring.

"Lovely, aren't they?" Henry said, grinning like a madman. He focused his eyes on Lenny. "You didn't think they were all extinct, did you?"

Lenny's eyes, along with the others, looked befuddled. And worried. "How?" Lenny asked.

"I'm a scientist, remember? Where there is a need, there is a way. I think it's rather genius. What do you think?"

"I think you've lost your damn mind," Lenny said, gritting his teeth.

Henry smiled and called out, "Dinnertime, ladies."

The physician's words were like ringing a bell to an all-you-can-eat buffet as the vampirish girls rushed onward, fangs bared, hissing and growling.

"Shit," Jace muttered, looking to the others for guidance. "They're practically kids. What the hell do we do?"

"Go!" Jena's lupine voice rose with power as her eyes darted over her Breedline companions. "Get out of here, all of you!"

Tim turned toward Jena, and before he had the chance to voice his opinion, one of the Biters leapt onto his back. He gasped in pain as she sank her fangs deep into his shoulder and greedily sucked his blood in hungry pulls.

As soon as Manuel got a clear shot, he fired his weapon. The silver bullet ripped through the vampire's flesh like a hot poker. Blood spattered and smoke rose. She immediately retracted her razor-sharp teeth and screamed in protest.

Tim quickly grabbed the girl by her long, matted hair and slung her to the floor. She instantly arched her back and bared her teeth at him. Crab-walking away, she hissed like a wounded feral cat.

The other fanged teens formed a circle around the group as if they were waiting for the right opportunity to spring into action.

Without warning, everything shifted as though time stood still, and the room erupted into chaos. A Biter at the far end lunged out like she'd been launched from a cannon and clung onto Jace's chest, using her catlike claws.

"Get the hell off me!" Jace shoved at the girl, who screeched like a banshee, but the vampire would not let go. She clawed at his shirt, ripping the material and the skin underneath. When she opened her mouth, he felt hot breath on his face and the stench of decay. The split second she went for his throat, he grabbed a clump of her ratty hair. He tugged and yanked at the long strands, straining to evade the sharp tips of her ivory fangs.

As Jem turned to rescue his brother, another Biter leaped into the air and landed on his back. "Son of a—" He grunted, doing his best to fight her off as she went to work on his back with her angry, sharp claws.

Roman kicked at two Biters who had slithered over like fast-moving serpents and attached themselves to his legs. He howled as one of them snaked her head around and sank her fangs deep into the muscle of his calf.

Drakon hurriedly grabbed one of Roman's attackers by the hair of her head and pried her loose. As he hoisted her up, her feet dangled. Instantaneously, she went into a full-blown tantrum, kicking, clawing, and screaming.

"For crying out loud," Drakon said, struggling to avoid the vampire's vicious assault. Then, in one swift motion, he snapped her neck like the crack of a whip and tossed her aside. The moment he went to free Roman from attacker number two, a pair of arms latched on to him from behind. He tightened the muscles in his neck as icy fingers clutched at his throat.

When Nicolas and Lenny took on four of the little blood-suckers all at once, it was like fighting a pack of mountain lions with their bare hands.

"Stay back!" Manuel shouted, pointing his weapon at the remaining Biters who looked at him and his partner with bloodthirsty eyes.

Beside him, Frank kept his gun raised. "Dear God..." He quickly made the sign of a cross, realizing their bullets were useless against the deadly creatures. "If you can hear us..." He quickly looked up, praying God was listening. "...please, give us a sign."

Right before Manuel and Frank decided to unload a few rounds into the vampires, who were now getting closer, a thunderous roar stopped them in their tracks. As they craned their heads to look, they saw Jena, still in the form of her wolfish creature, and stepped back with a sigh of relief.

When the vampires got a look at Jena, their terror was evident on their ghoulish faces. Little by little, they shrank back, hissing and cowering.

Jena sprang at the creatures, her powerful claws slashing their throats as swiftly as any animal of the wild moves to slay.

It all happened in a matter of a few seconds. Manuel and Frank stood stock-still watching the horror as it played out. What was left of the vampires, the ones who still had their heads, quickly backed away and retreated into the shadows.

Madness flashed before Henry as he took in all the decapitated vampires. "You'll pay for this!" Then he focused on Lenny with murderous intent. "You'll *all* pay for this!"

Fiona was crying, whimpering behind the palm of Henry's firm hand.

Lenny stepped closer. "Please..." He frantically looked at the terrified expression on Fiona's face and then back at Henry's wild, crazed eyes. "For God's sake. She's your mother."

Henry lowered his hand from Fiona's mouth, then raised the other, revealing a sharp-edged blade.

Fiona's eyes went wide. "Please, son. No..."

"Good-bye, Mother."

Lenny lunged, but it was too late. Henry sliced the blade through the side of Fiona's neck, slashing open to the bone. A gasp escaped her lips that turned into a wet gurgle. Time slowed, and in that drawn-out, terrible second, she went limp in Henry's arms. Slumping to her knees, Fiona's hands clasped her throat as dark liquid sprayed out from between her fingers. With her eyes staring blankly, and her mouth opening and closing, she finally fell forward where spurts of liquid pooled on the floor.

"NO!" Jena roared. She lunged, moving so fast, Henry never knew what hit him. She grabbed him by the scruff of his neck and opened her jaws. He opened his mouth to scream but was cut off as sharp teeth closed around his head and crunched down, turning his skull into a bloody mass of bone and brains. Then his lifeless body went limp and dropped to the floor in a grotesque heap.

Lenny stood paralyzed as deep sadness weighed on him, realizing his fate, and the fate of his beloved, had just been sealed.

Nicolas and the others watched as Lenny stared down at Henry's corpse. They could tell by the slump of his shoulders and the defeated expression on his face Lenny had just lost the last bit of hope he'd been clinging onto.

Jena approached him, wearing a look of sympathy marring her wolfish face. She gently placed her clawed hand on his arm. "I'm so sorry, Lenny. The curse... I couldn't stop myself."

He looked at Jena, glanced back at Henry, then at Jena once more. "He was our only hope. And now..." His eyes grew somber as he lowered them. "...my kind will cease to exist."

Jena held her wrist out, offering it to Lenny. "Take it. My blood is the cure."

Lenny stared at Jena's wrist in confusion. "But..." He turned to face her. "It's not been tested. How do you know it will work?"

"I don't," she said. "But what choice do you have?"

"I..." Lenny paused as the others approached. By all the scratches, bite marks, and torn clothing, everyone looked as though they'd gone a couple of rounds with a dozen wild cats.

Nicolas placed a comforting hand on Lenny's shoulder. "Have faith, my dear friend."

Chapter Thirty-Five

Lenny looked back at Jena as she positioned her wrist close to his lips. "Drink," she said, her rough wolfish voice given way to a softer, more soothing tone.

How perfectly terrifying she looked, her face a mask of dark fur, a long muzzle for a mouth, and pointed lupine ears atop her beastly head.

He nodded a silent understanding and took her wrist in his hands. He lowered his bloodred gaze and stared where the viable blood vessel was hidden beneath the thick layer of her dark fur. The rhythmic throbbing of her pulse and the drumming of her heart was like music to his ears. The sounds eased him in a way. The moment he peeled back his lips and bit into her flesh, blood flowed from the punctured vein and rushed into his mouth. At the barest taste of her blood, his eyes opened, growing more focused than before. Jena's blood possessed a powerful energy like nothing he'd ever tasted. He sucked gently at first, but then an overwhelming thirst took hold. Already he felt its healing abilities coursing through his veins.

As Lenny drew in deeper pulls, his tongue probing hungrily at the savory liquid, he felt the sickness inside of him slowly begin to fade. It was like an unknown force racing through his body as Jena's blood merged with his own. Then a renewed feeling washed over him, carrying away his weak and deteriorating state. As he released her wrist, a contented sigh escaped his lips, and for the first time in so many years, he felt alive again. And much more vibrant than ever.

He smiled up at her, the taste of her blood still on his lips. "It worked." Tears welled in his eyes. "I will forever be in your debt, Miss McCain." He dipped his head. "Thank you."

"You're welcome." Her mouth drew back into the most hideous wolfish grin, revealing rows of sharp-pointed teeth. "Now," she waved her clawed hand, "go fetch your beloved Athena. I will heal her too."

"What about the others?" Lenny asked.

"Others?" Jena tilted her head. "How many are we talking?"

"Now that Fiona is gone," Lenny paused, the look in his eyes expressing sadness, "Athena and her brother Augustus are the only two here in the facility. But there are still others in Manhattan, waiting for a cure."

"Well then," Jena began, "looks like I'll be taking a trip."

"What about the remaining Biters?" Lenny asked. "We can't have them wandering outside the facility. They're dangerous."

"They couldn't have gone far," Jena said. "I'm sure they're somewhere around here. Besides, didn't you say sunlight would kill them?"

When Lenny nodded, Jena pointed to a clock mounted on the wall at the far end of the room. "Well, considering it's already dawn, I believe they won't be leaving this place anytime soon."

"In that case," Lenny said, cocking a brow, "neither will I."

As Lenny turned to leave, he glanced down at his tattered shirt and was shocked by all the bloodstains covering the satiny material. He reached down and fingered the holes created by Henry's unruly little monsters. Beneath all the rips and tears, his skin showed no signs of trauma. It was as if they'd magically disappeared. If it weren't for Jena's blood, *her creature's blood*, he'd be near death by now. There was no way he could have withstood the vampires' attack in his previous condition. But now, he was good as new. The vampire virus that once took over his body, like a slow and painful cancer, was now a mere memory and no longer a death sentence.

He looked back at Jena once more, his expression grateful, and she noticed the changes in his appearance. The blue, webbed veins that had shown beneath his skin were no longer visible. Instead, they were replaced by the signs of youthfulness and immortality. Even the long strands of his platinum hair, which had previously looked bleak and dull, now glimmered with vitality and shine. And then she wondered what it had been like for Lenny all these years, living as a vampire. Surely, it hadn't been easy over the last two centuries, hiding in the shadows, never to see the sun.

Although she'd been cursed to live an immortal life, at least she could walk out in the day. Oddly, she felt sympathy for Lenny. She'd rather be dead than live forever in the darkness. To her it would be like an imprisonment.

Meanwhile, as Lenny went to retrieve Athena and Augustus, Nicolas and the others gathered around Jena. "You're not going after those Biters alone," Nicolas said. "I'm coming with you."

"I agree with Nicolas," Tim said. "There's at least half a dozen of them left."

"If we're planning on killing what's left of those little bloodsuckers," Jace said, "we're gonna need something real sharp."

"I agree," Roman chimed in. "Surely there's something around here we can use."

The second Jace took off, Jem called out, "Hold up, brother. Where do you think you're going?"

Jace looked over his shoulder. "To look for weapons."

"Okay, but don't go too far," Jem said, frowning. "You wouldn't want to run into those Biters. You'll be forced to shift. And it would be easier if we could avoid provoking your Beast."

"Whatever." Jace groaned under his breath as he walked off.

Roman tapped Jem on the shoulder. "I'll go with him."

Jem nodded. "Thanks, Roman."

As the guys weighed their options, mulling over the best way to destroy the remaining Biters without shifting, Jena looked toward the far side of the room where two bodies lay. She felt a twinge of sadness when she caught site of Fiona's blank, glossy stare. She was positioned on her side, her head nearly severed, lying in a pool of her own blood. Jena blinked a few times, and a single tear fell from the corner of her eye.

Not far from Fiona lay Henry's bloody corpse. Staring out of wide lunatic eyes were the gory remnants of the mad physician's head. Looking at the grotesquery, she felt no pity for the man. Dr. Henry Michaels deserved his fate and then some.

"What about Fiona?" Jena asked as she looked away from the carnage and refocused on the others. "We're not going to just leave her body here, are we?"

"This is a crime scene, Jena," Manuel said. "Detective Perkins and I should call this in. That is…" He paused, looking to Tim for some sort of guidance. "…unless you have a better idea."

Tim looked between the two detectives. "It's your call. But how are you going to explain all those hybrid wolves we destroyed, not to mention the Biters? And we still have to hunt the others down."

Manuel gave Tim a nod. "You're right. If we call this in, it will only complicate things. And I'm in no mood to deal with my captain. Besides, if he finds out Frank and I went against his orders in this investigation, and disregarded the feds, he'll have our heads on a chopping block."

"Yeah," Frank muttered, "Captain Hodge still hasn't gotten over Jena's kidnapping ordeal. When he found out we didn't notify him as soon as she turned up, all hell broke loose. And that reminds me…" Frank focused on Jena. "As soon as all this is over, Manuel and I are going to turn over Kian Adams, since she was involved with your kidnapping. Hopefully we'll find her sister alive in this ungodly place."

When Jena nodded, Manuel said, "And there's one more thing." He kept his eyes on her. "We'll need you to stop by the precinct to make a statement. About your kidnapping anyway. And in your human form, of course."

Frank rolled his eyes at Manuel. "I think that goes without saying, partner."

"What about the other two guys involved?" Tim asked. "Any word on them by chance?"

Manuel shook his head. "Nothing so far. But since we've identified them, I'm sure it won't be long before we locate their whereabouts."

"Well," Tim said with a shrug, "let's go find the rest of those Biters. The sooner we get this over with, the better. I don't know about the rest of you, but I've had enough of this place."

"I second that," Drakon said.

"Look what I found," Jace hollered as he made his way into the room with Roman trailing alongside him. They carried with them something long and sharp. It looked like surgical instruments of some kind. As they moved closer, Jace lifted whatever was in his hands and whooped, "Let's rock and roll."

Jem eyeballed the sharp objects. "What the hell are those?"

"Bone saws," Jace said, sporting a devilish grin.

"Where did you get them?"

Jace lowered his arms and nodded toward the corridor. "We found them in a room down the hall. The place looked like a freakin' torture chamber."

Roman visibly shivered. "And creepy as hell."

Jem grumbled low. "Let's just get this over with."

"What about your *special* powers?" Roman asked, his eyes focused on Jem, realizing how easily the guy could create a firebomb with one flick of his wrist. "I mean, couldn't you just turn those Biters to ashes?"

Jem looked from Roman to Nicolas, gauging his reaction. "I don't know. Maybe." He shrugged. "I guess I could try. Lenny didn't mention anything about fire."

"That's because it won't destroy them," Nicolas said. "It must be direct sunlight. They will heal with fire." He released a sigh. "Like it or not, we're going to have to behead the remaining Biters. Unless you can think of a way to herd them out into the daylight."

"These will work just fine," Jace said, flashing the sharp-edged blades. "Besides, I've got a score to settle." He peered down at his torn T-shirt. "This happens to be Metallica's signature album cover and one of my favorite shirts. Now look at it." He frowned. "It's freakin' ruined."

Jem groaned. "Then why the hell did you wear it?"

"I'd be upset too," came a soft, feminine voice laced with an English accent.

When everyone turned around, they saw Lenny standing in the open doorway. He was latched on to the arm of a young woman with long auburn hair and porcelain-white skin. She was petite, seemingly overly thin and frail, but still, she was a vision of beauty. Her rose-colored lips, plump and full, were drawn in a thin line, as if she were unsure of the occupants in the room. On the other side of her stood a broad-shouldered man who stood several inches taller than Lenny, putting him at about six-foot-three. He was handsome but appeared too lean for his frame. His pallid complexion matched the woman's, along with the color of his shoulder-length hair. And they both shared the same bloodred eyes as Lenny's. It was obvious what they were. *Vampires.*

Jena instantly inhaled the newcomers' scent. She was relieved to find nothing evil radiating from the two. Only fear and weariness.

"I'm a big fan of Metallica," the pale-faced woman said, pointing at Jace's T-shirt that was riddled with holes.

Jace stared into the woman's scarlet gaze and muttered, "Who the—?" His words were cut off by Nicolas as he stepped forward, clearly recognizing the couple as he reached out to the woman with open arms. "It's been so long, dear heart."

After a few moments, they pulled from their embrace and Nicolas extended his hand to the tall gentleman. "How have you been, my dear friend?"

The man took Nicolas's hand in a firm shake. "To be honest..." His accented voice matched his looks, pleasant but weary. "...I've had better days."

Nicolas shot him a look of empathy. Despite his thin frame and paleness, Augustus looked as he'd remembered him so many years ago. He was a true gentleman, as well as a powerful vampire who'd not only been a loyal friend to Lenny but to him as well. Augustus, along with Lenny and Athena, helped him adjust to living as an immortal when his brother, Ashton—who was cursed like Jena—had gone mad and abandoned him to go on a killing spree.

"Let me introduce you to everyone here," Nicolas said, his eyes focused on the couple standing close to Lenny.

When the couple nodded, Nicolas went down the line, starting with his beloved Jena, to all the members of the Breedline who were gathered, and finally the two detectives. Then he presented them to the newcomers. "This is Lenny's beautiful bride Athena, and her fraternal twin brother, Augustus Rutherford II."

Athena forced a smile, her eyes nervously settling on Jena's beastly features, and Augustus slightly bowed and said, "It's nice to make your acquaintance. Of course, I wish it were under better circumstances."

Jena noticed the dark worry in Athena's gaze as she moved forward and reached out to the overly thin, pale-faced woman.

"Please do not fear me," Jena said. "Although my appearance right now is a bit terrifying, I will not harm you."

Cautiously, as Athena took hold of Jena's outstretched hand, it looked gigantic against hers. "It's a pleasure," she said, her lips slowly curling up. "And thank you, Miss McCain." She swallowed back tears, fighting the urge to cry. "Thank you for saving my dear Lenny. God has surely answered my prayers."

"You're welcome, Miss Athena," Jena said, looking down at the woman's tiny hand. It was bony and coated with thick blue veins, like the hands of someone far older. She lifted her gaze, getting a closer look at the woman's pasty skin, to the color of her eyes, and the dark circles weighing beneath them.

When Jena released Athena's hand, she extended it to Augustus. It wasn't until he accepted her hand that she realized how considerably weak he was. It was like shaking the hand of an old man. But she knew it wasn't the case by what she'd previously learned from Nicolas about their past. They, along with Lenny, had stopped aging centuries ago.

"You're a saint for sore eyes, my dear," Augustus said, lightly squeezing her hand. "You came along just in the nick of time." He smiled brightly. "We are indeed grateful."

Chapter Thirty-Six

The morning sun had just peeked out as Joseph neared the steps that led to his apartment building. Sweat beaded on his forehead and soaked the back of his neck as he continued onward, his feet pounding against the sidewalk. Eager to get inside and take a shower, he forced himself to move faster. His lungs burned and the muscles in his calves ached. He could feel the beat of his heart begin to rise the moment he started to climb the stairs, taking two at a time.

The three-mile run through the park had been muggy and humid, but he'd managed without stopping to rest along the trails. It had been a miracle he'd even made it out of bed, much less have the energy to exercise. He'd been up most of the night, his thoughts consumed by the previous evening. No matter how hard he tried, he just couldn't shut them out. Images and flashbacks swirled inside his head like a never-ending nightmare.

He'd confided in Carrie, unveiling his dark secrets, starting with the death of his mother at the hands of his abusive father. At the time, Joseph was so young and impressionable, barely five years old. The brutality of his mother's death completely devastated him, leaving him heartbroken, followed by abandonment issues.

Next, he went on to tell her how social services took over the moment his father was arrested and sentenced to twenty years. He went from one foster family to another. It was apparent no one wanted him due to his developing violent behavior and the inability to express empathy. Not long after, Joseph suffered an emotional breakdown, affecting his ability to think, feel, and behave clearly. By the time he reached thirteen, he'd been diagnosed with a chronic mental disorder. He displayed all the traits of a psychopath and was carted off to a mental institute, where he spent most of his adolescent years. On top of that, he told her about the voice inside his head. He had no choice but to expose the Shadow—an evil, dark entity who had possessed him shortly following his mother's death—after the *thing* had revealed itself to Carrie.

At first, she was confused and uneasy. But to his surprise, Carrie believed him, expressing an unimaginable amount of compassion, pleading to let her help him. She'd even shown a remarkable understanding when he told her he'd killed his own father the day he'd been released from prison. But when he'd confessed to killing her ex-boyfriend, she instantly became frightened, wondering if the voice inside his head wanted him to kill her too. Although the Shadow taunted him relentlessly, demanding that he kill Carrie, he could never consciously or even physically harm her. He'd already fallen in love with her, but still, she would never be safe around him. That's when he'd told her she was in danger and better off without him. But she refused the notion, believing he was a good person. And she'd said those three little words he'd never forget.

He'd never dreamed anyone, much less someone as wonderful and beautiful as Carrie, could love a *monster* like him.

Finally, when Joseph found the courage to tell Carrie the truth about how he'd witnessed those two guys who had attacked her the night before they'd met, she was utterly shell-shocked. At first, she seemed surprised but also grateful, thinking he was the mysterious wolfish creature who had come to her rescue in the nick of time. But when he refuted her theory and admitted to stalking her that night, contemplating killing her before those two guys showed up, everything about Carrie's compassionate demeanor went out the door, sending him along with it.

Oh God... What have I done?

Each time Joseph remembered the look of devastation on Carrie's face and the raw emotion blazing in her eyes, it tore at his heart. The truth had leaked from his lips like someone else's story, something other than his own, and one you'd never imagine to be real. The instant he'd told her, he wished he could take it all back. His gut churned just thinking about it. Everything seemed like a nightmare. But instead of waking up, realizing that it had only been a dream, it had all been *real*.

Last night, he'd left Carrie's apartment in a daze, unable to think, or drive for that matter. The world around him appeared hazy like he was in some imaginary dream where nothing made sense. A half hour on foot, when his mind was a little clearer, he'd realized it would take hours to get home. His apartment was at least ten miles, and it was already close to midnight. That's when he decided to call for an Uber. He'd catch a ride back to Carrie's in the morning to retrieve his Jeep.

Then his brows pinched together. "Carrie's car..."

He'd completely forgotten about Carrie's Volkswagen Beetle. She'd left it at the restaurant last night. And he'd promised to pick her up this morning to retrieve it before work. *Should I call or just text her?*

As he made his way inside the apartment, the cool air came as a relief. It wasn't long before his breathing steadied and his heartbeat slowed to its normal tempo. Although his body was in tip-top shape, his mind felt defeated, overwhelmed, as if he were on the verge of a psychotic break.

The moment he decided to send her a text, his phone started to ring. He looked to the armband that was attached to his biceps, recognizing the number on the caller ID. *Shit!* His heart picked up the beat. It was Dr. Mendoza. He wanted nothing more than to let it go to voicemail.

During his last session, she had questioned him about the voices he'd heard as a child. He lied when she asked him if he was being truthful when he'd told her they no longer existed. Besides, if he divulged his secret, he'd most likely end up back in the nut house. But when she brought up hearing a mysterious third voice on their last recorded session, a sudden fear took hold. The moment she wanted to replay it so he could hear it for himself, his mind spiraled out of control.

Was it possible, he thought, *that it was the Shadow?* There was no conceivable way the voice inside his head could have been captured on Dr. Mendoza's recorder. Or could it? *No,* he thought. There had to be some other explanation. Perhaps a noise in the background mistaken for a voice or something malfunctioned with the recorder.

Nevertheless, he'd nearly thrown up right there in her office. He'd felt a desperate need to get away... away from Dr. Mendoza and away from the truth. The room seemed to be closing in on him. He remembered how his body trembled, how unsteady he felt the second he got to his feet, feverishly searching for an escape. The moment he rushed out of his therapist's office—promising to reschedule—he'd barely made it outside, spewing up all the contents of his stomach, reverse as it went down.

Joseph reached for his phone and stared at it, reluctant to take the call. He took a deep breath and swiped to answer. "Hello."

"Joseph, this is Dr. Mendoza. I hope I'm not calling at a bad time."

"No." He cleared his throat. "It's fine."

"Oh good." Her voice sounded relieved. "I've been a bit concerned. You seemed rather unwell during our last session, and you haven't rescheduled. Is everything all right?"

"Uh, yeah. I'm sorry about that. I've been meaning to call, but..." He paused, thinking of an excuse. "Work... it-it's been kind of hectic lately. I guess it just slipped my mind."

There was a beat of silence, then finally Dr. Mendoza said, "Joseph, are you sure you're okay?"

"Yeah," he quickly answered. "I'm fine. And I guess I should go ahead and make that appointment."

"How about this morning?"

"This morning?" Joseph said, his eyes rounding. "Uh, sure. What time?"

"I have an opening in an hour."

"Okay." The word squeaked from his dry throat. "I'll see you then."

"Perfect," she said. "I'll connect you to the receptionist's desk so they can pencil you in."

"Thank you, Dr. Mendoza."

"You're welcome, Joseph."

Shortly after Joseph confirmed his appointment, he ended the call and stripped out of his sweaty clothes. It was like his body immediately went into autopilot, but still, memories of Carrie's voice, filled with sorrow and betrayal, plagued his mind. And then his mind traveled back to her car. *I should call her,* he thought. *But would she even pick up?*

"No," he said out loud. "Bad idea." He exhaled a sigh. "I'll text her instead."

He swallowed back his nerves and sent her a text.

I'm stopping by your apartment to pick up my Jeep in half an hour. I will drive you to the restaurant to get your car like I promised.

He stared at his phone for what seemed forever, waiting to see if she'd respond. His heart ached as the minutes ticked by, feeling as though time stood still. He closed his eyes, praying she'd agree to his offer, like somehow God would feel sorry for him and answer his prayers. He didn't like the way things ended last night, realizing he'd broken her heart. And to top it off, he'd frightened her. He was desperate to apologize to Carrie, to make things right. Although deep down, he knew he couldn't repair the damage he'd done. The damage the Shadow had done. It was too late. It would take a miracle, but still, he could pray.

"Look at you, Joseph," the Shadow said, his spiteful voice compelling Joseph's lids back open. *"Praying to God. Do you honestly believe he cares about you?"*

"Get out of my head, dammit."

"Admit defeat, Joseph. You'll never hear from Carrie again."

Joseph snarled his upper lip. "Go. To. Hell."

"Oh, I plan on it. And I'm taking you with me."

Joseph ignored the voice, and before he stepped into the shower, his thoughts went back to Dr. Mendoza. Now, he had to face it all over again. In less than an hour, he'd be at the Jones Therapy Clinic, sitting across from his therapist, dreading whatever was on that recording.

"I warned you about your therapist. We need to take care of her."

"No." Joseph shook his head wearily. "I told you. I will not kill for you again."

"You say that as though you have a choice."

"You will no longer control me. And I promise, I will find a way to destroy you."

"Oh, we will see, Joseph. We. Will. See."

Nearly an hour later, Joseph pulled into the parking lot of the Jones Therapy Clinic. As soon as he put the Jeep in park, he leaned back in his seat and sighed. He felt like his mind was teetering on the edge of insanity, and his heart near the breaking point. Earlier, when he'd taken an Uber to Carrie's apartment complex to retrieve his vehicle, he still hadn't heard from her. No mention of her car. *Nada.*

Finally, after building up the courage, he went straight to her apartment to see if she needed a ride. His stomach did somersaults as he'd knocked and waited. When Carrie's roommate answered the door, she looked at him like a person about to deliver bad news. Unfortunately, it was. Jessica had explained that she'd already taken Carrie to pick up her car an hour ago, and that she'd left from the restaurant to go to work. She said something about Carrie having an early meeting this morning. He could tell the last part was a lie by the way Jessica lowered her gaze and fidgeted with her hands.

"Aww... I guess God didn't hear your prayers after all." The Shadow's smug voice brought Joseph back to focus, irritating him further. *"If you'd just killed her from the beginning, you would have saved yourself all this grief. Now, Carrie hates you. And she knows our secrets. Something must be done about it."*

"I won't allow you to harm her." Joseph's heart hammered inside his chest. "I swear..." He paused, swallowing hard. "I'll take my own life if that's what I have to do."

Joseph sat there, waiting for the Shadow to reply or threaten him in some way. But there was nothing. Only silence. It was so quiet he could have heard a pin drop. He should have been relieved, but instead, it made him nervous. And afraid. Afraid of what the Shadow might unexpectedly do.

When Joseph looked out the window and stared at the clinic, a sudden sick feeling settled into the pit of his gut. *I can do this,* he mentally tried to convince himself. He glanced down at his watch and took a deep breath. *I better get in there,* he thought as he opened his door, forcing himself to get out.

A few moments later, his heart went into overdrive as he went to push open the door that led into the clinic. He briefly paused and stared at his reflection in the door's glass. He looked like he'd been on a bender from hell. His face was pale, and dark circles rested below his eyes. The blue color of his irises appeared darker, haunted by a feeling of hopelessness. He was ready to say *the hell with it* and turn right back around. But Joseph knew he couldn't escape Dr. Mendoza. His therapy sessions were mandated by the institute the day he'd been discharged. Although it was only for a year, still, he found himself caught between a rock and a hard place.

He inhaled a deep breath, opened the door, and exhaled as he stepped inside. It wasn't long after he'd checked in at the front desk that the nurse had called his name and escorted him to the room he'd been dreading.

"Make yourself comfortable, Mr. Parker," the nurse said, holding the door open. "Dr. Mendoza will be with you shortly."

Joseph forced a smile. "Thanks."

He took a seat in an oversized chair directly across from his therapist's desk. Seconds later, the door opened, and Dr. Mendoza stepped into the room.

"Hello, Joseph." She greeted him with a smile, and the kindness in her warm brown eyes eased some of his bottled-up tension. "It's good to see you again."

Joseph rose from his chair and offered her his hand. "You too. And I'd like to apologize again for our last session. I didn't mean to run out on you like I did. I guess I had a stomach bug or something."

She took his hand in a brief shake, clearly noticing the exhausted look on his face. "There's no need for apologies. I completely understand." She tilted her head, staring at him with a concerned expression. "Joseph, are you sure you're feeling okay? Your face is white as a sheet."

"Uh, yeah," he said, releasing her hand. "I just haven't been sleeping well. But I'm fine."

Her brows drew together. "How long has this been going on?"

"A few days, that's all."

"Please." She gestured him to the oversized chair. "Let's get started, shall we?"

"Um, sure," he said, slowly sinking into the padded leather cushion, his nerves skyrocketing.

She took a seat behind her desk and faced him. "Joseph, I can tell something is on your mind. Would you like to talk about it? Perhaps whatever is keeping you up at night."

He leaned back, exhaling a small sigh of relief, praying this would take her focus off the recorded voice and she'd forget all about it.

The Shadow laughed inside Joseph's subconscious. *"Really, Joseph? Haven't you learned by now? Praying will get you nowhere. Besides, your shrink isn't letting that shit go."*

Silence hung in the air.

"Joseph..." Dr. Mendoza raised her voice. "Did you hear what I said?"

He snapped back to focus. "Sorry. Um, it's about Carrie."

"The young woman you've been seeing?"

Joseph nodded. "I *think* we broke up last night."

She leaned forward with her hands clasped and narrowed her gaze. "I'm sorry to hear that. Did something happen?"

He glanced down at his hands. "I-I told her."

"Careful Joseph," the Shadow warned. *"You're treading on thin ice."*

"Exactly what did you tell her?"

Joseph looked up, his eyes full of regret. "I told her about my past."

"The part about your parents or the institute?"

"Both," he said, swallowing hard.

"Oh, I see." She nodded. "And how did Carrie react?"

He nervously gripped the chair's armrests. "She seemed shocked at first, but then compassionate and considerably understanding."

"Well, that's good. So, what makes you think you've broken up?"

"Because..." His mind reeled, trying to come up with an answer. *She's in danger.* But he kept that to himself. "I think Carrie deserves someone better. Someone without a past. Someone normal."

"Did you tell her that?"

"Yes," he hesitantly said.

"Tell me why you believe you're unworthy of love, Joseph?"

"I don't know." He shrugged. "Probably because I'm damaged."

"Just because you've had a rough start at life doesn't mean you're unworthy of someone's love. Everyone has something in their past, Joseph. And I'm sure Carrie has things in hers as well. We all fight our own demons, but that doesn't mean we are damaged goods."

My demons are real, Joseph wanted to say, but instead he said, "But not just everyone has been institutionalized for most of their life. I mean, I've never experienced everyday things until only recently. My job at the Chronicle is the only employment I've ever had. I don't own anything, except for my vehicle. And Carrie..." He let out a weary sigh. "She's the first girl... I've ever..."

"So maybe you've had a late start in life," she said, straightening her shoulders. "It doesn't mean you're a bad person or abnormal. You're still so young, and you're selling yourself short, Joseph. I see an intelligent, handsome, responsible young man, worthy of love. And you have more than enough time to experience all those things. Most people don't have their life in order by age thirty. I think you're making good progress here."

Joseph's brows lifted. "You really think so?"

"Yes, I do. But you've got to give it a chance. Stop worrying about disappointing other people and start believing in yourself. Just because your life started out tragic doesn't mean it has to continue that way. You are worthy of so much, Joseph. Look how far you've come already."

They continued to talk about Joseph's relationship with Carrie and the new position at the Chronicle he'd been interested in applying for. Time seemed to slip by, until finally Dr. Mendoza glanced at the clock on the wall, realizing their session had ended thirty minutes ago.

"Oh dear," she said, moving to her feet. "Look at the time. I'm sorry, Joseph, but we'll have to end it here. I've got another appointment scheduled in ten minutes." Her expression grew serious as she moved from her desk. "I was really hoping we could discuss where we'd left off during our last session."

Joseph nodded and quickly rose from his chair. "I'll schedule another appointment before I leave. Besides," he paused, glancing down at his watch, "I need to get to work."

She came forward and took hold of Joseph's hand. "Of course. We'll discuss this another time."

"Lucky bastard," the Shadow said. *"And I was hoping for a reason to kill your shrink. But there's always next time."*

"And don't forget, Joseph. You deserve to be happy. And I hope things work out between you and Carrie."

"Thanks, Dr. Mendoza." Joseph's lips turned up into a half smile. "So do I."

Chapter Thirty-Seven

"Let's go," Tim said, motioning toward the others. "Those Biters couldn't have gotten far." He led the way, while Jace, Roman, Drakon, and Nicolas trailed close behind.

Jena, along with Lenny, Jem, and Detective Manuel Sanchez and his partner Frank Perkins, decided to hang back until Athena and her brother Augustus healed. Although they'd already consumed enough of Jena's blood to cure the mysterious and deadly vampire virus, it seemed to be taking longer to restore their bodies than it did Lenny's. Most likely it had something to do with them becoming ill months before Lenny had displayed any symptoms.

It was hard for Jena to watch the others go, her gut dreading the decision to stay behind, but it was the right thing to do. Not only were Athena and Augustus too weak in their current physical state, the two human detectives were defenseless and vulnerable to go up against the vampirish creatures. Someone had to protect them. In case they were attacked, between Jena, Lenny, and Jem, surely it was enough backup to keep them safe. Besides, they couldn't very well leave them alone to defend themselves.

* * *

"It's payback time," Jace said as he and his Breedline companions made their way down a dark, narrow hallway that seemed to go on forever. "Where are you?" He raised his voice, shining a flashlight in one hand and toting a jagged medical instrument in the other. "You *little* bloodsuckers."

"Speak up, Jace," Drakon said in a mock scolding voice, following directly behind Roman. "I don't think they heard you."

Jace glanced back at Drakon with a Clint Eastwood glare. "I don't know 'bout the rest of you, but *I'm* ready to get this shit over with."

"Me too, buddy," Roman whispered from behind Jace, nodding his head.

"I wonder how Jena and the others are doing," Jace said, glancing back at Roman. "Do you think—"

"Shhh…" Tim cut him off. "Would you please stop talking and keep your eyes ahead."

Jace raised a hand in defeat. "Okay, okay."

They moved slower now, keeping their eyes peeled, ready for something to spring out at any moment. But when Jace suddenly came to an abrupt halt, Roman, who wasn't paying attention, nearly bumped into him. He immediately threw his hands out. "What the hell, Jace?"

Tim looked at Jace with his brows pinched. "What's wrong?"

"I have to take a piss."

Tim heaved out an irritated breath. "Seriously?"

Jace nodded with a desperate look.

"Fine." Tim eyed the limited space. "Just go over there." He pointed toward the far end of the wall. "Make it quick. We'll cover your back."

A few minutes later, and what sounded like a raging river, Jace finally zipped up and jogged back over. "Much better." He let out a contented sigh. "Thanks, guys."

Finally, as they approached a tall steel door, it reminded Jace of the spine-chilling room where he and Roman had found all those sharp medical instruments. He cringed at the thought and wondered if that's where the nutty physician tortured his patients. He tucked the eerie notion in the back of his mind and moved next to Tim. Using the flashlight, Jace directed it alongside the door's frame. He flinched, cursing under his breath as a spider scurried down. Then he shined the light over a metal name plate. It had something written in black, bold letters.

Jace read it aloud, "Test room B." He rolled his eyes, trying his best to keep his voice to a minimum. "Pfft… This is probably where *Dr. Frankenstein* does all his freaky research. There's no telling what's in there. This could be where those creepy Biters slithered off to."

"Well…" Tim reached for the doorknob. "We're fixing to find out. Let's see if it's unlocked."

As soon as he gave the knob a twist, it turned. He quickly looked over his shoulder at the others, who had gathered behind him. "It's open." He kept his voice low and his hand clasped onto the door handle. "Get ready, guys." He took a few slow breaths, facing the door again. "Here goes nothing."

Tim eased the door open, his heart pausing a beat or two, relieved the hinges didn't creak. He silently signaled to Jace, nodding at the flashlight in his hand. Jace gave him a nod back and turned to face the dark room, preparing himself for whatever the hell was inside. The second he aimed the beam of light straight ahead, the hairs on the back of his neck stood on end. Something wasn't right. He instantly sensed danger. He took a couple of steps inside and immediately recoiled.

"Holy shit," Jace gasped, holding back his gag reflex. "What the *hell* is that smell?"

Tim moved in next to him, leaving the others standing inside the dark room. "Over there," Tim said, pointing toward the far side. "It's coming from that direction."

When Jace moved the beam of light across the room, cold dread hit him, and his jaw dangled slackly. There were rows of small cots with what looked to be Biters resting like rotting corpses. He recognized them by their long, dark, matted hair and the matching chiffon dresses. That's when the stringy-haired ghost girl in the horror film, *The Ring* suddenly came to mind. The pungent odor of death that hung in the air was so thick Jace could almost taste it. Hell, it was so rank he could probably cut the ungodly smell with a knife. He winced in disgust, crinkling his nose, and croaked out, "Filthy vampires."

Tim reached for Jace's flashlight and motioned everyone to gather. When they all got within earshot, he leaned in and spoke barely above a whisper. "Guys, look above those cots." He craned his head toward the sleeping vampires and aimed the light above them. The glow of the beam presented a large bay window that had been blacked out. Tim lowered the flashlight and faced them again. "We've got to find a way to break that window. Right now, daylight is our most powerful weapon, and it's just beyond that glass barrier."

"Please," came a strained whisper, "help me."

The voice startled Jace and he nearly jumped out of his skin. He instantly spun on the balls of his feet and faced the voice, with his hand firmly gripping the bone saw.

Tim whirled around with the flashlight extended, aimlessly searching the room. Drakon, Roman, and Nicolas kept their eyes focused, readying themselves to go toe-to-toe with the pack of teenage vampires. But when Tim trained the light toward the far end of the room, there was a man huddled in a corner, whimpering softly, wearing ratty clothes and no shoes. He was handcuffed to a chain embedded in the concrete floor. His eyes were wide and his pale face was a sunken mask of terror.

Tim stepped closer, cringed at what he saw, and instantly took a step back. All the muscles in his body went rigid. He couldn't move. He could only stare at the butchery lying only a few feet away. Not far from the man was a naked, bloody torso. Going by the way it smelled, it had obviously been here at least a few days. Although the person's head was no longer attached to its body, still Tim could easily identify it was a male.

Jace gasped in horror as he got a closer look. "My God..."

"Help me..." the stranger whispered, rattling the handcuffs.

Tim put his finger up to his lips, motioning for the guy to stay silent. Then he slowly moved closer and leaned over the man whose tattered clothes were caked in blood and gore. "Who are you?"

"M-Maximum," the man muttered quietly, swallowing hard. "Maximum Pierce."

Tim cocked a brow, wondering why that name sounded familiar. Then he noticed the trail of bite marks up and down the guy's arms and legs. Not even the exposed skin on his feet was left untouched. He reminded Tim of a dog's chew bone. "Who did this to you?"

"Those *things*..." Maximum glanced over at the sleeping vampires with fear in his eyes. "They've been taking turns, feeding on me for days."

"How'd you end up here?"

"Dr. Henry Michaels," Maximum answered. "Then he drugged me." He let out a dry, ragged breath. "When I came around, I found myself in here, handcuffed to the floor."

Tim turned toward the others and motioned for Nicolas. As Nicolas moved next to Tim, he knelt in front of Maximum. "Did you know this person?" Nicolas asked, gesturing to the decapitated body.

Maximum nodded. "H-his name was Adrian García. He was like a brother to me." Tears streamed down his cheeks. "Those cannibals killed him. They practically ate him alive."

Suddenly, the name registered in Nicolas like a beacon going off in his brain. Heat flared within him. He stood straight and faced Tim. "They're the two guys who were involved with Jena's kidnapping."

"Shit," Tim said, releasing a sigh. "Well, we can't just leave the poor bastard here."

"Hey, guys," Jace quietly muttered, feeling a sickening drop in his gut. When no one looked, he raised his voice. "Oh, guys, I believe someone is waking up."

When Tim and the others turned, they cringed as the clan of sleeping vampires began to rise. They came awake like animated corpses, hissing and growling. Deathly pale faces glistened beneath their myriad veils of black hair.

* * *

Tension began to seep into Manuel's body as he glanced down at his watch. *Dammit,* he cursed to himself. Nearly an hour had passed since Tim and the others went after those Biters. Now he was beginning to worry.

"You can't make time go any faster by looking at it," Frank said.

Manuel looked up. "What?"

"That's the fifth time you've checked your watch, partner."

Manuel sighed. "You'd think they'd be back by now."

"Don't worry." Frank smiled a little. "They're more than capable of taking care of themselves. Besides, they've got Jace with them. And I don't think there's a creature out there that can go toe-to-toe with his Beast. The guy shifts into a seven-foot werewolf for Pete's sake. Then there's Nicolas, who is not only immortal and super strong but he can also move faster than a bullet. And Roman is backing them up too. In addition, there's Drakon and Tim. The combination is impressive, wouldn't you say?"

Manuel nodded. "I guess you've got a point there."

Nonetheless Manuel checked his watch again and began pacing the floor.

As time passed, an eerie silence descended on the room, making the hairs on Frank's neck prickle up. They were still in the room where the bodies of the decapitated Biters lay, along with the very deceased physician, and Fiona. He still couldn't believe Henry killed his own mother. And thanks to Jena's creature, the mad physician and his savage little monsters had met their fate. Hopefully, Tim and the rest of the Breedline crew were taking care of the ones who managed to escape.

He looked to where Fiona's body lay underneath a sheet, feeling sympathy for the poor woman, although he'd never met her until today. Then he averted his eyes from the shroud covering Fiona and focused on Manuel, who finally stopped pacing. "Hey, partner, you still wearing the gold cross necklace Kathryn gave you for your birthday?"

Manuel nodded. "Yeah, why?"

"Well, I was thinking it might come in handy."

"It doesn't work on *real* vampires, remember?" Manuel said. "By what Nicolas said, there's only two things that can kill them. And that's sunlight and severing of the head."

Frank looked discouraged. "I guess you're right."

Manuel glanced over the room, feeling a shiver work its way up his spine. "Something doesn't feel right."

"What do you mean?"

"Call me crazy," Manuel said, "but for some strange reason, I feel like we're being watched. Don't you feel it?"

And Frank could. Something seemed off. It was too quiet, like something was lurking in the shadows, unseen to the eye. There was a presence somewhere. His mouth went dry, and he had to lick his lips before he could speak. "Yeah, I can feel it too."

Manuel looked past Frank to the open doorway when he heard faraway footsteps. When a dark figure appeared, his heart sank. "Shit... Looks like my intuition was right."

As Frank turned to look, he saw a tall, masculine woman, who was fast approaching. Her long red hair bounced with each stride. The blank expression in her eyes was chilling, like she was spellbound by something unknown. "Is that..." Frank swallowed in mid-sentence. "...who I think it is?"

"It's Karina Adams," Manuel said. "Kian's twin sister."

"She doesn't look human."

"No, she doesn't," Manuel replied.

Frank's stomach tightened into a hard knot as Karina's lips formed into an awful, menacing snarl, revealing tips of sharp-pointed teeth.

Before Manuel got the chance to call out to Jena, a small group of hissing Biters emerged from the shadows. They stalked behind Karina like she was the leader of the pack.

Frank drew his weapon. "Stay back!"

Karina halted in her tracks and growled in response, a guttural doglike sound.

The Biters followed close, their eyes alternating between Karina and the two detectives. The sounds coming from their grotesque mouths were inhuman chattering, like they were somehow communicating.

Jena, sensing them approaching minutes before the detectives had, managed to find a way through an exit on the far side of the room without being detected. While she found a way around, planning to attack the bloodsuckers from behind, the others moved in to protect the two detectives.

Manuel kept one hand close to his gun and extended the other, trying to keep Karina and her vampirish companions distracted. "Miss Adams, we have your sister. And we promised her we would bring you back with us unharmed."

Karina and her crew of vamps hungrily glared at Manuel, unaware of Jena as she slowly crept up, moving from the rear.

Waiting for the perfect opportunity, Jena sprang out with slashing claws. As she sank her deadly talons into one of the vampires, it let out an unearthly, high-pitched screech. In a matter of seconds, Jena dismembered the vampire's head.

Frank was stunned by the sheer brutality and cunning skills as Jena went from one creature to the next, ripping and tearing at their flesh. Then, before his eyes, Jem's body began to stretch as if something underneath his skin was trying to break free. The skin-twisting carnage seemed to end as fast as it began. In a flash, his clothes burst from his body. The tiny fragments of material scattered to the floor into pieces. It happened so fast Frank thought he'd only imagined it. Jem's human form simply vanished and was replaced by an enormous wolf with snow-white fur. It briefly looked between Manuel and Frank as though a silent understanding had taken place. Instantly, the wolf advanced on their enemies. It growled as it leapt forward, springing on its haunches, launching itself into the air.

The remaining vampires scrabbled on all fours, trying to escape death. Although Jena's creature and Jem's Breedline wolf had nearly taken them all, Karina managed to evade her fate. Lenny, Athena, Augustus, and the two detectives didn't notice as she quickly cut away from the group and slipped out of sight. Their eyes were focused on the savagery before them, praying their friends were powerful enough to destroy the bloodthirsty monstrosities.

Karina darted through the exit Jena had used, and when she snuck up behind the others, she threw both arms around Lenny's neck with a convulsive yell. And then, incredibly, she threw him across the room. He crashed into the corner, knocking the breath out of him.

Unexpectedly, Karina attacked Frank. He'd only caught a shadowed glimpse of her lunging on top of him, ripping at his shirt, and then the yawning of her jaws.

Manuel called out in desperation and threw himself at Karina. As he grabbed for her hair, he could hear the revolting sound of chopping lips, skin tearing, and Frank's despairing scream.

With gritted teeth, Manuel fisted a handful of Karina's hair and yanked her head upward. Her head spun around like the swiftness of an owl's, facing him with rage and blood coating her lips.

Manuel nearly gagged the instant she bared her fangs and hissed in his face. Her foul breath was beyond measure, like something had crawled down her throat and died. On pure instinct, he quickly released her hair and reached into the front of his shirt for the cross necklace. *Screw it,* he thought to himself. *Here goes nothing.* The moment he brought the cross up and flashed the gold pendant in her face, she looked stunned at first. Her eyes widened, and her jaw dropped like she was going to let out one hell of a protest. But instead, she burst into some ungodly cackle, the guttural sounds raising the hairs on the back of his neck. It was worse than the sound of fingernails scratching on a chalkboard.

Manuel grimaced. *Ah, hell!* He took a few steps back and drew his gun. "Come on, bitch." He taunted her. "Show me what you got."

Karina snarled her upper lip and before she had the chance to lunge at Manuel, something sharp sliced over her throat. Instinctively, her eyes bulged as she grasped hold, feeling a wet, sticky substance seeping between her fingers. A gurgling escaped her lips, realizing it was blood. And this time, it was her blood.

Karina looked up when a petite woman, holding a blood-soaked blade, stepped into view. In that instant, she knew it was her attacker. As the life drained from her throat, something clamped over her ears. It pressed against them with so much force, she thought her skull would burst. She tried to struggle, but the grip was too strong. It was as solid as Greek stone. Then she felt her neck begin to stretch, until finally, the opening in her skin snapped and gave way. Karina's vision soon faded into darkness.

Manuel looked to Augustus, who held Karina's head, and then to Athena with complete astonishment. He nodded a silent *thank-you* and focused his eyes on his partner. Frank was already on his feet, holding a hand to the side of his neck as blood seeped through his fingers. The dreadful image nearly brought Manuel to his knees.

"Sh-she bit me," Frank sputtered, his panic-stricken gaze bouncing back and forth between Manuel and Karina's decapitated head.

Chapter Thirty-Eight

Jace extended the bone saw and positioned himself into a fight stance as the pale-faced creatures started to stalk forward. Their lips were peeled back, revealing rows of ivory daggers.

The guy chained to the floor suddenly felt his bladder go full. Quickly, he went into fetal position and began to whimper.

Tim, Nicolas, Drakon, and Roman stood alongside Jace—each gripping a sharp-tipped weapon—readying themselves for the fight of their lives.

There was at least a dozen, if not more, of those putrid, walking corpses. And they looked hungry, feasting their crazed, dead-looking eyes upon them, hissing like a mass of snakes.

Tired of waiting, Jace made a move. With a deep-throated yell, he lunged at the closest vampire, preparing to chop off her head. With fast reflexes, she evaded the blade, but not fast enough. Jace reached out and snatched a wad of her long, matted hair. She howled and clawed, fighting to break free. In one swift motion, he shoved the blade deep into her jugular. As it tore through the back of her skull, wet ripping noises, like someone squishing overripe fruit, mingled with the sounds of bones cracking.

The horrific noises that came out of the vampire's mouth sounded like a squealing pig and ended with liquid bubbles. She went silent the moment her head finally tore free. Jace tossed it aside and glared at the remaining group of vampires, his eyes glittering with satisfaction.

While Jace went to work on another vampire, slicing and dicing, his comrades-in-arms sprang into action, wreaking havoc on a few vampirish ghouls of their own.

The pack of bloodsuckers fought like hell, fighting much harder than they would have expected, going by their petite, girlish frames. But they were no ordinary group of teenage girls. More like Satan's spawn.

Roman was thrown off guard when one of the vampires tackled him from behind. She climbed up his body as swiftly as a slithering serpent. When she bit into his shoulder, he let out a hell-fire scream. On instinct, he reached for the girl's hair, grabbed a chunk, and slung her to the floor. He heard the smack of her face as it hit the concrete hard. The moment he lifted the blade, preparing to strike, her head did a 360, reminding him of the possessed girl in the *Exorcist*.

When her head stopped spinning, her mouth juddered open in an awful, snarling hiss. The rank odor instantly assailed Roman's nostrils and sank deep in his gut. He forced down the dry heave lingering in the back of his throat and continued in his endeavor to lop off her head. But before he could strike, the girl covered her face and started to weep. "Please, sir," she said in a child's sobbing voice. "Please don't hurt me."

Roman slowly lowered his weapon, feeling a painful tug at his heart. He reached out halfway and muttered, "Little girl... are you okay?"

When she made no reply, he stood there waiting, his eyes focused on the girl, listening to the sounds of her heart-wrenching tears. It was as though all the chaotic noise surrounding him suddenly drifted away and silence took over the room. Carefully, he inched his hand closer.

"Don't touch her," Nicolas said, stopping Roman's hand from moving further. "She's using her powers to manipulate you."

Roman turned to Nicolas. "But—"

"No, Roman." Nicolas shook his head. "It's a trick."

He looked away from Nicolas and at the girl, with confusion set in his gaze. She seemed so small with her knees tucked in, and her hands shielding what he imagined was a tear-stained face. Roman turned back to Nicolas, his eyes racked with indecision as the girl's sobbing grew louder. "For Christ's sake," Roman said. "She's just a little—"

His words trailed off as the girl sprang forward, exploding in a fit of rage. Her bony fingers, hooked into claws, slashed across Roman's surprised face. She drew bloody scratches down the side of his cheeks like a feral cat. In a protective measure, Roman spun away, barely avoiding the claws aiming for his eyes.

Thinking fast, Nicolas grabbed the girl by the waist, still kicking and screaming, and tossed her sandbag style across the room. It wasn't long before she collided with the blacked-out window. As glass exploded, soft beams of the morning light engulfed the dark room. The girl's screams were deafening, echoing with raw, agonizing pain. When they finally faded into silence, dark smoke filtered inside, followed by bits and pieces of floating ash.

Roman looked at Nicolas in relief and nodded an approval.

Nicolas gave him a nod back.

The sunlight's burning rays were like a chain reaction, incinerating the remaining vampirish creatures with shrieks of agony.

Nicolas and his Breedline comrades watched in amazement as every single vampire went up in flames. All in the space of a minute, they turned to ash, silencing their horrid screams forever.

The stink of burnt flesh was thick in the air, and everyone in the room had just about reached their limits.

"I don't know 'bout the rest of you jokers," Jace said, "but I'm outta here."

"I'm right behind you," Roman said.

As the Breedline crew started for the door, a feeble voice called out, "Wait... You can't just leave me here."

As they turned to look, their eyes met Maximum's.

"How is it he's still alive?" Drakon asked. "He's been bitten. Shouldn't he be ash by now?"

"Biters only turn females," Nicolas explained. "Males are strictly a food source, so they don't secrete venom during feeding."

"If he's not going to be a threat," Tim said, "we need to get him out of here. And I'm going to need some help getting him out of those chains." He searched over the faces in the room. "Do I have any volunteers?"

"What about Jace?" Roman said. "He can break through those chains with his bare hands."

"No way man." Jace adamantly shook his head. "I'm seriously 'bout to hurl here, guys."

"I'll do it," Nicolas said.

"Thanks, buddy." Jace huffed a sigh of relief. "I'll go check on Jena and the others."

As Jace started for the door, Roman hollered, "Hold up. I'm coming with you."

* * *

As Frank dropped to his knees, his hand clutching his throat, blood oozed between the cracks of his fingers.

Manuel rushed over. "Frank—"

With his face contorted with pain, Frank held up a halting hand. "Don't come any closer."

"For crying out loud, Perkins," Manuel said, "you're bleeding like a stuck pig."

Lenny, who had managed to gather his bearings, moved to his feet and approached Manuel. "Your partner is right, Detective." He placed a reassuring hand on Manuel's shoulder. "Although the woman who bit him is dead, it's imperative you keep your distance. At least until we're sure she did not inject him with venom."

Manuel watched as Athena came to Frank's aid and placed a handkerchief to the gaping wound on his neck.

Manuel averted his eyes and looked to Lenny. "How long is that going to take?"

"Within the next twenty-four hours."

Augustus came forward and knelt in front of Frank. "Do you have a family?"

"Y-yes." Frank's eyes grew wide. "Why?"

"You'll need to avoid contact with them. Your family will be in danger until we know for sure you weren't exposed to the venom."

"But..." Frank swallowed. "I don't feel any different."

"It's still too early to tell," Augustus said.

Frank looked at Manuel and saw worry in his eyes. Then he refocused back on Augustus and said, "If Karina injected me with her venom, what's going to happen?"

"You'll have an insatiable craving for human blood."

Frank's eyes widened. "Please tell me I'm not going to turn into one of those *things*."

"Not unless you consume human blood," Athena said. "And I promise, you'll be human again, but the process..." She momentarily hesitated, keeping pressure on Frank's wound while thinking of the best way to explain without completely terrifying him. "I'm not going to lie, Detective. It may be a bit painful. But you must have faith."

"If that happens, how long will it take the venom to be out of my system?"

"At least two weeks," Athena replied. "It also depends on the amount of venom. But your body will eventually break it down."

Frank's mind was a complete whirlwind. He briefly closed his eyes and said a silent prayer.

"Don't worry, partner," Manuel said. "Come hell or high water, we're going to get you through this. You hear me?"

Frank looked up at his partner and gave him a slight nod.

"I don't think you have anything to worry about," Lenny said. "The worst-case scenario you'll have to come up with an explanation for the bite marks to your family."

A familiar voice called out, "What bite marks?"

Frank swore the voice came from Jace, but he couldn't be sure. He was too busy thinking of how he was going to explain all this to Missy. And what was he going to do if he was infected and couldn't go home for two weeks. Then he remembered his niece's birthday party. What reason would he give Carrie if he couldn't go? In addition, how would he explain the bite marks on his neck? *Dammit!* His wife would never buy some cockamamie story. Besides, could he really be untruthful to her? He'd never lied to her before. An icy panic hit his stomach just thinking about it.

When Jace and Roman came forward, they focused on Athena. She was crouched next to Frank, applying a bandage on his neck. And going by all the blood seeping through, it didn't look good.

"Don't worry," Frank said, noticing Jace's worried expression. "I'll be fine."

"Fine my ass," Jace said, eyeballing the bloody bandage on Frank's neck. "What the hell happened?"

"She's what happened," Frank explained, pointing to Karina's severed head.

Jace's mouth slacked open. "Shit... Is that who I think it is?"

"Yep," Manuel said. "That's Kian Adams' twin sister."

"Wait a minute," Jace said. "Are you telling me Karina was a vampire and she bit you?"

When Frank nodded, Jace said, "So, who hacked off her head?"

"I did," Augustus said, "but not before my sister cut her throat."

Jace's expression glimmered with approval, giving Augustus and his sister a thumbs-up. "You really went all medieval on that chick."

Roman's eyes nervously roamed over the occupants of the room. "Frank's not going to turn into a vampire, is he?"

"We think he'll be fine," Lenny said. "It's more than likely, since he's a male, Karina did not inject him with her venom. But just to be sure, he'll need to be monitored for the next twenty-four hours."

"You can hunker down at the Covenant," Jace said. "I'm sure Tessa won't mind."

Frank smiled a little. "I'd appreciate that, Jace. I just don't know what I'm going to tell my wife. If I've got to be away from home for two days, much less two weeks, how am I supposed to explain to her where I'm at?"

"You can tell Missy you're on a stakeout," Manuel suggested.

"I don't know. I'm not sure I can lie to her."

"You won't be lying," Manuel said. "As soon as we wrap this up, we've still got the Harris case to solve."

"But how is that considered a stakeout if I have to be held up at the Covenant for a few days?"

"We'll use a two-way radio," Manuel explained. "If I can get Joseph Harris's address from Dr. Katie Mendoza, I can stake out his place and still keep you on the receiving end.

Sure, you won't be there physically, but you'll be able to notify the Covenant if I run into any trouble and need backup."

Frank shrugged. "Yeah, I guess so."

"Keep your chin up," Jace said, smiling at Frank. Then he quickly noticed something in the room was off. "Hey, where's Jena?" He craned his head, searching. "And my brother?"

"They should be back any minute," Lenny said. "The woman who attacked Detective Perkins came with a pack of Biters. If it weren't for Jena and your brother, we would've been outnumbered."

"There was at least a dozen of those things," Manuel said. "Your brother shifted into his Breedline wolf and fought alongside Jena. They took out every Biter, except for that one." He pointed to Karina's head. "Somehow she managed to weasel her way around them. Hell, we didn't even see her. Although she got at Frank, she didn't get much further, thanks to Athena and Augustus."

"And I wasn't much help," Lenny regretfully said. "That redheaded devil woman caught me off guard. She grabbed me from behind and tossed me across the room like a rag doll."

"So, where did Jena and my brother make off to?" Jace asked.

"They're ditching what was left of those Biters," Lenny answered.

Jace shrugged a shoulder. "Where'd they take them?"

"Outside," Lenny said. "Daylight does serve its purposes."

"You can say that again," Roman said. "That's how we took out some the ones we found. Thanks to Nicolas, that is. After he tossed one out a window, they all went up in flames. Nothing was left but a bunch of ashes."

"Speaking of Nicolas," Manuel said, looking between Roman and Jace. "Where is he? And Tim and Drakon?"

"They stayed back to release a prisoner," Roman said. "Apparently, those Biters kept a guy chained to the floor, using him as food. And he wasn't the only one they kept prisoner. Unfortunately, the other guy wasn't so lucky. He lost his head, and I mean that literally."

"The good news is," Jace said, "by what Nicolas said, those two guys are the ones who kidnapped Jena. I believe the guy we found alive said his name was Maximum something or another. I can't remember his last name."

Frank's brows shot up. "You've got to be kidding?"

Jace grinned. "I kid you not."

"I believe you're referring to Maximum Pierce," Manuel said. "The other guy must be Adrian García."

"You mean, was Adrian García." Jace crinkled his nose. "Or what is left of the poor bastard."

"So, what are you planning to do, Detectives?" Roman asked. "I mean, do you plan on calling this one in?"

"If it were up to me," Manuel said, grinding his teeth, "I'd burn this place to the ground."

"That may not be such a bad idea," Frank pointed out. "How in the world are we going to explain everything we've witnessed? You really think the feds will buy our story? Think about it, partner. Are we really going to tell them we found vampires? They'll lock us in the nut house for sure."

"He's got a point, Detective," Lenny said. "Furthermore, how are you going to explain me, Athena, and Augustus? We cannot leave this place until sundown. If your people discover our species, do you really believe they'll let us live?"

"Well, whatever gets decided," Manuel said, "we won't do anything until you can safely leave this place. We've managed to keep the Breedline tight-lipped, and we'll do the same for all of you."

"Thank you, Detective." Lenny dipped his head. "We will forever be grateful."

Chapter Thirty-Nine

Detective Sanchez's knuckles turned white as he gripped the steering wheel of his unmarked car. Although his eyes were trained on the road ahead, his mind was miles away. He was thinking of everything that had occurred at A&E Pharmaceuticals. If he hadn't seen it with his own two eyes, he wouldn't have believed it. Sure, after he'd become aware of the Breedline species, he now viewed the world in an entirely different perspective. What he'd thought was only fictional, like something out of a fairy tale or believed to be a myth, was indeed real. But what Dr. Henry Michaels had done was on a whole new level of insanity. The physician, obviously nutty as a fruitcake, had gone too far.

Using young girls, the physician had created real-life vampires. And they were nothing like the vampires Manuel had previously met, who had practically saved his ass. Lenny, his wife Athena, and her brother Augustus had explained to him, the Breedline crew, and his partner all about the vampires Dr. Michaels had discovered. What remained a mystery was how he managed to reproduce the vampires.

Unfortunately, the Biters were just the tip of the iceberg. Dr. Michaels had used his own children, and his patients, as guinea pigs to devise what Manuel clearly saw as an abomination. What he'd done was incomprehensible and downright evil. How could anyone be so warped to do such a thing? He couldn't even fathom the thought. The whole thing was too surreal. Too unconscionable. Much less moral. And those poor families of all the victims. He couldn't imagine what they were going through, not knowing if their loved ones were dead or alive. It made him feel guilty because he knew what had happened to them all.

When his mind took him to the dreadful incident with his partner, he shifted uneasily in his seat, worried what the next twenty-four hours would be for Frank. Flashbacks, more like scenes out of a night terror, came rushing back. His head swam with images. Horrifying images of sharp-pointed teeth and blood. Lots of blood.

Manuel said a silent prayer for Frank. Then a sudden sense of relief washed over him, realizing his partner was in good hands. He'd be safe at the Breedline Covenant while they monitored him, making sure he hadn't been subjected to the vampire venom.

He stared at the road, continuing to think. Manuel kept wondering if he and his partner had made the right decision when they'd agreed to get rid of most of the evidence by torching A&E Pharmaceuticals. But before they burned the facility, they removed Fiona's body and secured enough documentation that tied Dr. Henry Michaels and his illegal research to the Summit Behavioral Institute for the feds to find. If they'd decided otherwise, it might jeopardize the Breedline Covenant. The more he thought about it, the more he knew it was the right decision on so many levels. Besides, what other choice did they have? If they tried to explain what really happened, and that vampires really existed, he and his partner would surely get carted off in straitjackets. He cringed as a new image came crashing down. It was of a small, white padded cell. *Yeah,* he thought. *We did the right thing.*

Despite their plan to keep the harrowing ordeal with A&E Pharmaceuticals a secret, they still had Maximum Pierce and Kian Adams to contend with. Both had been connected to Dr. Henry Michaels and with Jena's kidnapping, but they also knew way too much about Jena's creature and the Breedline. Most likely, they'd sing like a canary if they turned them over to the authorities. So instead, the Breedline had come up with a solution to their little dilemma. They offered to keep the two culprits in their custody until Manuel and Frank figured out what to do with them. And if the detectives couldn't solve the issue, the members of the Breedline council would decide their fate. Killing them was not an option. The Breedline species weren't cold-blooded murderers, but they did believe in justice. And they'd make damn sure Jena's assailants paid for their crimes.

Finally, Manuel came back to focus when he found a vacant spot in the parking lot at the Jones Therapy Clinic. Earlier, he'd made an appointment to speak with Dr. Katie Mendoza about the Harris case they'd been working. They were hoping to find the person responsible for Kevin Russo's bizarre murder.

While going through old files, Frank had discovered a homicide report that dated back twenty years. Dr. Katie Mendoza—formerly known as Officer Katie Mendoza—was the first responding officer to arrive at the crime scene. Going by the report, a Joe Harris had brutally beaten his wife while their five-year-old son, Joseph, was present. It stated in the report, after the little boy shot his father trying to defend his mother, he was later placed in foster care. There was no one else to care for the kid since his father was hauled off to prison for murder. After gathering all the information, and with the Breedline Covenant's help, it all pointed to this boy.

But there was something else. Something peculiar about this Joseph Harris guy, who for some reason, kept slipping through the cracks. According to what Roman had told them, his description of Joseph matched Jena's when she came across a stranger the night Frank's niece was attacked.

As Manuel cut the engine, unbuckled his seatbelt, and reached for the door to exit his vehicle, he prayed Katie had more information on this mysterious Joseph Harris.

He stood outside his vehicle, trying to relax despite his nerves. He exhaled a deep breath and surveyed the parking lot. It was early, but there were a few other cars. Aside from a silver Mercedes-Benz and the shiny red Porsche, there were a couple of older models, making his Ford Taurus seem so less economical. On a detective's salary, luxury cars were not affordable.

The moment he pushed his way into the Jones Therapy Clinic, his expression went from weary to surprised. Unexpectedly, the place seemed quiet and rather normal. Not what he'd imagined it would be. He stood in the entry, searching over the waiting area. The interior design was pleasant, and the neutral, off-white walls gave off a calming effect. There were several comfortable-looking, plaid cushioned chairs, a magazine rack, a few small tables decorated with floral arrangements, and a flat-screen TV mounted on the wall. A grey-haired couple sitting across the room, apparently waiting to see a therapist, appeared content watching an episode of *The Andy Griffith Show* in black and white. And somewhere nearby, the distinct scent of coffee brewing invaded his senses. The rich and soothing aroma instantly spiked his taste buds.

For some strange reason, he'd thought the inside would be noisy, and lunatic-like, seeing that it was a facility where you went for mental health treatment. Images of people, dressed in their pajamas, sitting at tables putting together puzzle pieces came to mind. But then it suddenly dawned on him. He'd been thinking of an institution for the mentally ill. This was a therapeutic clinic, not an insane asylum. *No white padded cells here,* Manuel thought as he approached the receptionist's desk.

"May I help you, sir?" a man sporting a polka-dotted bow tie asked.

"I'm Detective Sanchez. I have an appointment to speak with Dr. Mendoza."

"Ah, yes," the receptionist said. "Please, have a seat, Detective. I'll let her know you're here. Help yourself to a cup of coffee." He gestured to a table across the room. "I just made a fresh pot."

Manuel dipped his head. "Thank you."

It wasn't long after he topped off his second coffee and tossed the little Styrofoam cup into the trash when a young nurse, who had to be at least six feet, if not taller, appeared. Her platinum-blonde hair was neatly arranged in a bun on top of her head. "Detective Sanchez," she said, smiling perfectly white teeth. "Dr. Mendoza will see you now."

He smiled back at the blonde Amazonian and proceeded to follow her down a long hallway. When they came to a door at the end, she knocked once. "Dr. Mendoza." She peered inside. "Detective Sanchez is here to see you."

"Thank you, Nurse Flinn."

When the nurse pushed the door wider, Manuel instantly recognized the woman standing next to a desk. She had long dark braids and a welcoming smile on her lovely face. As soon as the nurse left, Manuel stepped inside with his hand outstretched.

"Hello, Detective Sanchez," she said, grasping his hand. "It's so nice to see you. I was so surprised to hear from you when you called. It's been a few years."

"It's nice to see you too, Dr. Mendoza. And yes, it's been a while since we last spoke."

"Oh, please." Her smile broadened. "Call me Katie."

"I'll make you a deal." Manuel released her hand. "I'll call you Katie as long as you call me by my given name."

"Deal." She chuckled, guiding him to an oversized chair. "Please, make yourself comfortable, Manuel."

As he settled in the chair, she took a seat in the one directly across from his. "So how have you been?" She looked at him curiously. "Married or children?"

He shook his head. "Neither."

"You've never married?"

"Just to the job," Manuel said. "How 'bout you? You and Oscar still together?"

She nodded. "We just celebrated our twenty-first anniversary."

"That's good to hear." Manuel grinned. "I always liked Oscar. And if I recall, the guy has one helluva right hook."

"Well, I guess you could say he used to." She laughed a little. "He gave up boxing five years ago. Nowadays, Oscar mostly hikes. And I'm glad. It's a lot safer and fewer trips to the dentist."

Manuel chuckled. "Yeah, you're probably right. Hell, I should know. Missing a few teeth myself." He smoothed his tongue over the empty space in the back of his mouth. "So, you two have kids?"

"We have a son, Hector. He's eleven now."

"That's great, Katie. And I have to say, you seem to be doing quite well for yourself. A rewarding career, and a family. I envy you."

"Thank you, Manuel." Her eyes beamed with pride. "How's Frank and his wife Missy doing? That is, last time I was on the force, you two were partners. Things are still the same, am I right?"

He went silent for a minute, thinking about Frank's current situation.

"Manuel?" Her eyes roamed over Manuel's face, noticing his blank stare. "Is something wrong? Did something happen to Frank?"

Her concerned voice snapped him back to focus. "Oh no." Manuel waved it off like it was nothing. "He's doing fine. Still married to Missy, and yes, we're still partners."

"Thank goodness." She placed a hand over her heart. "Going by the expression on your face, it worried me. When I asked you about Frank, you went pale as a ghost. Are you sure everything is all right?"

"Don't worry, Katie. Frank is perfectly fine," he reassured. "And so is Missy. It's just..." He paused and let out a sigh. "...this case we're working on. It's got us completely baffled. That's one of the reasons why I'm here."

"Oh?" She tilted her head. "How can I be any help?"

"I know it's been over twenty years, but do you remember that Harris case you worked? The one with the five-year-old boy who shot his father, trying to protect his mother?"

"Yes." Her shoulders tensed. "How could I ever forget that one? That case was the reason why I went back to school to get my degree in psychology. Why do you ask?"

"The little boy, Joseph," Manuel began. "After his mother died and his father was carted off to prison for her murder, do you know what happened to the kid?"

She thought about it, recalling that tragic day, wishing she had the power to change it, then finally said, "Since there was no other family member to care for Joseph, he was placed in foster care."

"Did you know the boy was later institutionalized?"

"Yes, I did, but..." Katie shifted uneasily in her chair. "What exactly are you asking, Manuel?"

"Frank and I believe Joseph may have something to do with a recent murder."

Her eyes rounded. "What—"

"Hold on, Katie." He held up a halting hand. "Let me explain. We know Joseph is no longer institutionalized, but the problem is, we can't seem to find the guy. I'm sure you've heard about the Summit Behavioral Institute getting shut down." When she nodded, he continued, "Well, my partner and I had a hand in that. Unfortunately, before we had a chance to question the head physician, he was murdered."

"Yes," she finally said, swallowing hard. "I was shocked when I found out. Those poor people. I just couldn't believe Dr. Leonard Manos could do such horrendous things to his patients."

"So, you knew the physician?"

She solemnly nodded. "He was one of the leading psychiatrists in the nation. We, along with other treatment facilities, care for some of his patients."

"We got into the institutions' files, but for some strange reason, we didn't find a single thing on Joseph Harris. It's as though he was never a patient there. No files, nothing."

"Joseph is now my patient," she hesitantly said. "His files are here. Although I probably shouldn't be telling you this, but since I trust you'll keep this confidential, he no longer goes by the name Harris. He's taken his mother's maiden name. It's Parker now."

His eyes rounded. "You've got to be kidding me?"

She shook her head.

"There's no way he legally changed his name," Manuel said. "If so, Frank and I would have found him in the data base. He must be using a fake ID."

"Maybe," she said. "But whatever the case, he's still my patient, so that's all the information I'm allowed to give you."

When his expression turned frustrated, she said, "I'm sorry, Manuel. But you, more than anyone, should know that I cannot divulge my patient's private records. I would be violating my doctor-patient confidentiality."

"You can if you believe your patient is a danger to himself or others," Manuel firmly stated.

Katie stared at him nervously, thinking about the unexplainable third voice on one of her and Joseph's recorded sessions. Then she looked down at her hands, remembering what *it* had said.

"Katie," Manuel said, his voice bringing her head up, "is there any reason for you to believe Joseph could be potentially dangerous in any way?"

"I just can't believe he would hurt anyone," she wearily said. "I don't deny Joseph has suffered a traumatic event. I mean, my God." She sighed. "Can you imagine what all he went through as a child? Seeing his mother being beat to death at the hands of his own father. But now, he's overcome so much. He's really made such remarkable progress."

Manuel leaned forward and placed his hand over hers. "I can tell you care a great deal for Joseph. Hell, I don't blame you. If I'd been the first officer to respond on that unfortunate day, there's no way I'd ever forget it. It just proves what kind of therapist you are, Katie." He smiled, removing his hand. "You're a good person with a big heart."

She smiled. "Manuel, do you believe in divine intervention?"

"You mean as in God and miracles?"

When she nodded, he said, "Yes. I believe God works in mysterious ways. We may not know why God does what he does, but deep down in my gut, I truly believe there are reasons for why things happen the way they do. Believe me, I've seen my share of mysterious things in my time."

"Me too," she said. "I may not understand why, but I don't think me ending up as Joseph's therapist after all these years is just a coincidence. I believe God brought me back in Joseph's life for a reason. Just like he sent me to him twenty-one years ago."

"You may be on to something there." Manuel leaned forward again. "Katie, can I tell you something confidential?"

"Of course. Anything you say goes no further than my ears. Consider it the same as doctor-patient confidentiality."

"Yeah, but you're not my physician."

"Oh, Manuel, you know you can trust me."

"I trust you, Katie. But what I'm about to say is a bit bizarre. I'm afraid you might want to institutionalize me after I tell you."

She smirked. "Nothing you say will make me think you're crazy. A workaholic maybe, and a little hot-headed as I recall, but not crazy."

"Okay, but remember I warned you." *Here goes nothing,* he thought. "Frank and I know this guy. He's a good friend, and we both know the guy's not a whack job. This friend of ours said he grew up in Joseph's neighborhood."

"So, you're saying this friend of yours..." She paused and did finger quotations. "...knew Joseph when he was a kid, right?"

Manuel nodded. "Our *friend* told us about a strange incident that happened after Joseph was institutionalized. Him and his family were concerned for Joseph's welfare. When they went to visit him in the institution, my friend was left alone with Joseph. He said Joseph attacked him and it took the strength of three guards to pry him off."

"Oh my," Katie said. "I had no idea this had happened. According to Dr. Manos, Joseph had no violent tendencies. His personality traits were identified as shy, timid, and scared. Of course, he'd been diagnosed with a mental illness, but there was nothing mentioned of anger or violent behavior in his files."

"There's more," Manuel said. "It's enough to concern me. Not only for the safety of others, but for yours, Katie."

"My safety?" She shrugged. "But why?"

"My friend described Joseph as if he'd been possessed."

"Are you talking about demon possession?"

"Yes," Manuel replied. "And this one refers to itself as the Shadow."

"The *Shadow*?"

Manuel nodded. "After Frank and I discovered this, we did some digging. This particular demon preys on the innocence of young children. It manipulates their minds and influences them to do things they wouldn't normally do. Think of this *thing* as a marionette and the child as its puppet."

"Are you saying it can hypnotize its victims?"

"I believe something to that nature."

Katie shook her head. "Do you know what it wants?"

"Human souls."

"Manuel..." Katie momentarily paused, thinking again about the strange voice on the recording. "There's something I think I should tell you. Or better yet, show you. And this too must never leave this room."

Chapter Forty

Veronica Hernandez wore the gaudiest green polyester, backless jumpsuit, a pair of black six-inch stiletto pumps, enormous gold hoop earrings, and several matching bracelets that noisily clanged together as she approached Carrie's desk. She looked like she was dressed to go out clubbing, not for the office.

"Good morning, Carrie." She flashed a red-lipstick smile. "I thought you'd like some coffee, so I stopped by King's Java." She extended a covered Styrofoam cup out to Carrie. "With cream and sugar just the way you like it."

"Uh, thanks," Carrie muttered, accepting her boss's bizarre act of kindness. It was as though an alien had taken over her body. She couldn't wrap her mind around it. Ever since that day Joseph took up for her, putting Miss Veronica Hernandez in her place, she'd completely changed. Before, she'd been a spiteful, selfish, manipulating person, lacking zero empathy, and now she was the complete opposite.

Aside from all the butt kissing, she'd given Carrie a big raise, an extra week of vacation, and more compliments than she could count. Whatever voodoo, sorcery, or incantation Joseph had conjured, she was liking her new and improved boss. Although Veronica's outlandish and obnoxious wardrobe could use a little magic. Her taste in clothes, makeup, and hairstyle was atrocious. Just looking at the woman made her eyes hurt.

"You didn't have to go to any trouble," Carrie said. "The coffee in the break room is perfectly fine."

"Oh, it was no trouble, really." Veronica waved it off, batting her long, false eyelashes. "Besides, you deserve it. Have I told you lately how much I appreciate all the hard work you do?"

Carrie shrugged. "I, uh—"

"Well, I do," Veronica bluntly stated. "And as a matter of fact, I'd like to give you an early birthday gift." Her voice rose with excitement. "I know it's this Saturday, and you probably already have plans, but I'd like to celebrate on Friday with all our coworkers. And you're perfectly welcome to invite anyone from out of the office. It'll be my way of saying thank-you."

"But—"

Veronica held up a hand. "I won't take no for an answer. Get me a list of who you'd like to attend. I'll have the party catered here in the office."

Carrie stood, shaking her head. "I appreciate this, but please, it's not necessary."

"Oh no," Veronica said, her voice taking on a serious tone. "I insist. It's the least I can do to make up for all my lack of appreciation in the past."

Not wanting to argue, Carrie finally gave in. "Okay, Veronica." She sank back down in her chair.

Veronica clapped her hands like a kid on Christmas morning, irritating Carrie with her noisy arm ornaments. "I can't wait to start planning." She reached out and patted Carrie's hand. "Don't forget about your guest list."

"Oh, I'd rather keep it work related," Carrie said. "I'm celebrating with family and friends on Saturday."

Veronica suddenly looked disappointed, her smile turning upside down. "Okay. If that's what you prefer. I mean, it's your party."

"Thanks, Veronica." Carrie smiled, lifting the Styrofoam cup to her lips. "And thanks for the coffee."

"Don't mention it, dear." She waved her arm, making her cheap imitation jewelry jingle.

Carrie cringed at the sound. She wanted to ask her if *Dollar General* had had a sale but thought better of it and kept it to herself.

"If you need anything," Veronica said, her lips turning back up, "you know where to find me."

When Veronica finally sauntered off in a nauseating wave of thick perfume and hair spray, Carrie's phone started vibrating. It made a buzzing sound on her desk. As she peered down, she saw her best friend's name on the caller ID. Curious to why Jessica was calling, especially since she'd just left their apartment not thirty minutes ago, she decided to answer. "Hey, Jess. What's up?"

"Have you seen the news?"

Carrie furrowed her brows. "No, why?"

"You know that pharmaceutical company called Adam and Eve?"

"Yeah." Carrie nodded against the phone. "What about it?"

"It burnt to the ground. According to the news media, they discovered a few bodies inside."

Carrie's mind went straight to Joseph, remembering that big story he was working on. He'd obviously landed the lead reporter position, since the article made the Chronicle's front page. When she'd read it, she immediately wanted to call and congratulate him, but instead decided against it. The article had to do with the mysterious death of Dr. Leonard Manos and the Summit Behavioral Institute getting shut down. Joseph had said his informant discovered something about the institute getting paid to do experiments on their patients. Although Joseph didn't know what kind of experiments they were doing, he suspected A&E Pharmaceuticals was involved.

"Have they identified them yet?" Carrie asked.

"No. The bodies were too charred to get fingerprints. The medical examiners or other forensic experts will have to go by dental records to identify them."

"Did they say how the fire started?"

"Nothing yet," Jessica said. "But they did say something about the feds. I guess they were investigating the facility."

"Do you know why they were being investigated?"

"Something about being linked to that car fire," Jessica said. "You know. The one that killed that physician."

"Are you talking about Dr. Manos?"

"Yep, that's the one. Didn't you say you knew him?"

"Yes, I did," Carrie said. "We counseled some of his patients. I'm still having a hard time comprehending the notion of him experimenting on his own patients."

"Sounds like a madman if you ask me," Jessica remarked. "Social media is calling him *Doctor Frankenstein.*"

"That figures," Carrie said, rolling her eyes. "If he really did all those things they're saying, he deserves it."

"Changing the subject," Jessica said. "Have you heard anything more from Joseph?"

"No," Carrie reluctantly said. "Not since the text he sent me the morning he stopped by the apartment to pick up his Jeep."

"That news article he did was outstanding. It made front page. I think Joseph is on his way to something big. Stuff like exposing government officials or uncovering foreign top secrets."

"You're probably right," Carrie said, thinking something entirely different. Something along the lines of a serial killer.

"Did you call and congratulate him?"

"No," Carrie said, releasing a sigh. "But I was thinking about it."

"I think you should call him," Jessica said, believing the couple had split over something silly, but in truth, it had been more than just a lover's quarrel. Little did she know, Joseph was possessed by some evil entity, but Carrie didn't have the guts to confide in her friend, worried Jessica would think she'd gone mad.

"He really seemed broken up when he stopped by to pick up his Jeep," Jessica continued, obviously trying to persuade her into forgiving Joseph. "Guys can be stupid sometimes. But I believe Joseph genuinely cares about you. Give him another chance, girl."

"I don't know. Maybe."

"I know, I know," Jessica spouted. "It's complicated, right?"

Complicated doesn't even begin to explain, Carrie feverishly thought.

"Sort of," Carrie muttered, sighing.

"Do you think he'll show up for your party?"

"I doubt it," Carrie said.

"Do you still want him to come?"

When Carrie didn't answer, Jessica said, "Want me to ask him?"

"No. Let him make the decision on his own."

"Okay," Jessica said. "But if you change your mind, just say the word. Besides, Ryan was looking forward to hanging out with Joseph."

"Well, I'll think about it. So, you and Ryan still getting along?"

"Things seem to be great so far," Jessica said, a clear smile in her voice.

"I'd say so," Carrie said, laughing a little. "I never hardly see you anymore. You're staying over at his place more and more these days. Has he asked you to move in with him yet?"

"He's hinted around a few times, but I'm not ready. Not yet anyway. Plus, what would you do without me?"

"Ryan just lives in the apartment upstairs from ours, silly," Carrie said. "But yeah, I'd miss having you around, especially our movie nights with a glass of wine."

"You mean a whole bottle of wine," Jessica pointed out, chuckling.

"So, you never told me," Carrie began, ignoring Jessica's cheeky remark. "Did you ever find out Ryan's big secret? I remember you saying you sensed he was keeping something from you."

"No. I figure he'll tell me when he's ready. There's no point in rushing things, right? I mean, it's not like we're engaged or anything. And I don't think it's anything serious, like he's a criminal or secretly an undercover spy. Although he did mention having a twin brother."

"Really?"

"Yep. And they're identical. If you're interested, I can ask Ryan if he's single."

"Nah, that's okay," Carrie said. "But thanks. Oh, by the way, seconds before you called, my boss decided to throw me a party here at the office this Friday. And she's having it catered."

"Good lord," Jessica groaned. "I can't believe that cow is still kissing your ass. Make her work for it, girl. You're not expecting me to go, are you?"

Carrie laughed again. "No. I'm strictly keeping the invitation list for coworkers only. Although Veronica did say I could invite anyone. But inviting my family and friends would make me feel uncomfortable, not to mention everyone else."

"Thanks," Jessica said, sounding relieved. "The thought of being around that woman makes my blood boil. I'll never forget the way she treated you."

"No worries. Well, I better get off here. I'll talk to you later. That is, if you ever take a break from Ryan."

"I'll be home tonight. Ryan has a double shift at the hospital. Later, girl."

When Carrie ended the call, she sat at her desk, staring at her phone with her thoughts tormenting her. Joseph was all she could think about. She was concerned for him. And what was that *thing* doing to him? Was it hurting him? Was it making him kill again? And did that thing... that monster... still want to kill her? She felt like she'd deserted Joseph, leaving him all alone to deal with this. *Should I call him? After all, his article did make the Chronicle's front page. No,* she thought, quickly changing her mind. *I'll send him a text. At least to say congratulations.*

* * *

Joseph sat at his desk, tired as hell, and couldn't seem to stop yawning. He stared blankly at his computer screen, trying to keep his mind off Carrie and focused on work. But no matter how hard he tried, she was all he could think about.

Although, he had to admit, he was a little psyched over his promotion. It offered many opportunities for the future, not to mention the raise that came with it. And yet, he couldn't stop those feelings he had for Carrie. He missed her. It felt like someone had stabbed him square in the heart. But deep down, he knew she was better off without him. And much safer.

Thank goodness his work kept him busy. His coworkers were all buzzing about the news report this morning on the fire at Adam and Eve Pharmaceuticals. His boss had already called him first thing this morning, giving him a run-down on the story. He'd briefly muddled through the facts, leaving it in Joseph's hands to get the rest of the scoop. Whatever it took, he had to concentrate on the task ahead. This story would either make or break his career.

After consuming large amounts of caffeine, enough to wake the dead, Joseph was finally able to stop yawning. He couldn't grasp why he was so tired. Sure, he had a million things on his mind and his workload had him staying after hours, then there was the unrelenting voice in his head, but all that wasn't out of the ordinary. He was used to it, and normally, after a few cups of coffee, he was revved up and rarin' to go. However, it wasn't the case this morning. He barely managed to get out of bed, which never happened. He even had to skip his early run just to make it to work on time. It was as though he hadn't slept a wink. And for some odd reason, his body felt like he'd been on one helluva bender.

Pushing the thought aside, he decided to contact his informant, praying he had more details on A&E Pharmaceuticals. As he reached for his phone, it suddenly dinged. His heart nearly went into overdrive when he saw it was a text from Carrie.

Hi, Joseph. I read your article and wanted to say congratulations. I hope it landed you that promotion. You deserve nothing less.

Joseph was so excited he could barely keep his hands from shaking.

He immediately texted her back. *Thank you, Carrie. And yes, I got the promotion. Thanks for asking. Everything OK with you? How's work?*

A moment later, Carrie responded. *I'm doing fine. Work has been busy.*

Joseph texted back. *What about your boss?*

I think an alien has taken over her body. She texted a laughing emoji. *Can you believe she is having an office party for me this Friday?*

Joseph smiled, thinking of her birthday. Then he texted her. *I'm happy for you, Carrie.*

After a few seconds, another text came from Carrie. *All thanks to you.*

Tears suddenly blurred his vision. Not tears of sorrow, he realized, but of joy. He was glad Carrie was finally getting the respect she deserved.

He texted back. *I didn't do anything. I believe it's just karma's way of saying you deserve good things.*

Thank you, Joseph. Are you still coming to my party?

Startled, he wiped at his eyes and read her text again, making sure he read it right. With nervous fingers, he quickly texted her. *I wouldn't miss it for the world. But are you sure?*

Yes. I would like to see you. We need to talk.

Thanks for inviting me. I'll be there. And I'll make sure I bring a bottle of your favorite rum.

Captain Morgan?

Of course. He texted a thumbs-up emoji.

See you on Saturday, Joseph.

I'm looking forward to it.

"Admit it, Joseph. That girl still has you wrapped around her little finger."

Ignoring the Shadow, Joseph kept his eyes forward and his mind on his work.

"I haven't forgotten about Carrie. I still want her, Joseph. And her beating heart."

"Stay out of my head," Joseph grumbled low, his hands trembling with rage.

"You okay, Parker?"

Joseph flinched and quickly looked up from his computer. His hard expression eased the second he saw his coworker staring down at him.

"Hey, Stewart." Joseph released a sigh. "Uh... I'm fine." He relaxed back into his chair. "Just a bit frustrated, that's all."

Stewart crossed his arms, looking concerned. "What's got you so flustered?"

"It's nothing out of the norm." Joseph shrugged. "You know, deadlines and all."

"I hear ya." Stewart nodded. "There for a minute, and by the look on your face, I thought you were 'bout to punch a hole through your monitor."

"*A hole through your chest is more like it,*" the Shadow said, further irritating Joseph. "*To eat your beating heart.*"

Joseph glanced down at his watch, noticing it was still early. "Hey, Stewart. You had breakfast yet?"

"Haven't had time. How 'bout you?"

"Same here. And I need something to fuel my tank." Joseph rose from his chair. "Whaddaya say we ditch this place and go get something? It'll be my treat."

"Heck yeah." Stewart's eyes lit up. "I'm game. Wanna give that new café on Montclair Boulevard a try?"

"Sounds like a plan." Joseph grabbed his keys. "Mildred's Café, here we come."

* * *

Manuel had just gotten into his unmarked car, fixing to give Tim Ross a call, when his phone went off. He wanted to relay what all he'd discovered from Dr. Katie Mendoza about Joseph Harris, in addition to the unexplainable mysterious voice on one of their recorded sessions.

"Well, shit," Manuel grumbled, noticing it was his Captain calling.

He swiped to answer. "What's up, Cap?"

"I need you at Montclair Boulevard ASAP. A body was found in an alley between Swinson's Bakery and Mildred's Café. It's another homicide, same as Kevin Russo's."

Joseph Parker's name instantly came to mind, giving Manuel all kinds of danger signals.

"Captain, are you saying the victim's heart is missing?"

"Looks that way. Since your partner requested a few days off, I sent Detective Ratcliff to the crime scene. As soon as you two wrap things up there, I want you guys back at the precinct pronto. We need to discuss all the details with this new homicide and the situation with A&E Pharmaceuticals."

Manuel silently cursed to himself. "Will do, Cap. And by the way, do we have anything on those remains at A&E yet?"

"Two of them were guards with an extensive criminal history. I haven't the slightest clue how they passed a background search. Although, considering who they were working for, it wouldn't surprise me if that part didn't matter. The other body was identified as Dr. Henry Michaels. And we also found some incriminating evidence that ties the physician to the Summit Behavioral Institute and the ungodly experimentations they were doing on their patients."

"Well," Manuel began, "hopefully this will give some of the victims' families some closure." Although he hated lying to his captain, he had no other choice. Besides, there was no way anyone in their right mind would buy his story of real live vampires or humans who could shift into wolves. He and his partner had promised to keep the Breedline species and their Covenant a secret, so they were forced to cover up all traces of vampires and anything that led to the Breedline. In truth, if knowledge of the Breedline species was to fall into the wrong hands, they could be put in danger. And this world needed them to survive. If they no longer existed, mankind would eventually perish. So far, they'd managed to save more lives than he could count.

"Maybe." Captain Hodge sighed into the phone. "But we still have some unanswered questions. Who was funding A&E Pharmaceuticals and Dr. Henry Michaels's research?"

Manuel had a pretty good idea the government was involved, but without proof he kept that thought to himself, and instead he said, "So, any idea what caused the fire?"

"Nothing definite yet. But it's leaning toward arson. Most likely it's connected to the two physicians' deaths and the Summit Behavioral Institute. Possibly a coverup. We'll go over the details later."

When Manuel ended the call, he wasted no time and headed straight for Mildred's Café. The moment he arrived, he saw flashing lights coming from two police cruisers, and recognized Detective Ratcliff's truck parked in front. As soon as he approached the crime scene, where it had already been roped off, a crowd of onlookers were starting to gather. Some were using their phones to try and capture a few photos.

"Who got killed?" a female bystander asked, sporting flamboyant pink hair. "Was it someone local?"

"Oh, dear God," another woman said, her bug-eyes peering up at Manuel. "I just live two blocks from here. Am I in danger?"

"It's that Valentine's killer," an older man said. "Same one that killed the son of Russo's Exotic Cars. I heard the guy's heart was tore clean from his chest."

"How do you know?" the pink-haired woman asked.

"Because..." the older man said, pausing with a distraught look on his face, "I'm the one who found that body this morning and called the police. The man's chest was ripped open just like the first victim that was found on Valentine's Day. And I'll bet anything his heart is missing too." He wearily placed his hand over his forehead. "I nearly fainted when I saw him lying there, staring out of those awful dead eyes."

"Valentine's killer, my ass," a baldheaded man said, whose arms were covered in ink. "No human is capable of that. I'd almost guarantee that werewolf is killing again."

"A werewolf?" the older man asked, his eyes bulging as big as an eight ball. "What are you talking about?"

"You know," the tatted bald guy said, "the one who attacked that young girl and slaughtered her friends in the Salem Cemetery last year."

"That was nothing but a bunch of made-up stories." The older guy grunted, rolling his eyes. "Everyone knows there's no such thing as a werewolf. Authorities said a bear was responsible for those attacks."

Joseph and Stewart stood behind the group of people, silently watching in utter disbelief.

"Great timing, wouldn't you say?" Stewart finally said to Joseph, keeping his voice low. "By the sound of it, we might just have ourselves a serial killer on the loose."

"You were wondering why you were so tired this morning," the Shadow said, his seething voice making the hairs on Joseph's neck prickle. *"Now you know the reason. And I have to say, that Texan's heart was simply scrumptious. Wouldn't you agree, Joseph?"*

Joseph kept silent, trying not to react to the voice inside his head. Then suddenly, he felt nauseous.

"What's a matter, Joseph? Cat got your tongue?"

Stewart turned toward Joseph, waiting for him to reply, but he said nothing. He just stared blankly off into the distance.

"Hey..." Stewart lightly nudged Joseph's arm. "You okay?"

No, I'm not okay, he wanted to say. *I'm possessed by a demon who makes me kill people*. Instead, he blinked and said, "Yeah. I'm fine." He let out a deep breath. "Just a bit rattled, that's all."

"I hear ya, man," Stewart said as the crowd continued to ramble on, their voices rising in the background. "The whole thing is terrible. Although it would make one hell of a story, right?"

Joseph's jaw knotted. Stewart's question reverberated eerily in his mind.

"Well, what do you think?" Stewart shrugged. "You want to do the story? I mean, you're the lead journalist now."

"Nah," Joseph said, shaking his head. "You go for it. Besides, I've got a full plate."

"You sure?"

Joseph nodded. "I'm sure."

Stewart's lips curved up. "Thanks."

"All right, everyone," Manuel said, waving his arms as though he was herding cattle. "I need all of you to move back." He raised his voice. "This is a crime scene."

Immediately, phones were lowered, and the group of nosy people hurriedly backed away, especially after Manuel threatened them with charges of obstruction.

Damn meddling people, Manuel thought, grinding his molars. He ducked under the yellow police tape and strode toward a large dumpster where two police officers stood. The minute he got closer, he noticed Detective Nicolas Ratcliff crouching to inspect the body.

The victim—a male who appeared to be in his early to mid-twenties—lying face up, had a giant hole smack dab in the middle of his chest, exactly like Kevin Russo had been found. And this poor guy's heart too appeared to be missing.

Manuel crouched next to Nicolas. "Do we have an ID on the victim?"

He turned toward Manuel and nodded. "Jerry Duffin. Twenty-four years of age. An out-of-towner. Driver's license says he's from Texas."

"Going by that hole," Manuel said, gesturing toward the dead man's chest, "I take it his heart is MIA."

"Yep. Same as Kevin Russo."

"Well shit," Manuel gritted out, then stood straight and looked between the two officers who stood nearby. "By chance, would either of you know if there's any working cameras close by?"

"Sorry, Detective," one of the officers said. "We already checked. There's nothing on these buildings close enough to get a visual of this alley."

"All right." Manuel released a heavy sigh. "Thanks, guys."

"If you two got this covered," the other officer said, looking between the two detectives, "we'll go maintain that crowd and wait for the coroner to arrive."

"Thanks, guys," Nicolas said, standing straight. "We'd appreciate it."

Manuel waited until the two officers were out of earshot then said, "Captain wants us back at the precinct as soon as we wrap this up."

Nicolas raised an inquisitive brow. "What's up?"

"He wants to discuss this ordeal and the fire at A&E Pharmaceuticals. They've already identified the bodies."

"Do they know if the fire was arson yet?"

"Nothing definite," Manuel said. "But they suspect it. And there's something else I just recently discovered."

"Oh?" Nicolas narrowed his gaze. "And what's that?"

"I found out some information on our perp."

"Are you talking about Joseph Harris?"

Manuel nodded. "Turns out, Joseph has changed his last name. It's Parker now."

"By the look on your face, something tells me that's not all you discovered."

Manuel's jaw clenched. "Yeah, and it's not good."

"Have you contacted the Covenant?"

"I was fixing to," Manuel said, "right before Captain called. I'll try again before I head over to the precinct."

"We're getting closer, thanks to you, Detective. Maybe we'll finally catch this guy."

"That's the easy part," Manuel said. "But figuring out how to destroy this thing is going to be the difficult part."

"Tessa mentioned something about Sebastian Crow finding some information on this particular demon," Nicolas pointed out. "If we're lucky, maybe he'll know how to destroy it."

"Keep your fingers crossed," Manuel said. "I have a feeling we're going to need it."

Chapter Forty-One

In the Covenant's guestroom, lying in a bed that would qualify as the world's most comfortable mattress, Frank stared up at the ceiling, filtering through all the events of the last few days. Although they were a bit muddled and lacking coherence, still the vampire who'd bitten him would forever haunt his memories. Each time his mind took him there, he saw the bloodlust in Karina's soulless eyes, smelt the stench of death, and felt the burning sensation as she sank her fangs into his flesh. Then there was the blood. *His* blood.

The dinging noise coming from his phone instantly brought his mind back. The moment he reached for it and looked at the screen, he saw there were two texts—one from Tim Ross, saying his twenty-four hours of isolation was up and that he was in the clear, which meant Karina hadn't injected him with vampire venom, *thank God*, and another from his partner letting him know he was headed his way with some new information on the murder case they were working on. Then he checked the time, noticing it was almost noon. His stomach instantly growled. *At least it's food I'm hungry for, not blood,* he thought, feeling an overwhelming sense of relief.

He heaved out a deep breath and positioned himself higher on the pillows. Before he rose out of bed, he reached for his neck and felt for the bandage where Helen had patched him up. Smoothing his fingers over the gauze, he wondered if the bite would leave a scar. Most likely, he thought, remembering Helen saying it took twelve stitches to seal the wound. Now all he had to do was explain to his wife how he managed such an injury. He didn't want to lie, but what other explanation could he give Missy? He couldn't very well tell her he'd been bitten by a vampire. She'd think he'd done lost his mind. He had to come up with something. She'd never believe he'd accidently cut himself shaving. No, that would be ridiculous. Maybe she'd come closer to believing he'd been attacked during an arrest, getting cut with a knife in the process. No, that would require too much detail and theatrics. Besides, that would make him a liar, and he was always honest with his wife.

Never in his life had he resented the limitations of being human until now. It'd be so much easier if he'd shared the DNA of his Breedline friends. Compared to humans, they had tremendous advantages when it came to dealing with wounds and illnesses. Their bodies healed super-fast, and they weren't subject to diseases or illnesses like cancer. Although silver was dangerous to the Breedline species. It was sort of like their kryptonite. It would slow their healing process, and one silver bullet to the brain was a death sentence. But some of the members of the Breedline Covenant, like Jace and Jem, were immune to silver.

A light tap at the door made him look up. "Detective..." A familiar voice called out. "It's Steven. Mind if I come in?"

"Sure," Frank said. His throat was dry. "It's open."

When the door creaked open and a tall man with a lean, muscular physique made his way inside, Frank pushed himself into a sitting position. Although Steven was Tessa's fraternal twin brother, the only commonalities they shared were the chestnut color of their hair and their shimmering emerald-green eyes.

Steven looked at Frank. "How are you feeling?"

"Much better. Especially now that I'm a free man."

"I heard." Steven smiled. "That's great news."

"You ain't a-kiddin'," Frank said, looking relieved. "There for a minute or two, I was worried I might become one of those *things*."

"You mean a vampire?"

Frank nodded. "I've got enough to explain to my wife when she sees this bandage on my neck. I'd hate to think how I'd explain the worst-case scenario. And whatever lame story I come up with, she'll know I'm keeping something from her. Missy can read me like a book."

"Well, maybe you won't have to explain anything."

Frank fixed Steven with an inquisitive stare. "What do you mean?"

"Tessa asked me if I'd heal your wound. That's why I'm here."

Frank's mouth hung open. He finally closed it and said, "Really?"

Steven crossed his arms over his chest. "Sure, why not? You and your partner have gone out of your way to help us out on more than one occasion, so why wouldn't we help you? Besides, you two are part of the Breedline family now."

"But how? Is it dangerous?"

"Normally, all I need to do is make physical contact," Steven explained. "I'll take on your wound, then heal myself. It won't take long. And don't worry. It's perfectly safe."

Frank felt his eyes go wide. The whole healing thing was too bizarre, too unreal. It was still hard for him to wrap his mind around knowing there were people who could shift into giant wolves, and now someone who had the power to heal. It didn't seem possible. "That's so unbelievable," he managed to croak out.

"It's a gift. I believe God gave it to me for a reason. So, what do you say, Detective?"

Relief surged through Frank once more. "I say, let's do it. What do I need to do?"

"Just relax," Steven instructed, "and close your eyes."

At first, as Steven sat down facing him and placed his hand over the bandage that covered his wound, Frank hadn't noticed anything different. Then, a few minutes later, his body filled with a tingling warmth. It spread to his head and traveled all the way down to his toes. Frank kept his eyes closed, knowing somehow Steven was working his magic. The stitches beneath the bandage softly prickled like tiny pins and needles, then began to itch.

Steven removed his hand. "You can open your eyes now."

Frank's lids snapped open and he drew in a breath. Instantly, he reached for the bandage and put his hand over it, fingers aimlessly searching for the wound beneath. "Unbeliev..." His words trailed off the moment he saw blood covering Steven's neck. "Y-your bleeding," he blurted, pointing at what looked to be a deep, bloody wound.

"It's okay," Steven said. His voice was shaky but there was a thread of steel infused into his words. "The wound will disappear soon."

Frank lowered his hand and watched in startled silence as he witnessed something remarkable happening right before his eyes. The open gash on Steven's neck miraculously began to grow smaller until finally it faded into nothing as though it had never been there. Even the blood had vanished like it had magically willed itself back inside.

"I-I can't believe it," Frank muttered. "The wound is gone."

Steven nodded. "And so is yours."

Frank quickly reached for the bandage covering his neck and peeled it off. The second he drew his hand over the area that had been previously lined with stitches, he was shocked to find the skin smooth and free of any existing sutures.

"I wouldn't believe it if I hadn't experienced it firsthand," Frank said. "What you did..." He paused, swallowing hard. "...that was truly a selfless act. And that's something that barely exists nowadays." His eyes beamed with an overwhelming expression of gratitude. "Thank you, Steven."

Steven stood. "It was my pleasure, Detective. And if you're hungry, Tessa and some of the others prepared a big lunch for everyone."

"That's music to my ears," Frank said, his stomach growling at the mere mention of food. "And to my stomach."

Steven gave Frank a pat on the shoulder. "I'll meet you downstairs in a few."

When the door closed behind Steven, Frank sat there for a few moments, thinking. As ridiculous as it sounded, he felt like some pieces of the puzzles he and his partner were diligently working so hard to solve were slowly starting to come together. If anything, the Breedline gave him hope when nothing else had been able to chip away at all the corrupt and diabolical beings of this world. And he was grateful they made a difference.

* * *

Joseph's legs moved faster than they'd ever had been able to before. He ran, his muscles pumping furiously, along the park trails as images of the other morning flooded his mind. The nightmarish crime scene he and his coworker had accidently come upon had unfortunately been his doing. The

Shadow had somehow taken control of his subconscious and physical state, forcing him to kill again. He felt dirty, *used*.

He racked his brain, trying to remember, but the events of the previous night were hazy and a blur now. And he knew it wasn't because he'd blocked it from his memory. It was because the Shadow had used his body to commit the heinous crime. Though his memory of killing his father and Carrie's ex-boyfriend were clear as the day, he couldn't see himself killing the innocent person someone had discovered in an alley near Mildred's Café.

I killed an innocent person.

He couldn't believe it. But denying it was useless. It had happened, and the realization of it all consumed his brain, pushing everything else aside. It was too much, and he didn't want to think about it. Hot tears sprang from his eyes and rolled down his cheeks. *I'm so sorry... Please forgive me, God.*

Finally, nearly exhausting himself, he slowed to a walk and checked his watch. Realizing he was already late for work, he stopped at a big oak and put his back against it. He leaned forward and lowered his head into the palm of his hands, thinking. *How am I going to stop all this madness? And how am I going to keep Carrie safe?*

He looked up and released a ragged breath. "God..." He helplessly pleaded. "I'm begging you. Please help me."

"You're wasting your breath, Joseph. God cannot help you now."

The Shadow's taunting voice continued to eat at his sanity, chipping it away bit by bit, leaving nothing behind but a body fueled with rage and desperation. Joseph straightened his shoulders and fisted his hands at his sides. "Instead of hiding inside my head," he said through gritted teeth, "why don't you face me, Shadow?" He whirled, his eyes searching. "So I can kill you."

Then, with incredible speed, Joseph was hoisted off the ground by some unknown force. Trying to gather his bearings, to get a grip on reality, he was violently tossed against a tree. The sudden impact knocked the breath out of him. As gravity took hold, he helplessly plunged downward, gasping for air. The moment his fall came to an abrupt halt, he winced in agony, and his vision flickered. But before he lost consciousness, certain the darkness would take hold, he fought against it, compelling his eyes to stay open. After a few moments, he gathered what strength he had left and slowly rose to his feet. On unsteady legs, he stood, supporting his weight against the sturdy oak, waiting for the invisible attacker in ready silence. But there was nothing. He was alone, feeling broken.

As it started to rain, Joseph lowered his head and simply checked out, his thoughts lingering beyond the rim of awareness. When the sky grew darker, and it began to pour, still he did not move. He didn't even register his soaked clothes sticking to his body like a second layer of skin, or that his socks and shoes were completely drenched.

A pulsing vibration coming from his phone snapped him into focus. As it continued to buzz in the armband he had attached to his biceps, he pulled it out and looked at the screen. When Carrie's name came up, he swallowed against the dryness in his throat and answered. "Carrie..."

"Joseph, she's dead."

"W-what?"

"Veronica." Her voice trembled. "My boss... she's dead."

Joseph's mind reeled and his hands began to shake. *Oh my God. Did I kill her?*

After a few beats of silence, Carrie raised her voice, "Joseph, are you still there?"

"I-I'm so sorry, Carrie. What happened?"

"Her body..." Carrie began, her voice filled with dread. "It was discovered by the cleaning staff first thing this morning. They found her in the parking lot, lying next to her car. I don't know all the details yet, but they think she was killed last night. She was working late and—"

"Carrie," Joseph abruptly said, "did they tell you how she was killed?"

"The same as Kevin."

Joseph said nothing. His thoughts shifted to the day he'd confronted Carrie's boss. She'd seen what he was. Witnessed the evil. He'd never forget the look on her face, the terror in her eyes, and her sobbing pleas. Then, for some strange reason, her fear transformed into sympathy. At that moment, he vowed he'd never take another life. And now, he was being forced to kill again.

"I warned you, Joseph," the Shadow gritted out. *"You no longer have a choice."*

"Please, Joseph," Carrie said. "Tell me it wasn't you."

No, no, no, no! Joseph closed his eyes, the words in his head repeating over and over. *I didn't kill her. I didn't kill her. I didn't...*

"Yes, Joseph. Together, WE killed her."

The Shadow's spine-chilling admission broke something inside of Joseph. For a moment, he just stood there, eyes wide, heart racing. Then suddenly, he felt dizzy as though the ground swayed, tipping the world side-to-side. He dropped to his knees; his face twisted into a mask of pain. He was a killer. *A killer!* The truth cut like a knife. Now it was real. And he had to accept what he was. But no, he couldn't. He *wouldn't*.

"Carrie..." He finally croaked out. "I-I swear. I can't remember. But I think..." He paused, clearing his throat. "I *killed* Veronica."

"If it's true, the Shadow made you do it," she said, anger evident in her voice. "Do you hear me, Joseph? You're not responsible for this."

"It needs to be stopped. Permanently." He swallowed around the lump in his throat. "I have to end this."

"What are you saying, Joseph?"

For a moment, he was silent, looking up at the cloudy sky as the rain subsided, shifting into a light mist. Finally, he opened his mouth, and said, "Don't you see, Carrie. There's no other way." He slowly maneuvered himself back on his feet. "If I continue to live, so will the Shadow."

"No, Joseph." Carrie's voice was panic-stricken. "I won't let you do this. There must be another way."

"I'm sorry," Joseph paused, fighting back the words, to say good-bye. "I have to go, Carrie."

Looking around wildly, heart hammering, not sure where to go, he took off running like an animal evading its predator. As he ran, he tried not to think of Carrie. Leaving her made his heart ache as though he was already dying. But he knew if he didn't stop the Shadow, she'd never be safe. And right now, that was all he cared about, all he could think about.

Chapter Forty-Two

While officers worked crowd control, Detectives Manuel Sanchez and Frank Perkins surveyed the roped-off crime scene. A canopy had been set up by first responders to preserve evidence from the morning rain. Located in the parking lot of New Hope Foundation was the body of Miss Veronica Hernandez. Not only was she the manager of a substance abuse counseling center, she was also the CEO's daughter, and Carrie Randall's boss.

Manuel, wearing latex gloves, crouched to get a closer look at the victim's wounds. "Looks like our guy's MO," he said, pointing at the ripped-out portion on Miss Hernandez's chest. "Same injuries as Kevin Russo and our recent victim on Montclair Boulevard." He averted his eyes from the body and looked up at Frank. "All three missing their hearts."

"Yeah," Frank said, looking between his partner and the bloody corpse, his stomach twisted in knots. "Now that there are three victims with the same MO, our perp will be considered a serial killer."

"I'm sure the media will have a field day over this," Manuel grumbled. "I can just see the headlines now." He stood straight, rolling his eyes. "Valentine's Day killer strikes again. But I suppose it's certainly more believable than the actual truth."

The Shadow. The words hung unspoken between them.

"This leaves us with no other choice," Frank pointed out. "We'll have to put out a warning and alert the area. Our hands will be tied until we find our killer. Have you heard anything from the Covenant on Joseph Parker's location?"

Manuel shook his head. "Nothing yet, but Drakon is doing some digging. Come to find out, the address Mr. Parker gave the Jones Center was bogus, and since nothing comes up in our data base and the guy won't answer his phone, Drakon is heading to Mr. Parker's place of employment, hoping to find something solid. So far, this guy is like a freakin' chameleon. And if it weren't for Katie, we'd still have nada on this guy. At least now we have the name he's going by, his contact info, and his place of employment. Just think..." He huffed out an aggravated sigh. "...all this time he was that journalist from the Chronicle who wrote the article on the institute we shut down. In addition, the damn thing made front page."

"I know, right?" Frank groaned. "Go figure. And speaking of Katie Mendoza, what are we planning on doing about that third voice on her and Joseph's recorded session? I mean, it was a bit disturbing. The Shadow, or *whatever* the hell this thing is, seems to want Katie dead. You don't think it will persuade Joseph to kill her, do you?"

"Katie told me their next therapy session isn't scheduled till the end of the month," Manuel explained. "That gives us two weeks. Besides, after I discussed the situation with the Covenant, they decided to put eyes on Katie twenty-four seven. Anything goes down, you can bet your ass she'll be protected."

"Well, at least Katie's in safe hands," Frank said, sighing in relief. "And hopefully the Breedline will put an end to all this madness before this *Shadow* kills again."

"Me too, partner," Manuel said. "I just hope they can destroy it without killing Joseph."

"I don't see how that's going to be possible," Frank said. "If Jena's creature has the power to destroy it, she'll have to kill Joseph in the process."

"I guess you're right." Manuel's brows lifted. "That poor guy has had it rough his entire life. Witnessing your father beat your mother to death is bad enough, then being tossed in and out of foster care until finally locked up in a mental institution is pretty messed up. And to come to find out, this whole time, instead of suffering with schizophrenia, he was possessed by a demon." He shook his head in regret. "I just can't imagine, especially as a child."

"I agree," Frank said, his expression grim. "This whole mess makes me sick to my stomach. So, when do you think the coroner will get here?" he asked, anxiously glancing down at his watch, trying to avoid Veronica's corpse lying below.

"Don't worry, buddy." Manuel shot Frank a look of empathy, realizing his partner had a hard time when it came to dead bodies, especially the bloody and gory parts. "As soon as she arrives, we'll get out of here."

Frank nervously began tapping his foot. "So, are you coming to my niece's birthday party?"

"Ah, damn," Manuel grumbled. "Is that this Saturday?"

When Frank nodded, Manuel said, "I'm glad you reminded me. I completely forgot. The days seem to go by in a blur lately."

Frank smiled as the shift in the conversation eased the tension a little. "Well, you are getting up there in age. They say the first thing to go is your memory."

"Oh, kiss my ass, Perkins." Manuel folded his arms and scoffed, "You're the same age as me."

Frank smirked. "Well, are you coming or not?"

"I promised Carrie I would stop by for a little while. Although, seeing her boss was just murdered, I doubt she'll be up to celebrating."

"I talked to her earlier, and as far as I know, she's still planning on having the party. She's pretty upset, as she should be, but still, she doesn't want to cancel, since Jessica and Ryan have already arranged things for the barbeque. Carrie's not the type to disappoint anyone, and if I know her like I think I do, she won't cancel."

"I'm sure she could use the moral support anyway," Manuel said. "Besides, isn't that new fella she's been seeing supposed to be there?" He squinted his eyes, looking at Frank, thinking. "What did you say his name was?"

"Heck, I don't know." Frank shrugged a shoulder. "I can barely remember Jessica's boyfriends' name."

Manuel chuckled. "You remember Ryan because we nearly arrested him when we thought he was sneaking into the back door to Carrie and Jessica's apartment."

"Probably," Frank said. "Plus, Carrie never mentioned the name of the guy she's seeing, and I didn't ask. I just gave her the benefit of the doubt, hoping she'd use better judgement this go-around. Don't you remember me telling you?"

"Oh yeah," Manuel grudgingly replied. "But for crying out loud, Perkins, it might've been a good idea to ask for the guy's name, seeing how nutty people are nowadays. Then you could've gotten a background check on this one. The last guy she dated wasn't exactly Prince Charming. And we both know where he ended up."

"Yeah," Frank hesitantly said, his expression grim. "Dead."

"Well, I don't know about you," Manuel said, "but I plan on asking this guy a few questions. At least find out his name, where he's originally from, where he works. You know, just to make sure he's on the up-and-up. Hell, for all we know, he could be some maniac with a criminal record, or a serial killer."

"Oh, come on." Frank grimaced. "Give Carrie a little more credit than that. And please don't embarrass her. She hates it when Missy and I grill her about personal things. We try our best to respect her privacy. And it's not like she's a child anymore. She's a grown adult who is fully capable of making her own decisions."

"I promise I won't embarrass her," Manuel said. "I'm just going to ask a few questions, that's all."

Frank reached out and clapped a hand over Manuel's shoulder. "I know you mean well, partner. It's nice to know someone else besides Missy and I is looking out for Carrie."

"Sure thing, buddy." Manuel's lips curved up. "Carrie's like family. And if anyone was to lay a finger on that girl..." He paused and patted his holster "...they'll have me to answer to."

"You *and* me both," Frank said.

The two detectives turned when they heard approaching footsteps. When they noticed a police officer heading in their direction in a hurried pace, their expressions grew serious.

"Detectives," the officer said, "we just got a call in. A male in his early to mid-twenties was struck by a vehicle. It's near the park, and going by the call, it sounds serious. Officers Channing and Taylor were the first responders on the scene. An ambulance is on the way."

"Do we have an ID on the victim?" Manuel asked.

"Yes, sir," the officer said. "Joseph Parker. We have a witness at the scene. Apparently, the victim was crossing the street when he was hit. He was jogging, I believe."

Instantly, the hairs on Manuel's neck stood on end. He traded glances with Frank, noticing the same look of bewilderment on his face. "That's our guy," Manuel finally said. "Let's go, partner."

* * *

As two male paramedics hustled from the back of an ambulance and rushed over with a gurney, a guy wearing a ball cap muttered, "H-he just came out of nowhere. I hit the brakes..." He continued to ramble, pointing at a body sprawled out on the side of the road, "...but it was too late."

A police officer came forward, motioning to the guy to stand back. "Please, sir." He held up a halting hand. "Step aside and let the EMTs do their job."

The guy gave the officer a look of understanding and moved back while the paramedics began checking the victim, whose breathing appeared to be shallow.

Joseph tasted blood. Not just any blood, he realized, but *his* blood. And the scent of it made his stomach churn. Suddenly, the world around him dimmed and began to spin, moving in slow circles, as though he was a lonely passenger on an endless carousel. Although his vision didn't seem to be working, he could hear voices trading back and forth, speaking in urgent tones.

"He's got a pulse," a medic called out, "but his blood pressure is sixty over forty and falling."

"Quick," another medic said, looking out of thick glasses, "let's get him on the gurney."

When Joseph felt his body being lifted, everything went utterly silent. Then his lungs began to burn painfully. His heart stuttered, and his breath came in gulping gasps, desperate for air. But no matter how hard he fought, he drifted further into the darkness. He could barely register the voice above him say, "He's losing consciousness."

It wasn't until now Joseph knew that death loomed near. He was finally ready to surrender himself to eternal emptiness, to the all-consuming nothingness.

Then, out of nowhere, snapshots of images flashed inside his head. They were like forgotten memories forged from his subconscious. It was as if he was a bystander, watching everything play out through someone else's eyes.

He was standing before Veronica, their faces mere inches apart, their breaths merging. Her eyes expressed uneasiness as his feral gaze bored into her, blazing with what looked to be hunger. His chest heaved, and his handsome face began to shift into something unnatural... something hideous. The color from his face drained, turning as pale as a corpse's. Black spider-webbed veins appeared on his ghostly skin like a mask of demonic horror. When he spoke, his voice was not his own. It was sinister, *evil.* "Hello, Veronica."

"Joseph, please..." She scrambled back, tripping over her stiletto heels as he inched closer, his eyes nothing but darkness and his teeth sharp as needles.

"Joseph cannot hear you."

"Who are—" Her words were cut off when he gripped her by the throat, paralyzing her with fear. She opened her mouth to scream but only a gasp managed to escape her lips.

Joseph begged his lids to open, to stop the nightmare, but his eyes would not obey. Then the Shadow's voice came to him in a whisper, *"Did you really think I'd let you die so easily, Joseph? Remember..."* His voice grew deeper, more demanding. *"I'm in control now."*

"He's coming back around," the first medic said, snapping Joseph back to reality.

As if woken from a nightmarish dream, his lids flew open, and his mouth parted with a gasp. At that moment, his faculties had returned, remembering what the Shadow had made him do. *Oh God,* he feverishly thought. *It's true. I killed her. I killed Veronica.*

"Hang on, sir," the medic said, looking down at Joseph with concern brimming through his coke-bottle glasses. "You're in good hands. We'll get you to the Bates Hospital in no time."

"Hospital?" Joseph groaned, slightly raising his head. "No..." He tried to push himself up, but something kept him confined. "No hospital."

"You need to relax," the other medic said, using a soothing voice. "You've been in an accident. I think it's best to get you checked out."

For a moment, Joseph wasn't sure where he was or what had happened. He remembered talking on the phone with Carrie about her boss being murdered, then shortly after, telling her good-bye, and next he took off sprinting. After that, everything seemed like a blur. Now he was strapped to a gurney, fixing to be hauled off to the hospital, and he felt like he'd been hit over the head with a baseball bat.

He put a hand over his pounding forehead, noticing there was a bandage. "W-what happened?" he croaked out.

Then a man wearing a ball cap, looking distraught, suddenly appeared in Joseph's field of vision. "Hey, man... Are you okay?" he asked, strolling alongside the paramedics as they wheeled him to the ambulance. "You ran out in front of me. I tried to stop." He stared at Joseph apologetically. "I'm so sorry. I didn't mean to hit you."

Joseph studied the guy's face, vaguely recalling the same panicked expression behind the wheel of a white Ford pickup right before it struck his body and everything faded into darkness.

"It's not your fault," Joseph said, his voice raspy. "I'm okay, I think." He looked down at himself, scanning over his torso and then his legs. Other than two skinned knees, scrapped elbows, and the pounding in his head, he seemed to be fine.

"Are you sure?" the guy asked, his brows arching high on his forehead. "I mean, don't you think you should see a doctor or something?"

"I'm sure," Joseph said, averting his eyes from the guy who'd accidently hit him to the medic who was at the foot of the gurney. "Please..." He shook his head. "I'll be fine. I don't want to go to the hospital."

The gurney came to an abrupt stop. "You'll have to sign a refusal of care form before we can release you," the medic who was facing him said. "But I highly recommend you see your regular physician for that head injury. There's a possibility you could have a concussion."

Joseph dipped his head. "I understand."

After Joseph signed the form and the ambulance drove away, two police officers had Joseph and the driver of the vehicle stay behind and sign an incident report.

"By the way," the driver said, extending his hand to Joseph, "my name is Jared Hunter."

"Nice to meet you, Jared." Joseph took hold of his hand. "I'm Joseph Parker."

"Well, Joseph," Jared said, shrugging, "would you like a ride? It's the least I can do, seeing I hit you and all."

"*Mmmm...*" The Shadow smacked his lips. *"I'm starving. Accept his offer."*

"Nah." Joseph waved it off. "I'll be okay to walk."

"You sure?" Jared pointed to the bandage on Joseph's head. "That looks a bit painful. At least let me drive you home."

Joseph considered. He *was* a little woozy, and his legs felt weak. Finally, he nodded and said, "Thanks. I'd appreciate it."

Jared smiled. "Great. Where we headed?"

"Not far. My apartment building is just a few miles from the park's entrance."

"Hillside Village." Jared beamed. "My sister lives there."

"Excellent..." the Shadow spouted, alarming Joseph. *"Two for the price of one."*

"On second thought," Joseph said. "Would you mind dropping me off at my girlfriend's place?"

Jared nodded. "No problem."

By the time the two detectives arrived, the white Ford pickup had already gone, driving away with Joseph Parker.

Realizing the ambulance had already left, and the only thing at the scene was a single police cruiser, Manuel turned to his partner with defeat etched into the grooves of his face. "Dammit..." he grumbled, gripping the steering wheel. "We must have missed the ambulance."

"Relax partner," Frank said, reaching for the door. "At least Officer Taylor is still here. I'm sure he knows what hospital Mr. Parker is being transported to."

Manuel nodded, trying to be patient. As he exited the vehicle and headed toward the police cruiser, Officer Taylor approached them halfway.

He tipped his hat. "What can I do for you, Detectives?"

"Would you happen to know what hospital the victim was being transported to?" Frank asked.

"Well..." the officer began, shaking his head. "It's the damnedest thing. Mr. Parker refused to go to the hospital, saying he didn't need to see a doctor. Hell, the way things were looking, I didn't think the guy was going to make it. Then he miraculously opened his eyes like nothing ever happened. If you ask me, he's one lucky bastard. I mean, who walks away from getting hit by a truck with just a few scrapes and bruises?"

Manuel groaned. "So, where the hell did he go?"

"Gets even crazier," the officer said, lightly chuckling. "He caught a ride with the fella who hit him."

"You've got to be kidding me," Manuel said. "What's the name of the driver?"

"Jared Hunter," the officer replied. "Nice guy too."

Frank raised an inquisitive brow. "Did either Mr. Hunter or Mr. Parker happen to mention where they were headed?"

"Sorry, Detective. Neither didn't say, but I did overhear Mr. Parker ask the driver something about dropping him off at his girlfriend's place."

Girlfriend? Manuel thought, glancing at Frank with a look of bewilderment. "You didn't happen to hear where that was, did you?"

Officer Taylor shook his head. "I'm sure you'll be able to catch up with him at his apartment building." He handed Manuel the incident report. "Mr. Parker lives at Hillside Village. It just a few miles from here."

"Yeah," Manuel said, his eyes searching over the report, locating Joseph's apartment number. "I know exactly where it's at."

Chapter Forty-Three

Carrie sat at the kitchen table, staring down at her phone, her mind whirling in all directions. Exhaling a deep breath, she cradled her face into the palms of her hands. She wanted to cry, to scream, to break things. She couldn't believe her boss was dead, murdered by the man she loved. But in truth, it wasn't Joseph who was responsible for the heinous act. It was the evil entity possessing his body.

Sure, Veronica deserved her share of karma for all the shitty things she'd said and done, but dear God, not death. Now Joseph blamed himself. And he was willing to end his own life to protect the innocent. To protect her.

She had to find a way to help Joseph, to stop him. To stop the *Shadow* from killing again. *There must be a way,* she thought.

The sound of a light knock coming from the back sliding glass door brought her head up. Her eyes widened in alarm, realizing she'd forgot to lock it. She'd left it open, leaving the screen in its place, savoring the cool breeze from the morning rain.

As she slowly rose, her shoulders tensed, and her heart pounded in anticipation. She cautiously crept toward the door, and the moment she caught sight of the person standing behind the screen, her heart nearly melted. She instantly released the breath she hadn't realized she'd been holding and softly murmured, "Joseph..."

He was soaked to the bone, hair falling to his shoulders in a wet, tangled mess, staring back at her with an expression of defeat etched into his handsome face. Dark shadows cast a haunted look in his sapphire eyes that told her he hadn't slept in days. Then Carrie became concerned when she noticed the bandage over his forehead. Although in retrospect, she should be terrified. Any woman in her right mind would be scared out of her mind. After all, the *thing* possessing the man she loved had wanted to kill her. Still wanted to kill her. But all she wanted to do was throw open the barrier that separated them and wrap her arms around him. She wanted nothing more than to tell him everything was going to be okay. If only it were true.

"Are you okay?" she asked, staring at his bandaged forehead. "What happened?"

"I'm fine. It was just an accident."

As she reached up to slide open the screen door, he held up a halting hand. "Wait..." he abruptly said. "If you open that door..." He paused, swallowing hard. "...I can't promise I won't hurt you, Carrie. I can't control the Shadow anymore."

"You won't hurt me," she said reassuringly, and that struck him as dangerously naive. "You've had enough chances to already. I trust you, Joseph."

"But how..." Confusion closed his mouth. "How can you trust me after everything that's happened? I've..." He swallowed back tears. "...killed people."

"You're not a killer, Joseph. It's the monster inside you."

"That's not entirely true, Carrie. It wasn't just the Shadow who chose to kill my father. I wanted him dead. And I would have killed you too."

"It doesn't matter now." Tears formed in her eyes. "I forgive you, Joseph. God will forgive you too."

He shook his head. "I'm not so sure about that."

"You didn't ask for this. And you surely don't deserve the life you've been dealt."

"I don't know what to do," he said in a trembling voice. "I don't know how to stop it."

"We'll figure this out." She slid open the screen and extended her hand. "There has to be a way."

When he took hold of her hand, she guided him inside, sensing his uneasiness. As they made their way past the kitchen and into the living room, she stopped and turned toward him. Tilting her head back, she stared into his tortured gaze and murmured, "Kiss me, Joseph."

He went rigid, her request creating an unsettling feeling in the pit of his gut.

"Don't worry," she whispered. "I'm not afraid of you. I'm not afraid of the Shadow."

He shook his head. "But—"

She placed a finger to his lips. "Just kiss me."

He closed the short distance between them, dipping low, and hesitated only for a moment before he gently pressed his mouth against hers. His lips were soft as suede, lingering, trembling.

She reached up, grabbed on to his shoulders, and tugged him closer. As their kiss deepened, and their tongues explored, she felt lost in him. After a few moments, she withdrew from their embrace and whipped her T-shirt over her head. The second she started to undo her bra, he reached out and took hold of her hand. "Carrie…" He visibly swallowed. "Are you sure?"

"Please…" Her eyes pleaded. "I want this."

Infusing himself with courage, he nodded and gently tugged at her hand. "Let's take this upstairs."

As soon as they made it upstairs and into her room, he asked, "Where's your roommate?"

"Jessica's at work," she replied, gazing up into his blue eyes. "We've got the entire day to ourselves. And probably the night, that is…" She paused, gauging his reaction. "…if you want to stay over."

"I'll stay as long as you'll have me."

In an endeavor to continue what she started downstairs, she kicked her shoes free and stripped out of her jeans. As she took off her bra and her panties, a yearning within him instantly stirred. "Oh God, Carrie…" His breath hitched as he took in the curves of her petite frame, nearly rendering him speechless. "You're beautiful."

His words brought a flush to her face. "Your turn," she said, slightly smiling as she sat on the edge of the mattress, waiting for Joseph to join her.

A moment later, the bed dipped as he sat down beside her, his clothes removed and his heart hammering. "I love you, Carrie." As he spoke, his voice changed. There was an achy pitch to his tone. It was so deep his words sounded a bit distorted. "You're everything to me."

When she turned to meet his gaze, two soulless orbs stared back at her. There was a spellbinding quality to them, an alluring persuasion she couldn't look away from, even though she knew it wasn't just Joseph that was present. It was the Shadow too. And for some strange reason, she didn't care. She wouldn't allow herself to be afraid. Not this time.

"I love you too, Joseph."

* * *

As soon as Manuel pulled into the apartment complex where Joseph lived, he immediately noticed Drakon's black Hummer H3 at the far end of the parking lot. Although the windows were tinted, he could still make out two dark figures in front and two passengers in the back.

"Looks like Drakon brought backup," Manuel pointed out, glancing at his partner who was sitting shotgun.

"Good thing," Frank said. "Considering what we're up against, we may need it."

Manuel snorted. "Oh, we're definitely going to need it."

The driver's door to the Hummer opened when Manuel hit the brakes and put the gear in park. When the two detectives exited their unmarked car, Drakon ducked out from behind the wheel of the H3, towering to the height of six-foot-seven, sporting a short-trimmed Mohawk and a pair of dark sunglasses. His expression was unreadable, hidden behind his Ray-Bans, but his presence read loud and clear. He had the aura of a trained assassin who could kill a man with his bare hands.

Tim Ross, the council head of the Breedline Covenant, stepped out from the passenger's side with a black satchel strapped over his shoulder and a note of seriousness stamped all over his face. Then Roman Kincaid and Jem Chamberlain emerged from the back, and they too wore the same momentous looks on their faces.

When the four men gathered near Manuel and Frank, Tim spoke out first, keeping his voice low. "Do you happen to know the type of vehicle Joseph drives?"

"His therapist," Manuel began, "says he drives a black, two-door Jeep Wrangler. She said it looked like an older model. Maybe a year 2000 make."

"You mean like that one," Drakon said, pointing to the far end of the parking lot.

When everyone turned to look, they noticed a vehicle matching Manuel's description.

"Well, it looks like we're finally getting somewhere," Manuel said, looking between Tim and Drakon. "Now that we know he's here, how you propose we go about this?"

"There's no easy way to do this," Tim said. "We're prepared to tranquilize Joseph if need be."

Manuel crossed his arms, his expression one of concern. "You think it'll be strong enough to sedate whatever the hell that *thing* is inside of him?"

Tim nodded, and Roman said, "I sure as hell hope so. We've got enough to tranquilize a ten-thousand-pound elephant."

"Are you sure that's safe?" Frank asked. "It won't kill him, will it?"

Tim shrugged. "What else would you suggest we do, Detective? This demon is killing innocent people. I know Joseph is a victim himself, but we've got to do whatever it takes to put an end to all this."

Jem clapped a hand over Frank's shoulder. "Tim's right, Detective. And don't worry. We're not planning on killing Joseph if it's not necessary. If we can get him tranquilized, and keep him sedated, it might give us enough time to figure out how to release him from this evil entity. We've still got Sebastian Crow doing some research. With his background in demonology, he might discover a way to destroy the Shadow."

"And if Sebastian doesn't succeed," Roman blurted, "we can always hire a priest."

Drakon smirked at Roman. "If only it was that easy, buddy."

"What about Jena?" Manuel asked, his eyes focusing on Tim. "Even if you manage to sedate Joseph and get him to the Covenant, won't she sense evil and attack him?"

"Jena is still in Manhattan with Lenny," Tim replied. "Since her blood is the cure for the vampire virus, she promised to heal the rest of his species who are infected."

"How in the world is Jena going to accomplish such a task?" Frank asked. "She's only one person and there must be several infected vampires."

"Helen has teamed up with Dr. Carl Eaves," Tim explained. "They managed to create a vaccine for the virus, using a minimal amount of Jena's blood. They're almost positive it will be successful."

"What if this doesn't work?" Manuel asked, focusing back on their main objective. "With Jena out of town, how are we going to stop this damn..." He shook his head, appearing frustrated. "...Shadow demon, or *whatever* the hell you call it?"

"That's why we brought this guy," Roman chimed in, jamming a thumb in Jem's direction. "If things get dicey, Jem can use those wicked hands of his and turn it to ash."

"That will be our last resort," Tim pointed out. "We won't kill Joseph if we don't have to. And that's *if* the demon can be destroyed. We're not even certain Jem's powers are strong enough."

"Let's get a move on, guys," Drakon interjected. "Time is ticking."

When they located Joseph's apartment, they patiently waited outside the door several knocks later. Finally, Drakon said, "Okay, guys. I'm running thin on patience here." He pointedly looked between the two detectives. "It's obvious he's ignoring us or he's not home. Either way, I'm kicking in the door."

"Go ahead," Manuel said, giving Drakon a nod of approval.

With one forceful thrust, Drakon managed to break open the door, nearly ripping it off the hinges. It didn't take long for them to search the place and find it empty. Joseph was MIA.

"Dammit," Manuel gritted out. "He's either on foot or he took an Uber."

"Wherever he is," Tim said, "it looks like he's planning on coming back. Unless he's replacing his entire wardrobe. Nothing seems to be missing from the bedroom closet or dresser drawers."

"His toothbrush is still here," Roman said, his voice echoing from the bathroom.

"And his laptop," Drakon added. "Surely, he wouldn't leave that behind. When I went to visit the Chronicle this morning, asking to speak with Joseph, one of his coworkers told me he'd just called in, saying something about being out of the office on a supposedly"—Drakon did finger quotations—"work assignment."

"Did the guy mention when Joseph would be back?" Manuel asked.

Drakon shook his head. "I asked, but the guy said he didn't know. Even if he did, I doubt he'd tell me. But I did leave him my name and number. I told the guy I had some information concerning an article Joseph is working on. Who knows?" He shrugged. "Maybe when Joseph gets my message, he'll be curious enough to give me a call."

"Maybe," Manuel said, arching a brow. "And I must admit, you are a bit intimidating, Drakon."

"You're probably right." Drakon nodded in agreement. "It might have been a better idea to send someone besides me. Come to think, the guy did look a little nervous when he saw me walking in." He lightly chuckled, then mockingly said, "You don't think it had anything to do with my hair, do you?"

Manuel laughed. "That's just the tip of the iceberg. Your presence alone is enough to scare the boogeyman."

Drakon pointedly looked in Tim's direction. "So..." He shrugged. "...what now?"

"We have no other choice but to wait for him to return."

"Frank and I will keep a lookout," Manuel said.

"You're not doing it alone," Drakon said. "We'll stick around as backup."

"Thanks, guys," Frank said. "If Joseph doesn't show up by tomorrow afternoon, my partner and I will have to slip out for a couple of hours. We've got a very important birthday party to go to. You think you'll be all right without us?"

"I'm sure we can handle it, Detective," Drakon said. "Who's having a birthday?"

"My niece, Carrie," Frank replied.

"Before we leave," Manuel said, "what the hell are we going to do about that?" He gestured to the door. "By the looks of it, Joseph will surely realize someone broke in."

"Don't worry," Drakon said, "I'll take care of it."

"All right, guys," Tim said. "Let's get this done."

* * *

As Joseph sat there, gazing into Carrie's eyes, taking in all of her, his first thought was to put his clothes back on and leave. It wasn't fair to her. He was putting her in danger just by being here. But his eyes just stayed on her face. God, she was so beautiful. The expression in her mesmerizing brown eyes held a lonely yearning as he stared into them, as if she was searching for something. *How could someone like her want someone like me?* She deserved better. Someone normal. But he couldn't bear the thought of living without her. It was selfish thinking on his part.

"Will you please tell me what happened?" Carrie asked, breaking the silence as she looked up at the bandage over his forehead.

He shrugged a shoulder. "It's kind of stupid, really."

"So, tell me anyway."

Okay, here goes nothing. He grimaced. "I was hit by a car."

"What!" Shocked, she reached for his hand. "My God, Joseph. Are you okay?"

"Actually, it was a truck," he said, correcting himself. "And don't worry." He faked a smile. "I'm fine."

"You didn't..." she began, staring at him with a concerned look in her eyes, "...intentionally mean for that to happen, did you?"

Joseph kept his eyes on hers, feeling trapped in her gaze, as though she knew the truth already. Finally, he nodded, his eyes conveying a look of regret.

"Why, Joseph?" She tightened her hand over his. "What were you thinking?"

"It was the only way I could keep you safe. I thought if I died, so would the Shadow."

"Promise me you'll never do something like that again."

"I promise," he said with sincerity. "Besides, *it* won't let me harm myself."

"What do you mean?"

"Carrie, there's no way any normal person would have walked away from that accident, much less with just a few cuts and bruises. I should be dead."

"Are you saying that *thing* inside you somehow kept you from dying?"

"I don't know." He shook his head. "But how else would you explain it?"

There was a knock across the room. Their eyes shot toward the bedroom door.

"Yeah," Carrie called out.

"It's me Jessica. Are you all right, Carrie?"

"I-I'm fine."

"I heard about your boss," Jessica said. "That really sucks. Veronica was a shitty person, but—"

"I'm okay, Jess," Carrie cut in. "Really."

"You sure?"

"Yeah, I'm sure. I just want to be alone for a bit."

"Okay." There was an awkward moment of silence. "Well... let me know if you want to talk, or just need some company."

"I will."

"I'll be at Ryan's if you need anything. I should be back around eight or nine tomorrow morning."

"Thanks, Jess."

"No problem, girl. You sure you don't want me to go ahead and cancel the party? I can contact everyone. I'm sure they'll understand, considering the circumstances."

"Nah," Carrie said, "let's keep it as planned. Besides, having friends and family around will lift my spirits."

"Okay, then. We'll talk in the morning."

As soon as Jessica's footsteps disappeared into the distance, Joseph said, "Maybe you should have told her about me."

"I'll mention it to her later," Carrie said. "I'm sure she'll be thrilled to know you're here and that you're coming to my birthday party tomorrow."

"Really?"

Carrie nodded. "Jessica and Ryan have been rooting for us to get back together."

Joseph cracked a smile. "In truth, so have I."

"You have?"

He dipped his head, keeping his eyes focused on her face. "I missed you like crazy, Carrie. When I'm away from you, I find it hard to focus. I can't eat. I can't sleep. Hell, I can barely breathe."

"Me too," she said, her voice trembling.

He intertwined his fingers with hers and lightly squeezed. "Carrie, how are we going to do this? I shouldn't be here. I mean, what if I—"

"It's worth the risk," she interjected. "You're worth the risk, Joseph."

"I couldn't live with myself if something happened to you. I'm afraid the Shadow will try to hurt you, and I won't be able to stop it."

"Is it..." She paused, swallowing hard. "...telling you to hurt me now?"

He shook his head. "It's strange, but I haven't heard *it* speak to me since I got here."

She looked at him, surprised. "Does this thing... I mean, the Shadow, speak to you every day?"

"Yes. And he's never been this quiet."

"The Shadow is a *he*?"

"I guess." He shrugged. "The voice sounds like a male. It reminds me of Hannibal Lector. You know, Anthony Hopkins in *Silence of the Lambs*."

Carrie nodded, looking disgusted by his description. "Well, maybe *he's* just giving us some privacy." Then she laughed a little. "This may sound weird, but you do realize we're having a casual conversation, talking about a demon, while sitting on my bed completely naked, right?"

"Yeah, I do." His face flushed. "And I swear, I'm having the hardest time keeping my eyes from wandering."

"I wouldn't mind if your eyes wandered."

Joseph took an unsteady breath and muttered, "Y-you wouldn't?"

She shook her head, staring at his mouth. "Would you like to kiss me, Joseph?"

Her breath caught as he lifted his hand to her mouth and gently trailed his thumb over her bottom lip. The moment he bent low and kissed her, she felt a warm sensation bloom throughout her body. Her heart pounded, and her skin prickled with goose bumps as his fingers slowly moved down her neck and then to her collarbone. And they didn't stop there. They kept going, softly tracing a path between her breasts.

"Is this okay?" he asked, keeping his voice low.

"Yes," she answered in a breathy tone.

Her body flushed as thoughts invaded her memory, thinking what it felt like to have his weight pressing down on her. Although this time, she wanted more. She wanted to feel his warm hands all over her, caressing, touching. And the heat of his bare skin atop hers, making love to her.

As if Joseph could read her thoughts, knowing what she wanted and prepared to deliver, he said, "I want you, Carrie." His hand went to her neck, and he slightly tilted her head back. He stared at her with such intensity it brought tears to her eyes. "And I'm never letting you go."

"Good, because I'm all yours," she whispered back.

Handling her as if she were a delicate piece of glass, he carefully guided her back against the bed. As soon as she settled onto the satin sheets, he moved between her legs. On impulse, her hands went to his shoulders. When she pulled him down, his pulse raced, and his heart nearly leapt from his chest. As their bodies came together, an arc of sexual tension exploded between them. God, she felt so good. Too good. Her warm breasts pressing against his chest ignited him further. He had to close his eyes. The skin-on-skin contact was almost more than he could bear. But this time when his lips came down on hers, a raw passion radiated between them, leaving them breathless.

As they ascended the heights of passion, holding on to each other, Joseph knew without a doubt it was fate that had brought them together. He was hers, and she was his. And that was something he'd only dreamt of having. Something he'd prayed for. Something he'd die for.

An hour later, after their lovemaking and drifting into a deep slumber, Carrie suddenly came awake with her bladder screaming in protest. She sat up in bed and looked down to see Joseph soundly sleeping next to her. The moon shining through the cracked blinds cast a glow over his handsome face. She smiled, noticing how content and peaceful he looked. If she hadn't already known, she would have never guessed this loving, yet tortured, man—a man she dearly loved, a man she could spend the rest of her life with—was possessed by something so evil.

Before she eased out of bed, she glanced back at Joseph and mentally said a silent prayer. *Please, God... if you can hear me, please free Joseph from this demonic entity who has plagued his body for so long. He's a good man who doesn't deserve this. He's suffered so much.* She released a deep breath and whispered, "Amen."

Carrie slipped out of bed, careful not to wake Joseph, and made her way into the bathroom. Quietly, she closed the door and switched on the light. After using the restroom, she went to the sink to wash her hands. At the same time, she reached for the soap and glanced up into the mirror. What she saw made her eyes go wide and her mouth open with a gasp. She tried to look away, tried to pull herself from the unholy image staring back at her. It was... *She* was... hideous.

"Oh, God." She instantly clamped her hand over her mouth to stifle her scream.

"Hello, Carrie," a sinister voice whispered inside her head.

Chapter Forty-Four

Drakon and Roman hung back in the shadows, surveying the Hillside Village—the apartment complex where Joseph stayed—inside the Hummer H3 while the two detectives waited in their unmarked car. The moon was full, illuminating the parking lot and the outer perimeter of the building, giving them enough light to see by.

Jem hid in the back of the complex behind rows of thick shrubbery, joined now by his twin brother Jace, where they had a good view of the door to Joseph's apartment. Every now and then, Jem peered through a pair of binoculars to get a closer look.

Jace leaned in close to Jem and nudged his arm. "Psst... Let me look."

"Hang on a minute," Jem whispered with a slight hint of irritation. "I think I see someone."

"Who is it?" Jace persisted, keeping his voice low. "Is it Joseph?"

"Shhh..." Jem held up a hand, motioning his brother to be quiet. "Hold on."

"False alarm." Jem finally lowered the binoculars. "It was just Joseph's next-door neighbor."

"Aw crap," Jace said, sounding disappointed. "I was ready for some action. I'm sick of waiting." He glanced down at his watch, noticing it was already after midnight. "Damn, it's nearly one in the morning. Where the hell is this guy, anyway?"

Jem shrugged. "How am I supposed to know?"

"Let me see those," Jace said, reaching for the binoculars. "I'm bored as hell."

"Here." Jem handed them over, rolling his eyes. "You're starting to get on my nerves."

"Oh, shut up," Jace grumbled, looking through the binoculars.

After a few moments of silence, Jace blurted, "Hey..." He snapped his fingers, trying to rouse his brother's attention.

Jem furrowed his brows. "What is it?"

"There's a dude standing outside Joseph's apartment door."

"Is it him?"

"I don't think so," Jace said, continuing to peer through the binoculars. "He's knocking on the door."

"Let me take a look."

When Jace handed Jem the binoculars, he put them up to his eyes. A few seconds later, he said, "Call Drakon. Give him the guy's description. He'll be heading toward the parking lot shortly. Right now, it looks like he's making a call. Probably trying to get ahold of Joseph."

As Jace made the call, Jem set the binoculars down. "Okay, the guy's making his way around to the front. I'm going to follow him from behind."

Before the guy had the chance to make it back to the parking lot, Drakon had already called the two detectives to give them a heads-up. Manuel had told Drakon and the others to sit tight. He thought it best if he and his partner went to check it out by themselves.

As the guy was about to get into his car, both detectives rushed over. "Hold up," Manuel called out, holding up his badge. "San Francisco PD. We're from homicide. I need to ask you a few questions, sir."

The guy spun around, his expression startled. "Wha-what—"

"I'm Detective Sanchez and this is my partner Detective Perkins. We're looking for a Joseph Parker. You know him?"

"Y-yeah," the guy said, nodding his head. "I work with him. Did something happen to Joseph?"

"Not that we are aware of," Manuel replied. "We just need to speak with him. Do you happen to know his whereabouts?"

"N-no." The guy nervously shook his head. "I was just looking for him myself. I thought since his Jeep was here, he'd be in his apartment. But I couldn't get anyone to answer the door. I've been trying to get ahold of him all day."

"And he hasn't returned any of your phone calls?" Manuel asked.

"All my calls just go to his voicemail."

"What's your name, son?" Frank chimed into the conversation as he approached the guy.

"Stewart Childs. I'm a reporter for the Chronicle."

Manuel suspiciously eyeballed the guy. "So, what brings you here at this hour?"

"I know it's late," Stewart said, looking nervously between the two detectives. "But I'm a little concerned for Joseph. You see, there was this guy…" He visibly swallowed. "A big guy with a Mohawk. He came to the Chronicle this morning looking for Joseph. He said something about having some information on an article Joseph is working on. But I don't think he was telling the truth. The guy looked a little sketchy, if you know what I mean."

"I get your meaning," Manuel said, trying his best to hold back a chuckle, imagining how Drakon would respond to Mr. Childs's comment. "So, did this Mohawked-guy happen to leave his name?"

Stewart nodded. "Yeah. He gave me his number too." He reached into the front pocket of his jeans. "I have it here."

When Stewart handed a folded piece of paper to the detective, he went on to say, "I was going to give it to Joseph, but when he never returned my calls, I got worried. That's why I decided to stop by his apartment."

Manuel looked at the piece of paper, surprised to see that Drakon had left his real name and number on it. Then he handed it back to Stewart. "Why did you wait so late to check on Mr. Parker?"

"I don't know." Stewart shrugged. "I guess I was afraid to get involved. It took me a while to build up the courage. That guy who came looking for Joseph scared the piss out of me."

"The guy you're referring to is an investigator," Manuel said, slightly fudging the truth. "He's working for us."

Stewart's eyes rounded. "Is Joseph in some kind of trouble?"

"No," Manuel quickly replied. "But it's important that we get in touch with Mr. Parker as soon as possible. Would you happen to know where we might find him? Maybe he's staying at a friend's place. Perhaps a family member or at a girlfriend's house."

Stewart's brows drew together. "What's this about, anyway?"

"I'm sorry, Mr. Childs," Frank spoke out, "but that information is classified."

"Well..." Stewart paused, thinking. "I really don't know much about Joseph's personal life. I haven't known him for long. Although I do recall him mentioning something about a girl he's been seeing. I think he said her name was..." He scratched his chin. "Carla... Casey... No, that's not it." He frowned, then a few seconds later, his eyes lit up. "It's Carrie. Yeah, that's her name." Then his expression dimmed. "But he didn't mention her last name."

Manuel faced Frank with a look of concern, then he refocused his eyes back on Stewart. "Thanks for all your help, Mr. Childs." He extended his hand. "Here's my card. Please contact us if you hear back from Mr. Parker."

Stewart took the card and nodded. "Sure thing, Detective."

The minute Stewart got into his car and drove off, Frank turned toward Manuel with a grim expression.

"I know what you're thinking," Manuel said. "I'm sure it's not your niece." He placed a hand over Frank's shoulder. "There's no telling how many other Carries are in the city."

Frank sighed. "God, I hope you're right. And right about now, I could kick my own ass for not asking Carrie more about this new boyfriend of hers. For crying out loud, what was I thinking? I should've at least got the guy's name."

"Don't beat yourself up, partner. We'll meet this guy soon enough. Then we're definitely going to do a thorough background check on him." He gestured toward Drakon's Hummer. "Come on. Let's go fill in the others."

Two hours later, they ordered Chinese takeout. When their food was delivered, the two detectives remained in their vehicle, keeping a lookout for Joseph, and ate as if it were their last meal.

As Frank finished the last of his kung pao chicken, he turned to Manuel. "I'm not waiting till noon for Carrie's party. I have a gut feeling something's not right, and before you ask, it doesn't have anything to do with the takeout."

Manuel checked his watch, then looked to the passenger's side at his partner. "It's four in the morning. You think it's a good idea to wake her at this hour?"

"We'll head over to her apartment close to nine," Frank said. "She should be up by then."

"Sure thing, buddy." Manuel smiled at Frank. "If it gives you peace of mind, then that's what we'll do."

* * *

Carrie quickly lowered her head, squeezed her eyes shut, and silently started to pray. *Please, God...* Her lips trembled. *I beg you. Please don't let this be real.* Then she began to whisper, repeating the words over and over, "This is not real... This is not real... This is not real..."

"I am real." The voice that spoke into Carrie's mind drew her attention, putting a halt to her words. It sounded sinister, *evil.*

She kept her head down and her eyes closed, pretending she didn't hear the voice. Dread instantly tightened her throat. With all the strength she could muster, she mentally tried to block out the voice. But the dark entity was too powerful. She had evil inside her, invading her subconscious.

"I know you can hear me, Carrie." The demanding voice echoed inside her head, *"Look upon me and see with your own eyes."*

Carrie lifted her chin and slowly opened her eyes. She swallowed compulsively as she looked at her reflection in the mirror. The face staring back at her wasn't exactly her own. It was a combination of her features and something else. Something unnatural and unholy. Black, bottomless orbs replaced her brown eyes, and dark, spider-webbed veins covered her pallid skin like a roadmap to hell.

The Shadow, she feverishly thought.

The evil voice laughed, although it sounded more like a cackle. *"So now you know I am real."*

"Please..." Carrie exhaled a weary breath as tears spilled down her cheeks. "What do you want with me?"

A bony, clawed hand suddenly emerged from the mirror like something out of a nightmare. Carrie froze as it reached out and wiped a tear from her cheek. The shimmer of wetness gleamed on its hideous finger, and Carrie wanted to scream, but when she opened her mouth, nothing came out. It was as though her voice had been stolen. Instead of a scream came a lizard-like tongue, lazily slithering between her parted lips. When it swirled around the tip of the repulsive extremity, she nearly lost the contents of her stomach. She watched in horror as the long, reptilian-looking appendage captured her tear and disappeared back into her mouth.

"Pity we don't have more time to get to know one another," the Shadow muttered. *"I was just starting to have fun. But there will be more time for you and me later. Now go back to sleep, Carrie."*

And like a puppet on strings, Carrie obeyed as if nothing had happened. On autopilot, she switched off the light, opened the door, and crept toward the bed in a sleepwalk haze. Moving slowly, she pulled back the covers and slid underneath.

As soon as the mattress dipped, squeaking in protest, the noise roused Joseph into wakefulness. He turned over and reached out, searching for Carrie in the dark. When his hand touched her arm, he shuddered. She was ice cold.

"Carrie?" He pushed himself up. "Are you okay?"

When there was no response, he moved closer, raising his voice. "Carrie..."

Finally, a sleepy voice said, "What's wrong, Joseph?"

As she spoke, her breath came out in a cloudy vapor as though the temperature in the room had dropped.

"Are you feeling okay?"

She nodded in the darkness. "I'm fine. Why?"

"Your skin." He rubbed his hand over her arm, trying to warm her. "It's like an icicle. And I can see your breath."

"What?" Carrie said, scooting higher on her pillow, watching her breath seep from her lips like puffs of smoke. Her eyes went wide. "W-what's happening?" She crossed her arms over her chest and shivered. "And why is it so cold in here?"

Joseph quickly turned toward the nightstand and reached for the lamp. The second he faced Carrie, his eyes grew wide, and his jaw slacked open. "Oh God, no," he finally managed to say.

Carrie's beautiful features had transformed into something demonic... *evil*. Her once enchanting brown eyes had shifted. They were like obsidian. *Empty. Soulless.* And the dark, webbed veins that showed beneath her pale face looked more like the dead than the living.

"What's the matter, Joseph?" she asked, cocking her head to the side. "You look like you've seen a ghost."

"Y-your face," he muttered, swallowing hard. "It's..."

Her brows furrowed. "What's wrong with my face?"

"Carrie..." He inched closer. "Is there a voice speaking to you? I mean, inside your head."

"A voice?" She looked at him confused. "What are you talking about? You're scaring me, Joseph."

"Come with me." He reached for her hand. "Let me show you."

As Joseph slid out of bed, he helped Carrie to her feet. She instantly snuggled against him. "I'm f-freezing," she muttered around her chattering teeth.

He snatched a blanket off the bed and wrapped it around her. "Is that better?"

She nodded, tugging the blanket more snugly around her.

Before Joseph guided Carrie inside the bathroom, he stopped outside the doorway.

She gazed up at him with a puzzled expression on her hideous face. "What's wrong?"

"I'm going to warn you before I turn on the light."

"Warn me?" Her black eyes narrowed. "About what? And why are you taking me into the bathroom?"

"Carrie, I think the Shadow somehow left my body and entered yours."

Her eyes bulged. "W-what?"

Joseph flipped on the light and when he pointed toward the mirror, Carrie blinked a few times, trying to get her eyes to adjust. The moment she saw the reflection staring back at her, she opened her mouth and screamed. The terror in her voice tore at his heart.

"Shhh..." He tugged her close. "It's okay. I've got you, Carrie."

"No..." She went all frantic, shoving at Joseph's shoulders, trying to break free of his hold. "It's not true. It can't be. I won't let that *thing* take me."

"Listen to me, Carrie. I'm not leaving you. We'll get help." What help? Who in the hell could help with this? A priest? For crying out loud, this wasn't something just anyone could get rid of. They were dealing with a demon. And the worst of it was the killing. *Would the Shadow make Carrie kill people like it did me?*

"No, no, no..." She continued to ramble, the incoherent words mixing with her sobs. "This can't be happening. It can't be—"

Joseph's face was pain-stricken. "I'm so sorry—dear God—I never meant for this to happen."

She struggled from his arms, and cried out, "Please, Joseph..." Her voice went guttural. "Just go."

"You don't mean that, Carrie." He followed her as she turned and walked away. "You're frightened and you have every right to be. But please, just let me help—"

"For God's sake, Joseph," she said, facing him. "Please, just leave."

As he tried to come close to her again, she rushed past him and locked herself in the bathroom. Bracing herself against the sink, she looked up and caught the horrible sight of herself in the mirror. Without thinking, she grabbed the nearest thing, an iron candle holder, and threw it against the mirror. Through despairing tears, she watched her reflection shatter as pieces of herself fell apart.

Joseph rushed toward the bathroom and tried to open the door. It was locked. On the other side, he could hear her crying. The sound was heartbreaking.

"Carrie..." He frantically called out. "Are you okay?"

A sense of panic set in when there was only silence. "Carrie?"

"I'm fine." The sadness in her voice made his eyes sting with tears. "I just need to be alone."

He leaned in, resting his head against the wood that separated them. "I'm so sorry..." His voice cracked, then he squeezed his eyes shut, his heart shattering. "Oh God..." He lightly beat the door with his fist. "This is all my fault."

After a few moments of silence, which felt like eternity, Carrie finally said, "It's not your fault, Joseph." Then the door slowly creaked open. When she appeared in the opening and lifted her gaze to meet his, relief instantly washed over him. Carrie no longer wore a mask of horror, but instead, the face of the beautiful person she was before. The one he loved so dearly.

"You're not to blame for this," she went on to say as more tears gathered at the corners of her eyes. "I knew the dangers involved. I'm sorry I took it out on you. I'd rather be dead than be without you."

The second he reached out to her, she took hold of his hand. He all but tugged her into his arms and held her close. "I love you, Carrie. And nothing you say or do will change that."

She lifted her chin and stared at him long and hard. Then smiled. "I love you too."

"I swear," he said, his eyes gleaming with sincerity, "we'll find a way to get through this. No matter what it takes, and even if I die trying, I'm going to destroy the Shadow."

Chapter Forty-Five

The next morning, as Joseph came awake, he suddenly felt uneasy. Remembering what had transpired with Carrie, he quickly pushed himself upright and nervously searched her side of the bed. A sense of relief settled over him the moment he saw her lying beside him, eyes closed, sleeping peacefully. He took a deep breath and continued to watch her. Although he was lying next to Carrie, he felt an emptiness in him. No voice inside his head, demanding him to kill. It was... just himself. Finally, there was silence. He reveled in the heavenly peace and quiet. Now, for the first time in so long, he was in control of his own body. The Shadow was gone.

But of course, he stressed, *now Carrie is cursed*. He thought about what she had undergone, taking on the evil entity that had possessed him for so many years. He'd always wanted his freedom, but not at the risk of losing Carrie. She didn't deserve this. The Shadow was his burden. His burden to carry, and his alone.

Then another panic set in. *Shit!* What time was it? As he went to grab his phone off the nightstand, realization hit him. He'd taken a few days off work, so it didn't matter how late it was. Still, he unlocked his phone and saw he had six missed calls, two text messages, and three voice messages. They were all from his coworker, Stewart. And two of the voice messages were sent at one o'clock this morning.

Carrie woke up with a moan. "Joseph?"

At the sound of Carrie's voice, he averted his eyes from his phone and looked to her in concern. "I'm right here." He placed a hand over hers. "How do you feel?"

"Okay, I guess." She flashed him a weary smile. "And if you're wondering if I'm hearing voices," she bluntly stated, "I'm not."

"We're going to get through this, Carrie." He squeezed her hand. "I promise."

She silently nodded. "How long have you been awake?"

"Not long." He focused back on his phone.

"How about some coffee?"

When there was no reply, she scooted higher on her pillow and said, "Is something wrong?"

"It's nothing, really. Well, I don't think anyway." As he looked at her, his blue eyes expressed a hint of worry. "Just some missed calls."

"From whom?"

"Apparently, one of my coworkers has been trying to get ahold of me. And he seems very persistent."

"Did he leave a message?"

"Yeah." He nodded. "Quite a few. The last two were at one o'clock this morning."

"Sounds urgent. Maybe you should see what's so important."

"I agree," Joseph said, opening his voicemail to the first message. He put it on speaker and hit play.

"Hey, Joseph. Thought I'd give you a heads up. Some guy came by the Chronicle looking for you this morning. He said he had some information on a story you've been working on. He left his name and number. I sent a screenshot of it to you. But..." There was a pause, followed by a sigh. *"This guy, well... not sure if he's legit. His name is Drakon Hexus. He looks like a freakin' hitman. If I had to take a guess, the guy stood at least six-seven or more. He has a Mohawk and a tattoo on his neck. Anyway, call me when you get a chance."*

Joseph turned toward Carrie and shrugged. "Wonder what that's all about. I have no idea who this Drakon guy is."

"By your coworker's description," Carrie said, "the guy sounds scary."

"Yeah, he does." His brows drew together. "I guess I should listen to the rest of Stewart's messages."

As soon as Joseph opened the next message, he raised the volume.

"Hey, it's Stewart again. I've been trying to reach you all day. It's nearly one in the morning and I'm at your apartment, but I guess you're not at home. I'm starting to worry about you, buddy. Call or text me. Just let me know you're all right."

Then Joseph played the last message. *"Listen, man."* Stewart's voice sounded nervous. *"I don't know what's going on, but as I was leaving your apartment, two homicide detectives from the San Francisco PD stopped me. They were asking if I knew where you were. Apparently, they want to ask you some questions. They wouldn't tell me what it's about, but they sounded serious. Said something about it being classified. When they questioned why I was here, I told them I was concerned since I hadn't heard from you all day and you hadn't returned my calls. I also mentioned that Drakon guy who stopped by the Chronicle looking for you this morning. Come to find out, that guy is an investigator, working with those two detectives. One of them left me his card. Anyway, I'll send you a screenshot of it. Maybe you should give 'im a call. And hey..."* There was a brief pause. *"If you're in some kind of trouble, you can trust me. I mean, if you're in a jam, maybe I can help. Later, buddy."*

As soon as the message ended, Carrie said, "Joseph..." She nervously swallowed. "Can I see that screenshot Stewart sent you?"

"Sure." He nodded and proceeded to check his text messages. When he found the two Stewart had sent, he handed his phone to Carrie. "Maybe you'll recognize the name of that detective since your uncle works for the San Francisco PD."

The second Carrie saw the name written on the business card, her eyes rounded. "I don't believe it."

"What is it?"

"That detective is my uncle's partner." She tore her eyes away from the phone and focused them on Joseph, looking completely stunned. "That means they're searching for you."

Joseph shook his head. "But I don't understand. What do they want with me?"

"Maybe they found something," she said, sitting the phone next to Joseph. "Like fingerprints. Maybe camera footage, or something that leads you to the crime scene."

"You mean, Veronica's murder?"

Shivers crept up the back of her neck. "Yes."

He reached out, trying to soothe her. "It's okay, Carrie. Everything is going to be okay."

"But..." Her eyes were desperate as she searched over his face. "How can you be so sure? And my uncle and his partner are both coming to my birthday party this afternoon. What are we going to do?"

"Maybe we should go to them for help. Since he's your uncle, and he and your aunt practically raised you, I'm sure he'll want to help."

"How are we supposed to explain all this?" She let out a deep breath. "I can't expect my Uncle Frank to believe we're dealing with a demon. He'll think we've both gone mad."

"What other choice do we have?"

Before she could say anything, he held up his hand. "Give it a chance, Carrie. Besides, your uncle knows you. It's not like you've said or done anything out of the ordinary before. He'll listen to what you have to say. You're his family."

Carrie put her head down and murmured, "Something out of the ordinary did happen to me."

Joseph cocked an eyebrow at her. "What do you mean?"

She lifted her chin and blinked tears. "It was a long time ago. When my parents died, something strange happened. It sounds crazy. Maybe I am crazy. When I told my aunt and uncle, they took me to a child psychologist. I was just five at the time, so they thought it was just my imagination. The psychologist chalked it up as a way of dealing with the death of my parents. But now, I'm not so sure."

He reached out and wiped at her tears. "Whatever it is, you know you can tell me. And I won't think you're crazy."

"Joseph..." She exhaled a deep breath. "I saw an angel. Her name was Lailah, and she saved me. If it wasn't for her, I would have died in that car accident along with my parents."

Joseph blinked as if her words had surprised him. "I believe you, Carrie."

"Y-you do?"

He smiled. "Of course, I do."

More tears clouded her eyes, but she wouldn't allow them to fall.

"Did she speak to you?" Joseph asked. "The angel, that is."

Carrie nodded. "I remember asking her if I could go to heaven to be with my parents, but Lailah said God needed me here for something important."

"And she didn't say what it was?"

"I asked, of course," Carrie said, her lips curving into a half smile. "At age five, I was full of questions. But she didn't know."

"Maybe this has something to do with the Shadow."

Carrie shrugged. "What do you mean?"

"Somehow the demon chose to leave my body and enter yours for a reason."

"But why?"

"I don't know, Carrie. But I do know we cannot do this alone. We're going to need help."

"You really think my Uncle Frank and his partner will believe us?"

"Yes," he said softly, then glanced down at his phone, realizing time was getting away from them. "Now go ahead and get dressed while I start a pot of coffee. I have a feeling we're going to need it. And stop worrying." He leaned in and kissed her forehead. "We'll figure this out."

"It won't take me long to get ready," Carrie said. "Then I'll drive you to your apartment so you can pick up a few things, like something other than what you had on yesterday."

He glanced down at his boxers, recalling the clothes he'd been wearing. Then he chuckled. "Yeah, a pair of jogging shorts and a T-shirt isn't exactly proper party attire. Plus, I don't want to make a bad impression when I meet your uncle."

"I think that ship has already sailed, buster," Carrie said, arching a brow. "I don't think he's going to be too focused on your fashion."

"Let's just pray he leaves his handcuffs behind and instead brings an open mind."

She sighed. "Me too."

Without another word, Carrie went into the bathroom. As soon as she shut the door behind her, Joseph slipped on the only clothes he had and headed for the kitchen. As he was about to reach into the cabinet where Carrie stored the coffee, there was a knock at the door. He stood there for a moment, wondering if he should answer it. He waited, hoping Carrie's roommate had returned from Ryan's while they were sleeping and would take care of it. But when the knock persisted, his wishful thinking took a nosedive.

I guess it's up to me, he thought, staring at the coffeepot in desperation. Before he went for the door, he pointed at the coffee maker and muttered, "I'll be back for *you* later."

When Joseph unlatched the lock and opened the door, he was greeted by two men. The taller one with a short-trimmed haircut was dressed in a tailored-fit jacket, a navy button-down shirt, and a matching striped tie. The other guy sported a James Dean hairdo and wore a brown leather jacket, jeans, and a pair of worn-out cowboy boots. They both looked to be in their late forties or early fifties, and by the expression on their faces, it was evident they were shocked to see him. Probably because they weren't expecting a guy to answer the door to Carrie and Jessica's apartment, he thought.

"Hi." Joseph shot them a tentative smile. "Can I help you?"

The taller guy narrowed his eyes and took a step forward. "Who are you?"

Suddenly, Joseph felt his adrenaline spike. "Uh..." His Adam's apple bobbed as he swallowed. "I'm Joseph. Carrie's boyfriend."

"Joseph Parker?" the other guy asked, his nostrils flaring.

"Y-yeah," Joseph nervously replied, nodding. "How did you know my—"

The guy with the James Dean look pushed his way inside. "Mr. Parker," he said, reaching inside his leather jacket, "don't move." When he brought his hand back, he held a gun.

Joseph froze. "W-what?"

As Carrie rushed into the room, she saw her Uncle Frank and his partner, Detective Manuel Sanchez, detaining Joseph in a pair of handcuffs.

Frank held up a halting hand. "Stay back, Carrie."

"Please, Uncle Frank," she pleaded. "Don't hurt him."

Uncle Frank? Joseph feverishly thought. *Shit!*

"We're not going to hurt him, sweetheart," Frank murmured. "But you have to understand. Joseph is not the person you think he is. He's very dangerous."

"No..." Carrie helplessly shook her head. "It's not his fault."

Jessica and Ryan, oblivious to the current situation, walked through the open doorway with their arms full of bags of groceries.

"Carrie, are you—" Jessica stopped in her tracks with her mouth agape when she saw Joseph with his hands cuffed behind his back and Manuel holding him at gunpoint.

"Guys," Frank called out, motioning toward Jessica and Ryan. "I need you two to move out of the way."

Jessica instantly dropped the bags to the floor and looked at Carrie, confused. "What the hell is going on?"

Ryan quickly set his bags down and looped his arm around Jessica. "Come on, honey." He pulled her aside. "Let's get out of their way."

Everything seemed to move in slow motion as Carrie stood there, watching the events surrounding her unfold into a nightmare. Then a voice deep within her subconscious spoke to her. *Kill them, Carrie. Kill them all.*

Frank reached into his jacket for his phone. As soon as he searched through his contacts, he initiated a call. "Tim," he began, "this is Detective Perkins. We've got Mr. Parker in our custody. As for now, he's not resisting. We're at my niece's apartment building on 1477 Fillmore Street. Carrie's apartment is on the second floor. Number 26B."

As Frank continued the phone call, Joseph looked at the man with the gun. "Please, listen to me." Joseph's voice sounded desperate. "Before you haul me off, there's something Carrie and I need to tell you in private." He averted his eyes, looking between Jessica and Ryan, then focused back to Manuel. "I'm begging you..." His expression was pleading. "This is urgent."

"We know more than you think, Mr. Parker," Manuel said. "If you cooperate with us, we'll do everything we can to help you. There's a special group of people on their way. And hopefully they can figure out how to get rid of *your* problem."

"What group of people?" Jessica interjected. "This is my apartment too, and I have the right to know what's going on?"

"Jessica..." Ryan tugged her closer. "I think we should stay out of this."

Jessica huffed, pulled away from Ryan, and crossed her arms. Then her eyes wandered in Carrie's direction. The second she caught sight of her best friend's face, she immediately placed a hand over her mouth and gasped. Carrie's sun-kissed complexion was deathly pale, and the whites of her eyes were nothing but ominous black orbs.

Unaware of Carrie's newfound appearance, Joseph kept his eyes trained on Manuel. "What sort of problem are you referring to?"

"You know..." Manuel said, trying not to say too much in front of Jessica and Ryan. "Your *Shadow* problem."

Joseph's eyes rounded and his jaw nearly hit the floor. He couldn't believe it. *How could they possibly know?*

Before Joseph managed to get another word out, a group of large men barged through the open doorway. Instantly, all eyes were on them. Jessica quickly latched on to Ryan's arm.

Joseph stiffened when a guy with a black, short-trimmed Mohawk entered, sporting a pair of dark-rimmed sunglasses. He towered to the height of at least six-seven, his intimidating stature alone frightening, not to mention his bulging, muscular arms. When he moved, Joseph spotted a word tattooed on his neck, but he couldn't make out what it said.

As the Mohawked-guy inched closer, Joseph noticed Ryan peer up at the guy like he recognized him. And by the expression on the guy's face, he looked surprised to see Ryan.

Joseph quickly averted his eyes from the scary Mohawked-guy as two more men entered. They looked identical, like twins, except one had a scar on the left side of his temple. Their long, blond hair made him think of musicians from an '80s rock band. Behind them, another guy emerged with a black satchel strapped over his shoulder. He had a menacing look about him, but not as much as the Mohawked-guy.

Then two more men stalked through the door's opening. Both had ink-black, shoulder-length hair, one with olive skin, dark set eyes, and his hair was slicked back into a ponytail. By his prominent features, he looked European. The other guy had a pale-ish complexion and a distinguished aura about him. His eyes were strange. They had to be colored contact lenses, Joseph thought. No one really had purple eyes.

When the group of hulking men crowded into the apartment, a tall, blonde woman stepped inside and moved next to the man with purple eyes. She squared her shoulders and focused on him with a narrowed stare. Although the woman had a petite frame, she gave off the vibe that she could take care of herself. Her facial expression was nothing but stone cold. The woman reeked of confidence and perseverance. Then she lifted her chin and deeply inhaled, her nostrils flaring as she sniffed the air. Joseph nervously watched as the woman shifted her attention away from him and focused her eyes on Carrie with a baleful glare.

The instant the woman tore her gaze away from Carrie, she looked to the men, who were obviously part of her crew, and said, "It's no longer possessing Joseph." She pointed toward Carrie. "The Shadow's in the girl."

How did she know? Joseph furrowed his brows, thinking. *Who are these people?*

When everyone focused on Carrie, the room went so quiet you could've heard a pin drop.

"Who the hell are you people?" Jessica spoke out as though she'd read Joseph's mind, her eyes roaming over all the unfamiliar faces. "And what the hell is going on here?"

Ignoring Jessica's outburst, Frank frantically looked back and forth from Carrie to Jena, until finally, his eyes feasted upon his niece in stunned disbelief. "Oh God..." His voice trembled. "C-Carrie..."

As the blonde woman started forward with her eyes locked on Carrie, the satchel-toting guy raised a hand. "Jena, wait..." His firm voice stopped her in her tracks. "Let's try our plan first."

With her lips drawn in a thin line, Jena nodded an understanding, then sternly said, "You got one shot at this, Tim." Her voice sounded guttural, ready for lethal force. "You better pray it works."

"If Tim's plan doesn't work," one of the guys who looked like an '80s rocker said, "I'll use my powers."

"No, Jem..." Frank blurted, his eyes pleading with the blond, long-haired rocker. "You'll kill her. Please... Carrie is like a daughter to me."

"Don't hurt her," Joseph finally said, struggling in the handcuffs. "This is not her fault."

The long-haired guy, who Frank addressed as Jem, looked between him and Frank with a grim expression. "I'm sorry. But we may have no choice. We must stop the demon."

"No." Joseph shook his head, his voice filled with tears. "There has to be another way."

The man with the satchel, ignoring their pleas, slipped it off his shoulders and reached inside. The moment he brought his hand out, he held what looked to be a tranquilizer gun.

"Everyone ready?" Tim asked, recalling Jena's statement, knowing he only had one shot to get this done. And if the tranquilizer wasn't enough to sedate the evil entity possessing Carrie, they would have to resort to using Jem's deadly powers. There just weren't any other options.

If anyone had any reservations about the plan, they didn't make them known. Instead, Tim received nothing but affirmative nods within his group.

Chapter Forty-Six

As Tim aimed the tranquilizer gun at Carrie, he prayed like hell it would be enough to sedate the demon, but in turn not enough that it would kill her.

Carrie just stood there as if waiting, her hands fisted at her sides. Her haunting stare chilled Tim's guts and made the hairs on the back of his neck rise. Worse still, as her lips peeled back, he saw the flash of sharp teeth.

Tim squared his shoulders and inhaled a deep breath. He paused only to better secure his grip, while Carrie's ominous eyes narrowed to slits. On the exhale, he squeezed the trigger. But to everyone's surprise, she reached out like time stood still and caught it with unimaginable speed.

"Ah, shit," Tim muttered.

Jem palpably tensed, readying himself for plan B, while his twin brother blurted, "What the f—"

His words trailed off when Carrie lifted off the floor and hovered in midair, hissing like a mass of snakes. Then a crackling sound—like the flames of a fire—perked her ears.

Jessica started sobbing, repeating the words *"oh God, oh God,"* until Ryan pulled her closer, cradling her head against his chest to silence her.

With his hands still cuffed behind his back, Joseph plodded a few steps forward. "Please, Carrie..." he said, gazing into her hellish eyes. "Don't listen to the Shadow. You can fight this." He swallowed back tears. "I-I love you."

Carrie looked in his direction, but it wasn't Joseph she was focused on.

It was Jem.

Her eyes fixed upon the other long-haired blond—who had somehow magically summoned a fireball in the palm of his hand—with an expression of rage, as if a gathering storm was building inside her.

As Jem extended his fiery hand, preparing to strike, Joseph hollered, "NO!"

But it was too late. The blazing inferno had already launched from the palm of his hand. As it made contact, Carrie's body ignited in flames. Her screams of agony brought

Joseph to his knees. When she reached out for him, the flames rose, blazing up like a column of fire. In the blink of an eye, her body shrank back as though the flames had swallowed her whole.

Joseph lowered his head and broke down as if his world had come to an end.

Ryan quickly steadied Jessica as her knees started to buckle.

Frank darted forward. "No!" he cried out. "Carrie!"

Manuel's hands were suddenly tight on Frank's arm.

"Let me go!" Frank protested, but Manuel tightened his grip, drawing him back even as Frank fought his way toward his niece.

An air of melancholy surrounded the room, and Jem felt an intangible weight of regret and responsibility bearing down on him. As he went to offer Frank some consolation, an eerie laughter halted him in his tracks. The voice echoed through the room, sending chills through Jem's veins. Then, out of nowhere, a figure from some haunted nightmare reached out with smoldering, bony fingers and gripped him by the throat. Instantly, the air in his lungs began to thicken.

In Jem's desperate attempts to tear away from the powerful clutch that held him, his efforts seemed useless. "Not possible—" he finally managed to choke out, his face tight with pain.

Everyone turned in unison, mouths dropping in utter disbelief as they gazed upon the horror before them. Carrie had somehow transformed into something far more wicked, but that wasn't the worst of it. The demonic Carrie-*thing* had Jem by the throat.

Jessica opened her mouth to scream, but her voice failed her, horror paralyzing her whole.

Wreathed in flames, an evil monstrosity resembling the Grim Reaper himself appeared above them with a scornful gaze. A ghoulish face of teeth and bone peered out from underneath a black-hooded robe, the empty eye sockets red with flames.

No, Carrie wanted to say, *don't hurt them,* but the words would not come. The Shadow had taken her body and her ability to speak. She fought with all her strength to find her way back to herself, to shift back into her true form, but she was lost in the blaze of fire. *Please, God,* she thought, *help me.*

Through gritted teeth, Jem struggled to catch his breath as the Shadow tightened his bone-crushing grip. His vision flickered and the world around him dimmed.

The growl that lit off across the room sounded like the roar of a revving engine, and at first Jem assumed Jena had shifted into her creature. He prayed like hell she was strong enough to destroy the Shadow, seeing that his powers didn't get the job done.

When a glimpse of white shaggy fur whizzed by, Jem's recollection told him it was a beast, just not Jena's. Instead, it was his brother's. And by the sound of it, Jace was good and pissed off.

Even his Breedline comrades seemed a bit taken back.

A werewolf, who towered to the height of at least seven feet, resembling the Abominable Snowman, suddenly raged across the living room. An end table toppled, and a lamp shattered in the path of the Beast's charging mass. As it launched itself toward the Shadow, readying for an attack, its blinding speed took the evil entity by surprise.

The Shadow's outstretched arm buckled upon impact, releasing Jem just as he was about to lose consciousness. As the infuriated white werewolf lashed out, the demon quickly regained its composure and slapped its snapping maw away.

The Beast howled at the jarring blow, sliding across the hardwood floor in a skitter of claws, leaving tattered rakes behind. As he collided into a coffee table, wood splintered, and glass exploded into pieces. The supernatural creature took the collision head on, absorbing the wreckage, taking the pain.

Leaning against Ryan for support, Jessica's tearstained eyes bulged in terror, her focus on the hulking werewolf. As it crashed through her apartment, leaving a trail of destruction and fur in its wake, she hadn't possessed the ability to scream, much less breathe. So instead, she clamped her hands to her face and released a quiet whimper into the palm of her hand.

"I promise," Ryan whispered, lightly squeezing Jessica's shoulder. "I *won't* let anything happen to you."

While Ryan vowed to protect Jessica, the Beast had already recovered. As he rose to his full height, he huffed and shook himself free of the fragments of glass clinging to his fur. As he prepared for round two, a deep-throated growl, coming from behind, broke his focus. He turned to look and saw the transformed face of Jena, sleek and black and hideous. There was no mistaking her creature, a cursed werewolf as big as his beast and as deadly, if not deadlier. Like him, she was impervious to silver and the last of her kind. She studied him with a look of valor and determination. In that fleeting moment, he knew he wasn't fighting this battle alone.

As they faced the demonic *thing*, its fiery orbs bore down on them, teeth bared, daring them to approach. Then it stepped from the flames and spoke, "If you mangy mutts think you can destroy me…" The Shadow paused and crooked a bony finger in an attempt to further egg them on. "…give it your best shot."

In a snarling rage, the two werewolves pushed off their hind legs and sprung into the air like they'd been vaulted from a catapult. The Shadow, who aimed to swat the furry duo away, failed miserably. As a massive surge of angry teeth and claws slammed into the demon, it tumbled backward like it had been hit by the weight of a moving train.

The Shadow came down hard, its bony spine connecting with the floor, sounding as though it had broken apart.

A large mass of dark fur and rippling muscle came into view and stood over the Shadow. In one fluid motion, Jena brought down a hairy fist and pounded into the Shadow's skull like a battering ram. The sound of bones cracking alerted her lupine ears, producing a smile on her wolfish face.

The werewolf's toothy grin intensified the Shadow's anger. Possessing a speed entirely unexpected, the demon's hands came up, fingers extended into bony hooks and grasped Jena by the throat. Its grip tightened, hard enough to open Jena's eyes, and nipped her airway shut. In a split second, the Shadow rose, lifting Jena's entire body off the floor.

With uncanny speed and eyes gleaming with malice, Jace's beast sped forward with his jaws open. But before he could reach the demon, it crushed Jena's windpipe with the force of a closing bear trap and flung her into the charging Beast. The two werewolves smacked into one another like a pair of bowling pins before crashing into a wall.

"Jena—" The man with purple eyes cried out, rushing toward the fallen werewolves. He knelt by the dark-furred female, who was lying on her side, and gently rolled her onto her back. She gasped in pain, but she controlled herself and gazed up at the man who was staring down at her. His expression appeared visibly concerned.

"I'm okay, Nicolas," she said in a puff of breath. "I'll heal."

"But—" he protested.

"*Go*," she gritted out, clenching her teeth. "Help the others... Destroy the *Shadow*."

Nicolas glanced over his shoulder, across the wreckage of the apartment, to the Shadow, who glared at him in mockery. Nicolas rose with his brows pinched then shifted his attention to Jace's beast. In a semiconscious daze, the werewolf grunted but still managed to get to his feet. Some of the hide on his shoulders and chest had been ripped away, coating his white fur in crimson. The bloody image reminded Nicolas of the first time he'd laid eyes on Jace's beast, back when they'd destroyed his older brother, Ashton.

Ashton had been cursed then. A savage killer. And he'd bitten Jena, spreading the lupine virus to her. But God had given his brother a second chance. He'd been chosen as the angel of holy fire, tasked to protect humanity and guard the outer limits of heaven. After all, Ashton wasn't born evil. Before he'd been cursed, he was an honorable man. A good, loving brother.

"Whaddya say we go kick some demon ass," Nicolas finally said, peering up at the Beast.

Infused with fury, Jace's beast looked at Nicolas narrow-eyed and nodded a ghastly affirmative.

"What's the holdup, guys," a guttural voice came from behind. "Let's do this thing."

As they turned, their eyes met Roman's. Although he no longer looked fully human. Now, he was twice the size, his distinctive European characteristics replaced by those resembling a man and a werewolf, a species unlike any of the others, with eyes that shimmered like diamonds. Though Nicolas had only witnessed such a creature on a few occasions, he knew what Roman was: an Adalwolf. And standing alongside him were two Breedline wolves. They were twice the size, if not bigger, than any average four-legged wolf. And their fur was as black as night, but Nicolas distinctly recognized Drakon. His rogue wolf was larger and had long curving canines like a saber-toothed tiger. So obviously, the other wolf had to be the Breedline council head, Tim Ross.

Although the odds were stacked against them, still the group banded together, readying themselves to go into battle.

Tension crackled in the air as the Shadow narrowed its evil eyes into hateful slits and fisted his bony fingers, waiting in silent fury.

While the group of supernatural beings glared at one another, preparing for war, Jessica huddled in Ryan's arms, blinking at the freakish sight. As if awakening from a dream, she lifted her chin and looked up at him with an expression of "what the hell is happening" on her features. Fearful of their outcome, she opened her mouth and tried to form words. But nothing came. She tried again and croaked out, "W-we're going to die, aren't we?"

For a moment, Ryan could only stare down at her, trying to make sense of it all.

She felt uneasy when he didn't readily answer. "R-Ryan?"

He took a deep breath and faked a half-smile. "No, Jessica. We're not—"

Ryan's words trailed off when the Shadow finally spoke. "You haven't the power to defeat me." His bright orbs remained fixed on Nicolas then darted over the others, his eyes flaring murderously. "You're nothing but a pack of dogs."

His words further angered Jace's three-hundred-pound Beast. He looked like a werewolf on steroids as he shot forward in a heated rage. With incredible speed, the Shadow grabbed the werewolf by the throat at the last possible second and held him at arm's length. The Beast thrashed and snarled but was unable to break free of the evil entity's hold.

Unexpectedly, something immense rammed into the Shadow from behind, knocking him off balance. The impact was enough to loosen his grip and set the Beast free. Growling in frustration, the Beast cricked his neck and rose on two legs once more. He glared at the demon and bunched his muscles. In a frenzy of teeth and claws, he bolted toward the Shadow. Its white coat was but a mere blur, covering the distance in a split second. The Shadow tried to react, but by the time his mind registered movement, the Beast was already on him, snapping at his throat.

The impact hurled the Shadow backward, and they both crashed to the floor. Claws tore into the bones of the demon's neck, ripping and snapping them.

The Beast's cunning maneuver took the demon by surprise, and for a moment, he found himself disorientated. But that feeling quickly faded and outrage took its place. Regaining the upper hand, the demon dug his bony fingers into the back of the Beast's neck and tossed the massive werewolf away.

As the Shadow watched the Beast collide into a wall, smacking his head with a wet crack, he caught a glimpse of two dark figures circling him. As the demon turned to look, he froze at the gaping jaws closing in. He regained his senses when something sharp pierced through his chest cavity. Suddenly, his entire body filled with a blinding pain. The demon roared in agony as the bones crumbled under the force of the bite. Before he could counter-attack, his wrists became pinned to the floor as another set of teeth fastened around his neck. Canines the size of daggers crunched through bone and tore away pieces of vertebrae.

Then a voice called out, "Nicolas!"

Nicolas looked up from where he kept one of the demon's wrists locked in place while Roman pinned the other. Instantly, he recognized the man who had appeared out of nowhere. The combination of pale skin, golden eyes, and long, jet black hair was a dead giveaway. It was Jace and Jem's half-brother, Sebastian Crow. When he held up a silver dagger, he said, "Use this." Then Sebastian tossed it to him, and added, "Aim for the eyes."

With fast reflexes, Nicolas snatched up the blade and quickly plunged it into the thing's eye socket. The Shadow bucked and let out a hellish shriek. In a desperate attempt it clutched the hilt with its bony claws and tried to pluck it free. Finally, unable to retrieve the weapon, the demon went limp, hands falling to its sides, and died with a defeated grimace on its evil face.

Breathing hard, Nicolas plucked out the dagger and backed away, taking in the grisly scene just as the Shadow's skeletal form began to shift back into Carrie's body.

An expression of shocked disbelief emerged from Nicolas's face, and all the others gathered in the apartment.

Carrie! Joseph screamed her name in his mind. His throat clenched, squeezing until he felt he could not breathe. When he finally got his voice to work, he yelled her name aloud. There was such an overwhelming sense of heartache and devastation in his tone.

Eager to get to her, Joseph struggled with the cuffs that were still bound to his wrists. Finally, he looked between the two detectives in frustration. "Please..." He staggered, his legs wobbling like he was on the verge of collapsing. "...take these things off."

The second Manuel uncuffed him, he rushed to Carrie's side, with her Uncle Frank trailing behind. Joseph dropped to his knees and bit back tears, forcing himself to look at her wounds. The damage to her eye had been catastrophic, and she did not appear to be healing. That's when realization struck him. Carrie had died the moment the Shadow had been destroyed.

As Frank fell to his knees and broke into fits of sobs, Joseph fought back his own urge to break down. Instead, he swallowed back tears and reached out to Carrie. Gently, he picked up her head and placed it on his lap. "Oh, God," he said, stroking her hair. "This is all my fault." He lowered his face to hers. "Please, Carrie..." Tears trickled down his cheeks. "Please come back to me."

A voice from above softly addressed Joseph. "I may be able to help."

When Joseph lifted his head, the tall man with long, blond hair—who had just moments ago shot fire out of the palm of his hand attempting to destroy the Shadow—stood above him with compassion in his gaze.

"It's too late," Joseph said, slumping his shoulders. Inhaling sharply, as if to gain courage, he went on to say, "She's already gone."

"My name is Jem Chamberlain," the blond-haired guy said. "I'm a friend of Carrie's uncle." He looked at Frank with a sympathetic smile, then back at Joseph. "Not only can I heal, but I also have the gift to bring back the dead. Although I have healed fatal injuries and illnesses, I have never actually used my powers for this before."

Joseph's eyes flew open, and his mouth made the shape of an O. But before he could utter a reply, Frank said, "Please, Jem..." He paused, using the back of his hand to wipe the tears off his face. "...you've got to try to bring my little girl back. She means the world to me."

"And me too," Jessica said, crouching next to Frank, her voice stricken with tears. Then her focus shifted to Joseph. Her eyes displayed empathy and a hint of hope in them. As she looked back at Jem, she continued with sheer determination in her voice. "I don't know who you people are, or rather *what* you are, but all I care about is my best friend. If you can bring her back, then do it."

"I second that," Manuel said as he came up behind Frank, his lips trembling and his eyes wet with tears.

Jem's eyes roamed over the grieving faces surrounding him and nodded. "I can't guarantee it will work, but I'll do everything in my power to bring her back."

Jem lowered himself to the floor and carefully gathered Carrie into his arms. He stared wearily into her lifeless, pale face, and at the bloody wound to her eye. He drew in a deep breath, closed his eyes, and used his mind to reach out to Carrie's soul. And he prayed to God it hadn't already left her body. Although he feared the worst, he was determined.

"Carrie, can you hear me?"

He waited, cradling her limp body against his, praying for even the slightest sign. When there was nothing, only dead silence, he tried again. *"Carrie... listen to my voice. If you can hear me, let it be your guide. Follow the sound of my voice."*

As Jem remained patient, holding on with every bit of hope, he merged more forcefully with her one last time. *"Carrie, hear my voice. Let it guide you back to the light. Come back to us. Come back to the people who love you. Your Uncle Frank needs you. Jessica needs you. And Joseph needs you."*

It took all Jem's strength and concentration to search for Carrie's soul. But all that remained was darkness, nothing but an empty void.

Jem squeezed his eyes in frustration, just before he gave up, and finally lifted his lids. The moment he looked up, tears fell from his eyes. He felt like a failure and shook his head sadly. "I'm sorry, but—"

"I can bring her back," a voice echoed, cutting off Jem's words.

When everyone looked to the unfamiliar voice, as if by magic, a giant man angel with black wings, ducked his upper torso and made his way through the open doorway. He was tall, maybe ten feet, and his shoulder-length hair was ink black. He was bare-chested with a lean, muscular physique and wore tight, black leather pants with matching boots.

Everyone remained speechless, taking in the gigantic angel who stood inside the apartment, his head nearly touching the vaulted ceiling. As he faced the occupants of the room, his eyes zeroed in on a creature sitting on the floor with its back propped up against the wall. It looked like a werewolf, but much bigger. By the blood covering its white fur, and its hide ripped in places, it was evident the wolfish creature had been wounded. Instantly, a spark of awareness came to him. He remembered battling this creature before. But that was a different time. A time when he was evil. *Cursed.*

When the Beast registered his towering presence, its white hairs quickly retreated into flesh. Bones cracked and reformed. Within seconds, the werewolf was gone, and the naked body of a blond, long-haired male took its place. The bloody, ragged wounds that covered the man's head and torso began to fade until finally they miraculously vanished as though they had never been there.

The sounds of heavy breathing, with the faintest hint of a growl, brought the angel's head around. Lying on the other side of the room was a massive creature similar to the white werewolf, except coarse black fur covered its muscular body. For some strange reason, he sensed the identity of the human beneath the wolfish exterior. He moved closer and dropped into a crouch as the werewolf began its transformation. When the form of a naked woman emerged, silence hung like a shroud, broken only by the pounding beat of his own heart. Time seemed to slow as realization hit him. This was the young woman he had bitten and cursed.

Then a flicker of his human past came to him suddenly. Memories of their brief, intimate encounter brought forth emotions he'd forgotten. As he stared at her beautiful features, regretting how he'd wronged her, something inside of him twisted and knotted. Shifting back to reality, he reached for a chair that was toppled over and grabbed the crocheted blanket lying over the back cushion. Carefully, he draped it over her bare skin and hovered at her side. His instincts dug deep, driving him to beg her for forgiveness. Before he reached out with his hand to touch her cheek, she opened her eyes and managed a weak smile. "Hello, Ashton."

He froze for a moment, too shocked to react. Then he regained his senses and smiled back. "Hello, Jena."

Jena shook her head, refusing the angel's hand when he offered it. "I forgive you," she said as though his thoughts had drifted into her mind. "Please, don't worry about me. I'll be fine. Go help the girl."

He nodded and rose to his feet. As he prepared to use his gift to bring Carrie back to the living, he heard a familiar voice call out. "Brother? Is it really you?"

Ashton paused and turned his head. A tall man with purple eyes and ink-black hair stood among a group of people who surrounded the body of the dead girl. Lurking close by the others were two hulking wolves and another two-footed wolfish creature he remembered from not so long ago.

Momentarily, the angel was distracted when a tall man with pale skin and long, black hair stepped into his field of vision. The moment Ashton caught sight of his golden eyes, the name *Sebastian* registered in his mind. Then, like magic, the guy extended his hand and a flash of light appeared out of nowhere. It was like a portal leading to some unknown destination. As it grew and lengthened, Sebastian motioned for Jena and the naked, long-haired man to enter. Not long after they disappeared into the opening, a man who looked identical to the long-haired guy, except for the naked part, followed suit. Shortly after, the two hulking wolves shot through. The second Sebastian stepped into the portal, it closed without a trace.

Ashton looked away and refocused his attention toward the familiar voice. That's when he couldn't believe what he was seeing. The man who had called out to him was indeed his little brother. He looked across at Nicolas and grinned. "Yes, little brother," he finally said, his words laced with a southern drawl. "It is I... Ashton."

When Nicolas moved toward him, Ashton closed the distance with his arms outstretched. As they hugged, Nicolas felt like a child crushed up against his brother's superhuman size.

Pulling from their embrace, Nicolas looked up, meeting his brother's gaze, who was now the angel of holy fire, and said, "How did you know to come here?"

Ashton nodded toward the ceiling. "God sent me."

"To bring the girl back?" Nicolas asked.

Ashton nodded. "It's not her time."

When the angel moved next to Carrie and knelt beside her, Joseph muttered, "Wh-who are you?"

The man angel did not answer, but there was a flutter near his back. Joseph and the others surrounding Carrie quickly scrambled back as Ashton's huge wings began to unfold. As the dark plumage unsheathed to their fullest, they wrapped around Carrie's limp body and began to glow.

Joseph looked at Nicolas with a puzzled expression. "What is he doing?"

Nicolas smiled at Joseph and simply said, "He's saving her."

Chapter Forty-Seven

"Please, God." Carrie heard Joseph say. *"Bring Carrie back to me."*

She could hear the heartache in the tone of his voice, feel his pain. She desperately wanted to open her eyes, to reach out to him, but her eyes would not obey, and her arms felt heavy at her sides.

Then, as if a miracle, Carrie's lifeless body began to stir. Her eyelids fluttered, until finally, they opened. Miraculously, her ruined eye had healed, but her vision was a little blurry. It took a few seconds for it to clear, and when she was able to focus, the first thing she saw was... feathers?

The angel's expanded wings slowly withdrew from Carrie's body and then tucked behind his back again. He gently brushed his knuckles against her cheek and murmured in a soft voice, "Welcome back, Carrie."

She was mesmerized by the man angel staring down at her. His body was like a giant, but his features were so beautiful she had to blink a couple of times. Then, distant memories suddenly flashed before her eyes. They were childhood memories of Lailah—the angel who had saved her—and the last day she'd seen her parents alive. After all these years thinking Lailah had been a silly figment of her imagination, now she truly believed that angels existed and what she'd experienced as a child *was* real.

"A-are you," Carrie began, "an angel?"

He nodded. "I am the angel of holy fire."

A look of bewilderment crossed her face. "Angel of holy fire?" She shook her head. "I thought Lailah—"

"I took her place," he said with a smile.

"But why?"

"God granted Lailah her mortal life back."

Her eyes widened. "You mean, she's human again, and here on earth?"

"Yes, Carrie."

Joseph watched and worried as he anxiously stood back, waiting for his cue to approach Carrie. Finally, when the angel motioned to him and the others, he blew out a sigh of relief and came forward. His heart turned over in his chest the moment he looked down at her. She was pale, but not deathly so, which wasn't bad considering all she'd been through. Before he spoke, he mentally told himself, *I can be strong for her.* Instilling himself with courage, he muttered, "Carrie..."

Her head turned slowly toward him. "Joseph?"

He immediately dropped to his knees and scanned her face, searching for evidence of injury. "Are you okay? Are you hurt?"

"Don't worry," she said, flashing him a weak smile. "Thanks to the angel, I'm almost as good as new."

Joseph briefly closed his eyes. *Thank you, God.* Then he faced the gigantic angel and said, "Thank you. How can I ever repay you? You saved the love of my life."

The angel dipped his head. "Just take care of one another."

Joseph nodded. "I will."

"*We* will," Carrie abruptly said.

When the angel stepped away and moved toward Nicolas to say his good-byes, Joseph refocused his eyes on Carrie. "I thought I'd lost you," he said as a tear rolled down his cheek.

"Remember what I said to you earlier this morning?" She reached up and wiped at his tear. "That you were stuck with me?"

Her words made him chuckle. "I believe I can make the sacrifice." Then he closed the distance between them and kissed her. When he drew away at last, he murmured, "I love you, Carrie."

"I love you too," she said, smiling at him before leaning up to kiss him again.

"You okay, sweetheart?"

Carrie looked up to see her Uncle Frank suddenly looming over her, a worried expression etched into his face. Standing close by was his partner, Detective Manuel Sanchez, her best friend, Jessica, and Jessica's boyfriend, Ryan. And they all looked every bit as concerned as her uncle.

"I'm fine," Carrie said, trying to infuse strength into her words. Although by the gloomy look on their faces, she doubted they believed her. "Really," she went on to say, slowly pushing herself upright. "So, stop worrying."

"You scared the shit out of me, girl," Jessica said, wiping the tears from her eyes. "I thought you were dead."

"I'm so sorry, Jess."

"Although I haven't the faintest idea what all just happened here," Jessica said, "I'm just relieved you're alive. Hell, there for a minute, I didn't even think I'd survive."

Ryan wrapped a comforting arm around Jessica, and Carrie said, "I'm pretty clueless myself. But I promise to do my best to explain what I do know."

Jessica nodded. "We'll talk later."

Frank bent down and took hold of Carrie's hand. "I'm just grateful to have you back."

"Me too," Carrie said as Joseph helped her to her feet. "You're not still planning on arresting Joseph, are you?"

"No, sweetheart," Frank said, averting his eyes from Carrie then focusing on Joseph as he lumbered back up. "We were never going to arrest you, Joseph. With some help from our friends, we found out about the Shadow. We were just trying to get you to a safe place, and at the same time avoid further casualties."

"I'll have to admit," Manuel chimed into the conversation, "you took us on one helluva goose chase, Mr. Parker." He arched a brow, then continued to say, "In all my years on the force, you've been the most difficult person to locate."

When Joseph tensed, as though he wasn't sure how to respond to Manuel's and her uncle's statements, Carrie piped in and said, "Before you arrived this morning, we'd already made a decision." Her eyes went back and forth between Manuel and her uncle. "We decided to come to you two for help. I was unsure at first, worried you wouldn't believe us, but Joseph assured me it was the right thing to do. And honestly, it was our last resort. Neither of us had a clue on how to deal with a demon."

"This was my burden," Joseph spoke out. "I never meant for anyone to get hurt, especially Carrie."

"You didn't ask for any of this," Carrie said, studying Joseph intently, wondering if he'd ever stop blaming himself. "None of this is your fault."

A deep voice came from behind. "She's right, Joseph."

When everyone turned, a barefooted, European-looking guy with ripped and tattered clothes came up to Joseph with his hand outstretched. "I'm not sure if you remember me," he said, eyeing Joseph sharply. "We were just kids back then. But I lived in your neighborhood and—"

"Roman?" Joseph blurted, looking befuddled. "Is it really you?"

"In the flesh," Roman stated, smiling perfectly white teeth.

Joseph smiled back, and there was a wealth of emotion in his eyes. As he took hold of Roman's hand, he said, "I can't tell you how glad I am to see you. But how are you connected with—"

"I'll explain the details later," Roman said, squeezing his hand. "For now, let's just call it divine intervention."

Joseph nodded. "I'll graciously accept that answer. It's good to see you again."

"You too, buddy," Roman said, giving his hand another squeeze.

A knock at the door took them by surprise. As Carrie and the others shifted their attention toward the open doorway, a dark-complexioned young woman with thick black hair pulled up into a curly, poufy ponytail peeked her head inside. She was a talented author who lived in the apartment upstairs next to Ryan's. "Carrie... Jessica..." She called out. "Are you home?"

"Oh shit," Jessica whispered, looking at Carrie wide-eyed. "It's AJ. I completely forgot she was coming early to help me get ready for your party." She kept her voice low. "Thank goodness the angel and the others aren't still here. They made their exit in the nick of time."

"Oh no." Carrie gasped. "The apartment is a mess."

"You sure you're still up to having the party?" Joseph asked, keeping his voice low.

"Why not." Carrie held up her hands in defeat. "After everything, I think I'm ready to get back to some sort of normalcy. Not to mention a few rounds of drinks," she tacked on.

"I'll second that," Jessica said.

"Come on in," Carrie called out, motioning AJ inside. "And sorry for the mess."

When AJ moved further inside and caught sight of the disheveled apartment, her eyes rounded in startled disbelief. "Oh my gosh." She flinched, nearly dropping the covered dish in her grasp. "What happened?"

"Uh..." Carrie muttered, her eyes roaming over all the wreckage, trying to come up with some sort of explanation. "Raccoons got in."

"Raccoons did all this?" AJ asked, her head swiveling between Carrie and to all the overturned chairs and broken glass littering the living room.

"It was a family of raccoons," Ryan blurted.

"Yeah," Jessica said. "We accidently left a window open last night."

AJ frantically looked around. "They're not still here, are they?"

"Don't worry," Carrie said. "They're all gone."

"Thank goodness," AJ replied, sighing in relief.

"How 'bout we move the party upstairs to my apartment," Ryan suggested. "I'll get the grill fired up for the barbeque."

Jessica winked at Ryan and Carrie silently mouthed, *thank you.*

"Sounds like a plan," Joseph said. "I'll help Ryan get the ribs prepped."

Roman nudged Joseph's arm and whispered, "You wouldn't happen to have an extra set of clothes and shoes I could borrow, do you?" He gestured to his torn clothes and bare feet. "I kind of ripped these..." He paused and lowered his voice even more, "...you know, when I shifted."

Before Joseph could answer, Ryan stepped closer and said, "I think I've got something in your size."

Roman clapped a hand over Ryan's shoulder. "Thanks, man."

"You think you can lend me something too?" Joseph asked, looking down at his wrinkled T-shirt and jogging shorts. "I didn't get the chance to grab a change of clothes last night, and this is all I have."

"Don't worry," Ryan said. "I got you both covered."

"Thanks," Joseph said, smiling up at Ryan.

While everyone started gathering everything for the party, Frank wrapped an arm around Carrie and whispered close to her ear, "Raccoons?" He chuckled lightly. "Where in the world did that come from? And I can't believe your neighbor bought that."

"Well..." Carrie said with a shrug. "They have been getting into everyone's trash lately."

Frank pulled her close. "I love you, silly goose." He kissed the top of her head. "And happy birthday."

"Thanks, Uncle Frank. I love you too."

Chapter Forty-Eight

Four months later...

As Roman and Lailah said their vows, promising to love and cherish one another till death do them part, the minister continued to proceed with the ceremony. The moment he pronounced the happy couple as husband and wife, Roman bent his head and kissed his beautiful bride.

The crowd surrounding them, consisting of family and friends, instantly erupted into applause. When the kiss lingered a bit longer than expected, Roman's best men cheered and Jace gave his approval with a high-pitched whistle.

Finally, as the newlyweds pulled from their embrace and turned to face their guests, they started to make their way down the aisle, hand in hand.

Immediately they were greeted with compliments and congratulations, passed from one loving embrace to another.

They were halfway down the aisle when they saw Tessa and Tim standing together. On cue, both waved and smiled at them. Like everyone else, they were dressed formally, Tim in a sleek, black Brioni suit, looking like James Bond, and Tessa had on the most elegant lavender gown that accentuated her already slim figure.

"Look at you," Tessa said, extending her arms out to Lailah. "You're absolutely stunning."

Lailah, who wore a strapless, flowing, classic white bridal gown with lace floral details, picked up her skirting and met her with a hug. "Thank you, Tessa."

As Tim and Roman shook hands, Tim said, "I couldn't be happier for you both."

"The same goes for me," Tessa said, pulling away from Lailah. "You two make a perfect couple." Then she focused on Roman's spectacular attire. "You look dashing." She held out her arms. "Come here, I have to hug you too."

Roman hugged her instantly, as he, or anyone for that matter, was incapable of denying the Breedline queen anything, especially a hug. It was an honor just to be in her presence.

The second Lailah came upon her brother's outstretched arms, her face lit up with a smile. When she moved closer, Manuel grinned broadly, looking her over from head to toe before tugging her into his arms. "You're too beautiful for words. Congratulations, sis. I'm so happy for you."

"Thank you, Manuel," she said, squeezing his neck.

As they hugged, Lailah blinked tears, recalling childhood memories. Even though she was the oldest of the two, Manuel had always looked after her like a big brother. He was like her shadow, always watching over her, protecting her. She regretted not being able to see him grow into the man he is today. And deep down, she knew he'd blamed himself for her death. It pained her to know he'd carried that guilt for so many years. But now that her mortal life had been graciously restored by the hand of God, they could let go of the past. Although she'd been honored to have served as one of His chosen battle angels, she was ready for a new beginning. Ready to make up for lost time.

When Manuel pulled back, he reached up and tucked a loose strand of her long, red hair behind her ear. "I love you, Lailah."

"I love you too, little brother."

The moment Roman came forward, Manuel greeted him with an extended hand. "I'm leaving her in your hands now." He looked at Roman with an arched brow. "I'll expect you'll keep her safe."

"You can count on it," Roman said, taking Manuel's hand in a firm shake. "I'll protect her with my life."

Manuel nodded, then turned to the pretty blonde standing next to him. "I'd like to introduce someone very special," he said, his gaze focused on the woman he was falling head over heels for. "This is Kathryn Hobbs..." He cleared his throat. "My girlfriend."

Kathryn extended her hand to Lailah. "It's a pleasure to finally meet you," she said, smiling. "And congratulations. You look beautiful."

"Thank you, Kathryn," Lailah said, shaking her hand. "And yes, it's wonderful to meet you too." She quickly shot her brother a look of approval. "We'll have to do lunch soon."

"Of course," Kathryn said. "I'd love to."

While Kathryn shook Roman's hand, Frank stepped forward and wrapped his arms around Lailah. "Congratulations, dear heart."

She hugged him back. "Thank you, Frank."

As Lailah eased back, she caught sight of a young girl who stood next to Frank. Her features appeared familiar as though she'd seen her somewhere before. "I'm sorry," Lailah said, "but have we met before?"

Frank put his arm around the girl's shoulders and pulled her close, noticing how nervous she looked.

"This is my niece," Frank spoke out, "Carrie Randall."

"Y-you're the angel," Carrie muttered, bowing her head. "The one who saved me."

In response, Lailah placed a hand over her mouth. "Oh my…" Then she reached for Carrie's hand. "Please, that's not necessary."

Carrie slowly lifted her chin, and when her eyes met Lailah's, tears trickled down her face. "All my life, I thought I'd only imagined you. But you were real. You *are* real."

Lailah smiled. "I thought I recognized you. Although you were a bit smaller back then. But your eyes…" She lightly squeezed Carrie's hand. "I could never forget those big brown eyes of yours."

Carrie smiled back. "Do you remember when I asked if I could go to heaven to be with my parents and you said God needed me here for something important?"

"Yes." Lailah dipped her head. "I remember."

"Did I—?"

"Yes, Carrie," Lailah said, releasing Carrie's hand, then focusing on the handsome young man standing directly behind her. "Joseph needed you. He is your destiny."

Carrie beamed at Lailah's answer, and Joseph moved closer with a look of bewilderment stamped all over his face. "H-how did you know my name?"

"God may have mentioned it once," Lailah said, winking at the couple. "But that's our little secret," she added, keeping her voice low.

"I'm just glad I got to see you again," Carrie said. "And congratulations. Everything is simply beautiful, especially you."

"Thank you," Lailah said. "The ladies in the Covenant did all this for us. It reminds me of the Garden of Eden." She looked up at the large white canopy that was set up on the backside of the Covenant's estate. Draped over the arch was a splendor of overflowing garden roses mixed with foliage and varieties of greenery. Twinkling lights glimmered in several trees like thousands of tiny fireflies. There were rows of white, satin-draped chairs and colorful flowers that hung in garlands, decorated with satiny white ribbons. Finally, she shifted her eyes back on Carrie and said, "It's like a fairytale wedding come true."

"Congratulations to the both of you," Joseph said, grinning as Roman approached them. "You've got yourself a good guy," he tacked on, jabbing a thumb in Roman's direction.

"I completely agree," Lailah murmured, peering up at Roman with a big smile stretched across her face. "Not to mention very handsome."

Roman leaned forward and kissed Lailah on the forehead. Then he offered his hand to Joseph. "Thanks, buddy. It means a lot that you two came to celebrate our special day."

Joseph shook his hand. "Thanks for including us."

"So, how is Jessica faring?" Roman asked, keeping his eyes on Carrie. "I heard the Covenant gave Ryan permission to reveal his big secret to her."

"It took her a minute," Carrie said, "but after it all finally sank in, she's accepting the fact that the guy she loves is from an entirely different species who can shift into a wolf."

"I think they'll be just fine," Joseph said. "Besides, when you found out I was possessed by a demon, it didn't scare you off. Well, at first maybe," he added with a chuckle.

Carrie arched a brow. "You've got a point there. I guess it's true what they say."

"And what's that?" Joseph asked.

"True love conquers all."

"Yes, it does," Joseph said as he reached for Carrie's hand, intertwining his fingers with hers.

"Congrats, you two," Jem said as he approached, leaning toward Lailah with his arms extended.

Lailah returned the hug. "Thank you, Jem."

When Jem pulled away, he offered his hand to Roman. As they shook hands, Jem's twin brother, Jace, was next in line to congratulate the couple, followed by Drakon, Nicolas, Steven, and Roman's best man, Lawrence. All six men were acting as Roman's groomsmen, wearing stylish, grey three-piece suits, sporting navy bow ties and pocket squares.

Jena sauntered through the crowd of groomsmen with the rest of Lailah's bridesmaids in tow that consisted of Lila, Abbey, Angel, Celina, and Lawrence's wife, Tara. Their matching white, V-neck chiffon bridesmaid dresses with slits up the thigh and silk, navy belt sashes, complemented their youthful figures. After they returned hugs and congratulations, more guests began to form, so the wedding attendants, along with the others who had already congratulated the newlyweds, moved toward the reception area.

Lailah smiled as she took in all the members of the Covenant. As the wedding party mingled, enjoying each other's company, they made her feel like one big happy family. Of all the couples, only five were married, which now included her and Roman. Though she could tell by the way the bonded couples looked at one another it wouldn't be long before they too were joined in holy matrimony.

So far, Lawrence and his wife, Tara, were the only married couple, aside from her and Roman, who hadn't yet produced a child. Jace and Tessa had two adorable, rambunctious twin boys who kept them on their toes. Jem and Mia had a beautiful little girl who went from crawling to running in a remarkable amount of time. Then there was Drakon and his wife, Cassie who were expecting their first child any day now. And some of the couples who weren't married already bore children. Tim and Angel's daughter, Natalie, was the oldest of all the kiddos in the Covenant. She was an adorable toddler who everyone doted on, especially Jace's pet cat, Buddy. Sebastian and Eve had a set of twin boys who were growing like weeds. Steven and Abbey were the last couple to have a child. Their son, Jonah, was the spitting image of his father, just a smaller version.

"The ceremony was absolutely wonderful."

Lailah blinked and looked up to see Dr. Helen Carrington, her eyes wet with tears. Standing next to Helen was her bonded mate, Alexander Crest.

"Thank you," Lailah said as Helen and Alexander embraced her.

Roman took turns hugging Eve and Mia as they came by to give their best wishes. It was hard for him to tell the two twin sisters apart. They were both tall, with flawless, porcelain skin, crimson eyes, and black hair that hung past their hips. Even their chiffon gowns were similar, except Eve's was a dusty rose and Mia wore powder blue.

"Oh my," came a bubbly voice. "I'm so happy I could cry."

Roman and Lailah turned toward the voice just as Drakon's *very* pregnant wife reached out to embrace Roman, then Lailah.

"Thank you, Cassie." Lailah pulled away, her eyes glancing down at Cassie's rounded belly. "So, have you decided on a name yet?"

"Since we're almost positive it's a girl," Cassie began, "Drakon and I have decided to name her Sara Eloise."

"That's a beautiful name," Lailah praised. "I'm curious. Where did you come up with the names?"

"Sara is after my adoptive mother," Cassie said, "and Eloise is Drakon's mother. But we'll probably call her Ella for short."

"I love the idea," Roman said. "I'm sure Drakon can't wait—"

"Oh, no..." Cassie gasped, placing a hand over her belly, feeling a deep pressure in her lower abdomen, followed by a sudden gush of fluid between her legs. "M-my water just broke."

Cassie didn't remember much about being rushed to the Covenant's examination room, except for the persistent pressure in her lower abdomen and Drakon, who was right by her side, holding her hand. "Don't worry, honey," he reassured. "You're in good hands. Everything is going to be just fine."

Then Dr. Helen Carrington and Kathryn Hobbs appeared as Drakon gently transferred Cassie onto a padded examination table. The two ladies had already changed out of their evening gowns and were wearing scrubs. Since Kathryn was a nurse, Helen was grateful Manuel had brought her to Roman and Lailah's wedding. In emergencies like these, Helen had always counted on Cassie for assistance due to her profession as a nurse practitioner specializing in the neonatal intensive care unit at the Bates Hospital. But this time, she was the patient.

Helen reached down and took hold of Cassie's hand. "You ready for this?"

Cassie exhaled a deep breath and managed a tight smile. "Ready as ever."

Helen nodded and averted her eyes toward Drakon. "How's Daddy doing? You ready to meet your daughter?"

Drakon smiled at Helen. "I'm fine." Then he peered down at Cassie and lightly squeezed her hand. "And I can't wait to meet my little girl."

"My contractions..." Cassie groaned, "...are really starting to kick in."

"All right," Helen said, placing her free hand on Cassie's belly. "Let's see how far you're dilated."

Drakon remained by Cassie's side, his fingers intertwined with hers while Helen did an examination and Kathryn did a quick blood pressure check.

Drakon leaned down and kissed Cassie's forehead. "I love you," he said in a voice that cracked, "so much."

Cassie's eyes snapped in his direction. "I love you too." She squeezed his hand. "Don't worry. I've got this."

Helen came back into view. "Well, you're fully dilated. You ready to push this baby out?"

With her face scrunched painfully, Cassie bobbed her head and gritted out, "Ready."

As time seemed to tick by at an agonizing pace, Drakon was relieved to finally hear Helen say, "Okay, I've got her."

"Is she okay?" Cassie asked.

Before Helen could reply, the sound of wailing brought attention to everyone in the room.

As Helen held up baby Ella, she continued to cry, and so did Cassie, tears of joy. A moment later, Helen handed the baby over to Kathryn and said, "That's definitely the sound of a healthy baby."

Kathryn quickly wiped off the baby, and when she wrapped the tiny infant into a warm blanket, her crying calmed. She handed the small bundle to Drakon first and said, "She's beautiful. Congratulations, you two."

Drakon cradled the newborn, carefully supporting her head. "Happy birthday, sweet-pea," he whispered, cherishing this precious moment. Then he looked over at Cassie, smiling broadly. "She's perfect."

As Cassie reached out, Drakon gently placed the baby into her arms. And when baby Ella opened her eyes and looked up at her mother with the deepest blue eyes, Cassie's expression beamed. "Oh, Drakon..." Her voice trembled. "She has your eyes."

Baby Ella cooed, and that's when Drakon lost it. He wiped at the tears with the back of his hand as they began to trickle down his cheeks.

"Don't worry," Helen said, offering Drakon a tissue. "This place is a little like Las Vegas." She chuckled. "What goes on here, stays here. So go on. Cry all you want."

"Thanks, Helen." He took the tissue and wiped his eyes. As his gaze drifted back down, the sight of their daughter nestled lovingly in her mother's arms tugged at his heart.

More tears came, but he didn't care. This was the happiest moment of his life. That's when he made a promise to God and himself. Every single day he awoke, he'd say a prayer of thanks that he'd found redemption, and another chance at true love.

To be continued...

"The strength of my soul
was born on the backs
of moments
that brought me
to my knees."

–S.L. Heaton

Read on for a sneak peek into the next book,
LIVING NIGHTMARES/A Novel of the Breedline series
by Shana Congrove. Coming soon!

Shay Conrad, an aspiring writer, who—healing from a broken heart—suddenly finds her life changed forever. Her dream of becoming a best-selling author finally comes true. During her journey into this fast-paced world filled with fame and fortune, she unexpectedly gets a second chance at love.

Despite her guarded exterior and damaged past, Shay surrenders to her inner desires she feels for Cain Peterson—a gorgeous Canadian rock musician who has just signed on with one of the top recording studios in Los Angeles, California. And yet, just as their relationship blossoms, Shay's world completely turns upside down. The life she once knew is quickly shifting beyond the realm of reason. Her Paranormal Romance Series—*Living Nightmares*—a spine-chilling story of the undead, mysteriously starts to unfold into real life.

Haunted and tormented by her own terrifying novels, Shay seeks refuge in Cain, and for the first time... true love. But the nightmares are far from over. Cain has a secret. And when the truth is revealed, Shay begins to doubt her own sanity.

With the help of an eccentric group—a secret society comprised of humans born with the power to shapeshift into wolves, an eighteenth-century vampire, and a cursed werewolf—will the two lovers survive the dangers that are fast closing in, or succumb to the evil which seeks to destroy them?

Reference for terms and cast of characters

BREEDLINE – A secret species of humans created to protect humanity. Born with an identical twin, they have the power to shapeshift into wolves. They are not like the old legend of the lycanthropy myth. The Breedline species can shift into their wolf at will. The moon has no power over them. They do not pass their ability to other humans. In wolf form, they have superstrength, speed, and heightened senses. Compared to humans, Breedlines have tremendous advantages when it comes to health. Their bodies heal fast and are not subject to illness or diseases. The only thing that slows their healing process is silver. It is their kryptonite. Besides old age, a silver bullet to the brain is the only way to kill a Breedline.

All male Breedlines, born with an identical twin, shift into their first wolf at the age of eighteen. Female Breedline twins do not go through the change until they make love to their bonded mate.

BREEDLINE TWINS – They have the power to shapeshift into wolves, born with a strong, unbreakable bond. They share telepathic abilities with the power to sense their twin's emotions or injuries. In some cases, the bond between twins is so strong they cannot live without the other.

BREEDLINE BONDING – The male Breedline spends his life searching for their bonded mate. When two Breedline species experience a bond, they instantly feel a simultaneous, desirable attraction. The bond is for life. It is possible for them to have more than one mate in their life span.

BELOVED – A word used by a Breedline to express the bond to their mate.

DOUBLE BONDED – In some cases, male Breedline twins bond with the same female.

BREEDLINE COVENANT – The Breedline species must live within the boundaries of their Covenant. There is one in every state. A council governs its laws and oversees the species population.

THE BREEDLINE QUEEN – A Breedline queen is born once a century. Her massive stature, black fur, and red eyes are the queen's trademarks. Her alpha wolf has twice the strength, speed, and size of any Breedline. She rules over all the Breedline Covenants. She is their absolute law.

TRUE LAW – All Breedline Covenants have a book of laws. If disobeyed, they must face the Breedline council. A Breedline who takes a life out of revenge, or evil—other than protecting their life and the life of another—will be shunned by their Covenant, forced to remain as a rogue wolf.

ROGUE WOLF – A Breedline wolf who has killed with the intent of evil. They can never shift back into their human form.

RED (BLOOD) MOON – During this time, all Breedline species have a strong desire to create offspring. This is a time when Breedline females are more fertile for the conception of twins.

CHIANG-SHIH DEMON (Kiang shi, a.k.a. Ramael Arminius) – An ancient demon that can inhabit the body of a Breedline fetus or during a Breedline's death. It continues to take the soul over the natural lifespan of a child or the deceased Breedline. When the demon possesses a fetus, it breaks the bonding and telepathic abilities with its twin. If the demon possesses a deceased Breedline's body, it must do so before the soul passes on. If the soul is not intact, the body will soon die. The demon's sole purpose is to seek world domination.

THE BEAST – It is the second-born son of the Chiang-Shih demon. When provoked into a rage, he will shift into the Beast instead of the Breedline wolf. The Beast is also known as the Great White due to his white fur and enormous, seven-foot stature.

ZADKIEL (Tzadqiel, a.k.a. "Righteousness of God")– The archangel of freedom, benevolence, and mercy, and the patron angel of all who forgives. The Breedline species considers Zadkiel the Angel of Mercy.

SUCCUBUS (a.k.a. Creepers) – A succubus feeds off the blood of a Breedline species. They are skilled with hypnotic abilities and capable of using their beautiful features to influence the thoughts of the Breedline species and humans.

HALF-BREED – A species born with the genes from both a Breedline and a succubus. They can bond with either species. Although they cannot shift into a wolf, they need blood from a Breedline to survive.

WICCA (or Wise One) – According to the Breedline species, a Wicca is the goddess of magic, witchcraft, the night, the moon, ghosts, and necromancy. They can do white magic (good) or dark (evil).

GUARDIANS (a.k.a. Spirits of the Forest) – They originated during the Middle Ages with the purpose of protecting the Breedline from the destruction of any creation of a dark Wicca. They can stay invisible, with the power to move through any barrier and over any distance instantly.

THERIOMORPH – They are born with the genes of a Breedline but do not shift into a wolf. They shapeshift into an enormous black panther. They possess powers of mind manipulation and random visions of the future. They must use the drug dopamine to suppress their urges. In some cases, the Breedline see them as a threat to their species.

ADALWOLF – A species that has the power to shift from their human form into a beautiful creature twice the size, resembling half man and half wolf. Born with superstrength, they can move from one place to another at supernatural speed. Their eyes take on the appearance of two shimmering diamonds. With the power to regenerate their own cells, an Adalwolf will stop aging at thirty. The moon has no power over them, and they are immune to silver. They can bond with any species.

LUPA (she-wolf) – The ancestors descended from the old legend of the lycanthrope, but the moon has no power over them. The species only affects female offspring. A lupa is a dangerous creature which shapeshifts into a therianthropic hybrid wolf-like creature.

Jace Chamberlain (a.k.a. the Beast) – He is a Breedline species who later discovers he was born with a curse of the Beast, inherited by the Chiang-Shih demon. His bonded mate is Tessa. He's an IT engineer and the lead singer and plays acoustic guitar in the band Chaos.

Jem Chamberlain (a.k.a. the Chosen Son) – He is a Breedline species and Jace's identical twin brother. He carries the gene of the Chiang-Shih demon, which gives him the power to create a portal, the power to heal, and a force of electrical energy used as a weapon. His bonded mate is Mia. He's an IT engineer and the drummer in the band Chaos.

Tessa Chamberlain (a.k.a. the Breedline Queen) – An inspiring artist who discovers she is the Breedline queen after she meets and bonds with Jace Chamberlain.

Jax and Jem Chamberlain – Jace and Tessa's identical twin boys. Both have inherited the Breedline genes.

Dr. John and Sarah Chamberlain – They are Jace, Jem, and Cassie's adoptive human parents. They are physicians in a children's unit, donating their time to the emergency center.

Chester and Amelia Ewan – They are called Guardians—a species originated during the Middle Ages—with the purpose of protecting the Breedline from the destruction of any creation made by a dark Wiccan.

Katlyn Gray – She is a Breedline and Jace and Jem's biological mother. She was accidently killed by the Chiang-Shih demon.

Jackson Gray – He is Jace and Jem's uncle. Although he carries the gene of the Breedline, he does not shift into a wolf. He's a medical supply pilot.

Mia Blackwood – She is a half-breed and Jem's bonded mate. She is Eve's twin sister.

Eve – She is a half-breed and Sebastian's bonded mate.

Sebastian Crow – He is a half-breed and Eve's bonded mate. He has the power to summon a portal.

Arius and Tidus – They are Sebastian and Eve's identical twin boys. Both have inherited their parents' genetics of a half-breed. Arius carries the mark of the Chiang-Shih demon, with the power to create a portal and the ability to heal others.

Alexander Crest – He is a Breedline species who was possessed by the Chiang-Shih demon at birth. With the help of the Breedline Covenant, he was released from the demon's possession and reunited with his twin sons, Jace and Jem Chamberlain, and their half-brother, Sebastian Crow. He is bonded to Dr. Helen Carrington.

Tim Ross – He is a Breedline species and the council head of the California Covenant.

Angel – She is a half-breed and Tim Ross's bonded mate.

Natalie – She is a half-breed and Tim and Angel's daughter.

Kyle Jones – He is a Breedline species that resides in the California Covenant. Celina Baldolf is his bonded mate. He's a mechanic and plays bass in the rock band Chaos.

Casey Barton – He is a Theriomorph and lives in the California Covenant. He is a clothing model and plays backup bass and keyboards in the band Chaos. He is bonded to Lila Demont.

Dr. Helen Carrington – She is a Breedline species and a physician at the California Bates Hospital for both Breedlines and humans. She is bonded to Alexander Crest.

Drakon Hexus – He is a Breedline species and bonded to Cassie Chamberlain.

Cassie Chamberlain – Adopted at age two by Jace and Jem's adoptive parents, she later discovers she is a Breedline species when she bonds with Drakon Hexus. She is a nurse practitioner, specializing in the neonatal intensive care unit.

Celina Baldolf – She is a Breedline species with the power of a Wiccan but only practices white witchcraft. Dr. Helen Carrington is her aunt, and Kyle Jones is her bonded mate. She is an editor for a local publishing company.

Steven Craven – He inherited the genes of a Breedline and an Adalwolf. He is Tessa's fraternal twin and is Abigail Winthrop's bonded mate.

Abbey (a.k.a. Abigail Winthrop) – She inherited the genetics of a Lupa from her mother and is bonded with Steven Craven. They have a son named Jonah.

Dr. Kenneth Craven – He is a Breedline and an orthopedic surgeon at the San Francisco General Hospital. He is Steven and Tessa's father.

Lisa Wellington (a.k.a. Lilith) – She is a Breedline with the gift to heal. She is Steven and Tessa's biological mother. She tragically died saving Sebastian Crow.

Lila Demont – She is a Breedline, born into a wealthy, prestigious family. She is a lab technician and assists Dr. Helen Carrington. She is bonded to Casey Barton.

Victor Demont – He is a Breedline and Lila's father. He is a retired council member of the Pennsylvania Breedline Covenant.

Raphael (a.k.a. Buddy the cat) – He is the angel of healing who secretly disguises himself as a black cat who resides in the Breedline Covenant as their pet. He guards the children in the Covenant.

Nathan Gage (a.k.a. Nate) – He is a Breedline and the owner of several upscale night clubs in the largest metropolitan areas of Northern California.

Zeke Rizzo – He is a Breedline, born with a curse of a sin-eater, and the owner of the Cat Club. He is bonded with Anna Saeni.

Yelena Smirnov – A full-blooded succubus from Russia. She is bonded with Apollyon.

Anna Saeni – She was born with the genetics of a Breedline from her father's side, who died when Anna was a baby, but she does not shift into a wolf. She is like a sister to Sebastian Crow and bonded with Zeke Rizzo.

Roman Kincaid – He is an Adalwolf trained in military tactics, hired as a special breed of warriors from Brazil. He has a team of Breedline soldiers who work for a private Special Ops group contracted by the military for missions that no one else can or will do. He resides in the California Breedline Covenant along with team members, Lawrence, Bull, Justice, and Lena.

Lawrence Colbert – He is a Breedline, trained in military tactics and as a medic who works alongside Roman Kincaid and the Breedline Covenant. He is married to Tara Blackmon.

Lena – She is a Breedline, highly trained in survival skills, martial arts, and anything dealing with weapons, hand-to-hand combat. She is also Bull's little sister and is bonded to Justice.

Bull (a.k.a. Benjamin Allen Calvero) – He is a Breedline, highly trained and an expert in a variety of military tactics, who is part of Roman Kincaid's team. He gets his nickname because of his size. He is bonded to Jena McCain's best friend, Angie.

Justice – He is a Breedline who is part of Roman Kincaid's team. He's highly trained in military tactics, an expert with explosives, hand-to-hand combat, sniper training, and is a pilot. He is bonded to Lena.

Detective Manuel Sanchez – He is a homicide detective at the San Francisco Police Department who discovers he carries the Breedline genetics. His partner is Detective Frank Perkins. His sister is Lailah.

Detective Frank Perkins – He is Manuel Sanchez's partner and discovers the secret world of the Breedline. Born as a human, Frank pledges his loyalty to the Breedline. Fighting alongside his partner, they take an oath to help the Breedline protect the world from corruption and unknown creatures who prey on the innocent.

Captain James Hodge – Unaware of the Breedline species, he is Detective Manuel Sanchez's and Detective Frank

Perkins's superior at the San Francisco, California, Police Department.

The Fury – Three fraternal twins—Apollyon, Electra, and Callisto—created by an evil German scientist named Dr. Hans Autenburg. Using his own DNA, he mixed it with the genetics of a Breedline, an Adalwolf, and a powerful Wiccan.

Battle angels – Their one purpose for existence is to serve the Creator in the war against demons and evil havoc on earth. The battle angels are unlike any of the Creator's other angels. The indigenous battle angels, on average, stand ten feet tall, although a few tower to the height of twelve feet with a more muscular build. Tattooed with unique warrior markings, the black-winged warriors are suited with armor typical of ancient heroes, and they wield a type of sword associated with a long-gone empire. They are the bravest of angels, who consider only the importance of their mission, and are perfectly willing to give their life in the service of righteousness. Gifted with special powers, they fight against the dark side. They are particularly fond of the human race, considering themselves humanity's special protectors.

Jena McCain – She is an aspiring artist with the ability to speak with the dead. She was attacked and bitten by an age-old creature and cursed with a lust for human blood. Now that she is cursed to hunt humans, God has granted her the ability to only destroy evil.

Nicolas Ratcliff – He is immortal with the power of invisibility and supernatural speed. He is a detective for the San Francisco Police Department and is bonded with Jena McCain.

About the Author

Shana Congrove has always had a passion for fantasy, romance, and the supernatural world, and her idea of heaven is creating new adventures for her Breedline characters. In 2019, Shana ranked the second novelist in FanStory.com and continues in 2022 to rank in the top ten. In 2022, her books won the Literary Titan Book Award. She lives in Northwest Arkansas with her family and loves to interact with new readers on Instagram and Facebook/A Novel of the Breedline Series. Visit her website: shanacongrove.com

9 781737 047834